INFATUATE

AIMEE AGRESTI

HARCOURT
Houghton Mifflin Harcourt
Boston   New York   2013

Harcourt is an imprint of Houghton Mifflin Harcourt Publishing Company.

www.hmhbooks.com

Text set in ITC Kallos Pro

Library of Congress Cataloging-in-Publication Data is available.
ISBN 978-0-547-62615-4

Manufactured in the United States of America
DOC 10 9 8 7 6 5 4 3 2 1
4500397135

FOR BRIAN AND SAWYER

There was something strange in my sensations, something indescribably sweet. I felt younger, lighter, happier in body; within I was conscious of a heady recklessness, a current of disordered sensual images running like a mill-race in my fancy, a solution of the bonds of obligation, an unknown but not innocent freedom of the soul.

— Robert Louis Stevenson, *Dr. Jekyll and Mr. Hyde*

Part One

1

The Calm Before the Storm

I hadn't expected the end of high school to feel this way. Sure, there was a certain fizzy exuberance warming the chilly hallways of Evanston Township High School. There were joyous squeals and heartfelt hugs. There were colorful tatters of festive wrapping from token gifts littering the floor. There was that spirited roar of hundreds of our classmates simultaneously buzzing about their plans for the coming week. But all of that had nothing to do with the milestone I had reached with the ring of that final bell seconds earlier, and *everything* to do with the winter white blanketing the football field outside the window, where cars screeched out of the parking lot, their horns honking wildly. The holiday break was upon us all. That Dante, Lance, and I wouldn't be back here until June's graduation ceremony wasn't news on anyone else's radar. I gazed out the window again as the Chicago wind wrapped a wayward sheet of newsprint around the goalpost. In my mind, memories swirled in the same reckless way. Graduating early had to be the ultimate anticlimax.

The locker next to me slammed and Dante appeared. "Sooooo, everyone seems to be going to Jason Abington's Christmas party tonight," he needled me, eyebrows twitching up down, up down. He was making fun of me in the way that only best friends can get away with.

"Fantastic," I said with the full dose of necessary sarcasm. I pulled off the taped photos from the inside of my locker door and gave them a last glance—all featured me with either Dante or Lance—then grabbed my bag and coat. I nodded at the now empty locker, then closed it one last time. *Bang.* I flashed Dante a look that said I wouldn't be sweet-talked into any party-crashing expeditions. "Spend the evening with a house full of sloppy drunks in Santa hats while Jason and Courtney hook up in every room?" I had gotten over my longtime crush, but I still didn't feel like watching Jason paw at his brainless bombshell of a girlfriend. No thank you.

After the conflagration that was our prom—no metaphors here: the entire event really had gone down in flames, taking with it the historic Lexington Hotel downtown in what had been dubbed "the Great Chicago Fire, Part Two" by the *Chicago Tribune* —Jason had actually called me once. It was soon after school let out for the summer. I had thought it was Dante playing a trick on me, and by the time Jason convinced me it was him, I was too shocked to speak. It didn't really matter, though—by then I was uncharacteristically settled in the boyfriend department. Maybe boys have some sort of radar for when you no longer need them and that is precisely when they finally start noticing you.

"So, then that's a no?" Dante asked with mock innocence.

"That's a 'not-if-everyone's-life-depended-on-it' no . . . *again.*" I couldn't resist adding that last bit. It sometimes felt like Dante, Lance, and I lived in an entirely different universe from everyone else at school. We had played this odd role in, well, saving them from losing their souls this past spring, but it's not as though any of them knew. I was beginning to think I had hallu-cinated it all. Our lives—Dante's, mine, Lance's—had changed, but no one else's had.

"Okay, okay, got it." He put his hands up in surrender. "You're no fun." He paused, and then asked with a smirk, "How 'bout a Christmas carol?"

I scanned the area around us, but as usual none of the bodies bouncing like charged atoms along the crowded hallway paid us any mind, so I played along, with just the slightest roll of the eyes: "'Angels We Have Heard on High'?"

Dante gave me a friendly smack on the arm. "Ha! Am I crazy or do these jokes never get old?" He fixed his attention over my shoulder. "You're still coming over for holiday movie madness, right?"

"Sure thing." It was Lance's voice behind me. Two vinelike arms wound around my waist and held me close. He leaned his chin on my shoulder. "What time do you want us?

"Happy graduation, by the way," he said. He turned to me, lunging, to peck me fast and firm on the lips.

"And to you, too," I said, just flirtatious enough, kissing him back.

"Ugh. I swear, sometimes you guys are worse than Courtney and Jason."

"I'm offended," I said in mock protest.

"I'm not!" Lance said, squeezing me. He planted an exagger-ated smack of a kiss on my neck but then straightened up just as fast. He pushed his clunky black glasses farther up on his nose, his gaze darting. From the corner of my eye, I saw my favorite English teacher passing, trying not to see us, it seemed. Even af-ter Lance and I had been together so many months, I still blushed when we had these moments at school. I never would've guessed I would be the type to even *have* moments like this at school. I had proved to be anything but this type for my entire high school career up until this last semester.

Dante shook his head. "The things I put up with in the name of friendship." It was true. The three of us had one another and we were grateful. Dante and I had been pals since we were little kids. Lance had been something of a loner until that fateful internship brought us all together in our junior year. It had been his idea for us to do summer school and graduate early. "What would we miss? Another prom?" he'd joked. And so we had spent those sunny months studying, writing papers, taking tests, and now we were done.

After we cleaned out our lockers, we set off down the hall, Lance's warm hand in mine. "I was starting to think this one might be a flight risk tonight," Dante said, nodding in my direction.

"Fine, I'll be there." I sighed. "I just have to finish my college applications," I explained to Lance. "We can't all be evil geniuses like Dante, who can write application essays in his sleep." I was done with the ones I really wanted—Northwestern, University of Chicago, Princeton, and Harvard and Yale (those last two were just for kicks)—but I still had my safety schools left. I had waited till the last minute on those in the hopes that I wouldn't really need them.

"Whatever, there's plenty of time," said Dante, who seemed to score perfect grades without breaking a sweat.

"They're due in, like, a week." Lance laughed. He was also brilliant, but was supremely organized and had sent his off back in September.

"Exactly! Plenty o' time!" Dante flashed that wide, winning smile. "Dude, I'm finishing mine on the way to the airport. I'll send 'em before the plane takes off." I slapped his arm playfully. He was kidding now.

The hallways had mostly cleared by the time we made it to the door. I wrapped my scarf around my neck and Lance held the door for me. The three of us stepped out, and a gust of wind swooped to meet us. Heads down, we pushed on to the L station.

Over the summer we had started taking the L to that familiar stop downtown and then walked through a pile of rubble to the ruins of the glamorous hotel we had once called home. At first, we just needed to be near it, like anyone visiting a grave site. We would sit wordlessly sorting through all our memories of the horrific and the good—because, despite it all, there had still been some good—we had witnessed there.

We picked up hot chocolate from a weathered convenience store underneath the L tracks and made our way to South Michigan Avenue along grungy streets that grew emptier and emptier by the block. Every inch of sky appeared gray as the wind whipped us enough to convince me that even if we weren't going to be soon boarding a plane and heading south for the next few months, we probably wouldn't have had too many more pilgrimages here before the frigid depths of a cruel Chicago winter would have kept us away.

Louisiana. In just over a week, we would be on our way there. We were volunteering in a student program in New Orleans, doing a host of community service projects and, I could only imagine, having an adventure or two. I had once been to Florida —Disney World—with my adoptive mother, Joan, but otherwise, I had never been farther south than our cousins' place in Evansville, Indiana. And sure, I had lived away from home, at the hotel, but that was in Chicago. No matter what had happened at the

Lexington, at least the proximity to home had been a comfort. But now . . . New Orleans? My pulse picked up.

I pulled my jacket closer around me and glanced from behind a curtain of my hair to Dante on my left, who was watching the sky, and Lance on my right, hands in his pockets and his eyes on the pavement. None of us had spoken since boarding the L in Evanston. That, in itself, seemed to be a sign that our thoughts would have been nearly identical.

We turned the corner and found ourselves at the foot of the Lexington Hotel debris. Whenever I stood here, it was almost impossible to imagine what the entrance, with its swooping awning and stately steps, had once looked like, or how row after row of windows had reached ten stories into the sky. The building had been decimated in such a way that it seemed a bomb had gone off inside. Only jagged portions of the first level remained, spiky bits of the façade jutting up and out. The rest of this behemoth had been reduced to no more than a series of mountainous piles of oddly shaped fragments, like one of those 3-D puzzles of architectural landmarks that Lance liked to put together and display in his room.

There had been endless news stories about the tragedy. In the immediate aftermath, they eulogized the impossibly glamorous owner, Aurelia Brown; her second in command, Lucian Grove; and their beautiful but sinister staff, known to us as the "Outfit" —all assumed to have been turned to dust in the flames. *Lucian.* Even now, it was hard to think of him, to imagine what had become of him. Whenever he crept into my mind, I had to swat those memories away. The loss of him stung. I had printed out every article, read them just once, and tucked them away in an envelope under my bed.

Far easier to read were those more recent pieces speculating about what might be done with this hallowed ground. There was talk of reopening the hotel one day, but now the site stood completely untouched. At least like this it still felt like ours.

With charred chunks of terra cotta, stone, and brick crunching beneath our sneakers, we wound our way up our favorite hill of debris to nestle in against a twisted metal beam that was like a bleacher seat. From here we could look down into a gully where, on a sunny day, you could see the crystals of the chandelier sparkling from where it had crashed to the floor of the lobby. It was the very last sign of the opulence of the place where each of us had been swept off our feet, had fallen in love, before discovering that the people we were so enamored with were trying to recruit us for their dark ways. And in fact, they weren't people at all; they were devils, who had started out like us but had lost their way and were now in the business of buying souls, granting grand wishes, and finally committing their converts to an eternity below.

In a matter of days, we would, I had no doubt, be thrust back into some version of that world all over again. That's what awaited us in New Orleans and we all knew it, even if we hadn't spoken of it yet. It just made sense. I touched my necklace—a golden angel wing—for strength, then warmed my hands around my paper cup. Lance tightened his arm around me as I huddled close.

"To easier times in the Big Easy," Dante said, his voice heavy as he held out his cup of hot chocolate in a toast.

"To voluntourism, New Orleans–style," I offered, holding mine out too.

"Cheers," said Lance.

Added Dante, before sipping: "Thank you, Mr. Connor Mills, student coordinator extraordinaire."

Volunteer tourism, or voluntourism, had been a brainstorm of ours last summer. If we were graduating early, we reasoned, we needed to do *something* with all that time. The three of us were far too Type A to sit around for a semester, and we hadn't really wanted to race off to college early. That felt like . . . too much. We already had enough on our minds without jumping into any sort of intense academic pursuit just yet.

The idea originated when I had returned to my old candy striper job at Evanston General Hospital in June, working alongside Joan. One afternoon, a pickup basketball game landed an out-of-towner, one Connor Mills, in the ER after he took an elbow to the eye. It was ugly, but it could have been much worse. It didn't hurt that he was the type who could pull off the disheveled look: rugged and athletic, he had dirty blond hair, the scruffy good looks of a pro mountain climber, and an easy charm, even after a head injury. It was a busy day at the hospital, and since they wanted to monitor him for a concussion, he was there until after nightfall. I was removing his dinner tray, enjoying a fleeting lull in the day's activity, when he started talking.

"So, you're in med school over at Northwestern?" he asked me in a southern drawl. He wore a gauze patch over one eye. "How long y'think till this heals up?"

"You must not be able to see very well," I said, smiling. "I'm just a volunteer here. I'm in high school. So I can't give any medical advice but I *can* hook you up with the really good cookies from the break room down the hall if you're still hungry. Sometimes the night nurses steal 'em, so I always hide a few."

"I might take you up on that." He laughed.

"Where's the guy who did that to you?"

"My buddy." Connor shook his head. "I'm in town a few days, seeing friends. Didn't expect to spend it here."

I felt sort of bad for him, and since I wasn't needed anywhere else at that moment, I hung around and challenged him to a game of poker.

I had just won a round and was gathering up the vending machine M&M's we used for betting when Connor said, "So you're a volunteer? I help run a program in New Orleans. City kids, Katrina victims, all sorts of community outreach. Bet you'd like it."

"How much would you bet?" I held out a handful of M&M's.

He laughed, taking one and popping it in his mouth. "We call it voluntourism down there."

"That's catchy."

"You should apply. You can come hang out. Winter's much nicer there."

By the time Connor was released, he had won me over, and he promised to e-mail me the application. Dante and Lance hadn't needed much convincing to join me. As soon as we were accepted we began wondering what might really be waiting for us in New Orleans.

"So . . ." Someone had to break this silence as we stared at the ruins. "Anyone getting any fabulous graduation gifts?" I asked, my voice as light as possible. Joan was taking me for a girls' day of shopping and spa treatments in the city before I left, in her continuing effort to make me less of a tomboy. I loved her for that.

"Still trying to convince my mom the chef's table at Alinea is a worthwhile investment." Dante, our resident gourmand, laughed quietly to himself.

Lance pulled his arm from me and leaned forward, elbows on his knees as he studied the building's mountainous remains. A harsh gust blew a gritty spray of brick and mortar dust into our faces. "No," he said finally, his tone flat. "But actually, I kind of have something for you guys . . ."

How about *Seventeen*? And one of the gossip magazines; those are fun. *Us Weekly*? I should've raided the hospital gift shop." Joan shook her gray ponytail and grabbed the magazines off the newsstand in front of the cashier.

"I feel so bad I'm leaving again. You're sure they're all okay?" For the second time in a year I was taking a leave of absence from my volunteer hospital job and I couldn't help but feel guilty—I grew up at that place, and I didn't like to let down the people there. They were like my extended family.

"It's fine. They love you," Joan assured me as she scanned the titles again. "How long is the flight?"

"Just under three hours. Not bad."

She plucked a third magazine—*Entertainment Weekly*—and slapped it on the counter. "We'll take this one too," she said to the woman ringing everything up. "Nothing worse than running out of reading material on a flight."

"Thanks, Joan."

"Of course, sweetie, it's the least I can do." She paid for the magazines and handed me the bag, then put one arm around me, wheeling my suitcase with her other arm as we walked out and found seats near the security checkpoint. "I'm very proud of you, you know." She squeezed my arm. "Even if I'm not one hundred percent thrilled with this trip." I nodded. Joan had had to put up with a lot in the years she'd spent with me, aside from watching the place where I interned in the spring burn to the ground. She had taken me in when I was just a five-year-old kid left for dead on the side of Lake Shore Drive with no memory and no one looking for me. It probably hadn't been the easiest way for her, then a single nurse working the late shift, to begin her tenure as an adoptive mom.

"I still don't really know why this is so important to you, but I do understand it's a good opportunity," Joan continued. "But I did tell you that New Orleans happens to be the murder capital of the world right now, didn't I?" She whispered this last part, as though she didn't want to offend the city. And, yes, she had told me this a million times, and it wasn't even true.

"It's not the murder capital of *the world*. It's more like it sort of leads the nation." I wasn't exactly helping my cause. I tried again. "Every city has crime."

"Well, it should be leading the nation in SAT scores. Or random acts of kindness."

"I don't think there's any way to measure for that. Who knows, maybe it does."

She put her hands on my cheeks, looking in my eyes. "I'm just going to miss you so much."

"Me too." I tried to steady my voice and steel my nerves, but O'Hare Airport wasn't exactly the most Zen-like place. Lines snaking endlessly, people running for their gates as though competing in a track and field event. I felt a sharp pang, wishing to be under the covers of my bed at home, but fought it back. "You really don't have to wait, though. Dante and Lance will be here soon, I'm sure. I mean"—I checked my watch—"they have to be here by ten fifteen or they're getting left behind." I hoped Dante, forever fashionably late, wouldn't make us like those frantic people racing for their flights.

"I don't want you waiting here alone. Besides, I've got to soak up all the time I can with you." She put both arms around me.

"And, by the way, can I get a little credit for letting you go on this trip with your boyfriend?"

"Joan," I said, rolling my eyes. This was also well-covered territory. "You love Lance."

"I know, I know. I just can't believe I won't see you for so long." We had planned for her to come visit midway through the trip, since she'd never been to New Orleans.

I nodded but was instantly distracted by four numbers—proclaiming the new year, which was about fourteen hours away—bobbing toward me. They were attached to springs and a headband atop Dante's head. I always felt relieved having him near. It settled my queasy stomach.

"Hey, Ms. T!" He reached down and gave Joan a hug.

"So good to see you, dear! And aren't we looking festive?"

"Thanks!" He shook his head for effect.

"Will they let you through security like that?" I joked, flicking one of the numbers. "You look like a threat for sure."

"Flattery will get you everywhere! And relax, I brought a pair for you, too."

I had to laugh. "Lance oughtta be here soon."

"I saw him. He's, like, two minutes behind me. He was still trying to talk his mom out of escorting him in here. I had to run to keep mine from following."

"See, Hav, I'm not the only one," Joan piped up.

"I can't get rid of this one." I pointed to her. I couldn't help but feel how I'd miss her. I still wasn't entirely sure about this new life I was leading, and I didn't like keeping secrets from her. But what was I supposed to say? *So, it turns out I really have to go because, you see, I'm an angel in training—all three of us are—and this trip is somehow part of the second of three tests we need to pass to get our wings. And, by the way, if*

I fail, I basically . . . I couldn't even finish the thought. My stomach churned and I broke out into a cold sweat.

Joan was still talking: "And besides, you wouldn't want to have to buy your own magazines, would you?"

"There he is," Dante piped up as Lance ambled in through the doors with his oversize duffel bag.

"Sorry, guys," he said. "Hi, Ms. Terra. How are you?"

"Why, hello, Lance! So good to see you. You're looking dapper today," she said, sparkling. He wore jeans and a hoodie poking out from under his fleece.

"Um, thanks, Ms. Terra." He smiled shyly. "Hey, lemme get these," he said as he grabbed my bags.

"Oh, thanks, you don't—" He just shook his head. I still tended to protest gestures like that out of habit, but I was secretly glad that Lance didn't listen. "So, I guess we should probably get going, right?" I proposed. Joan gave the boys hugs and wished us luck and then, as they started walking off to security, she held me in a long embrace.

"I'm proud of you, Haven, honey. Remember to call."

"Promise." I nodded and, with a wave, began walking away, to catch up with the guys.

In the distance, Joan called out: "Let the good times roll, sweetie!"

I waved again. *"Laissez les bon temps rouler,"* I said to my compatriots. Lance slowed his pace a second to give me the quickest of kisses.

"But not too much!" Joan's voice rang out again.

2

Laissez Les Bon Temps Rouler

I let Dante have the window seat, taking the middle myself, and within moments of nestling in, he already had all three of my magazines in his grip and a pillow tucked beneath his closely cropped hair, with his eyes closed. On the other side of me, Lance pulled out his copy of *Popular Mechanics* and his earbuds. He leaned in, his eyes alive with excitement and what looked like an undercurrent of fear. "Next stop, New Orleans . . ."

"Your second attraction on the Metamorfosi tour," I whispered back, using the word we had learned in the spring for the passage of angels and devils earning their respective stripes. A chill swept over me.

"We got this," Lance whispered. "Promise." He craned his neck for a peek at Dante slumbering then inched closer to me, resting his hand at my jaw and kissing me. It was enough to make me forget for just a moment about what lay ahead. He cradled my neck and placed one of his earbuds in my ear, the other in his, and slouched in his seat, then opened his magazine as one of his favorite songs cued up. I watched him for a moment and noticed a crease forming between his brows, evidence that he was losing himself in the details of an article on math and science and architecture, subjects that made sense to him.

I sat back and fooled with my mysterious new smartphone. Lance had presented the phones to Dante and me at the Lexington ruins on the last day of school.

"Wow, this is a pretty extravagant graduation gift. Maybe I should've treated to the hot chocolates?" I said, puzzled, when he handed mine to me. Like theirs, it had the initial of my first name engraved in gold on its black case. I still had a strictly utilitarian cell phone. Joan always said she didn't think a high school kid needed all the bells and whistles. Maybe she had a point, but nevertheless, it could be embarrassing to take out my completely boring little phone at school.

The eyes of gadget-obsessed Dante lit up instantly. "This is sweet!" He grabbed his phone and began hitting buttons. Then he frowned, shaking it as though he might hear something loose inside. "Dude, I think mine's broken already."

Lance shrugged. "Yeah, I took mine apart and put it back together again and still can't get it to operate. But I have a feeling they'll start working soon enough." Dante and I looked at him. "The story is, we're getting an upgrade."

He said he'd gotten home from school and found three phones on his bed along with a typed note that read:

No more postcards, no more books . . .
    For each of you. Further instruction to
follow.

That was it. But it was enough. We could only imagine that we would be receiving some sort of guidance from these phones, just as I had once had a book that automatically wrote new pages for me, advising me how to stay alive through our first angel test at the Lexington. Lance received postcards that did the same thing. They never gave us all the answers—they seemed to want us to think for ourselves. But they gave us hints and, more important, convinced us that something, somewhere, was looking out for us.

In the middle of the flight I tried the on/off button a few times, but still got nothing.

"I'm afraid you'll need to put that away, miss." A honey blond flight attendant leaned in with the bright smile of a pageant finalist. Not a single strand of hair had escaped her precise bun. I couldn't quite fathom how this level of perfection was achieved. But hadn't I learned by now that you never really know what's going on beneath all that? Tucking the phone away in my backpack, I then dug out my new copy of *Dr. Jekyll and Mr. Hyde,* one of the books from AP English Lit that I had brought along to reread.

The plane shifted direction, my ears popping as it careened through the sky, just as Dante snarfled a snore and repositioned his head on my shoulder. I glanced over to see if Lance had heard him, hoping we could share a comforting laugh, but saw his eyelids were struggling to stay open. His glasses slid just enough to make that scar beneath his eye more visible. On his wrist he wore a leather cuff bearing an angel wing that matched the one on my necklace. My fingers felt for it now around my neck, as though it had the power to transport me back to prom night. We had shared a core-shaking episode that night, almost getting killed in the process. I couldn't imagine many relationships started that way. And it had changed us too.

We were scarred—and not just on our shoulder blades with

their matching marks that seemed to be waiting for wings to be fastened on. Nor merely by the three slashes above my heart or the swipe below Lance's eye or the sweep on Dante's arm. We were equally marred on the inside. We couldn't have gone through what we had and not been.

We had been inseparable ever since. We just needed to be near one another, in our own odd little angel support group. We were in a sort of purgatory, a limbo of being on constant guard for the next challenge. All summer we were skittish, edgy. At first we felt rundown from this endless waiting to be attacked. Then we started looking for ways to get strong again: we ran around the track at school for hours at a time after summer classes. Lance and Dante would sometimes join me at the hospital unloading and lifting boxes of heavy supplies.

When school started, we manically raced through our course work. We were not typical sixteen-year-olds. I still felt unsure of how exactly to navigate a remotely normal romantic relation- ship with Lance. I thought perhaps I was some kind of adrenaline junkie, operating at my best only under the threat of imminent death. And it was with that in my mind that I let my head rest on Lance's shoulder and I drifted off. I didn't wake until the pilot's voice crept into my subconscious and I took a drowsy peek out the window to see that we were beginning our descent.

The cab weaved through streets studded with revelers sipping mixed drinks outside on a sunny weekday afternoon, loops of purple, green, and gold beads shining from their necks. Jaunty trumpet-heavy jazz poured out of the open doors of every bar we whizzed past. It was exactly as I had imagined New Orleans would be. But I hadn't anticipated the heat. Sticky and sweet-smelling, the thick humid air smothered us as soon as we set foot outside the airport. By the time we found the car that had been sent for us, I had already stripped down to the T-shirt under my sweater. I hoped I'd packed enough of my summer clothes.

"This is hot, even for us, so don't y'all worry. It's not just you northerners," said the driver, clearly a native judging by his tanned and glistening skin. His lilting twang sounded so welcoming that it convinced me I would be one of those people who went on vacation and inadvertently picked up the accent of the locals and came home sounding ridiculous.

"Where's good shopping around here, sir?" Dante was already thinking ahead. Lance busied himself cleaning his glasses, which had steamed up instantly, on his shirttail.

"Canal Street, Magazine Street, all over the Quarter. Y'all are gonna love it."

The city unspooling outside my window could not have looked less like Chicago. Shops and eateries lined every street. Wrought-iron balconies were wrapped around precious row houses, some painted in candy colors. A horse-drawn carriage pulled out in front of us, clomping along at a pace far slower than I walked even when I was relaxed. But no one seemed to mind. Time moved differently here, I could already tell. I breathed deep, taking it all in.

"Your house is a short walk from Jackson Square, real pretty —"

"And just a block or so from Bourbon Street, right?" I piped up. From my guidebook, it looked like our new home was within striking distance of the famous strip, which pretty much sounded like a nonstop party.

"Please, what are *you* going to be doing on Bourbon Street?" Dante laughed.

"Unleashing my wild side maybe, you never know."

"Because you really let your hair down at the Vault," he volleyed back, a reference to our evenings as underage fish out of water at the Lexington's posh nightspot.

Lance turned around in the front seat and smiled at me. "You can take the girl out of the club but you can't take the club out of the girl," he said. "But, culturally speaking, Bourbon Street is definitely worth a look."

The driver pulled to a stop outside a quaint red brick building on Royal Street. The two-story home seemed perfectly charming and plenty exotic to me, even sandwiched between what looked to be two sprawling mansions. Our residence had one of those delicate balconies I'd already admired so much and featured two sets of tall double doors flanking a metal gateway designed to look like leafy vines. An old-fashioned lantern—like something out of Sherlock Holmes—dangled above the doors, waiting to be lit as soon as the blazing sun set.

Our driver lined our bags up on the curb. *"Bienvenue!"* he said. "This is a great location, heart of the French Quarter." I liked how he said *Quarter,* drawing it out—*Caaaaahrter*—and I had been lulled into such a state of calm by the city's relaxed pace that I had to ask him to repeat what he said next because I thought I'd heard him wrong. "Just said, y'all are right next door to that haunted house." He pointed toward the gray house next to ours, spanning the corner of Governor Nicholls Street. "LaLaurie mansion. Watch out. Oooo." He waved his fingers, a show of mock spookiness.

"Why am I not surprised?" I whispered to Lance.

Lance smirked, looking at me from the corner of his eye. I studied the imposing mansion. Rising a full story above our hostel, it had black-lacquered shutters framing the windows and a grand balcony wrapping all the way around the corner. The dove-gray paint of its façade was chipped and there were a few boarded-up windows on the upper level. A honking horn pierced my thoughts, and I looked back to see the cab disappearing down the street, a hand waving goodbye out the window.

"Haunted house? Please. That's nothin'." Dante brushed it off and gathered his tiger-striped bags. "After where we've been?"

Luggage in hand, we turned our attention back to our own residence and clustered around the center gateway. We peeked inside and could see through an arched walkway back to what appeared to be a patio. There was no one anywhere in sight. I nudged the gate, and it creaked open.

"Well, shall we?" I asked.

"Let's do it!" Dante said.

Lance shrugged, but proclaimed, *"Laissez les bon temps rouler."*

I led the way through the passage until we came out into what would be our own secret garden. I had never seen anything like it: the courtyard was hemmed in by the sides of the building, but above was sun-soaked sky. An ornately carved stone fountain gurgled in the center, with a ledge around its circular pool that seemed the perfect place to sit and read a book. A wrought-iron table and matching chairs stood to one side with a cushioned chaise longue beside it. All around the garden, patches of tropical plants flourished, their giant leaves fanning in the hot breeze. Technicolor flowers in luscious candy-apple reds, hot pinks, and citrus shades blossomed up trellises that lined all four interior walls. I tried to call up anything I could remember from my last trip to the Chicago Botanic Garden, where Joan would take me each summer. I let my fingers sweep a wall of magenta blooms. "Bougainvillea," I said, almost to myself.

"Gesundheit," said Dante, who'd already sat on the chaise and put his feet up.

"You're good." Lance came to my side and leaned in for a closer look. "I think you're right."

"There are banana trees too. Anyone interested?" Dante asked. He was on his feet now, trying to reach a cluster.

"Um, maybe we should have a look around before we start eating the landscape," I said, scanning to see if there was anyone to notice that we were about to tear the place apart.

"Suit yourself," he said, wiping his dirtied hands on his jeans. "But I'm totally coming back for a snack later."

Two staircases beckoned from either side of the entranceway, each leading up to the balcony level. We climbed the stairs on the right side to a green-shellacked door, and knocked. Strands of my shoulder-length caramel hair were matted to my hot neck and slick temples, and I prayed I wouldn't be forced to meet a whole house full of people looking this way. Lance leaned to peek into a window just a few feet away and shook his head to confirm there were no signs of life. I tried the door and it was open, so in we went.

We instantly entered a hall of mirrors—a short walkway lined floor to ceiling with square mirrored panels the size of pizza boxes. "Kind of fun-house chic," Dante muttered, as we walked through into a sprawling living room. It looked like a carnival come to life. The walls were painted slate gray, but that was the only subtle thing about the décor. One wall was dominated by a giant mask, crafted of some sort of shiny lacquer, in a riot of eggplant, gold, and emerald shades. It wore a smirking expression and had almond-shaped slits where enormous eyes would have gone. A tufted purple velvet sectional sat curved around one corner of the room near windows that looked out onto Royal Street. Elsewhere, distressed gold leaf side tables and a matching coffee table caught my eye. Expertly mismatched low-slung chairs and a love seat in the hue of the walls and speckled with cushy, oversize pillows echoing the mask's colors gave the whole place the feel of some very modern—bordering on psychedelic—lounge. Two golden scepters the length of golf clubs hung in an X above a mammoth mounted flat-screen TV.

"This sort of feels too cool for us, don'tcha think?" I had to ask softly. But it wasn't just us. Now I noticed the murmur of voices in the distance, the thump of music, and the clomp of shoes, jogging . . . toward us. A pair of guys talking to each other walked down the hallway off the living room, one of them spinning a basketball on his fingers. From the other direction, a scarlet-haired girl carried a box that looked too heavy for her.

"Thought I heard the door!" came a deep, cheery, panting voice attached to the running feet. "Sorry for the delayed welcome but . . . welcome!" Connor approached us with his hand extended. He wore an olive green Tulane T-shirt and jeans and had a bright, toothy smile. He had a clipboard and pen and his eye seemed perfectly healed and entirely scar-free. "Hey, I'm Connor. How's it going?" he said to Lance and Dante, shaking their hands. "And, Haven, good to see ya again. And I mean, really see ya this time." He pointed to his eye.

"Hey. Looking good. I'm glad it's all better."

"Thanks to my good friends at Evanston General."

"So you're the poker guy with the busted eye," Lance said, and pushed his glasses up. He looked at me as if I had failed to impart some vital bit of information.

"Yep, guilty as charged. So, hello, Chicago. Let's getcha settled in." Connor waved us to follow him as he led us down a narrow hallway adorned with framed frayed-edged maps of old New Orleans, black-and-white pictures of men dressed as kings, shots of the city streets at night, and abstract interpretations of the fleur-de-lis.

"He's just, you know, heartier than I expected for a guy who gets knocked out playing basketball," Lance whispered as he wheeled my suitcase.

"Oh?" I said, not sure what to make of it. Then: "Ohhh." I tried to stifle a grin at the thought of him being protective.

"You didn't mention he was so cute, Hav," Dante, being no help, said under his breath, before speeding ahead to catch up with Connor.

"He didn't need stitches but he was pretty beat-up," I offered to Lance, matter-of-factly.

"Good," he said. "Or, I mean . . . you know." I felt his free hand on the small of my back as we walked on.

I peeked into the open doorways we passed—a kitchen here, a dining room there—but we were going too fast to take much in. Connor had that slight bounce to his quick step that implied friendliness; there was something comforting about him. "So, I'm gonna be sort of the resident advisor here. I'll keep everything running smoothly, answer all your questions, make sure everyone plays nice, that kinda thing," he explained as he walked. "I go to Tulane. You guys should totally tour the place while you're here —great school. Still time to apply. You're seniors, right?"

"Just graduated," Dante said.

"Of course, I knew that. Well, just so y'all know, wherever you go to school, this will spoil you for dorm life—college doesn't really look like this." He laughed as we turned a corner. Now the doors had plastic street signs posted on them. "This is a rich donor's pad. He lets us use the place for events and prospective student visits and stuff. Okay—" He stopped in front of a door marked DECATUR STREET and consulted his clipboard. "Lance and Dante, looks like we've got you guys in here. Get settled. New Year's bash and welcome party tonight at eight. We'll leave here at seven thirty if you wanna go as a group." He slapped Lance on the back. "Enjoy. And Haven, you're a few doors down at the end of the hall. Here, I'll take that." He grabbed the bag from my shoulder and my suitcase from Lance and wheeled it himself, whistling as he walked.

"Southern gentlemen, gotta love 'em." Dante shrugged, like it was no big deal, as if sensing the ripple pass between Lance and me. He pushed past Lance into their room.

"I'm gonna unpack," Lance announced. He kissed me on the cheek, then followed Dante as I rushed ahead. Connor had stopped outside a door with a sign reading TCHOUPITOULAS, which I had seen in my guidebook but hoped to avoid ever having to pronounce. He opened the door.

"Just out of curiosity . . ." I pointed to the sign.

He smiled. "The *T* is silent."

"Good to know, thanks."

The room looked like it belonged in a dollhouse: eggplant-hued, with a tall, skinny window looking out onto the courtyard, one long silver desk, two chairs, a closet running the length of one wall . . . and one bed. I breathed a sigh of relief. It looked like I would be rooming solo.

"So, these rooms are all a little bit quirky," Connor started as he set my suitcase beside the bed. He walked over to a gauzy curtain hanging along the wall. He whipped it open to reveal a ladder and a loft carved into the wall with a mattress inside and a small night table. The ceilings were high and airy enough, but even so, you wouldn't be able to stand up in this nook. It was a cozy little spot — and a nice bit of privacy — but I knew what it meant. "A bunch of the rooms have this loft situation. I'll let you and Sabine decide who's bunkin' where."

"Sabine?"

"She got here a little while ago and went out. She's from"—he consulted his clipboard once more—"Boston, looks like."

"Sabine from Boston," I repeated, starting to feel nervous.

"Right, so seven thirty in the common room," he said, pointing at me. "There's a welcome kit for each of you in the dressers."

"Got it." He opened up the closet to reveal two identical silver dressers, the size of filing cabinets, and a suitcase and matching bag. "Thanks."

He let himself out and said, "Need anything, lemme know." I smiled and thanked him.

I poked around the room. Sabine had claimed one of the dressers and unpacked already, her clothes folded in precise rows. I hopped onto the bed to survey the room and heard a crunch. I gazed at the crisp sheet of paper that had been left:

Hi!
   I'm Sabine. Nice to meet you! A few of us went to get some beignets. Here's my number if you want to join up. Otherwise, look forward to meeting you tonight!
   Yours, Sabine

Her handwriting was pretty and full of uniformly round, bubble-shaped letters. I thought of calling the number she'd left, but something—nerves?—held me back. Instead, I simply set to work unpacking.

3

You'll Be One of Us Soon

At 7:25 p.m. Dante and I emerged simultaneously from our rooms ready to make our way to that color-splashed living room, my stomach a little queasy at the thought of meeting so many new people, and just the newness of it all, of learning to navigate this town, period. I felt like I was standing in a field waiting to be struck by lightning—again—with nowhere to go for cover, and I just wasn't sure I was ready to dodge and outrun it yet again.

Dante, as usual, helped shake me out of it as soon as he saw me. "You're welcome," he said, preemptively, staring at my outfit.

"Thank you, Dante," I said flatly, embarrassed, fanning out the gauzy layers of my knee-length plum chiffon dress to curtsy my appreciation. It was the sort of thing I never would have chosen myself—nipped in at the waist, it had jeweled straps and a sprinkling of clear crystals that made it shimmer all over. But, girly as it was, when I put it on, I actually liked it.

"You know you didn't *really* want to wear that old homecoming dress." He turned up his nose at the thought. He was forever calling me out for my sartorial choices; when our information packets had arrived in Chicago labeling these New Year's festivities as "semiformal," he had forced me out to the mall. He was now wearing the satin violet tie from that shopping trip.

"Please, being your stylist is the best distraction from, like, real life, you know?" he said lightly, but with a twinge that showed there was some dread beneath the surface. He fluffed my hair, as the door to his room opened.

"Hey," Lance said. He fished for something in his pocket. Like Dante, he wore a dark suit, but his tie was a muted gray.

"Well, I picked out the shoes on my own. A little credit please? I'm wearing heels at least." I gestured to my metallic sandals.

"I had to convince you to go silver. Partial credit," Dante joked.

"I thought you seemed taller. Two and a quarter inches?" Lance calculated, as was his way. Then he stepped in, pulling me by the arm just enough so his lips were level with my eyes. He tilted up his chin so it rested on the top of my head. "Yeah, usually it's easier to do this." I playfully swatted him away.

"It's just a matter of time before I'm kicked out of my room by you *lovebirds,* I know it." Dante sighed. "Ugh. See, birds are trouble. I'm beginning to understand why Hitchcock made a horror movie about them."

"Dan!" I rolled my eyes. Lance didn't seem to be listening. He had already dug out his new monogrammed phone, testing it once more, with a furrowed brow that said it still wasn't working.

There were voices up ahead. I could sense a wave of anxiety pass through the three of us, our posture collectively stiffening.

"Still no sign of the roommate?" Dante asked. Lance had popped out the battery in the back of the phone and some other piece and held them up to his eye. He saw me looking and just shook his head, slipping the components back into the pocket of his slightly wrinkled suit jacket.

"Nope, not yet," I replied. "Is it weird that I'm nervous to meet her?" Sabine hadn't come back all day and I felt slight pangs of guilt now that I hadn't called her to at least say hello and thank her for the invitation to roam the city—her note had been so welcoming. But, really, the day had flown by, consumed by all the usual mundanities of christening a new place home, followed by a lengthy primping session with Dante.

"Honestly, nothing's weird anymore," Lance offered. He had a point.

"Loosen up, Hav!" Dante kneaded my shoulders and slapped me on the back, just as we reached the living room.

Our fellow housemates were already gathered. The basketball players from earlier chatted easily—I assumed they had come from the same school, like we had. Others—like that redhead, who now wore a jade halter-top dress—sat perched with stiff backs on the sleek furniture, looking like they hoped to blend in with the décor. They glanced side to side, debating, it seemed, whether to strike up a conversation or wait for someone else to make the first move. The three of us took our places standing along the periphery, against the wall with the TV. Before we could get too social, we were startled by a few loud claps from the side hallway.

"Hey, team!" Connor called, standing in the center of the room. He was dressed in a suit and tie, but he held his jacket and his rolled-up shirt sleeves exposed his tan forearms. "The other folks'll have to meet us there. Let's roll out!"

The St. Charles streetcar rattled along the center of the tree-lined avenue. Here and there, a few strands of shiny beads, no doubt remnants of last year's Mardi Gras, still hung entwined in the branches of the trees above. They reminded me of my phone call with Joan earlier, when I confirmed we had arrived safely in New Orleans. "Promise you won't do anything nutty just to get someone to throw those plastic beads at you?" she said. I laughed and assured her I hadn't gotten too wild yet.

Dante slid into me on the wooden bench seat, angling to get a better view of the mansions dotting the way. No two were alike, each with special touches like ornate gates out front, bay windows, delicately crafted balconies and porticos, and charming little detached pool houses nestled in back. "The Garden District totally rocks," he said.

"Kind of awesome that this was all one huge estate back in the day," Lance said, eyes trained outside, his fingers drumming on my leg.

"Good to know," I said. "I feel like the trivia gauntlet is being thrown down." Lance and I liked to get competitive about our facts—it was just our thing. This constituted flirting for us.

"Just sharing," he said, with a mocking faux innocence.

"Ugh, have we forgotten we're outta school?" Dante groaned. "Here, this one!" He pointed out the window at what looked like a small castle. "Let's move here, Hav."

"I'm in," I joked. Lance suddenly pulled out his phone again, as if an idea had just struck him. Dante shook his head and continued surveying.

"Check this out." Dante, ever the gossip, flicked his head toward the front of the streetcar where Connor sat chatting with the driver. The redhead beside him quietly looked on, nodding at something he was saying, hanging on his every word.

"It seems this streetcar may indeed be named Desire," I whispered back.

"I know, right? Looks like someone is already trying to line up that midnight kiss. Good for her," he declared in a sincere, even serious tone. I thought I could feel a trace of loneliness creeping out from beneath that confident armor of his.

From the corner of my eye I watched Lance fiddling with his phone. There were plenty of dark clouds obscuring our thoughts. But tonight, I wanted to be like everyone else. For the first time ever, I had someone to make midnight matter.

As if on cue, Lance gave up on the phone and emerged from his interior world to rejoin us. "Anyone want to check out Tennessee Williams's old pad tomorrow?" he piped up as he cleaned the lenses of his glasses on his sleeve. "It's near our place. And William Faulkner's too."

"Faulk yeah!" said Dante. I gave him a playful slap on the shoulder.

The streetcar stopped and Connor called for us all to jump out.

After we walked a few of the leafiest, quietest streets I'd ever seen, Connor turned a corner and we were greeted by a pristine white mansion with sprawling, manicured grounds of lush hedges and sweet white rosebushes that spanned the full block. A porch wrapped around the entire first floor of the place and even from where we stood, we could hear the strains of a jazz band playing. Darkness had fallen, a chill settling in the air, reminding us that even here in the South, it was still winter. But a warm, buttery glow from the black-shuttered windows beckoned us in. A banner reading WELCOME, VOLUNTEERS! had been unfurled over the pillars. We crossed beneath an archway of greenery and went up the steep front steps.

"Whoa, pretty nice digs," Lance said under his breath as we

entered, our senses enveloped by the festivities. Jaunty music and the scent of spicy food filled the air. Scores and scores of other high school students, college types, and well-dressed adults milled around, chatting, holding aloft tiny plates of towering fried foods and sipping from delicate stemware. Our group dispersed, everyone heading off in separate directions. Dante, Lance, and I wound our way to the back of the great hall, taking it all in, and continued on to a mahogany-outfitted grand living room complete with a buffet and white-coated chefs in crisp, cylindrical hats. A long line of people waited patiently to be served all manner of southern comfort food.

"I'm dying for that gumbo," Dante said, his eyes glued on the buffet tables. "Did I tell you I've almost perfected my roux? I'll have to make it for you guys." He seemed to be thinking, then he grabbed Lance and me by the arm. "That's it, come 'ere." He tugged us toward a less populated corner of the packed room. As we followed him, weaving through the clusters of people snacking, I caught the slightest glimpse of . . . no, I mean, what was wrong with me? My heart stopped for a moment, and then he was gone. That golden hair, the suit, a drink in his hand. I blinked my eyes, shook out my jumbled head. There were a ton of people here. I was seeing things.

Dante huddled us up, his back to the crowd as he dug a small tin of mints out of his pocket. "Got something for you guys," he said. "You'll thank me."

"Should we be offended?" I checked my breath in my palm. It was still pepperminty from brushing my teeth before we left. Lance turned around and did the same thing over his shoulder.

"No, no, no." Dante rolled his eyes and opened up the case: three tiny brown leaves, each no bigger than a postage stamp, were nestled inside. "I only have a few of these left from, you know, the Lex. Let them dissolve on your tongue and you can eat whatever you want for the next twenty-four hours and you should be immune to any toxins." His eyes darted past us, hoping no one heard. He didn't have to explain. Before the hotel had been destroyed, Dante had pilfered all sorts of mysterious ingredients from the Lexington's pantry—powerful plants and herbs harvested straight from the underworld.

"Thanks, man. But, I don't know, isn't it a little reckless to use them so soon?" Lance asked what I'd been thinking.

Dante just shook the tin at us. "There's no point waiting. We have to play it safe. We'll figure something out, but let's try to fit in tonight, whaddya say?"

I liked that idea. "You convinced me," I said, taking one of the wispy, translucent leaves in my fingertips. *"Laissez les bon temps rouler."* I placed it on my tongue; it tasted like cinnamon and bubbled up then dissolved in a split second. Lance shrugged and did the same thing; Dante took the last leaf, snapping the tin shut.

"Okay, I don't care how long that line is, who's with me?"

In no time, we had staked out a tall cocktail table where we stood silently tucking into the fiery gumbo. Dante had accumulated a staggering array of plates and little ramekins of other spicy, saucy dishes that he introduced us to: étouffée with its plump little shrimp and clouds of rice; chicken and sausage jambalaya that had a potent kick. Lance had stacked his small plate full of fried pickles and seemed content to eat his weight in those, while I had collected a handful of building-block-size pieces of cornbread.

After we had consumed it all and camped out in the room with the band to watch them play for a while, then investigated the various species of plant life in the greenhouse, peeked into the scores of first editions and autographed books in the study ("This Mark Twain could pay for college for all three of us," Lance said, pointing at an open tome inside a locked cabinet), and finally wandered back into the rollicking grand hall at half an hour to midnight, it occurred to me that we had missed the whole point of this occasion.

"I guess we should be, like, getting to know people, right?" I said, a little embarrassed, food coma setting in. "I mean it's kind of a mixer."

"The only mixers I'm interested in are the ones that go into the virgin hurricanes out there." Dante flicked his head toward a drink station set up near the French doors leading to the side porch. I grabbed my water-filled wineglass—I was still parched from the spicy selections we'd been scarfing down all night—and we slithered through the crowd to that bustling spot where the fruity signature concoction was being blended by the gallon.

"I wonder how many liters it takes to quench a crowd this size on New Year's Eve, taking into account that people are especially in the mood to imbibe, and factoring in the ratio of alcohol drinkers to nondrinkers." Lance scanned the crowd, wheels turning in his head to compute, thinking, thinking.

And it hit me again. A flash. I saw him. Across the way. It *was* him.

My head spun, keeping him in my sights. I stopped in my tracks, the crowd clearing enough for me to see without a doubt those eyes that had been burned into my memory. The eyes that I had last seen looking back at me as he fell down, reclaimed by the fiery depths below, and breaking my heart. They pierced right through me now, rooting me to my spot, looking at nothing but me for those long seconds as the bodies flowed in the vast space between us.

Chiming bells shook me out of it, and I dropped my glass. It shattered at my feet and I averted my eyes from his. Everyone near me scattered. Dante and Lance were already at the hurricane station. "Omigod, I'm so sorry," I said to everyone around me, as glass crunched under my shoes. A black-and-white-attired waiter was already at my side with a broom.

I looked up, standing on my tiptoes to find him again. His eyes lassoed my attention once more and he beelined straight back toward the solarium. A chipper, disembodied voice then rang out, amplified from another room: "If everyone could please gather in the ballroom!" The masses surged in the opposite direction. I pushed upstream through the crowd, desperate to follow him, not thinking at all. Something else beyond even reflex or instinct took over, this animal need to not let him get away.

I made it back through to the glass-enclosed solarium, where the doors to the patio had been left open. The dark-suited figure cut across the lawn and disappeared into the maze of high hedges in the garden. I scurried down the steps, hoping to not lose my footing, and broke into a jog as I entered the labyrinth. My heels sank into the ground with each step, making me run harder. I could hear the soft crush of his quick footsteps as he slipped farther into the maze's twists. I did my best to follow, the crisp night air chilling my sweat-slicked skin as I turned the dark corners, the prickly shoots of the hedges reaching out to me, until a light glimmered in the distance.

I ran toward it, those scars above my heart beginning to flare. But I had to keep going forward; I just couldn't stop myself. A last burst of energy and I turned the final corner, onto a stone patio with a lit fountain trickling softly at its center.

And there was Lucian, bathed in a halo of warm light, the glow reflecting off his skin, outlining the sharpness of his jaw and giving an extra sparkle to his eyes. I had no words.

"Haven . . ." he said softly, and only then did I realize how much I had missed that voice all these months even though I shouldn't have. I took one step forward but as I did, my world crumbled. It was as though I had set foot into a trap and had triggered a force yanking away this façade. Before my eyes, he morphed into something else. His form grew taller and filled out, his hair darkening, and the bones of his face restructuring until it wasn't Lucian at all.

It was the Prince standing before me now, a smile on his lips telling me that I had been deceived, and so easily. I spun around to run away, but he grabbed my arm, clenching it in his hand so firmly I felt welded to him.

He tugged me so close I could feel the heat radiating from him. What little I had ever seen of him at the Lexington had always been at a distance. I had never had to feel his wrath—he had only sent his underlings to deal with me. But this level of fear I couldn't even process. My stomach dropped, my heart throbbed, every inch of my skin crawled. In the distance I could hear the murmur of a toast going on back in the house, and then everyone joining in, counting down to the new year. If only I were in there now. If only I had paid attention to the message my scars were sending me.

This dashing, deadly monster leaned in to my ear. I could hear his breathing, so deafening. "Lucian sends his love," he whispered in a sweet voice. "You'll be one of us soon, Haven. No use trying to fight it."

With that, he planted a kiss on my cheek. Though his lips barely touched my skin, it stung so hot and sharp I felt like I'd been branded.

In a flash, he disappeared, leaving me standing alone on that stone patio, in the center of a circle of fire. The sounds of cheers and noisemakers wafted from the party. Dazed, I rubbed at my aching arm, bringing it back to life after being in his death grip. I shook myself out and leapt over that low flame, running, until I found my way out of the maze, up those steps, and back inside to the safety of so many strangers.

4

Boom

I didn't stop running until I had made it all the way back to the great hall, where the sound of applause fluttered out from the ballroom to the end notes of "Auld Lang Syne." It didn't occur to my legs to stop moving until I felt myself slam right into someone's chest, my face landing flush against his white cotton dress shirt. His arm latched on to mine. Around us, party guests flowed from the direction of the ballroom, chattering spiritedly, wishing one another a Happy New Year as music cued up. I righted myself, murmuring an apology. My hand flew to my angel-wing necklace for comfort.

"Haven! Whoa! Just the girl I was looking for," Connor said, laughing. "This is your roommate, Sabine. Sabine, Haven."

"Hi! So great to finally meet you!" The raven-haired girl with delicate features threw her arms around me. She wore a simple black slipdress and heels that made her my height.

"Hi." I tried to sound normal. "Great to meet you too. I—"

Connor seemed to spot someone across the way. "Hey, man!" he said over my shoulder, with a big wave, then looked at the two of us again. "Have fun. Happy New Year. I'll catch you guys later, okay?"

"See you later!" Sabine said. I just smiled. I was still catching my breath and struggling to regulate my heartbeat. I wanted to sit down, or lie down, or just disappear and forget about the Prince and Lucian and whatever else might be coming for me.

"He's totally hot, right?" Sabine whispered conspiratorially, a mischievous glint in her eyes.

"Definitely not a bad-looking guy." I had to smile.

"Have you seen some of the other RAs? Eeek. Trolls. No, that's terrible. Bad Sabine." She shook her head, scanning the crowd as she sipped from her hurricane. "But, let's just say . . . we're lucky."

"Agreed." I chuckled. "No complaints here for sure. So . . . how were the beignets?" I worked hard to manufacture a tone far sunnier than I felt. "Thanks for your note and all. By the time I got in, it was late so I figured . . . But that was so nice of you—"

"Omigod, don't worry about it. But they were to die for." She grabbed my forearm to drive home the point. "I have to go back. We'll have to go tomorrow. Or maybe they're still open later to-night—Café Du Monde, do you know it?" Sabine seemed a little like a flirtatious, female Dante. She possessed a warmth I appreciated, especially at that moment. She was petite like me, but with jet-black hair, porcelain skin, and a willowy frame. I felt more athletic these days, stronger, though I don't know if I looked to others as hearty as I felt in my skin. And, of course, right now, I was feeling more than a little fragile and powerless and . . . scared. I tried to lose myself in simple conversation.

"I don't know it. It's my first time in New Orleans."

"Anyway, they were amazing. So you're from Chicago? I love it there, my—" she launched in, but was quickly interrupted.

"Hey, there you are. What happened to you?" Lance asked, appearing at my side.

"We've been looking for you, like, everywhere!" Dante said. He downed the last of his drink. I wanted to send them messages with my eyes, but there was no way to communicate what I had just been through.

"Oh, hey, yeah, so this is Sabine, my roommate," I said, ignoring Lance's question. I made the introductions and smiles were exchanged and more hugs administered.

"Have you met Max and Brody yet?" Sabine asked us.

"No, I don't think—"

"You'll love them." She stood on her tiptoes glancing around the room. "I'm going to find them. Don't you go anywhere!" And with that she wandered off.

"So, you missed midnight. What gives?" Lance asked as soon as she left. "Happy New Year, belatedly." He leaned in to quickly kiss me on the lips, and it made me wish I had never run outside. I wanted to rewind. I wanted midnight back and to spend the rest of the evening like this. But Dante was talking now.

"And you missed a scintillating speech, too."

"Oh?"

"Welcome to the city, go forth and conquer, blah blah. They introduced a bunch of people."

"You want a drink or something?" Lance asked, worry clouding his eyes.

"Um." I looked around to be sure no one could overhear but by now the crowd was relaxed enough that they were completely immersed in their own worlds—the adults all tipsy and our peers hyped up on plates of sugary confections that must've been unveiled in a neighboring room.

"What he means is, were you, like, running laps or something?" Dante cut in. "You're looking a little . . . *rough*."

"No, I know, I know . . ." I smoothed my hair back behind my ears, patting it down, and wiped my moist brow with the back of my hand.

Dante reached for my cheek. "What is this smudge on you? Is it lipstick?"

It stung still. I held his wrist to stop him. "No, it's just . . . he's here," I said, soft and serious, as though I had just placed a ticking bomb in their hands. I looked from one to the other, my eyes stabbing them with this news so there could be no mistake. "He's here. The Prince."

Lance took a step closer to me, his hand on my upper arm. His steady gaze flickered immediately to the space above my head and behind me, searching, a secret service agent sussing out a threat. "What do you mean? How do you know? What happened?" he demanded, his voice firm.

"Or he was here, but he's not now. They're here in the city, coming for us. I—we were going to get the drinks and then, you know, I thought I saw . . ." I was trying to find a way to make myself *not* sound like the complete fool I'd been.

"Hav! C'mon, what's the deal?" Dante whispered but the desperation in his voice poked through. He shook me to get me going.

"I thought I saw . . . Lucian." I didn't want to tell them, Lance especially, and yet keeping it from him made it seem like it was something that needed to be hidden, which felt even more toxic.

"Lucian." Lance snarled the name.

"Lucian? But you said—" Dante started.

"No, I know. So I saw Lucian and then I sort of followed him, because, I don't know. I thought I was going crazy. I just had to see what . . . I don't know, I just followed him. Outside."

"Outside." Lance didn't like this either. "Of course," he snapped. "Why would you follow him? What would ever possess—"

"Lance." Dante stopped him. "Not productive." He turned to me. "Tell us everything, every single thing."

I told them what had happened, what the Prince had said, and they asked questions I had no answers to. But they didn't have much time to absorb it all before Sabine found her way back to us, with two guys in tow. She introduced the guy who looked like a skateboarder—with a wide streak of electric blue running through his chin-length dark blond hair—as Brody and the one with the golden complexion and short black hair poking out from beneath a fedora as Max.

"So you guys are from Boston?" Dante asked.

"No, man, just her," Brody jumped in. "I'm San Diego and he's Phoenix."

"We just met, you know, today," Max clarified. It occurred to me that Sabine was one of those people who somehow instantly become friends with everyone. She rummaged through her purse and extracted a tube of lip-gloss.

"So, anyway," she started, coating her lips and smacking them. "We have a proposition. It's early, I mean, for New Year's. Let's get outta here and hit Bourbon Street for a look around before all the craziness dies down."

"Who's with us?" asked Brody.

In no time, we were hopping off the streetcar and winding through the French Quarter, following the roar of revelers. Bourbon Street, entirely closed off to traffic, swarmed with stumbling good-timers, many donning party hats and tiaras and dancing in the streets to the music pouring out of every bar and eatery.

Scantily clad women perched in doorways made catcalls to the men walking by. A voluptuous woman in the shortest jean shorts I'd ever seen, ice-pick-like heels, and a leopard halter-top that barely contained her waved to a pack of guys all decked out in plastic New Year's top hats and glasses fashioned out of the numbers of the new year. "Yep, I bet she's sorry she didn't wear a coat out tonight too. Brrrr!" I joked, folding my arms in the crisp air.

"I'm sure outerwear isn't her primary concern." Max laughed, then, turning to Dante, he pointed to me. "She's so cute!"

Dante smacked him playfully on the arm, already pals. "I know, right?" He grabbed Max's fedora. "This is totally badass, by the way." Soon, they were in their own world, talking about where to go shopping.

"Seriously," Lance piped up. "There are, like, per capita, a *lot* of, ahem, adult entertainers in this town."

I heard a splash and whipped my head in its direction. Brody had gotten entirely sloshed with a beer by some guy in a green feather boa, spray even landing on Sabine beside him. She patted at her damp arm. The offending drunk shouted his apologies as he stumbled by.

"No sweat, dude," Brody yelled, turning to us, soaked. "A rite of passage, right?"

"It's a baptism," I shouted back in agreement. "We should all be so lucky." He shook his head, smiling, a good sport. Sabine looked at me with wide have-you-ever-seen-anything-like-this?! eyes.

Another posse caught my eye, coming down the center of the street and led by a young woman who looked like she belonged on the runway of a lingerie fashion show. She had an ice-blond pixie haircut, cheekbones carved of stone, and a sinewy frame. She wore the tiniest white strapless minidress, sky-high white heels with straps that crisscrossed again and again almost up to her knees, and a fluffy white feather boa around her neck. In one hand she held up a sparkler in the night air. It crackled and spit its tiny charges like fireflies. Though the crowd was so densely packed it was difficult to move very fast or far, this group had no trouble as their leader strutted along, commanding all of Bourbon Street's attention. Her merry band of fellow provocateurs, all with sparklers blazing, was made up of statuesque women in short, dark sequined dresses and lean, athletic men in black pants and partially undone button-downs, their sleeves rolled up.

We couldn't take our eyes off them and watched silently for a few long minutes, getting jostled from all sides. As raucous as this drunken Bourbon Street crowd was, it still felt comforting to be among them. To be just one little person embedded in this massive group seemed safer than I ever would have expected. I almost dreaded having to go back to our new residence, where I would, at some point, be forced to be alone with my thoughts in those awful minutes of darkness before falling asleep—if I would be lucky enough to fall asleep.

The parading group threw beads as they passed, but we were too entranced for the necessary hand-eye coordination to kick in to catch them. We just let them drop at our feet as we watched the procession. The pixie twirled her sparkler as though it were a baton, somehow managing not to singe herself or those nearby. She looked as if she was leading a marching band. Finally, she made a swooping motion, unleashing the sparkler skyward, so high it seemed it might kiss the moon. She stopped in front of me for a moment, looked right in my eyes, and said with a wild, wide smile, "Boom."

A second later, the sparkler ignited with the *BOOM!* she had promised. It exploded above us into a kaleidoscope of shimmering colors, then twinkled as it burned out, like rain in lamplight. I felt my jaw drop. When I turned my gaze back to street level, she had moved on, making her way down Bourbon. She grabbed the sparkler from the man beside her and tossed that one too. Up, up, up until it bloomed as vibrant as the one before it.

"Whoa," Lance said, then pushed his glasses up on his nose.

"I'm pretty sure that kind of thing is illegal where we're from," I offered.

Dante grinned. "We're definitely not in Evanston anymore."

"She's gorgeous," Sabine whispered, wistful. "Don't you feel like you have to be absolutely perfect to have that hair?" She pulled back her lustrous locks and mugged. "I would kill to look good with that cut, but I could never, ever do it."

"You totally could," I assured her as we began walking again. I was secretly glad that I wasn't the only one who could feel intimidated like that. I felt unsettled by beautiful things for so many reasons, a reflex after my time at the Lexington. "You would look great."

"Really?" Sabine sounded truly touched. I nodded. She looped her arm in mine. "So would you!" I didn't even care if she meant it or whether it was true. It was just nice to hear.

We all walked on together silently those last few blocks to Royal Street. The house pulsed with activity when we returned—the TV blared in the living room, music and conversation trickled out of a couple of open bedroom doors, someone foraged for snacks in the kitchen. Our group split into three pairs, all of us retiring to our respective rooms, exhausted by what we'd seen tonight.

I let Sabine go ahead and said good night to Lance at his doorway—Dante had already gone inside.

"You know you can stay in here if you want, right? Or . . ." He didn't finish his thought and what he managed to get out he said with a halting awkwardness.

"Yeah. Thanks," I said. The truth was, I didn't want to be

alone. I would've liked nothing more than to just drift off to sleep in Lance's arms. But on our first night in this new place, I didn't want to be that girl who was spotted leaving a guy's room at some strange hour of the morning. "I feel like I'd better be in my own bed. First night and all."

"Yeah, no, got it, I figured," he said, agreeing too eagerly. "Good thinking." He kissed me good night and I could feel him watch me walk to my room before retreating into his.

H e's supercute," Sabine said with a mischievous smile when I returned. "Well done, you!"

"Thanks," I said, with a little laugh.

"You've been dating how long?" She pulled on sweatpants and a tee as I changed into a pair of my aquamarine scrubs, relieved to be out of my heels.

"Just a few months, but friends for a while."

"Cute," she said. "I dated a friend once . . ." I waited for more but she didn't seem anxious to offer it up so I let it go. She took in my outfit. "Are you on call tonight?" she joked, tying her hair back and taking a seat at the desk as I hung up my clothes.

"New Year's *is* one of the most dangerous holidays," I quipped. "Old volunteer job. It's actually where I met Connor. It's a long story but—"

"Omigod, me too!" she interrupted. "I mean, I wasn't exactly saving lives. It was an ice cream shop on the Cape." She shook her head, as though details weren't that important. "But, you know, he came in a couple times or whatever."

"Seriously?" I asked. She nodded, seeming to be excited by this odd coincidence. I didn't know why I felt disappointed. Secretly, I kind of liked the idea that Connor had seen something special in me and told me to apply for the program. I wished that I didn't need that kind of reassurance, but sometimes it's just nice to feel wanted. "That's really funny." It came out more flatly than I would have liked.

"Anyway, he's a mint chocolate chip guy," Sabine said.

"Good to know."

"I'm totally dying to know where we're working first," she said as she searched in her bag. "Do you have any idea?" She pulled out her phone and gave it a look, scrolling.

"No." I drifted off in thought for a moment. The idea sent the slightest shiver down my spine, as I recalled my last boss, the stunning and lethal Aurelia Brown. I couldn't imagine what tomorrow would bring.

"Awww." She smiled at her phone then quickly flashed it at me: it was a photo of a handful of girls in someone's living room, a HAPPY NEW YEAR banner behind them. The text message read *Miss you!!!!* "Weird not to be home tonight, right?" she asked, her thumbs tapping out a response.

"Yeah, I know," I said, even though I didn't exactly feel that I had missed out on anything. Back home, I still would have spent the evening with Lance and Dante; we just wouldn't have been dressed as nicely.

"How late is it there?" she said to herself, thinking.

"Boston? It's an hour back so, wow, like two?" I answered.

She nodded and began dialing. "Have you ever been to Boston?"

"No. For me it's like there's an electric fence keeping me in the Midwest. It's amazing I managed to convince Joan to let me go this far."

"I think it's so cool that you call your mom Joan." I had told

Sabine I was adopted, but that's all she knew, and really all she needed to. I was good at not sharing a whole lot about my past. "Anyway, it's a great town. You have to visit. We're just outside of it, but it's a short ride in to Newbury Street, all the good shopping." She put the phone to her ear. "Hey you! Happy New Year! How *are* you?! . . . I know, I just got it. So cute!" Moonlight trickled in from outside our window, reflecting off the glossy-white wraparound balcony. Might as well give her privacy. I unlocked the latch, pushing the window open. I sat on the sill and then just scooted my legs over to the other side to climb out. The air had grown chillier and I felt the goose bumps rise on my skin. I could still hear the dull roar of Bourbon Street in the distance.

"You know there's a door right there?" someone yelled from part of the balcony diagonally across the courtyard, an arm waving. I leaned over the railing and could see him in the hazy light. Connor. I waved back. He pointed off somewhere to my left. I looked over to a door that must've been located at the end of our hallway.

"Yeah, you know, I don't like to make things too easy," I called back.

"I like that about you," he answered, then, with another wave, said, "Night!" He turned and let himself in through a similar door over on his side of the building. Muffled voices from another section of the balcony traveled my way. It was dark over there, but I could see two figures sitting, talking, and watching the courtyard below. Above them, the third story of the mansion next door loomed over our more modest home, like a bully in the shadows.

"Get a room down there!" shouted one of the people from across the way.

I leaned over and spied two figures entwined on the chaise. I squinted to see who it might be. Two faces looked skyward, and both bodies sprang up and scurried inside.

Behind me the window whooshed open. "Hey!" Sabine said. "Whatcha doin' out here?"

"I do believe I just witnessed the first dorm hookup."

"No way." She stomped her foot in mock outrage. "I'm jealous. Get in here and give me the scoop. You can fill me in while we fight over the beds. Don't know about you but I'm totally zonked," she said.

I climbed back in and we negotiated the most equitable division of sleeping arrangements possible: A coin toss determined that I got the loft. We both nestled in and turned off our bedside lamps.

"Next project," she said, yawning in the darkness. "I think we've gotta decorate somehow, you know? Maybe hit those antique stores nearby, find something fun?"

"Did you see the one with the giant, like, stone camel in the front window?" I asked, laughing.

"Perfect," she said, though I knew she was only kidding. "Night."

"G'night." I lay on my back, my eyes wide open. This was the least tired I'd felt all day. If I hadn't had a roommate, I likely would've flipped the light back on and tried to read, but that didn't seem like a nice thing to do on our first night here. Much as I'd tried to push it aside all night, now all I could see when I closed my eyes was the image of the Prince. Or Lucian becoming the Prince.

Through the sheer, gauzy curtain shrouding the front of the lofted space, I was at just the right height and angle to see the full moon shimmering outside the window. I locked on to it, glad for any bit of light to illuminate those dark places now in my mind, and I hoped its peacefulness would cocoon around me.

Then I saw it and bolted straight up in bed.

A low glow flickered in the top corner window of the mansion next door and a light sparked on. It hadn't been there before—I would have noticed it while I was outside. It had only *just* gone on. I crawled forward on my bed and slid open the curtain in a quick whoosh. Below, I heard Sabine roll over, then deep breaths of sleep followed. Leaning forward now, I could make out a shadow. Someone stood in the window next door. But before I could see anything more clearly, the light went out again. I stared at that darkened window, waiting, unable to move. Finally, after many minutes, I slipped back under the covers, pulling them tight around me.

5

Everything Okay in Here?

I managed to doze off at some point, but my sleep couldn't be called restful. It was more a series of nightmares, except they all happened in real life: my mind replayed a loop of every horrific event I'd encountered during my first test of angelhood. Every moment—and there were a lot of them—when I had narrowly cheated death. Every poisoning, every fire bolt launched my way, every one of those beautiful, evil creatures I'd had to battle. My skin could still feel their hot claws on me. My heart remembered the ferocity of its beating when a pack of them had stolen into my bedroom to attack me. That's when my eyes finally sprang open.

I peeked at my alarm clock: almost five o'clock. Outside the sky was still inky black, just the slightest ribbon of midnight blue creeping up from the horizon. Sabine was sleeping peacefully. It was still too dark to read, so I grabbed the book from my night table, crept down the ladder, and, not bothering to change out of my scrubs, quietly let myself out of the room.

The stark emptiness and pure silence of the hallway did

nothing to settle my frayed nerves. But as I turned the corner, I caught the clang of silverware and the vacuum swoosh of the refrigerator being opened. I smoothed my hair and poked my head into the kitchen just as Connor turned around.

"Whoa!" he said, startled, almost losing the two-liter bottle of diet soda tucked under one arm, and the steaming cup of ramen noodles and the apple in his hands.

"Sorry. Hi," I said, also sorry that I hadn't bothered to get dressed. He looked sufficiently messy himself, but wore it well, from his fresh-from-bed hair sticking up every which way and heavy-lidded eyes to his mesh soccer shorts and a fraternity T-shirt with a ripped sleeve.

"Haven. Hey, didn't expect to see anyone up this early. I've got a paper due. What's your excuse?" He crunched into his apple.

"Just, you know, in the middle of a good book." I held it up. It could've been the truth.

"I like a girl who gets up early to read. That says something about you, you know?" He nodded in praise. "I knew what I was doing when I drafted you at the hospital."

"Yeah, guess so," I said, thinking about how he also had recruited Sabine but saying nothing.

"Anyway, make yourself at home. And just lemme know if you need anything." He waved his apple as a goodbye.

I leaned against the counter, thinking, then called out, "Connor?"

He popped his head back in.

I did my best to sound nonchalant. "So what's the deal with the house next door?"

"Ahhh, the haunted one?" he asked, in a loaded way. "The

LaLaurie pad? The tourists love it, of course. But it's just some well-marketed folklore. Nothing to worry about."

"No, totally, I know," I said, trying too hard to sound cool. "So is it, like, abandoned?"

"Right now, yeah. But actually it's gonna get fixed up soon. Some of you guys will be working on it, as one of the group projects."

"Right. Thanks."

"House meeting at nine o'clock," he reminded me, then ambled down the hall, polishing off his apple. I poked around inside the fridge and opened the cupboards in the hopes that some sort of comfort food would appear and soothe me. I found some of those single-serve packs of Oreos, like Joan used to put in my lunches in grade school, and couldn't resist tearing one open.

That's when I heard the scream. It came from somewhere out front: a male voice, deep, expletive-laced, accompanied by rattling metal. Then footsteps running through the hall. I lunged out of the kitchen.

"You heard it too?" Connor asked. I nodded. "Stay here." He jogged down the mirrored hall to the back entranceway.

Despite his instruction, I trailed behind him. The sun had only just begun its ascent, the sky brightening to a deep indigo as we clomped down the wooden staircase to the courtyard and through the lantern-lit archway to the locked front gate. One of the guys from our house, the one I had seen yesterday with a basketball, stood there, hands clasping the metal bars, trying to get in.

Connor slowed his pace, his alarm lessening. "Jimmy, dude, what're the deal? What're ya doin' out here?"

"You gotta let me in. Lemme in, lemme in!" He was frantic.

"Where're your keys? If you lost 'em already, we're gonna have to charge you," Connor said, unhitching the lock and opening up. I hung back in the shadows of the archway.

"Call nine-one-one," Jimmy said. He raced in, letting the gate crash. He ran right past us.

"What are you talking about?" Connor called out to him.

Jimmy paused just a moment, shouting back from the courtyard, "There's a body out there. An eff-ing body!" We could hear him stumbling up the steps and slamming the door. Connor and I stood stunned in the lantern-lit haze. He sighed and scratched at the back of his head, like he was psyching himself up, then unlocked the gate once more. Silently, he stepped out onto Royal Street, as I followed a few paces behind.

By the time I reached the sidewalk, he was walking back toward me stone-faced. With a firm voice, he ordered: "Haven, go back upstairs."

It was too late. My eyes flashed to the ground, and a scream, involuntary and raw, escaped my lips. My hand rose to my mouth. In front of our house lay a battered body in a pool of blood. Much as the sight shook my every nerve, I still couldn't manage to look away. The victim looked like he could've been a college student, or someone we'd seen last night at the welcoming party or run into celebrating with the masses as we shuffled home. He wore jeans and a T-shirt with the remnants of a hooded sweatshirt in tatters around him. In the brightening morning light, as the city still slept, our block felt so tranquil, not the kind of place you would expect to find this. It just didn't belong. The asphalt of Royal Street had been hosed down since last night, all traces of the evening carousing wiped clean.

Connor pushed me back, away from the scene. "C'mon, we're going back upstairs," he said. I took one last look and something glinted back at me. Just beside the man's flung-out arm, some kind of wispy plumage, a few white feathers, had gotten matted to the ground, blood working as the adhesive.

S o, there's a midnight curfew here now. And you just have to keep your wits about you. New Orleans is a great place, but it's still a big and wild city," Connor said with a furrowed brow and in a voice that made him seem much older than he actually was. "Be smart, guys. And if you need anything, I'm here."

The meeting in the common room had begun much differently than anyone had anticipated. We were all ready to start the day, seated on the sofas and chairs and floor, with notebooks and pens and, now, serious expressions.

Some residents had continued to sleep through all the commotion of the morning. Others had awoken to witness the cops outside talking into radios and unfurling that bright yellow crime-scene tape; the body was finally sheathed and taken away.

Sabine had still been sleeping when I got back to the room, and my knocks on Lance and Dante's door had been met with silence, so I had busied myself getting showered and dressed until I could finally talk to someone about what had happened. When we had all convened for the meeting, there hadn't been nearly enough catch-up time. Lance had only managed to whisper, "Check your phone," before Connor had launched in. I knew exactly which phone he meant.

Connor seemed understandably anxious to be done with this unfortunate discussion. "It's easy to get into trouble in this town, take it from me. But . . . just, you know, be careful." He paused. "So, are we all good? Any questions or anything?" He scanned the room. No one moved; we all just stared blankly. "Okay, well, I'm here to talk anytime." He sighed. "I know it's a pretty horrific welcome, and I'm sorry for that, but we're gonna be fine."

He picked up a stack of papers at his feet. "All right, so let's try to remember why we're here: voluntourism. When I come at ya, tell us your name and where you're from." He made his way around the room, handing out thick stapled information packets as we introduced ourselves to the group.

Finally, Connor returned to the front of the room. "Great, so here's the deal: there's no shortage of community service to be done in this town. We're gonna mix things up and let y'all lend a hand doing everything from tutoring and peer counseling to running trips for kids and building some homes for Hurricane Katrina victims who are still living in temporary quarters. You'll find a schedule in here." He held up the leftover packets. "Every day'll be a little different, but no day will be boring. You'll be all over the place, from way out in the bayou to as close as next door —where some of you will be fixing up that old LaLaurie mansion. The city's turning it into an event space—"

I thought of anyone having to spend all day in that place, and my whole body shivered for just a second, enough that Lance gave me a curious look. I couldn't help it: my mind flashed to what I'd seen in the window. I had been tired—had I just been seeing things? I couldn't deal with it now. I went through my packet and looked at the maps, calendars of the next several months, listings of so many businesses and locations and contact people.

But Connor wasn't quite done with his speech. "So, if y'all are ready, let's roll out in five, okay?" He held up one hand. "I'll meet ya in the courtyard. First stop: the Latter branch library in the Uptown area." With that, we all dispersed to our rooms, buzzing about all we'd just heard, gathering our things. I climbed up to my bed in the loft to find my phone. While Sabine was occupied switching most of her possessions from one purse into another, I summoned the courage to look at the screen. A message popped on instantly, no indication from whom or from where. The time-date stamp read January I at seven o'clock sharp. It simply said:

Good morning, Haven. Happy New Year. We are reunited, and I hope you will find comfort in that. But I regret to have to tell you that, once again, your soul is in grave danger. Be strong, winged one. Trust your instincts and you will conquer again. Remember what you've already learned. Draw upon the lessons you've been taught, the tests you've mastered.

"Ready, Hav?" Sabine called. I hit the button at the bottom of the phone to clear the screen. Instead of the usual array of icons I was used to seeing on a smartphone, there was nothing but a blank screen. I tapped it again and an image appeared . . . of me. It was that portrait that had burned up at the Lexington, in the office of Aurelia Brown. In it, I was recast as the subject of a painting I loved, *La Jeune Martyre,* lying in the shallow water of a darkened ditch, a halo above my head and a shadowy figure in the distance looking on. I stopped breathing for a moment. I flung the phone in my backpack, anxious to get it out of my hands.

I t wasn't until we were on the streetcar, rattling along tree-lined St. Charles Avenue again, that Lance and I had a moment alone, so he could whisper, "Anything?"

I nodded. "Vague, but yeah."

He nodded back. "Good." He looked relieved that the phones were working, that no matter what might be in store for us, at least we would have some sort of guidance. Something somewhere would look out for us in even the slightest way.

Connor waved us all off, and we filed out into the pretty

perfection of the leafy Uptown streets. The sun lit up the morning sky now, the air already moist and surprisingly warm. Walking just a few blocks, I could feel sweat glistening on my forehead, though it may not have been entirely from the temperature. That text message was the surest of signals that we had to be on guard now.

Lance and I walked silently, the rest of our group chatting around us. I imagined his mind was racing as much as mine was. Dante managed to break away from Max and sidled up to me. He watched his feet as he walked. If he was quiet, there always had to be a reason.

"Hey, Hav," he finally said. He kicked at a rock, knocking it along the sidewalk. "Are you, like, I don't know, kind of freaked out? By everything here, already?"

"Um, yeah." I laughed, knocking into him with my shoulder. "I think that's a pretty normal reaction." I thought for a moment. "So, are you getting the messages now too?"

"Yeah, omigod, what's the deal with these? Didn't you guys used to get these all the time? Why don't they tell us things straight up? Where are they coming from?"

"I wish I knew. Believe me, it would make all of this a whole lot easier. But you'll get the hang of how to follow them and they will start telling us useful things." I wasn't sure which one of us I was trying to reassure.

"I guess I'm just a little, I don't know, *scarred* from before."

"And rightfully so. But we're tougher now, you know?" I offered. We followed the group up a walkway toward what looked like a mansion set back from the road on a patch of supremely green grass.

"Yeah." Dante didn't sound entirely convinced.

"It'll be fine. We'll be fine. This time around we have the

advantage of knowing that everything is suspect. We're looking through different eyes, more educated eyes. That's got to help us. Right?"

He just nodded. Connor held the door open and we strolled inside, gathering in a dark wood foyer with a sweeping staircase. The rooms on either side of us were filled with racks and racks of cataloged books, but the grand estate certainly wasn't like any public library I'd ever seen. It was empty save for two gray-haired women shelving books from a cart. I grabbed a fact sheet from the stack on a table near the door.

"Pretty awesome, right, guys?" Connor said in a loud whisper, waving to the ladies then leading us up the creaky wooden staircase.

"Totally," Max said.

Lance craned his neck, trying to take in every bit of the place.

"Is this French?" Sabine asked, running her hand along the curved banister. "I love all the French stuff here." I glanced at the sheet of paper I'd taken.

"You would think either that or Spanish, given the influences when New Orleans was settled, but the architecture and styling are Italianate," Lance said with the joy of someone unwrapping an unexpected gift.

"Former home, gifted to the city to be used as a library," I read aloud.

"Add this one to the list, Hav. I would live here too," Dante said. I nodded, but I was too busy listening to the harsh, hushed voices quibbling behind us. I peeked over my shoulder to see the redhead—Emma was her name—arguing with Jimmy. He still seemed on edge from this morning, and I couldn't blame him.

" . . . but what were you *doing?*" she snapped. "Where the hell were you all night?"

"I was at the party and then, I don't know."

"I can't believe you don't even have the decency to be honest with me. Is that it? Is that how you treat me after a year?" Expletives followed, then she brushed past me, hustling up the stairs to Connor's side. Jimmy put his head in his hands like he had just been struck with a monster migraine.

"This is sorta our headquarters," Connor announced as we reached the second floor. "All the tutoring and counseling happen up here."

We followed him down the worn carpeting to a room with a half-moon-shaped window looking out onto the grounds, a high ceiling with delicate moldings, and framed paintings of pale people from the Victorian era. Long folding tables and chairs were clustered in a heap at the center of the room, waiting to be set up. A bare metal bookcase on wheels sat in a corner. Connor handed us each a lengthy checklist and explained that we would be spending a few hours here every afternoon for any local kids, elementary through high school, looking for homework help. A few nights a week the room would also be used for a teen crisis hotline. And, indeed, a row of desks in the back was outfitted with a quartet of very ancient-looking phones.

"As you may have noticed, today's a holiday—they let us in here special to set up. You folks over here"—he pointed to where I stood—"take a look at this list of books and gather a copy of each to stock our little library up here. While you guys"—he gestured to the rest—"are going to set up the workstations. Hop to it, folks!" He clapped, signaling us to start.

Our group had two others in addition to Lance, Dante, and Max. The first was a black-attired, goth-inspired girl with nose piercings named River. "Yes, it's my real name," she had said, rolling her eyes after introducing herself back at the house, even though no one had questioned her. The other was Drew, an earthy type in flared jeans and a weathered turquoise tunic, with the kind of wavy, sun-kissed locks that begged to be pinned with daisies.

"So, Haven and I will take science, math, and biographies," Lance proposed. The others split up the remaining subjects, and returned downstairs in search of fiction and children's books. I headed that way too, until Lance grabbed my arm. "Science and math are up here." He looked over his shoulder to be sure the others were gone. "I have to tell you something."

"Ohhhkay," I said, following.

We climbed one more flight of stairs to find a stuffy, dark-paneled room, musty because of so many yellowed tomes.

"So, what did you see this morning, anyway?" he asked quietly as we made our way through the towering stacks, scanning for the titles we needed. We had the room entirely to ourselves.

"Just, you know, a dead body." The thought of it made me shiver all over again. I pried out one of the books on the list.

"I think you should start taking pictures again," he said in a serious tone. "Just to make sure we know who we're dealing with all the time." He crouched down to pull out a biology textbook.

"Yeah, I was thinking that too." I had, of course, brought my camera—it was nothing special, a used digital model I'd gotten a while back. But I had learned over the past year that the equipment didn't matter: I was a soul illuminator. When I took a photo of someone, anyone, their true aura shone through. My photos showed inner beauty or, just the opposite, could detect a decrepit spirit, a decaying soul.

"Is that all?" I asked, still somber, but a lightness was creeping in, as it sometimes did when we had these kinds of conversations that other people just didn't have.

"Yeah, you know, no big deal," he said as if kidding with me. We smiled at each other.

"No sweat, right?" I shook my head and returned to my sheet. "Okay, then, just four more and Darwin." I looked at Lance and noticed that a hint of worry lingered behind those heavy frames. Perhaps I could change that. "I'll take the bottom two, you take the top two and"—I took a slow step backwards—"I'll race you for Darwin!" I dropped the books in my hands and took off running. His face brightened instantly.

"Not fair, you got a head start!" he called after me from the end of the aisle.

"Sounds like something a loser would say!" I snaked through the next aisle, yanking a book from the shelves, and I saw his face on the other side. In a burst, we sprinted again, agile and silent. I grabbed my other book—astronomy—and whipped around a corner, closing in on Darwin. Lance shot out from the opposite side. I scanned the numbers on the spines. *The Origin of Species* was going to be on the top shelf, which I couldn't even reach. I dropped the books in my hands, ran and launched myself up, pulling it out while airborne. I should have landed on my feet. But Lance caught me, bringing me back to the ground.

"I still won, you know," I needled him. I held the book behind my back, while he clasped his hands around my waist.

"I'd say it was a team effort."

"We'll agree to disagree." I smiled as he leaned me against the bookcase to kiss me.

After the books were gathered, we all set up the tutoring room, and Connor gave us a crash course in teaching tips. "Don't make anyone feel stupid and, on the flip side, if you find you're actually not as knowledgeable as you thought on something, don't be afraid to admit it and we'll assign someone else," he advised us.

"Why are you looking at me?" a jock named Tom, in a Lakers jersey, piped up. "I was kidding. I know gym isn't actually one of the subjects."

Then Connor walked us through a handbook on counseling. "Or, as I like to call it, 'knowing when to call the cops,'" he said in a joking tone. Drew raised her hand. "You don't have to raise your hand, Drew."

"Oh, sorry," she said meekly. "But isn't there, like, doctor/patient confidentiality?"

"I once talked someone off a ledge," River said, stone-faced and a shade confrontational.

"I bet you did," Brody quipped.

"I think you mean 'down from a ledge,'" Dante prompted.

"That's what I said," she said, sniping back.

And the afternoon went on until we were all well enough prepared to not inflict any scholastic or psychological damage. The rest of the day and evening passed uneventfully. Then again, when a day starts as that one had, it really couldn't get much more . . . *eventful,* thankfully.

6

The City of the Dead

The next morning the schedule simply read, *Tour of Community Service Projects, Part 1.*

"Some of the locals need some free labor, and a lot of folks are still trying to rebuild their businesses and lives or maintain public spaces with limited resources," Connor explained as he shepherded us out of the house. "So before reporting for tutoring and counseling duties every afternoon, you'll be on a rotation aiding New Orleanians near and far." He stopped before the mansion next door. My pulse picked up. "Lance, Brody, and Tom, you're here today." I breathed a quiet sigh of relief. Lance gave a wave as he went inside.

"Between you and me, I'm kinda glad not to be in that place," I whispered to Dante.

Connor led the rest of our group on a walk winding through the streets. When we reached wide, bustling Rampart Street, he stopped.

"Haven, Sabine, and Drew, you're at Saint Louis Cemetery Number One, just past that church there. They're expectin' ya."

"Huh?" I asked. Dante let out a single staccato cackle, then flung his hand over his mouth. Connor looked up but didn't say a word.

"Yeah, way better than a haunted house, Hav," Dante said. "Enjoy."

"Dante and Max, you're at Priestess Mariette's Voodoo Temple." Connor pointed down the street to a sign blowing in the warm breeze.

"Are you serious?" Max asked.

"Yep. Go on! That's a lady you do *not* want to keep waitin'."

"Awesome," Dante said cheerfully.

"The rest of you guys, come with me. We're hitting a food bank a few blocks down for some Meals on Wheels action. See y'all later at the library. Make me proud!" he instructed as he left us.

The smooth gray façade of Our Lady of Guadalupe Church beckoned from across Rampart Street, its spire piercing the cloudless morning sky. According to our packets, the contact here was a Sister Catherine. Well, a nun would certainly be a change from my last boss.

Just inside the church's heavy white-painted doors, a small tour group had gathered, their guide spouting facts in a whisper amplified by the vaulted ceiling. The only other sounds came from the creaks of the dozen or so parishioners shifting ever so slightly in their wooden pews, lost in their own thoughts and prayers. Light streamed in through stained-glass windows, speckling bits of color against the sharp white walls. I hadn't actually spent a ton of time in any church, with the exception of the small, cozy chapel nestled within the hospital, where I had often escorted the family members of patients or, better yet, been dispatched to retrieve loved ones when there was good news. The silence here was so deep it made me aware of every clumsy step and noisy breath I took. I felt like everyone was looking at me. Sabine was slightly less concerned about that sort of thing.

"I totally love this," she whispered to Drew, tugging on her burlap-like messenger bag. "Hav, you need one of these. Get rid of that backpack."

"I was going for, you know, geek chic," I whispered back, embarrassed.

"I think it's nice," Drew said. I liked that she was one of those people who could be counted on to be polite no matter what.

"Yeah, no." Sabine shook her head at me. "We'll work on it. But what is this? Hemp?"

"Yeah, but it's really softer than it looks," Drew said, holding it out for Sabine to pet. "I love a good hemp. Connor actually talked me into it."

I was suddenly paying attention. "You went shopping with Connor?"

Drew shook her head. "No, I met him back home at this vegan shop I used to go to a lot, and he convinced me I had to get one. I guess he has one too."

Sabine and I looked at each other. "That guy gets around," she said.

"What?" Drew asked, confused. But we didn't get to explain.

I felt the lightest tap on my shoulder, like a bird landing there, and couldn't help being startled. I spun around to find a tiny woman in a habit, only her milky, moon-shaped face exposed. Hands clasped before her, she smiled with pruned lips. She looked to be in her seventies, at least.

"Hello, girls. You must be from the student program," she

greeted us in a delicate voice that crackled with age, like Joan's old vinyl records, and was tinged with the sweetness of her native drawl. Crepelike folds of skin hung at her neck and creases were nestled into pockets around her eyes and mouth. Hers was a fragile face whose years gave it an added warmth. A vein-vined hand extended from beneath her robe to meet mine.

"Sister Catherine, hi, so nice to meet you. I'm Haven." Her grip was as gentle as her presence. The others shook her soft hand and whispered hellos too.

"A pleasure to have you here, my dears. We appreciate your service. Have you seen Saint Louis Number One yet?"

"No, ma'am," said a serious Sabine.

"It will be celebrating its two hundred and twenty-fifth anniversary next year so we're sprucing it up. It's quite beautiful, but will be far more stunning from the contributions of your able hands and warm hearts."

"Thank you, we look forward to helping out," I said, as Drew smiled. She was several inches taller than all three of us and was hunched over now, which made her look even shier.

Sister Catherine led us back outside into the warm sunshine. Her back curved slightly, making her just about my height. I wondered how tall she had once been and whether she was very hot shrouded in the drapes of that robe and headpiece.

"You'll be spending most of your time in our city of the dead," she began. Those words chilled my blood for a split second. She continued, "But there are such wonders in our little church. You're welcome to explore as much as you like. You'll find in our garden"—she pointed to an area behind the church, where a life-size statue, probably of a saint or apostle I should have known, stood watch—"the most delightful grotto. Feel free to light candles or leave messages there. We find that many prayers are answered."

"Good to know, thank you," I said after a while, just to fill the silence, since my compatriots didn't say a word. I felt a bit out of my element with this particular breed of spiritual small talk, but I tried my best. "Now, Saint Catherine, she was the patron saint of . . ." I hoped the nun would complete my sentence, because I sure had no idea what the answer was. We reached Basin Street, where a fortress-like whitewashed wall extended the full block. The sun glared off of it in blinding rays.

"Fire," Drew said, with surprising authority.

"Why, yes, very good. Saint Catherine wards off fire, illness, and temptations."

My eyes darted to Sabine, a smile curling her lips. If I could have read her thoughts, they probably would have been along the lines of: *Why would you want to ward off temptation?* I just shook my head.

"Our church was founded during the great yellow fever epidemic here in the late seventeen hundreds."

We followed Sister Catherine across the street, her pace slow and steady. She walked with the security of someone who knows that her outfit can literally stop traffic; no one's going to run down a nun. Eventually we reached the open front gate of the cemetery. We heard voices, footsteps, and the fluttering of movement and activity just beyond it.

"Bringing you kids here is like having All Souls' Day all over again, and I've always thought how nice it would be if every day were All Souls' Day." Sister Catherine stopped, looking at us with penetrating dusty blue eyes.

"All Souls' Day?" Sabine asked.

"When people come to fix up the graves, right?" I said, recalling a mention I'd seen in my guidebook.

"Very good," Sister Catherine said as we entered the grounds. We followed her along a narrow walkway lined with crypts of all sizes, some of crumbling brick just a few feet from the ground and boxy, the length of a casket, and others glistening white and easily the size of garden sheds. Pointed fences of thin metal spokes and black peeling paint surrounded many of them. Narrow walkways and alleys formed intersections in the gravel and dirt, as the cemetery unfolded in its miniature grid system.

We walked silently and somberly for a few long minutes, at one point needing to pull off to the side to allow a group of nearly two dozen tourists to pass. "It's certainly the most famous and infamous of Saint Louis Number One, right this way . . ." the guide said to his followers, all shielded beneath hats and sunglasses.

Finally Sister Catherine continued. "On All Souls' Day—and All Saints' Day, for that matter—loved ones come to pay their respects and freshen up the grave sites." She stopped before a beat-up crypt with patches of faded brick peeking out beneath dingy gray cement. "It's lovely to have help on these two days, of course, but so many of these are left with no one to care for them. The truth is, our city of the dead has been suffering. I've been the caretaker here for many years, but I'm quite old and I can't do the restoration work myself. With the help of kind volunteers like yourselves, we're hoping to bring back its glory and to honor those buried here. So you'll start right here and then you'll be following a list of tombs we're going to have you focus on. At some point I'm hoping to bring a contractor in to actually rebuild a few that are in particularly bad shape."

"Great," I said, studying our first target. The name chiseled into a marble slab in front read BARTHELEMY LAFON and a plaque described him as an architect. I'd have to tell Lance. I wondered how he was doing in that eerie house right now. It felt strange not to be working alongside him. "Looking forward to getting started," I added.

"Cool," Sabine seconded.

"I have some materials for you in the caretaker's cottage out front." Sister Catherine began to hobble back the way we'd come. "And I have some T-shirts and painter's pants you can change into as well." I was glad to not have to paint in my lone pair of khakis and one of my nicer blouses. Then the nun stopped in her tracks for a moment, looking at me as another tour group passed us by. "One more bit of the job, if you don't mind," she said. She touched my arm then waved a finger to lead us back the way we'd come; we turned down another narrow pathway. "We have a number of well-known New Orleanians represented here, which is why we get the tours," she said in her low, rich crackle. "But really there's just one tomb everyone comes for, as you might well know. Marie Laveau."

We stopped before a tall, slim crypt reaching far above our heads. Much of its smooth white stone surface had been doodled on with notes of thanks, or, more commonly, *X*s. So many past visitors had scrawled sets of *XXX*, three *X*s together all across the tomb, in an array of colored markers or paint or pen. Around its base lay an assortment of items I could make no sense of: flowers (some of them dead), stones, bottles, bricks (some covered in foil), fruit that had been there long enough to rot (only the pits of peaches had been left in some cases), containers that seemed to hold leftovers from restaurant meals, books, pens, breath mints, maps, handwritten notes, candles, photos, bones, and plastic bags of herbs. "This tomb you will never paint," Sister Catherine said sternly. "Are you familiar with Miss Laveau?"

No one said anything. I didn't want to be that awful kid with her hand constantly up in class, but I didn't want her to think we weren't interested. Both Sabine and Drew looked nervous.

"Well, I do know she was a voodoo queen and also, I think, a nurse during the yellow fever outbreaks?" I offered.

"Yes, dear, excellent," Sister Catherine said, looking at me and nodding.

"What's with all these?" Sabine pointed to a cluster of Xs. Drew leaned in to inspect some that had been painted on, running her finger over them.

"That's a fine question," Sister Catherine said to Sabine, who looked proud of herself. "Well, there's quite a bit of lore associated with her, as you can imagine. Many believe that if they leave these markings they'll have various wishes granted. You may also see some visitors knocking three times on the tomb." She did this herself. "There are so many stories like this, so many superstitions, and people come looking for help. We all have our own beliefs about where to find aid when we need it, don't we?" She shook her head, suggesting that she wished everyone who came here would just cross the street and hit up the church instead. But I could certainly understand; after seeing what I had, I knew that you needed to find hope anywhere you could.

"At any rate," she continued, "people also leave these various items as offerings, to entice Miss Laveau's spirit to assist them. Unfortunately, as you can see, some insist on leaving perishable goods, which don't stand much chance of lasting in this warm climate, and make a mess of things. Each day, if you might do a pass collecting anything rotten from here, it would be greatly appreciated." With that she gave one final look at the site and walked away at her easy pace.

We followed her to a tiny gray shack that seemed barely larger than some of the more elaborate crypts. She jiggled the key in the door and we entered a single, sparse room. Inside sat a wooden desk and chair, a lamp, a metal storage cabinet, and a phone. And that's about all that could fit. I didn't feel any air conditioning, but just being out of the sun's rays was a welcome relief. Sister Catherine pulled sharply folded clothes from the cabinet along with several papers bearing yellow highlighting.

"Here you are. This should be everything you need. This"— she shuffled through the papers, pulling one aside—"gives some basic painting tips. All the supplies are in here."

"Thank you, Sister," we said in unison.

She nodded slowly, eyes downcast, in that way that nuns always seemed to in movies, like when Joan and I would watch *The Sound of Music* at Christmastime. She shuffled toward the door and then turned around once more. "And please don't remain in the cemetery past sundown. For . . . safety reasons," she said, her voice taking on a heavy, chilling tone for a moment.

"What do you . . ." Sabine started. But before we could ask any more, Sister Catherine slipped out, the last trace of her long black robe slithering away like a tail as the door shut.

"Nuns freak me out," Sabine said after she left, giving a shimmy like she had the chills.

"C'mon, she was . . . sweet," I said. Drew just giggled at us. We changed into the white cotton painter's pants—which dwarfed Sabine and me, since they were apparently made for people twice our height—and equally enormous T-shirts with a drawing of the church on the front and STAFF in giant letters across the back. Sabine tugged at the extra material of her tee, trying to tie it all into a knot. Having little luck, she scowled.

"I know, these outfits are pretty hot, right?" I joked, and she laughed at herself.

With paint cans, rollers, brushes, and newspapers in hand, we made our way back to a trio of graves on our hit list. The sun seemed to have grown hotter than it had any right to be in January. I spread out sheets of newspaper on the ground around Lafon's grave site and set to work rolling out the thick pastelike paint over the crypt. The thirsty cement soaked it up. I rolled layer after layer and I tried, above all else, to keep my mind from wandering too far down corridors I didn't want it exploring.

By midafternoon, I had rolled my final coat and had Lafon positively gleaming. At one point my fellow painters had given me cash and sent me on an expedition to round up some lunch, during which I discovered that the mysterious muffuletta, which I had seen mentioned in signs all around town and sounded like a species of small animal, was just a fancy name for a sandwich.

As we were cleaning up, Drew, who looked graceful with her long, lean limbs but was surprisingly clumsy, managed to spill a can of paint all over her sneakers.

"Well, at least white goes with everything," Sabine offered.

"Totally coulda been worse," I said, trying to be nice since she looked a little upset.

I told her and Sabine to go ahead, that I would close up the caretaker's cottage and put things away so they could have a head start getting home to let Drew clean up before our tutoring session. With an organ droning in the distance, I dropped the keys off in the church's main office. A kind, bespectacled, fifty-ish administrative assistant named Susan directed me to leave them in a trophy-shaped urn, which looked eerily like ones used for holding remains. On the way out, my phone, the old-fashioned one, buzzed with a text message from Dante: He and Max wanted to walk back home with me but were running a few minutes late and asked if I didn't mind waiting.

In search of a place to kill time, I wandered around the side of the church to that garden with the imposing statue and a small bench. But something else caught my eye, and I kept right on walking toward it. Lights flickered ahead from within a darkened passageway. As I got closer, I could see it looked like a cave, a cozy little hollowed-out rock formation. This had to be the grotto Sister Catherine had mentioned. Inside, the space was barely wider than my arm span, but had been outfitted with shelves that now held hundreds of lit candles. The burning scent mingled with a mustiness, but nevertheless, it felt comforting, like an old blanket found at the bottom of a chest. Along the rough walls, handwritten notes had been taped up, and small engraved plaques offering thanks mounted, some with the names of those whose wishes had been fulfilled. I scanned these messages. I wondered what they had all asked for. A warm breeze swirled outside, whistling against the cave's opening. A quick gust whipped past me into the grotto and the flames of all the candles bent at once but only one blew out. I didn't like the idea of someone somewhere potentially losing a wish on my watch. I removed the candle from its crimson glass bed on the shelf and tipped its wick into the flame of its neighbor. It ignited bright and strong.

You've got no idea what kinda business a voodoo shop can do." Dante, excited, rattled on a mile a minute. "We just got this tour group, totally went wild, and it's tough because the place only just opened and she's still getting her pantry stocked and her temple set up. You haven't lived until you've seen two sweaty sunburned women from Alabama get in a tug of war over the last voodoo doll for attracting marriage."

"I pity their future husbands," I said.

"No kidding." Max shook his head, whistling.

"And not that I'm in the market for it, but they actually have dolls for that?"

"There are dolls for everything. Love, luck, money, revenge, you name it. Someday my prince will come," Dante joked quietly, fluttering his eyelashes. Max was scrolling through the texts in his phone, not paying attention.

"Lemme tell you," I said under my breath. "I saw a prince on New Year's and they're not all that great." Max was on the phone now.

"Sorry, sweetie. Didn't mean to bring that all—"

"No, no, it's cool. Besides, we're in it together."

"I know, thanks for that," he said. His playful sarcasm had a way of making everything seem okay.

"So what's your boss like?" I asked, trying to navigate away from dark topics.

"Mariette. She's superhot but, you know, obviously not my type. She's gorgeous and kind of mysterious. There's this whole crazy backroom of stuff she uses in her spells and readings. We were unpacking it today and setting it up and labeling things like, literally, jars of chicken bones and alligator teeth."

"Whoa. Hardcore." I stopped for a minute. I wasn't quite sure how to broach it, but I couldn't help it when the alarms went off. "Do you think Mariette is . . ." I started softly. "One of, you know, *them?*"

"Totally good question," Dante said quietly, his tone darkening just a shade as he thought it over. He had somehow survived being poisoned, brainwashed, and almost drafted into devilhood earlier this year. He played it so cool, though, that I sometimes forgot how harrowing it had all been. It made me shiver now, even in this midday heat. "I don't know. I just don't get a vibe from her that she's like them. But it's too early to know. What about your boss? Any hotties where you are?" he asked in all seriousness.

At this, I had to smile. "She's a nun. An old nun. Sister Catherine."

He burst out laughing. "That made my day! Very glamorous, indeed."

Max was off the phone now, shaking his head. "Sorry, my mom, you know, checking in all the time."

"I was just telling Hav about Mariette," Dante said.

"She's really cool," Max confirmed. "I guess she had a shop years ago in another part of town that got wiped out by Hurricane Katrina and she's finally rebuilding in this new spot. She's a tough lady."

"She sounds really, I don't know, *wild*," I said, imagining that supply of bones and teeth.

"Yeah. I think she's gonna be awesome," Dante said gushing, his eyes dancing, as we neared home.

"I'm gonna run in and grab Lance," I said when we stopped in front of the LaLaurie mansion.

"Good. You guys are too PG-13 for your own good," Dante said, laughing.

"You know what I mean." I smacked his arm, rolling my eyes. "Do you wanna come in? C'mon, how often do you get to check out a haunted house?" Even in the bright, comforting light of day I still felt like it was somehow taunting me.

"Okay." Dante nodded. "You convinced us." He stepped up

to the door and let himself right in. Max turned a wary gaze to the threshold, not quite as gung ho as Dante but following him nonetheless.

We entered into a construction site—exposed rafters above, plastic sheeting in place of walls, a paper-strewn drafting table in one corner, and all manner of scaffolding and platforms that had been rigged up.

"Lance?" I called out.

"This place is totally the ugly 'before' picture of a makeover. Bleh," Dante said, touching the plastic and cringing like it might bite. The soundtrack of banging hammers and buzzing saws echoed from another wing.

"We're back here!" Lance's voice strained to be heard above all the activity. Dante and Max disappeared down a darkened hallway, anxious to inspect. I was about to follow when a flicker caught my eye.

The foyer window had been left open and a lit votive candle burned on the sill. It reminded me of the ones I had just seen in the grotto. A gust swirled in, and the flame put up a fight, flickering before it was finally extinguished. That's when I noticed something peeking from beneath it: a corner of white paper under the crystal holder. Perhaps it was a wish, I joked with myself. Though I figured it was probably just a receipt from the convenience store across the street, or a list of what the contractors had to tackle next, I couldn't resist. I slid out the crisply folded square of smooth ivory paper, thick and luscious like cotton. And there it was, as though branded into the paper: *H.*

My heart stopped, as if it already knew something my brain didn't. I leaned against the windowsill for support and opened up the slip of paper. It read:

Haven,
I'm here and I'm watching you.
Always,
L

The words swirled in my head. They terrified me and thrilled me at once. I knew that handwriting. It had once accompanied a dress, a gift for me to wear on my first and last date with him. Yes, I knew who that L. was, without any doubt. The realization chilled me, and yet I felt myself breaking into a sweat. I was much more comfortable with Lucian safely confined to my thoughts and memories, not here in this world with me. I didn't know who he was now or how his penance in the underworld might have changed him. I really didn't even know whose side he was on. Enough time had passed to take with it all the good things he had once been, allowing only the bad to remain. There was too much I didn't know.

I read it again. Then, without another thought, I crumpled it in my hand, as though it might disappear if I could hold it tight enough, suffocate it. I stuffed it in my wallet, as voices bounded down the corridor, inching closer. Lance, Dante, the whole group appeared.

"See you tomorrow, John," Brody said to a burly, mustachioed man in a T-shirt that looked too tight and wearing a tool belt slung low on his hips. I figured he must be the supervisor at this site.

"Take it easy, guys," the man said. Sawdust and sweat coated his face and meaty arms.

"Hey you, did you get lost?" Lance asked with a laugh. "You should see it back there."

"Hi, no, sorry, I was . . . trying to call Joan." I didn't mean to lie, but I wasn't prepared to tell the truth. "I'm . . . how are you?"

"Geez, Hav, man up. You really are scared of this place, huh? You look like you saw a ghost."

I couldn't find the words. Luckily I didn't have to.

Max elbowed him. "You're so mean. C'mon, Haven, I'm with you. Let's get outta here." He led the way and we all followed. I cast one last look before the door closed, as though he might appear.

7

I Have to Tell You Something

It had already begun to eat away at me, this note nestled in my wallet. Even I could tell I was acting weird, like when I gazed spacily out the window of the streetcar or zoned out talking to Lance and Dante as we wandered those picturesque blocks to the library.

As soon as we reached the tutoring room upstairs, which was already full of more than a dozen kids of all different ages, I hung back and let Lance go in with the others, then grabbed the back of Dante's shirt, pulling him out to the hall.

"Hey!" he said in protest.

"I have to tell you something," I whispered. There was no mistaking my tone. He noticed the serious set of my eyes and reflected it back to me, ready to listen. In sixty seconds, he was up to speed.

"Wow," was all he could say at first, as he looked at the note.

"Do you sense a sinister undertone or maybe just something more informative? Like, 'By the way, just so you know, I'm around'?"

"Um . . ." He bit his lip like he didn't quite want to answer, which I could only take to mean something sinister.

"And, I thought I sort of saw something in the window of the mansion one night, but I may have just hallucinated."

Dante hung his head, processing, then looked up as he handed back the note. "Look, Haven, you said it yourself. There's no telling what might've happened to Lucian during his time, you know, *below*. The Prince is obviously still gunning for you—for us," he added, trying in his own way to be comforting. "And really all we can do—"

"I know, I know, we have to operate under the assumption that everyone, *everyone*, is against us. We have no reason to think otherwise." I sighed. "But the real question is—"

"Lance," Dante finished my thought.

"My gut tells me that I can't *not* tell him but . . . I can't tell him. I don't know why . . ."

"I know why. He'll freak the heck out."

"Yeah. Right?" I said, defeated.

"Yeah, for any number of reasons. I mean, *wow.*"

"But it doesn't seem right to not tell him. From a security standpoint alone, this is kinda something we need to share, right?"

"Um, yeah, I'd say so," Dante confirmed. "And then on the other hand, it's kind of a classic ex-boyfriend problem. You don't want to lie but . . ."

"But I didn't go looking for this. And Lucian wasn't really a boyfriend . . ."

"Whatever, Hav. Maybe you didn't, like, go out on date nights much, but there was enough there that Lance would sorta flip out, in my humble opinion." I knew he was right, of course. "Give me the note," he demanded.

I hadn't realized I was holding it pressed to my heart. I handed it back to Dante. He flattened it, read it fast, and looked at me, as though searching for some sort of answer to a question I hadn't asked. Then with a sharp swoosh, he tore off the lettering with my name at the top of the note, which included the *H* on the flip side. I gasped, surprised at myself. For some reason, it felt like he was tearing a hole in my heart.

Dante handed me the scrap with my name on it. Though I missed the weight—physical and otherwise—of the full note, I saw his point; now it was no longer *mine*. Now it could have been intended for any of us, all of us. In fact, without my name at the top, the tone shifted. It felt more ominous.

"'Hey. Look at this note *I* found,'" Dante said in the exaggerated, robotic delivery of someone reading a script badly. "'It's really creepy. See? What do you think it means?'" He flipped back into his normal voice: "I'll show it to Lance and say I gave it to you first, and since you know Lucian's handwriting, it makes sense that you could identify the author. We'll do it tonight when we get back."

When we finally got to tell Lance later that night, we did exactly as we had rehearsed. I felt guilty. Lance took the paper from Dante and stared at it for a good long time, running his hand through his messy dark locks. Finally he handed it back, a faraway look in his eyes.

"That's it then. We're just going to have to look out for one another. All the time. Because they know how to get to us when they want us." He was quiet the rest of the night. He said he was just tired and turned in early. I didn't press him.

That night when I saw the flash from next door, I sat up in bed, staring at that corner of the mansion. At midnight the light flicked on. A figure appeared, framed by the window. I could see the ghostly form of a man the way the moonlight hit but only in hazy silhouette. I could tell that he was facing my direction, his head at the exact angle it would need to be to see my room. I shuddered, my skin crawling, but, even so, I found myself descending that ladder and taking a place at my window. I opened it and climbed out onto the balcony, which, like the courtyard, was deserted. I watched until the light flared out and the window went dark.

But the next two nights it was illuminated again, like clockwork.

Connor had announced he was treating us all to a Friday night feast at a New Orleans landmark to celebrate our first week of work. Antoine's was packed, every table filled with boisterous patrons, as the host led us back through a series of dining rooms to our own private spot. Bathed in a deep green with gold trim, and a glimmering chandelier cascading down from the ceiling, the ornate room seemed to double as a museum. Glass display cases lined the walls, showing off ball gowns, tiaras, crowns, and capes worn by past Mardi Gras kings and queens, along with their scepters. I positioned myself at the end of the table where Emma sat, far away from both Connor *and* Jimmy. I wondered for a moment if she had been late to arrive or if she was intentionally avoiding them.

I offered to take photos of everyone seated along the banquet table. "Okay, I'm good with this side. Thanks, guys," I said, checking the photo in the viewfinder and confirming I'd clearly gotten a solid half of the group in one shot.

I had decided to take my phone's advice and return to old lessons learned. Back in Chicago, I had discovered that my photos could expose people's true nature, cut down to their soul, and show what was there. If there was evil, the image in the photo would rot; it was that simple. I had been entrusted with the power to destroy these photos and banish these beings to the underworld. There was nothing simple about that; they would fight to the death—and they certainly had earlier this year—but I could do it.

"Okay, smile on three. One, two, three!" I called out in my perkiest voice, which sounded so unnatural to my own ears, and snapped the shot. I reviewed it fast. Another good one. "Thanks!" I returned to my seat beside Lance.

"So you got some good shots?" he asked, knowingly.

"Yeah, all set," I answered, tucking my camera in my bag. I set it back on the empty chair beside me. I was saving a seat for Sabine, who had texted that she was just a block away. She had insisted on going home after tutoring to change before dinner. Emma, it seemed, had paid her the ultimate compliment. "Are you sure you're not southern?" the redhead had asked in a delicate drawl when she had broken off from our group to head home. Sabine, flattered, had blushed.

Dante sat across from me, beside Max, and the two of them seemed completely lost in their own world, talking and laughing like old friends. You never would've guessed they'd met only last week. The other guys had clustered at the half of the table near Connor.

"So," I said to Lance, "anything new next door?"

He had already drained his Diet Coke and was crunching on pieces of ice, thinking. "Same old. The whole thing is a mess," he said flatly, adjusting his glasses.

"The foyer was bad enough."

"The rest is much worse. Parts of it were burned. Other parts are just these rotted beams. It's like an x-ray of a building. You can see in between the different floors, hollow spots everywhere."

"Could you tell at all if anyone had, um, been upstairs?" I whispered, my fingers dancing over my necklace.

"I don't really know. There sort of *isn't* an upstairs right now." He wasn't looking straight at me, the way spies meeting up in movies rarely look at each other but talk into that space in front of them with their eyes scanning from side to side. "The place is so structurally unsound that we have to work our way up with the restoration. But I'll get up there soon, one way or another."

Tuxedo-clad waiters appeared bearing overflowing baskets of bread. Dante excused himself to go to the men's room. Lance and I traded quick glances and I rose from my seat and slipped away without a word. I found Dante fooling with his cell phone outside the restrooms, at the end of a dim hallway. He looked up at the sound of my footsteps approaching, shoving the phone back in his pocket and pulling out a tiny tin.

"I can't help but feel like we're wasting this," I whispered as I got closer.

"I'll figure something out, I swear. But for now, I just think it's the best thing to do." I knew he was right, but I lived in fear of when those precious antidotes would run out. We had been taking them daily since the first night.

"For now, here," he said. I reached in to pick out a leaf, thin as a moth's wing, and let it dissolve on my tongue.

Lance appeared at the end of the hallway, as expected, striding toward us. Dante offered the tin to Lance too. But just as he reached in to take a tiny leaf, a door opened, the light suddenly shining on us, and Sabine appeared behind him.

"Hey, guys!" she greeted us. "So here's the real party!" Lance quickly popped the leaf into his mouth. "Did I miss anything? Oooh, are those mints? Can I snag one?"

Dante snapped the tin shut. "That was my last one, sorry," he said with an easy smile. I, on the other hand, felt completely rattled. "See you in there," he pointed in the direction of the dining room. "I'm starved!" And with that he slipped away to rejoin the group.

"You're just in time for dinner," I said, trying to play it cool. "Didn't miss a thing."

"I'll catch up with you," Lance said, continuing on to the men's room.

"I just had to put myself together. I feel so *blah* from the long day in the city of the dead, you know?" Sabine smoothed her silky hair, and, of course, didn't look the least bit blah.

"Yeah, it's surprisingly good exercise, all that painting. It works more muscle groups than I expected," I said as we started heading back to the dining room.

"Totally." Sabine didn't look like she was paying the least bit of attention. Her eyes flitted around, her hand fidgeting with the clasp of her bracelet. Just outside the doorway, she slowed her pace and grabbed my arm, pulling me back a few steps. "Haven, I need to talk to you about something." She stopped when we were clearly out of sight from the guests inside the dining room. Waiters scurried past us with trays full of savory delicacies.

"Sure?" I said, not meaning to sound so unsure. She let go of my arm. Her nervous eyes could barely look at mine. "Is everything okay?"

"I saw what Dante had," she whispered.

My heart nearly stopped. "Whaddya mean?" I tried to play dumb.

"Those leaves. I saw them. I know what they do. I have some but I'm almost all out."

The questions overflowed in my mind, setting off warning bells. But the heaviness of her tone told me that she was telling the truth. Beneath the strain in her voice lay a softer intention, the need to be understood and to share a secret. I had to choose whether to let her in. So I asked, "What do they do?"

"They protect you. They keep the toxins away, out of your system."

"How do you know that?"

"I had a friend who learned the hard way what can happen if you don't take them."

As I thought of more questions to ask, I saw Lance coming down the hall. He shot me a confused look as he approached. I answered it with a blank stare. He passed us wordlessly and ducked back into the dining room. Sabine spoke again before I had formulated a response.

"I wasn't sure whether to say anything," she said, shaking her head, her eyes pleading. "I didn't plan on ever telling anyone, really, but . . . it's hard." She paused for a moment, collecting her thoughts. "And when I saw that leaf in Lance's hand, I just . . . I had to try."

"I understand," I said. And I did. More waiters streamed into the room.

"I know it's not the best time for a bombshell." She rolled her eyes and almost laughed, reminding me of that lighthearted, easygoing girl I had assumed she was before this.

"No, I mean, hey, when is it ever a good time, right?" I smiled.

"No kidding." She shook her head. The waiters hustled past us with empty trays.

"I feel like we should get back in there," I said, even though it was the last thing I cared to do. I wanted to grill her, ask every burning question, and then tell it all to Lance and Dante and try to make sense of it. Did all this mean Sabine was one of us? An angel in training? She had to be, didn't she?

"You're right," she said, sighing. "But later . . . ?"

"Definitely," I promised her. "We've got a lot to talk about."

We nodded at each other, signaling silently that we would go back in that room and revert to these other versions of ourselves for the duration of the evening until we could safely speak again.

"I saved you a seat," I said, pointing, as we stepped inside. "We're over here in the middle." My bag and napkin sat on the two chairs between Lance and Tom, who was almost always dressed like he was on his way to the gym but had managed to wear khakis tonight. Sabine took the seat beside Lance. I couldn't help but feel a little disappointed; she would have had no way of knowing that I had been sitting there, and I certainly didn't want to make a big deal out of it. Salads had been set at each place, along with small cups of gumbo, while several platters of an oyster dish, some kind of almond-encrusted seafood, and a saucy chicken dish were scattered across the table.

The clinking of knife against glass quieted all the wild threads of conversation. Connor stood, his cola-filled stemware in hand. "Hey guys! Just wanted to say I hope everyone had a good first week despite a little bit of a rough start." My mind set on an image of that dead man in the street on New Year's Day. I had been trying to snuff it out all week long. "But we're glad you're here, and here's to a great few months ahead! Cheers!" A chorus of *pings* broke out as everyone knocked their glasses together. Sabine turned to Lance, toasting him and then saying something that made him smile. "And also," Connor went on, "I hope y'all enjoy being treated like kings tonight because we're going on a retreat this weekend—"

A chorus of curious *What?*s and *Huh?*s swept the table.

"And it's a little rustic. More to come but—"

"Aren't we kind of already on a retreat? Here in New Orleans?" Brody, laughing, looked around the table for agreement. He leaned back his chair so it was balanced on its two back legs.

"Oh, y'think this is a retreat?" Connor smiled at him, perfectly calm.

"I mean, yeah, kinda," Brody said with another staccato laugh.

Still smiling, Connor kicked one of the legs of Brody's chair in a sharp and quick movement. It slid to the floor, taking Brody with it. He looked up from the ground for a second, like he didn't know what hit him. Sabine gasped. The whole table fell silent.

"Are you insane?" Brody snapped at Connor, clumsily getting back up on his feet.

"No, man," he said, entirely affable. "I'm just bein' me. Why don't you take a lap around the block and come back, okay?"

"Are you serious?"

"Deadly," he said. "Go on. Look, now you've gone and made all your friends nervous. Come back in a better mood." I glanced over at Lance, who looked stricken. There was something so jarring, terrifying even, about seeing someone say and do harsh things with a smile. The disconnect rattled me. Without another word, Brody stormed away, letting his hand slap against the doorframe. Connor sat back down, still grinning. "More food for us, right?" he said. Then to Tom: "Can ya pass the oysters? You guys gotta try these. They're famous here."

"They look great," Dante said, trying to break the silence. "I'm gonna steal one before they disappear." He grabbed one with a spoon just before Tom swooped up the plate. Connor started talking sports with Jimmy and slowly, the conversations began again, all of us making a group effort to act as though nothing had happened.

Sabine and Lance were already locked in some sort of tête-à-tête, Dante and Max were equally engaged with each other, so that left me and Tom.

"Glad that wasn't me," he said. He shoveled some salad into his mouth.

"Yeah, me too," I said quietly. "I didn't take Connor for such a tough guy. I don't know why; must be the accent."

"Yeah, I know what you mean, and he's pretty cool all around. But he's fierce on the court, which I also never woulda guessed. Usually I can tell just by lookin'."

"The court?"

"Basketball?" He rolled his eyes like I was some kind of idiot. "I've played a pickup game or two with him in my time and that guy is fast and scrappy."

"When have you had time to play basketball?" I stopped eating to look at him. "They've been keeping us pretty busy."

"Yeah, but I mean, back home."

"You know Connor from home?" Now he had my interest.

"Met him this summer. We worked out at the same place."

"You're from . . ." I tried to remember. "LA?"

"Seattle."

"Oh, I was thinking, you had a Lakers top on the other day."

Tom rolled his eyes again, frustrated with me. "First of all, it's a *jersey*, not a top. Second, Seattle lost its basketball team a few years ago — it was ugly — so I changed my allegiance. Desperate times."

If that qualified as a desperate time in Tom's life, then clearly we had little in common.

"Right. But about Connor . . ." I started again, wondering how one guy covered so much ground in a summer. Maybe he was on one of those soul-searching cross-country road trips I heard people were always taking in college. I hoped that someday I would get around to learning how to drive.

I had already lost Tom's attention, though. He swiveled his head and became instantly engrossed in some proper guy talk. I spent the rest of the evening flitting in and out of the innocuous getting-to-know-you conversations at the girls' end of the table.

"I don't like the sound of rustic," Emma said. She was from Nashville, as was Jimmy.

Drew lit up. "Near where I'm from there's this amazing resort where you stay in treehouses."

"See, that sounds like a nightmare to me." Emma laughed.

But for the most part, I found myself too distracted to really pay attention. I needed to talk to Sabine. I looked over, but her epic discussion with Lance wore on. I anxiously tapped my foot, ready for this party to end and for an opportunity to ask all my questions.

8

That's Just the Krewe

It was nearly ten o'clock by the time they cleared away the last of the dishes. We ambled out of Antoine's en masse, and I found my way to Lance's side.

"So are you going to this thing?" he asked.

Before I could ask what he was talking about, Sabine materialized. "Brody says that Jimmy knows someone who can totally get us into that bar on St. Peter Street with the crazy courtyard, you know?" Her eyes were bright and shining at the prospect.

After Sabine approached Connor with a chirpy, childlike "Can we get ice cream?" she secured the green light we needed to break off from the group.

Connor looked the seven of us over and begrudgingly warned, "Curfew's midnight," while a scowling Emma shot daggers at us —or, at least, at Jimmy—and turned back in the direction of the house. And so we set off, following Jimmy through streets that were nearly as packed as they'd been New Year's Eve. I was getting the idea that was just how it was in New Orleans: every night was a party even if there wasn't anything in particular to celebrate. Everyone we passed had smiles on their faces and many had drinks in their hands. Here in the French Quarter a feeling of liberation swirled around you and swept you up, roughing off your frayed edges and leaving you aglow.

We could hear the music and the crowd even before we turned the corner onto St. Peter Street. Jimmy whispered a few words to the burly guy at the door and we were magically granted safe passage through a carriageway entrance into the sprawling courtyard. Lance had convinced me it made sense to go, deeming it a fact-finding mission, to get our bearings in this city and have a look around the nightlife scene. This place certainly had its charm. Lantern lights twinkled, wrought-iron tables were surrounded by spirited revelers who looked to be having the time of their lives. I thought I even recognized a few faces from the New Year's Eve party in the Garden District. Were they counselors? Students? Either way, like us, they looked too young to be allowed in here. Perhaps everyone knew Jimmy's connection. Jimmy . . . I looked around our group but he had wandered off somewhere. It seemed we were on our own to navigate through the drunken throng. Lance said something into my ear, but I couldn't really hear it. I could barely make out my own thoughts. He pointed ahead of us. At the center of the patio, water cascaded from a lit fountain, shaped almost like a martini glass with angelic carved figures at the top. In an odd union of elements, a low-burning fire flamed up from the center of the fountain's pool.

"Hey, you've got your camera, right?" he said, breaking me out of my reverie.

"Oh, yeah." I pulled it out of my bag. I planned to snap everything and everyone in sight. It couldn't hurt. I wished it were quieter here, though, so I could tell Lance about Sabine.

From several feet away, she called over to us. "Hey! Haven! Will you get us?" She put her arms around Brody and Max on either side of her. I never would have known that this was the same girl who had entrusted me with her deepest secret just hours before. It seemed as if she had simply told herself she wasn't going to think about any of that right now and she shifted into the old, fun Sabine. I was always trying to lock things away at times when I couldn't afford to be brought down by them, to compartmentalize my moods, but I never felt I succeeded.

I trained my camera on them and zoomed in. Dante leaned into Max in a way that almost made me laugh. I snapped, the flash blinding everyone in the general vicinity. Dante shot over to me.

"You have to e-mail that to me," he whispered.

I snapped all around us, capturing as many faces as I could. Our group colonized a cozy, dimly lit area of the patio amid a backdrop of drooping broad-leaved trees. Dante, Max, and Brody were dispatched to round up drinks. Sabine had positioned herself beside Lance again. The music got even louder—a peppy, jaunty style like nothing I'd heard before.

"Hey!" Sabine and Lance both looked over at me. "Name that tune." I leaned forward, around Sabine, to try to stump Lance in one of our favorite games. "Classic Cajun music. The entire genre."

"Uhh . . ." He put his hands up, not playing along.

"Zydeco," I said, shaking my head, feeling shot down.

"Oh! So that's what zydeco is," Sabine said. "You know your stuff, Haven."

"Thanks," I said, trying to conceal my disappointment. She and Lance resumed whatever it was they were talking about while I allowed myself a sip of my fruity hurricane—which was so dangerously good, its alcohol so well camouflaged by sweetness, I knew too many sips could easily get me into plenty of trouble.

A man in a straw hat strolled out from inside the bar with

a washboard strapped to his chest and a spoon in each hand. He strummed against the rippled surface, earning cheers for his scratchy percussion from those patrons, ready to live it up, streaming in.

A group wandered in amid the newcomers, but stood out from the T-shirts and beer bellies and even the low-cut tops and tight jeans. The girl leading them wore a spaghetti-strap floral minidress hitting at her midthigh, her tanned and taut legs in expertly beat-up brown leather cowboy boots. There was a small pink bloom perched behind her ear, softening the severity of her short-cropped blond hair and accentuating her perfect features. I recognized her in an instant: the girl with the sparklers on New Year's Eve. With no warning, she grabbed the hand of the man with the washboard and pulled him into a dance, spinning herself under his arm, stepping and prancing to the music.

The entire outdoor crowd turned its attention to their dancing as though this had been part of the night's planned entertainment. The sparkler girl's group was made up of dressed-down jeans-clad guys and girls who seemed like they exerted zero effort to look the way they did—their faces had no makeup and yet appeared flawless; while their outfits generally were unremarkable, it didn't matter—everyone still looked at them. They clapped and hooted and hollered as the group's leader whirled around. Before long, the revelers in the courtyard were clapping, and other patrons who trickled out from the bar to see what the fuss was about quickly joined in. Two members of the band from inside —a trumpeter and fiddler—even came out playing, bopping to the music.

I was so transfixed that I didn't realize I had actually given voice to my thoughts: "Who is she?"

A rosy-faced man in a stained T-shirt piped up beside me. "That's just the Krewe," he said, his eyes glued to the show playing out before us as he took a swig from his beer.

"The Krewe?"

I sorted through my mental files. "I thought krewes only came out during Mardi Gras time—there are a bunch of krewes, right? They put together the floats and march in the parade?" I remembered reading that there were a host of different groups; people paid dues to be part of them and they had all sorts of wild names.

"Yeah, yeah, those are the real krewes. Rex, Bacchus, whatever. But *this* Krewe," he said, gesturing with his beer toward the group, "isn't really a krewe at all. It's just a name they've sorta been given unofficially since they have this way of riling people up—just look at 'em." He yelped and whistled, tucking his beer bottle under his arm to clap along.

Watching the hubbub, I was so engrossed I almost forgot to take pictures. I dug my camera out again and clicked off a bunch of shots of the scene. As the blonde twirled, smiling so brightly, I noticed a mark on the inside of her wrist. I zoomed my camera and managed to snap a photo of the fleur-de-lis, that symbol we'd seen so much of since arriving, branded proudly on her skin. This one had been drawn to look like it was made of flames. I thought I could feel a tattoo needle burning at my back and in that marred space above my heart. My scars were suddenly flaring in a way I couldn't ignore.

As the song ended, with a great sawing flourish from the fiddler and a flutter of notes from the trumpeter, the girl embraced the washboard player and gave a bow to the jubilant, applauding crowd. She transformed the whole feel of the party, like some sort of good infection. Everyone was dancing now.

"She's amazing," Sabine said gushing, and leaned over me as we both watched her return to her group and go back inside. "Gorgeous, too. Where do you think she got that dress?"

"No idea."

"It looks kind of vintagey, you know? And the boots. I bet she's one of those girls who shops in thrift stores and some-how looks better than people who dress head to toe in designer everything even though she spends, like, three dollars. I hate those girls."

"I'm sorry, that's just how some of us roll," I said as a joke. Sabine nudged her shoulder into me, acknowledging that me as a fashion plate was a humorous idea.

"That's it. We're going to find the nearest thrift shop and hit it together," she said. Then, just as quickly, she turned back to Lance. They seemed to have so much to talk about tonight. I couldn't help but feel a little jealous. I didn't like this feeling. I had had the sense, since earlier in the year, that he belonged to me, that we belonged to each other in some strange, unspoken way that transcended any typical, ephemeral high school relation-ship. We had gone through so much together, things that no one else could really, completely understand. I didn't like the idea that I could be the kind of girl who would become so possessive.

Sabine's voice interrupted my thoughts. "I'm running to the ladies', be right back."

Lance slouched in his seat, taking a sip from a hurricane. "She seems cool," he said.

"I have crazy stuff to tell you," I blurted out, unable to control myself now that Sabine was out of earshot. His face fell, not in fear but in disappointment, as though reality was trespassing on his good time.

"Is it life threatening?" he asked.

I thought for a moment. "No. I guess it's not."

"Then, later. Join me in being totally normal for a few minutes." He looked around. "All of these people have nothing to worry about," he said, shaking his head like it was a revelation. "That one"—he pointed in the direction Sabine had gone—"has no worries." This, of course, couldn't be further from the truth. But even so, I changed tack.

"So what do you know about Barthelemy Lafon?" I asked.

"What do I know about Lafon? What do *you* know about Lafon?"

"I know that he was an architect and city planner in New Orleans and that he's resting much more comfortably tonight in a stunningly painted tomb, thanks to yours truly."

"Is that right?"

"Yep, I painted his grave the other day."

"You don't have to be too obliging. I mean, what he did with the Garden District and the city's grid system is awesome, but he ended up becoming a pirate and a smuggler." With a straw, he speared at the ice left in his glass.

"Well, in that case, I'll scuff it up a little tomorrow."

"Now, if you get to Benjamin Latrobe, then let me know."

"He did the U.S. Capitol, right? He's on my list."

"He's a rock star in the architecture world."

"I'll take good care of him."

The chair between us scraped back and Sabine plunked down in it, guzzling a hurricane. "Whaddid I miss?" she asked both of us, but didn't wait for an answer. She pointed to her already half-empty glass. "These are amazing, especially when they're free!"

"Um, not to be—" I started.

"*Narc!*" Dante shouted, suddenly listening in. "*Narc!* Over here!"

I glared at him but turned back to Sabine. "I just mean, I think they . . . pack a punch." I stirred my nearly full drink with my straw.

"That's the idea!" she said brightly.

"So who bought it for you?" Max asked, leaning in.

"One of the guys who was with that hot blond girl." She jerked her head in the direction of the interior bar. "His name is Wylie." Her eyes danced as she said it.

"Of course it is," I said.

"He's *so* cute. I mean, did you see him?"

"He is. I don't think ugly Wylies exist." I was torn—I wanted to encourage Sabine, but without feeling like I was feeding her to the wolves. My scars were warning me that there was something off with that group. So I added quietly, "I don't know about his friends, though."

But Sabine was barely paying attention. "And I don't see what the big deal is with these." She held up her drink. "It doesn't taste so strong. It just tastes delicious! What's in here?"

"Rum," Lance answered. "Careful." That was the Lance I knew.

"Lots of rum," I added.

"Huh." She studied it, shrugged, and lowered her head to keep drinking. The level of the liquid sank fast. She popped back up. "I think I'm going to need another."

Soon after Sabine pounded down her third hurricane, our group quickly reached the consensus that it was time to go. She had slumped back in her chair like a rag doll, on the verge of sleep. With Brody and Lance holding her upright, she stumbled out of the bar. The walk back to the house was just a few blocks, but it took a while, punctuated by some dry heaving that had us worried. We missed curfew. The house lay quiet, and if Connor heard our late arrival, he didn't bother confronting us about it.

Brody flopped Sabine into her bed, where she landed flat on her back, limbs sprawled. I nestled a bottle of water into bed beside her, and we all said our good nights. As soon as everyone left our room, she rolled slowly onto her side, moaning as though she was about to be sick.

"You okay over there?" I asked, pulling my scrubs out of the dresser. I was sorry the night had ended this way. Clearly, we wouldn't be having any serious talks with her in this state.

"Yeeeeeah," she groaned. "I just need to sleep it off."

A thought occurred to me: "Hey, you don't think there was anything in your drink, do you? You took one of those leaves today, right?"

"Yeahyeahyeah, this morning. I have a few left. Don't worry. This is all the booze." She slurred her words. "I know the difference." This came out sounding certain, without question. I was impressed. I still wasn't sure if I would've been able to tell the difference between the toxins we'd once fallen prey to and just average, run-of-the-mill alcohol or food poisoning.

"Good, just making sure."

"I'm not a bad person, you know," she piped up, catching me off-guard.

"I know." I laughed. "Of course not. I'm just sorry you're feeling bad."

"I gotta let off steam sometimes, you know?"

"Sure." I didn't know where this was coming from. But she probably wouldn't remember any of it in the morning, anyway.

"Don't you ever have nights like this?" she asked in a whimper.

The answer, of course, was no, for better or worse. But I pretended to think about it longer than I needed to as I finished getting dressed. "Well, I could argue that it's a character flaw on my part that I don't have enough nights like this. Maybe that makes me . . . *weird*." I was being honest. Fitting in had never been my strong suit, but I was kind of used to it at this point.

"Lance thinks you're insanely perfect." She said it in such a way that it didn't seem like a compliment.

I stopped. And turned around. "Whaddya mean?"

"He thinks you're perfect. That's what he said," she went on, drowsily. "He thinks you're too tough for your own good sometimes."

Much as I wanted to hear more, I didn't want Sabine to know how much I cared what Lance thought. "You're crazy," I said, trying to smile. "Get some sleep, okay?" I gathered my things to brush my teeth and was almost out the door when she let out a hopeless heavy sigh.

"Don't you need a break from it all sometimes?" Her tone had softened. "To just forget about it?" I knew she was talking about us in the grander sense, what we were and this secret we shared. "Isn't what's on our shoulders kind of a lot? I don't know why we got stuck with this." She sounded defeated. I closed the door and sat down on the floor by her bed.

"I don't know either. But I guess I feel like if I let my guard down for one minute, then that's it for me," I tried to explain. "I just, like, don't trust the world anymore, you know? I feel like a target. I can't afford to be anything less than completely present and ready for anything." Fun seemed like a luxury I didn't quite get to have, at least not in any sort of abundance.

"It's so freaking exhausting, though." Her lifeless arm hung over the edge of the bed. "Why aren't you worn-out by it all?"

"I am. Trust me!" I shook my head. But getting to talk about this with someone new, someone besides Dante and Lance, was comforting.

Her heavy lids fluttered closed. "So sleepy . . ."

"Good, go to bed." I tucked her arm back onto the bed and flipped off the light.

When I finally nestled into my bed, waiting for sleep to overtake me, I suddenly remembered to check my cell. Reaching down to my bag on the floor, I fumbled around and pulled out my phone. A new message lit up, received just after ten o'clock tonight.

Tomorrow you will begin training once more. Prepare for the unexpected, but trust in the merit of even the most unorthodox of practices.

Those few words found a home at the pit of my stomach. I was so lost in my worries that I almost missed the flicker of light — on-off, so fast tonight — from that house across the way.

9

I'm Sorry I Had to Do That

The relentless pounding on the door just wouldn't stop. It shook the entire wall, then the entire room. I even felt it rattling in my head. I expected to open my eyes and be back at the Lexington Hotel, when plenty of bad dreams, and worse realities, had begun that way. But this time it was outside our door.

"Get up!" a voice shouted, punctuated by a *BANG BANG BANG*. I sprang up in bed. Sabine just moaned and rolled over. The room was still pitch-black, probably hours before dawn. My clock confirmed it: 4:04 a.m. The pounding came again. I flew down the ladder to answer it, but before I could get there, the door burst open from a swift kick. I gasped as Connor shone a flashlight at Sabine in bed—she just turned her head away—and then at me, standing there frozen.

"Get up, ladies!" he barked at us. It was the version of Connor we had glimpsed at dinner, not the easygoing college guy who played pickup basketball games. "Never seen anyone move so slow! Five minutes to pack for the retreat. Meet in the common room. Go, go, *go!*"

I was too stunned to even string words together but hungover Sabine managed to croak, "Where are we going?"

"Four minutes!" he called on his way out the door.

"But we don't even know what to bring!" she cried out after him.

"Three minutes!" He continued banging on other doors as he made his way down the hall.

I finally found my voice again. "What's with that guy? He started out so nice."

"Lunatic." Sabine shook her head, then put her hand to it. "Owww."

Minutes later, Connor ushered us all outside, with hastily packed duffel bags and suitcases in tow. Fast, fast, fast, he marched us down to a van waiting in front of our house.

The streets were deserted, the sky still black. No one spoke. The only sound was the soft, steady whoosh of tires on pavement as we rolled out of the city and onto empty country roads. Dante and a few others dozed. Brody played games on his phone. Lance and I took turns gazing out the window and watching Connor, who drove stone-faced. Even when our eyes connected in the rearview mirror, his glance betrayed not the slightest emotion. My mind raced through a million scenarios, all horrific, most involving some variation of Connor being one of *them*. As the first light of day broke on the horizon, we pulled off onto a dirt path leading back through lush tree-canopied land, the ground saturated beneath our wheels. "Off-roading, all right!" Brody whispered.

Connor pulled right up to a small dock with a lone boat awaiting passengers. He stopped the van, opened the door, and waved us out. "All aboard!" he shouted.

The deck swerved beneath me as I lunged to step in the boat, trying to secure my footing. A wooden bench ran down the middle of it, with seats on both sides. I took my place between Lance and Dante, who whispered, "So awesome. I've been dying for a swamp tour!"

Thick cypress trees lined both banks, their heavy branches drooping to touch the wet ground. From the wild, overgrown vegetation surrounding us to the murky swamp water below, the world here consisted solely of a palette of greens, some vibrant, others viscous. Birds called out at the rising sun; a chorus of insects chirped in unison. Sabine was the last to board the boat, hesitating on the narrow, warped pier. At first I thought she was going to be sick—she was so hungover—but her ashen face seemed to register true fear.

"C'mon, time to roll out," Connor said, cutting her no slack. She shook her head, her feet rooted in place. Finally, he scooped her up in what would've been a bear hug under different circumstances and lifted her right into the boat. The rest of us watched, mouths agape. I squeezed closer to Lance and waved Sabine over to sit between me and Dante. She looked in my eyes only a second, then let her lids close. Her hands, folded primly on her lap, trembled. Connor took the helm and the motor sputtered and roared as we set off, skimming along the algae-coated water, cool wind whipping and a soft spray kicking up at us.

Sabine looked like she was in pain; eyes still closed, she sat hunched, arms crossed. I put my hand on her back and asked, "Are you seasick? If you lean down and get blood rushing to your head, you'll feel better."

"That's not it," she said flatly.

Connor steered us into a narrow bend where a tree seemed to

be growing right out of the water, and he cut the engine. Dante walked over to the railing, reaching out and letting his fingertips graze the Spanish moss hanging like fringed sleeves over the cypress branches. Max joined him. Collectively, our group loosened up.

"I want y'all to breathe in that fresh swampy air!" Connor said, taking a deep breath. He pulled out a long stick propped against the engine and grabbed a white bag from the floor, tearing it open with his teeth. "Look alive," he called to Dante, tossing something his way. Dante caught it and held it up: a campfire-suitable marshmallow.

"Yum! Are we making s'mores?" he asked.

"Nope!" Connor said cheerily. He speared a marshmallow with the stick and leaned over, tapping it in the water. "Check this out." He waved. Everyone looked over, craning their necks. River got up to stand near Connor.

"He looks like a mean motherf—" she said with a smile.

"River," Connor cut her off, with a laugh. "A quarter in the swear jar for you."

That's when I saw its long pebbled form stealthily inching up in the water. It reached the marshmallow and rose, its jaw snapping at the stick and stealing the treat before sinking back into the swamp. Drew yelped. Max jumped back a step, looking sheepish. He fanned himself with his hat. There was applause and someone exclaimed, "Whoa!"

"Hey, Lafitte, just wanted you to meet some friends," Connor said to the gator.

Lance chuckled. "He's named after the pirate? Jean Lafitte? That's hilarious."

"Smart man, thank you," Connor said. "Yeah, there was always talk his treasure was buried here somewhere, so I thought it fit. Anyway, there are plenty more where Lafitte came from, along with all sorts of other wildlife that make this guy look like a kitten. We'll be running trips here with some elementary school kids from the Ninth Ward. We'll bring 'em out here next weekend, give 'em a tour, then go into town to this place famous for their fried catfish . . ." As he explained the details, baiting a stick with a marshmallow, I felt the tension in my body ease: it seemed the old Connor was back. I breathed a sigh of relief. Sabine had opened her eyes, but focused them on her feet, still looking pained.

"Just wanna direct your attention over that way." Connor pointed to a shack on stilts in the distance, perhaps a football field or two away. "That's where we're headed." He paused. "But I'm afraid this is as far as I'm taking you." We all looked at one another. It seemed everyone thought they had heard him wrong. Connor smiled, a devilish grin. "What? Y'all thought I was gonna give you door-to-door service? Gotta work for things around here."

"Um, do you want me to drive?" Max offered. "My uncle has a boat like this in Florida. I could—"

Connor started laughing. "You're a sweet one, Max. But I don't think y'all are getting it." He walked the length of the boat. "You. Are. Going. To. Swim." With each word he slammed the stick against the side railing, making us all jump. Then he stopped and smiled again.

"We'll be eaten alive," Brody said, scowling in disbelief.

"You can go first, buddy," Connor said calmly.

"You're a nutcase."

"You're going. Now." With that, he smashed the stick against the railing, breaking it in two. "Get in there!" he yelled at Brody.

"Why the hell would I do that?" Brody said, standing up, looking him in the eye. Lance stood now too, like he was ready to pounce. I sized everything up, thinking *How can I get out of here? What's my escape route?*

"Maybe because your life depends on it. All of you. Your lives depend on getting the hell in that water right now. Go, now!" he shouted. Brody still stood there and Connor grabbed him by the shirt, dragged him, kicking and flailing, to the railing and, in one swift motion, flung him in the swamp. Brody screamed as he splashed into the water. Connor lunged at Tom next, but Tom just sprang up and leapt off the railing himself, joining Brody, who had already begun swimming feverishly to shore. We were all on our feet now. Except Sabine, who dropped to her knees, breathing ragged. She was hyperventilating.

"Go! Go! Go!" Connor yelled at us. Sticks in both hands now, he crashed them against every possible surface, swinging wildly, trying to hit us all like he was swatting flies. Everyone fled, sustaining sharp, stinging smacks in the process, some already flinging themselves from the railing to greet the horrors of the swamp rather than be left with Connor.

Across the deck, Dante and Max, exchanging a quick glance, synchronized their jump, hitting the water together. Wailing now, Sabine cried, "I can't go! I can't!" amid the frenzied splashing below. Alligator jaws snapped across the water pursuing this stream of new prey. Connor had just finished pushing Drew in and he set his crazed eyes on me, Lance, and Sabine. Sabine's body shook with fear and she had broken out into a sweat. Being pushed seemed a much worse way to go and no one had successfully fought Connor off yet. Lance jumped in and Connor turned his attention to me, swiping at my head then my feet. I pulled Sabine up onto the metal railing and tugged her until she fell over the side with me, screaming.

The warm water washed over us, our legs kicking against so many obstacles: the brush of tangled plants reaching out, creatures traveling along beside us. Were they alligators? Or worse? I could feel them as I kicked to propel myself. We seemed surrounded. There was so much splashing it was impossible to tell who was responsible, man or beast. Connor ripped the boat's engine back on and zipped past, spraying us. His eyes were fixed in the distance as he left us for dead without so much as a glance back.

I had never been such a strong swimmer but I pushed through the water, relentless, my arms and legs burning, and caught up with the front of the pack. Sabine was a body length behind me, and her head bobbed under the water. She gasped, arms waving. I swam back, grabbing her around the waist, intending to swim ahead with her, when Lance appeared on the other side.

"It's okay, go on. I'll take her in," he said, his arm weaving around her, like a lifeguard. "Meet you on the shore."

I swam ahead, my limbs stinging. I could feel the gators clipping at my feet. I heard that pop of their snapping jaws all around us, and it only made me swim faster, overtaking Brody to reach land, where I dodged a trio of boars scavenging for food along the water's edge.

I saw something unusual halfway up toward that elevated shack —which looked as if it was made of rotting wood—and ran toward it, through wet, thick soil, tripping over the vinelike plants that ensnared me with each step. My left foot felt twice its normal size, stinging each time it hit the ground, but still I ran. Finally I reached it, regaining my breath as the others grew closer. A branch had been speared into the earth, like a javelin, with a sheet of paper hanging off one of its limbs. I ripped it off and read:

Welcome Wing-Seekers,
I'm your trainer and your guide. And I'm sorry I had to do that to you. Come on up, and I'll explain everything. Promise.
Connor

Brody caught up with me first, then seconds later the rest of the group trickled in, fanning out around me. My mind tried to make sense of what I read in those few short sentences. Lance stepped forward from his perch beside Sabine, who sat on the ground. He took the paper from my hands, read it, and furrowed his brow in a way that said he couldn't believe it either. I turned around, looking into each set of eyes as if it was my first time seeing them. How was it possible? Now, suddenly, different as my housemates all were, they felt like a part of me. I was comforted and yet . . . intimidated, too.

The cabin was larger and far better appointed than I might've guessed from the outside. A long wooden table had been set with an array of sandwiches. The fridge had been fully stocked. All of our bags sat in a neat row in a spacious alcove where at least a dozen hammocks had been strung up on wooden posts. We had wandered up in complete silence, passing the note to one another, as though each of us felt that something so weighty needed to be experienced individually. It had been enough to think that Sabine was like Dante, Lance, and me, but *this* was more than I could begin to understand.

"So we've got some stuff to talk about, huh, guys?" Connor's voice had greeted us as we entered the cabin, all of us soaking wet and reeking of swamp water—a peculiar mix of fresh, overgrown plant life and something rancid. None of us said anything about being hungry or wanting to change out of our wet, miserable clothes. Instead, we all gathered quietly around the fireplace where Connor stood.

"I want you all to take a look at yourselves," he started. "You swam with alligators today. I watched you and you all got bitten. Every single one of you. Haven," he singled me out. I jumped, startled to hear my name. "How's your foot?"

"Huh?" I asked. I had my legs curled under me on the floor, my wet jeans stiffening now as they dried. I stretched myself out and discovered a hole had been taken out of the side of my sneaker. I put my fingers through the gaping opening.

"Yeah, you got a bite from a snapping turtle—those things are so nasty they eat gators. But what's going on there? You're missing part of a shoe and you've got a couple scratches."

I pulled up the leg of my jeans: no blood, just some red slashes. I nodded.

"Check your limbs everyone—no one's *missing* any limbs, right? Digits all intact? Anyone have anything more than a scrape?" We all looked ourselves over, watching one another from the corners of our eyes. "There's a reason for that. You're not human. Not anymore, at least." He paused to let that fully sink in. "Everyone here has already passed a test. Am I right that you all faced some tough times last year?" He scanned our serious faces. After some shifting of eyes, a collective reluctance to give ourselves away, we all nodded. "You had to fight to save your souls? Well, sorry to say, the fight is going to get tougher. But you're on your way to getting your wings. And I'm here to help. Any questions so far?" One by one, every hand went up.

"All right, I'm not surprised." He exhaled, gearing up for the attack. "Shoot."

What followed was the kind of rapid-fire press conference that happens on the news after some sort of crisis or natural disaster, when the networks need to preempt regularly scheduled programming.

"Who the heck *are* you? What's your story?" Brody called out.

"Good question. All you need to know is I'm your best friend and occasionally, like today, your worst nightmare. I'm with the administration," Connor said with finality, as if that was supposed to mean something to us. When he got no reaction, he went on. "They're the governing body."

"Of, like, angels?" Dante asked in a tone that suggested he couldn't believe he was actually asking a question like this out loud. He received a nod in confirmation. "Are there elections? How do they work?"

"Who cares," River cut in. "Are you stronger than us?"

Then miscellaneous questions from the rest of the group.

Tom: "Why should we believe you?"

Drew: "How do we get our wings?"

Jimmy: "Whoa, so *everyone* went through crazy stuff before getting here?"

"That was the first test," Emma said, rolling her eyes, then she turned back to Connor. "There are three tests? So what's the second one?"

Max: "Do you know how we got this way?"

Lance: "What can you tell us about the training we'll be doing? And why, exactly, wasn't even one of us eaten alive today?

Given the speed of alligators, the sheer quantity of them, and the number of us invading their space, I don't entirely understand why we're all still breathing."

"Why did you *do that* to us?" Sabine spat the words, the bitterness in her voice putting a sudden stop to the barrage of questioning. I thought of Lance clutching Sabine, pulling her to safety through the water, and I felt a sickness at the pit of my stomach, which I wasn't proud of.

"Sabine." Connor sighed, looking away for a moment, guilt setting into his eyes. "I didn't want to have to do that. There will be more things I may do that I wish I didn't have to. But to answer you both, a big part of our work together is on cultivating your overall sense of fearlessness. When you conquer your fear, you won't believe what you'll be capable of. But it's much harder than you might think."

It finally hit me, and I had to ask. "So, that's it then: we really are immortal now?" I felt everyone's eyes on me and a deep hush fall over the room.

"Yes," Connor said, giving a mighty weight to the word. "Yes, you are."

Lance leaned forward, pushing his glasses up on his nose. "But then what does that *mean?* We can't be killed?"

"That means that the kinds of things that might kill a mortal —swimming with alligators, getting shot, jumping out of a plane with no parachute—will not kill you. You may still get some injuries, like your scratches today, but whatever you receive will be nothing compared to what should have happened."

"So we're invincible. Awesome!" Brody clapped his hands once.

"That's where I gotta stop you," Connor said in a stern voice. "No. You *can* still be destroyed by representatives of the underworld. They can seize your souls and then you'll be committed to an eternity of . . ." He seemed to be searching for the words. "It's worse than being killed." He sat down, hands on his knees, leveling with us. "Listen to me: They're looking for you. You're being hunted. They *are* going to find you. Look to your right and to your left . . ." He paused as we all did this. I glanced at Sabine and then Lance, whose eyes read pure concern. I could feel his mind working, sorting through all this. "One of them may not be among us in a few months," Connor said in a tone that chilled me. "It's going to be up to all of us, working together, to keep one another safe. Hear me?" Everyone nodded.

"Pardon the question, but dude, *how?*" Dante asked.

Connor thought a minute before replying. "That's something we're gonna spend every minute of every day trying to figure out."

10

The Thrill of the Chase

After giving us a chance to wash the reek of the swamp off ourselves, change, and eat something, Connor led us out of the cabin and over to a patch of grassy, mossy land where five objects had been set along a fallen tree trunk.

"Hey, my suitcase!" Dante said the minute we got close enough to make out the animal print. "That thing better not have a scratch on it."

Connor stood in front of the tree trunk. "Sorry, buddy," he said. "As Dante noticed, I helped myself to some of your things for this exercise." In addition to the suitcase, there was a can of hair spray, Max's fedora (which, according to Dante, was one of many since Max preferred to cover up the scar on his head), a basketball, and, as Lance pointed out to me, one of my worn gray T-shirts. I didn't like the idea that Connor had gone through our bags. I was surprised people had managed to pack such frivolous, fun things at four in the morning. I hadn't even been clearheaded enough to grab one of my nicer shirts. I was just grateful Connor hadn't taken my phone. No one had asked about those mysterious messages. It seemed every other major question had come up, even though Connor hadn't answered them all. I wondered if there was any significance to those omissions.

"One part of our training will be working on skills every angel should have in some capacity."

Dante already had his hand raised. "Are we gonna learn to fly now? I'm dying to fly." Max and I exchanged looks and smiles.

"Dante, man, you've gotta crawl before you can walk." Connor laughed. Dante looked disappointed, and Max patted him on the back. "Flying comes way later, guys. Relax, okay? Today we're just gonna try levitating some stuff. Trust me, it comes in handy. So let's start small and see what ya got. Who's up first? Emma? Since it's your hair spray?"

She stood opposite the metallic can, staring it down, but succeeded only in making it shake.

"I mean, how do we do this? Are we supposed to make any movements or think about anything in particular to make this happen?" I asked. I wondered if everyone else had done this kind of thing before.

"Nope, just don't think so much, Haven. Everyone has a different way of doing things. You'll figure it out," Connor said, but I felt helpless. "Like anything else, some of you will be better than others. But hang in there. With practice you'll all master it."

One by one he had each of us try to raise Emma's hair spray. Nearly everyone had lifted it at least an inch for a moment before it was my turn. I focused on it, steadying my gaze and tuning out everything around me. I imagined it aloft, taking flight. But there it sat, refusing to budge. I stared some more but after a few long, painful minutes, I had succeeded only in making the heat rise in my skin.

Connor cut me off. "Okay, let's keep moving. Brody?"

"But I'm not done," I said, frustrated.

"Haven, there'll be time. Don't worry."

Brody, who'd been busy chatting with Tom, took his place before the can. In the blink of an eye, he had it floating. Connor applauded.

"And that's how it's done," Brody said, giving a bow.

"Nice work," Connor said. Sabine went next and even in her shaken state, she lifted it too, though not for quite as long as Brody had. Connor had the two of them try the other objects, and they made it through everything but the basketball and suitcase. I tried to dissect how they did it, but there was nothing to study. It was such quiet, internal work. Brody seemed downright relaxed about it—with the larger items, he extended his arm, but that was as much exertion as he showed. And though Sabine's concentration was clear, she didn't seem on the surface to be doing anything differently than I had.

We worked at it until nightfall, some of us—like Lance—improving and some, like me, not improving and growing angrier, more sullen with each attempt. "Shake it off, baby," Dante said, kneading my shoulders and patting me on the back. But something else was eating away at me too.

When we finally climbed into our hammocks to go to sleep, my mind and muscles felt equally weary. Connor had retreated to a room in the back of the cabin, leaving us unsupervised. Some had already fallen asleep—I could make out Dante's trademark snore cutting through the still air. No sooner had I nestled into my brightly patterned hammock, the tightly woven nylon molding to hold my body, than I heard a giggle and footsteps, followed by the creak of a wooden post. I could only imagine it might be

Emma creeping over to join Jimmy. Their ups and downs were dizzying. But the room was oppressively dark, and it hit me: what if it wasn't Emma and Jimmy? The events of the day had set me off balance, and now it was difficult letting myself fall asleep while having to wonder about this.

As light-footed as possible, I hopped down from my hammock and felt in the darkness until I reached the one in front of mine. "Are you awake?" I whispered.

"Hey. No, I'm asleep," Lance whispered back with a soft, woozy chuckle. Relief set in. I had been paranoid, which I could blame on exhaustion.

"Want some company?"

"Yes, please."

I climbed up, and he enveloped me instantly. The strong arms that rescued Sabine were mine now, again. His lips found mine and for a few moments everything else, and everyone else, melted away. He kissed my neck and pulled me close and I drifted off to sleep.

I awoke to the clanking of dishes in the kitchen, a sizzling stove, and spirited voices. Sabine was seated on the counter watching Connor flip pancakes. Only half of the group was up.

"We're trading stories," Brody said. "What's yours? Who tried to recruit you for the underworld? Mine was a hot librarian."

"Really?" I asked. I grabbed an apple from the fridge. "I wouldn't think that would be your type."

"I know, go figure. Max's was a hot history teacher on a model United Nations summit trip."

"Hot camp counselor." Drew shrugged. "I think Tom's was something like that too."

"No, his was a tennis coach," Jimmy said. "But I think it was at a tennis camp, so that's close."

"Hot band frontman," River said, angry still.

"Oh, cool, ours—Emma's and mine—were a couple of owners of the coffeehouse we played at," Jimmy said.

"Played?" I asked.

"We have sort of a country music act going. I play guitar, she sings," he said like it was no big deal. "What about you?"

I was unaccustomed to talking about this, but everyone had been so open. "Mine was a hot internship boss," I declared, feeling like I'd completed the secret handshake and belonged to the group now. And then a different impulse hit me: that note from Lucian. I had the scrap with my name in my wallet right now.

"Me too," said Sabine, nibbling from a bowl of blueberries.

"Wow, what was the internship?"

She ignored the question. "And Lance and Dante were with you, right?"

"Yeah." Everyone in the kitchen looked at me as though I'd said something truly shocking. Connor glanced up from making the pancakes.

"That's crazy," River said, a hint of venom. I wasn't sure exactly what part of that had been so upsetting to her.

"See, I told you: amazing, right?" Sabine said.

River shook her head. "I mean, you guys are enough," she said to Jimmy. "But all three of them? All three?" She stormed off, as though offended.

Unable to make sense of it, I tried to change the subject. "So what was your job like? I don't know about you, but my internship would've been pretty cool if not for, you know, the whole soul-buying business." It was actually kind of comforting to be able to talk about it. Maybe I could get used to this sharing stuff, I told myself. "We were working at a hotel."

"That's cool," Sabine said flatly. She didn't offer anything about her experience. Then she perked up again just as fast. "By the way, you've got a great guy there." She pointed as Lance stepped into the room. She hopped down from the counter and grabbed a plate of pancakes from Connor.

"Yeah, he's okay," I joked, blushing.

"Thanks for the help yesterday," she said. On her way to the dining table, she gave Lance a quick peck on the cheek.

"Anytime," he said shyly. I just smiled, trying to suppress that feeling in my gut. Sabine had already taken a seat beside Brody and sat chatting and laughing with him. It was hard to believe this was the same girl who had fallen apart yesterday.

As the last few late risers drifted in for breakfast, we convinced Emma and Jimmy to perform for us. There was a guitar in the corner of the cabin's living room, and Jimmy began to play and sing. He seemed to transform as he strummed, his voice carrying the melancholy tune; Emma joined in, her notes so delicate and rich. It was a familiar old song, from the eighties, with lyrics about someone loved and left behind. I had found my mind wandering during their performance, thinking back, and it had taken me a few seconds to realize when they had finished singing to join the rest of the group in applauding.

After everyone was dressed and nourished, Connor announced we'd be spending the afternoon doing some more levitating and then climbing cypresses and leaping from the highest branches because, as he explained when we gathered to head outside, "Even though you're not gonna get hurt, you've gotta learn to land on your feet. And no taking the stairs out here. I want everyone jumping off the porch. You've gotta look for every opportunity to use your strength."

I looked to Lance, who read my mind and had already calculated the distance from the porch to the ground: "Twenty feet." He shrugged, like it was no big deal.

Then came the scream.

Emma had just opened the door. I thought maybe she had fallen from the porch, but she still stood there, at the front of our pack. We all spilled out, crowding around her. Connor rushed to her side.

I pushed through and saw on the worn, splintered wood of the porch a pair of angel wings drawn in blood.

There were many serious faces in the van on the way back, everyone, I suspected, with the same thoughts running through their heads. Once in a while someone would shout a question to Connor, but it would be one we had already heard the answer to at least ten times that afternoon and yet still needed confirmation on.

"If they knew where we were, why wouldn't they just attack us right then?" Dante piped up at one point.

"That's not how they roll. There's a thrill in the chase for them," Connor explained. I watched him in the rearview mirror, his brows knit. "Let's not sell ourselves short. You guys are actually an exceptional group. My gut tells me that they aren't confident about taking you all on at once. They'll want to divide and conquer."

"So there really is safety in numbers?" I called out, hopeful.

"You'd be surprised," he said.

By the time we got back to Royal Street, dusk had fallen and

Connor had informed us of a new addition to our daily schedules: each night two of us would stand watch over the house, walking the halls, peeking into the courtyard, keeping an eye out lest anyone—or anything—should leave a stealthy message as they had at the cabin. Or, of course, make their presence known in even clearer ways.

Part Two

11

You Are Going to Be Taken

Though we now all knew our real purpose in New Orleans, we still had to keep up our volunteer cover. Over the course of the next week, we each made a couple trips to the swamp in smaller groups. We would arrive early and do that treacherous swim again, then we would climb the cypress trees, swing on the hanging moss, and leap to the ground, over and over. By mid-morning the buses would arrive carrying a group of school kids ready for their tour. We would ride the boat with them, teaching them about the various creatures we had secretly been swimming alongside only hours before. For lunch, we would take them out for the best po'boys anyone could ask for and then we would send them home, fed and entertained.

The week brought some other new assignments as well. Lance and the guys at the house next door would be taking a hiatus from that renovation project to work on some Habitat for Humanity homes on the outskirts of town. Max, Drew, and Sabine would be joining them. Dante and I would be planting a community garden.

But today, I was still stationed in the city of the dead. Lance kissed me goodbye, leaning in and whispering in my ear, "Careful, okay? I don't love having you in that cemetery alone all day."

"I'm not alone, you know. There are all those dead people." I tried to laugh, but he didn't quite appreciate the humor. A few yards away, Dante slapped Max on the back. We stood on the curb, waving goodbye as the group boarded Connor's shuttle and pulled away.

Dante and I were left to wander to work together. It was our first chance to talk, just the two of us, since our world had been turned upside down.

"So, what's new?" I said, deadpan.

"Yeah, you know, not much," he replied in a kidding tone.

"Yeah. Living with a whole bunch of angels. Devils are drawing bloody wings on the doorstep, the usual."

"Good times," he chirped. It was comforting that, no matter what went on, Dante and I could always make each other smile.

"Ohhh, where to begin, Dan?" I sighed, shaking my head. We recounted all that had happened in the past forty-eight hours.

"And to think on Friday night we were chowing down at Antoine's, not a care in the world," he said. "Or I mean fewer cares than now, at least."

And then something struck me. "Remember that group Friday night? The Krewe or whatever?" I asked him. "You know, the one girl had a fleur-de-lis right here." I held up my wrist.

"Hav, we can't run around declaring everyone with a tattoo a devil. I mean, have you looked around this place? That would be, like, this whole city. And half the people at school back home," Dante argued as we made our way toward Rampart Street, the morning sun already beating down on us. "Mariette has a tattoo. It's a sort of snake coiled around her upper arm. But I don't feel like *she's* one of *them*. Come by later, snap her picture, see for yourself."

Something else I'd forgotten: the pictures from the other night. I hadn't printed them yet. "Okay, if you think she won't mind."

"And I'm just going on the record as saying, with the other inked hottie, from the Krewe, I think you're being a little crazy with this one, and I say that with great love and respect," he said. "Why would they be so out in the open? Even the Outfit was really, you know, tucked away in their little hotel, waiting for the souls to come to them."

But I wasn't ready to let it go. "Dan, I'm just saying, I got that feeling, that flare, you know, right here." I patted that place above my heart where I had those scars, three sharp slashes. "That group feels to me like it's who we're looking for. There were feathers left by that dead guy on New Year's, D. They were white like her outfit that night."

He was quiet for several seconds and then: "I just don't want you to be right, that's all."

I nodded. "I know. I don't want to be right either. But this is how it is." We reached the corner where we would need to part.

"Hey, can I ask you a totally frivolous *girl* question?" I said, embarrassed.

He lit up. "My favorite kind!"

"Do you think . . . I mean . . . it probably doesn't mean anything but . . . Sabine, I think, kind of has a crush on Lance, and I wondered—"

"Please, that's nothing. Whatever. He saved her from being gator food, and she's grateful. It's fine."

I exhaled. "Thanks, D."

The cemetery positively bustled today, for a cemetery at least. I spotted not one but two tour groups winding through the narrow walkways near Marie Laveau's grave in such close proximity to each other that I worried a shoving match might break out. I set my paint, tray, brush, and roller by the tomb I was assigned to, spread my newspaper on the ground, and set to work. I had been there nearly an hour, rolling out a second coat of paint, my muscles straining as I reached to finish up the top of the tomb. Already I had begun to feel encased in a film of sweat, which wasn't the best start to the day, when I felt the stinging. I patted at the scar on my chest and glanced around me, noticing nothing out of the ordinary. More tour groups filtered through, business as usual. I felt for my wing necklace and found it beneath my shirt. Perhaps it had irritated that scar. I pulled it in front of my shirt, then returned to work.

The voice came from behind me, no warning: "Good morning, Haven, dear."

Though she couldn't have sounded more soothing, she startled me enough that I fumbled, dropping the roller right back into the tray and splattering myself with white paint.

"I'm so sorry. Good morning, Sister Catherine." I scurried up to my feet, wiping my sticky, speckled hands on my pants. "Oh, I hope I didn't get any on you."

"No, dear, I'm fine. Besides, I have plenty of these." She smoothed her habit. I had to smile. "It looks like you're making lovely progress."

"Thanks. I'm almost done with this one and I'll be starting the next in no time—I might tackle the Protestant section." I pointed toward the back of the cemetery, where a great expanse of grass that seemed to be awaiting new graves sprawled beside a series of low-lying ancient brick crypts. "Unless, of course, there's anything else you'd like me to get to first?"

"No, that sounds excellent. I appreciate your initiative. Our city of the dead is so lucky to have you. I hope you consider it your new home."

"Of course," I said, but actually, I didn't like the idea of finding a home in the city of the dead at all. With a goodbye nod, Sister Catherine swooshed to turn around, making her slow, steady way back out.

I missed Sabine and Drew, and by midday, I had had enough alone time in the cemetery. I packed it in early and headed to the voodoo shop to take Dante up on his offer. I had my camera in my backpack, so why not take that picture? Dante had his back to the shop's front window, adjusting a display of voodoo dolls. When the bells on the door jingled announcing my arrival, he spun around.

"I can't wait for you to meet Mariette! We've been working on putting together her altar room all day. It's still getting there, but you'll get the idea." He took me back through the shop, past a cramped pantry whose door was cracked open just enough for me to see rows and rows of jars containing all manner of mysterious ingredients, arranged along floor-to-ceiling shelves. Finally, we reached a closed nicked-up wooden door with a snake painted on the front. I didn't like the way it seemed to be staring at me.

Dante knocked and a voice, deep and rich, called slowly, "Come, my child."

He wiggled his eyebrows up and down, giving me that look that said I was in store for quite a show. Gently, he creaked the door open to reveal a beautiful woman seated on a silk tapestry on the floor. She looked to be in her late twenties and had a long, luscious black onyx mane, sharp features, and flawless cocoa skin. She wore a tank dress long enough to fan out around her and she sat behind a low circular wooden table with candles flickering on top of it. This whole windowless chamber smelled of spices and herbs difficult to place. The room itself was a riot of colors and knickknacks, and every square inch seemed to be occupied: voodoo dolls, candles of every height and width, a skeleton, a few skulls, toy dolls, stones, masks, beads, dollar bills, a small trickling fountain. It was all too much to take in at once.

"Come," Mariette said, waving us in with a long, sinewy arm, the gold bangles on her wrist clanging. "Please, be seated." We took our places on the floor on the other side of the felt-covered table. "You must be Haven. I've heard so much about you," she said in a slow, soothing tone that could possibly lull me to sleep or hypnotize me. She held out her hand, but not for a formal handshake. Instead she presented her left hand palm up. When I reached mine out too, she seized it, wrapped both hands around it, and squeezed. "I am Priestess Mariette."

"So good to meet you," I said softly, trying to match her serenity. She closed her eyes for a moment. I glanced at Dante but he was just watching her. The seconds felt incredibly long. As I waited, I internally debated when the right time might be to take that photo. There probably wasn't one, I decided. So, when she finally opened her eyes, I went for it.

"Um, I wondered, I'm kind of an amateur photographer. Would it be possible to take a picture of you here? It's just so . . . beautiful."

"Of course. I understand completely," she said, a response I didn't expect, but everything here was a little strange. As quickly as possible, I pulled out my camera and snapped a few shots.

Mariette didn't bother smiling or posing, but she didn't need to; she was the type who could look stunning in a setting like this, even with that terrifying snake tattoo engulfing her arm.

"Now, perhaps you will you do something for me in return. Can I read you, Haven?" she asked in such a smooth intonation, it almost didn't seem like a question at all.

"Excuse me?"

"Would you like a reading? Because I would very much like to read you." Her smile was so sparkling white it nearly blinded me. "Your aura is demanding it. I think I may have to . . . regardless."

"Oh, um, okay? Okay. Sure," I said, because there seemed no way around it. With careful fingers, she unfolded each layer of a red satin scarf as though it were made of tissue and spread it out on the table. She lit a pair of black candles, easily the size of two-liter soda bottles, and pulled a white sketchpad and metal tin from a drawer in the table and handed it to Dante. He opened the pad to a clean page and pulled a sharpened pencil from the tin. When he was situated, Mariette took the black velvet sack that had been tucked off to the side, lifted it to her mouth, and whispered into the soft material words in a language I couldn't understand. She clasped the bag between both hands, shook it, and chanted something low and guttural. I found my eyes unable to look away from her tattoo. All the shaking made the snake appear to be slithering up her tight, firm arm. The serpent was black with a blood-red forked tongue. Her bracelets jangled, until all at once, she stopped. She kissed the bag, loosened its braided tie, and let the contents spill out onto the silky table covering.

Littered before us now was an array of bones: a few hearty ones, like long fat fingers; others wispy like twigs; and a broken one, but not completely in two pieces. Also among them were two stones, one brown and one smooth and red. Dante began sketching, his pencil quickly scraping against the paper. Mariette held her palms in the air above this collection, as though the pieces might levitate into her hands, and closed her eyes for a moment. When she opened them, she leaned down to study the formation they had made. A few bones had landed overlapping one another, while two others were by themselves. The red stone touched the broken bone and the brown stone sat away from the rest of the group. She looked at me.

"You are destined to fly," she said. "But you already know this."

I said nothing, not wanting to out myself in case she was speaking purely metaphorically.

"There are certain curses that must first be broken before this can be achieved. Your lifeline is interrupted." She pointed to the broken bone. "You yourself are not cursed, but you must save those who have had curses placed upon them. Or you must defeat them. This is how you grow to your full potential."

I didn't say a word.

"You are right to be afraid." She pointed to the red stone now. "You have to be careful, Haven." She looked deep into my eyes. "You are going to be taken. It is inevitable. But if you keep your spirit strong, you will defeat the forces working against you. This strength is part of the natural order of what you are."

I hardly knew where to begin, so I started with the most basic question: "What do you mean, what I am?" My head whipped to Dante beside me and he looked away.

"Don't blame him. I knew the very moment he set foot in here, just as I know it's true of you. You're both special, and here we protect angels. I am grateful to be working with Dante. And he will be vital to your survival and your success, as I'm sure you already know. I will guide him on his journey and he will supply you with the materials you need as you face your challenges."

All of a sudden, everyone seemed to know everything there was to know about me.

"And, wait, who is going to take me? I don't understand what you mean."

"Those who oppose you."

"What am I supposed to do, though?" I asked, the hopelessness setting in, releasing itself into my system and making me instantly lethargic.

Mariette didn't respond. She simply turned to Dante: "Please bring me the three ingredients you put away on the second shelf this morning and the oil there, along with one of the bags." He nodded and scurried away.

She motioned for my hand. I reached out, and she took it in hers and spoke with the urgency of someone who desperately wants for you to do as you're told. "Promise me you'll come back for another reading soon. Promise me you will. I'm worried and I need you to stay close so I can help you guard against them."

I just nodded.

Dante returned with three Mason jars and a tiny eyedropper bottle lined up like soldiers on a small silver tray beside three teaspoons, a thick plastic bag, and a ribbon. He presented the tray to Mariette and she placed it on the floor.

"You've finished?" she asked him, gesturing to the bones.

"Yes, Priestess."

"Very well." She delicately gathered the items on the table and placed them back in the velvet sack, then lifted the tray onto the table. The jars were half-filled with what looked to be sand, each jar containing a different color: green, red, and blue. She put two scoops of each into the bag, shook it up, and then added three drops of the amber oil.

"This gris-gris bag," pronouncing it *gree-gree,* which I had never heard before, "won't protect you from *them,*" she explained, tying the ribbon tightly around the bag. "But it will guard you against general, everyday wickedness and malevolence." She handed it to me. "It will have to do for now," she said, apologetic. "Dante has shared with me your message from one of the demons. May I see the missing piece?"

I was puzzled for a moment and then it occurred to me. I dug into my bag and pulled out my wallet, finding that crinkled scrap of paper, and holding it out. "Oh, you mean this." She made no move for it. Instead, she pulled from beneath one of the candles the rest of the note, which Dante had been keeping.

"It may be too much to ask, but may I retain this portion?" she asked respectfully, unfolding it on the table. "I will do my best to make something to help ward them off. It's exceedingly difficult to deter them. But if I have an object one of them has touched then I could possibly hit upon something."

"Of course," I said, trying not to show my disappointment at letting it go for good. I set the scrap on the table, knowing it was for the best. "It's yours, if it can help."

"Thank you. I hope you know that this should always be a safe place for you. You are always welcome here."

"Thank you," I said, anxious to go. I rose to my feet.

"If that's all today, I'll see you tomorrow," Dante said to Mariette. I had already fled, winding my way back to the front of the store. He caught up with me just as I had made it to the street.

"Hey! Hav!" he called, when I didn't stop. I turned around. "Are you okay?"

"Define 'okay,'" I said, not bothering to mask my huffiness.

"I'm really sorry," he pleaded. "I didn't know she was going to do all that. I had no idea."

"I don't really need another source telling me I'm in trouble." This weekend had been enough. I felt I was losing my grip.

"I know, I know." He tried to calm me. "Maybe Mariette really will be able to help. Maybe she'll be able to make something, you know?" We walked on and boarded the streetcar to the library for tutoring.

12

A Zydeco Birthday

I was glad to spend the rest of the afternoon lost in algebra problems. Lance and the Habitat for Humanity group had been relieved of their tutoring duties for the rest of the week, so I was juggling a trio of math-challenged girls, who seemed a little disappointed to be stuck with me instead of Lance.

When we arrived home, the house-building crew had beat us there. The TV was on in the living room, though no one was watching, and there was all sorts of rattling going on in the kitchen. Dante peeled off, looking for Max, and I went to my room. I turned down the hallway just as Jimmy stormed past, looking angry. Ramming into my shoulder, he almost knocked me over. "Geez, Jimbo!" Tom laughed, passing us both. But Jimmy stalked off without apologizing. Seconds later, Emma appeared, tears in her eyes. She seemed to be hurrying after him.

"Are you okay?" I asked as she hustled by. But she just wiped her wet face and kept going.

I reached Lance's door and knocked. He called out in his deep voice, "C'mon in." I opened up and found him perched on his bed, his back against the wall and a book face-down beside him. On the other side of the bed was Sabine, playing one of his handheld video games.

"Hey, you," Lance said, smiling.

"Hey, Haven!" Sabine perked right up.

The game made one of those electronic descending-scale *beep-beep-beep*s like someone had just died.

"Hey." I tried not to sound shocked to find her there. An orange glow of late-day sunlight pouring in through the window framed them perfectly. I felt like a guest here.

"So, what's up?" Lance asked.

"Oh, me, nothing, or, I mean . . ." I struggled to find anything, anything at all, that might make me sound like everything was fine and I was unbothered by this scene. "So, I just saw Emma, like, crying."

"Yeah. She and Jimmy broke up," Sabine said matter-of-factly, like I was clearly the last to know. "They're so hot and cold . . . crazy." She shook her head. "Come hang out. Lance is telling me all about life at Evanston High."

"Yeah, it's a pretty exciting place," I said, no life in my voice. "I'm just gonna toss my bag, be right back." But I knew I didn't mean it. For some reason, my instinct was to retreat.

"Yay!" she said, perfectly friendly. She started the game up again.

Lance glanced at the screen and said, "Whoa! You're about to die." I let the door close behind me.

What was she doing in there? Why did I feel this way? *Remember what Dante said,* I told myself. *You're just blowing things out of proportion. You're not thinking clearly. You've had an intense few days.* I cut myself some slack, but it all chipped away at me.

Back in my room, I grabbed my camera and its peripheral cords. I scowled as I passed Lance's room again, and continued on to the study room with the computers. I had it all to myself. I didn't need to be wasting time playing video games or whatever Lance and Sabine were doing. I pulled up my e-mail first; among the highlights were three messages from Joan (she had written daily). Then I set to work printing those pictures from the other night and the one today of Mariette.

I had to inventory the souls around me and then start monitoring them. This was the only way I knew how to chart who might pose a threat to us. Slowly, I would learn who I could trust, who I should fear, and who would eventually need to be banished to the underworld.

I opened the few shots of the volunteer group as a whole and isolated in new files each tiny face seated around that dinner table from Friday night so I could print each on its own. If there was anyone here to worry about, I would need to know most urgently.

By the time I finished, amassing a thick stack of images, the outdoor sky had gone dark. Sabine still wasn't back in our room. I tucked the photos into the bottom of the drawer in my nightstand and vowed to check them daily for any mutations or disfigurements, the telltale signs that indicated those in the pictures were losing their souls. Being an angel with no wings didn't get you very far, but being a soul illuminator, as I had been dubbed, seemed to bring with it at least a tiny bit of power. I wondered if anyone else here shared that skill. I hoped not. I had only just gotten accustomed to the idea of being different and special, and now to suddenly find out that there was a whole houseful of *mes* here, well, it would be an adjustment.

I t was nearly midnight when Lance came knocking on my door. I had left it unlocked and he let himself in and climbed up the ladder.

"Hey, what happened to you tonight?" he asked, lounging at the foot of my bed.

"Oh! I know, I totally got carried away printing." I tried my best to sound normal, breezy, but it came out too excited. I opened the drawer and pulled out the stack, fanning the sheets.

He took them and flipped through the photos. "Anything yet?"

I shook my head. "Who knows, it could take a little while."

He lay on his back, looking up at the ceiling. "Have you noticed people are kind of weird about how the three of us came into this together?"

I thought about River in the cabin and replied, "Now that you mention it, yeah, actually."

"Sabine said it's because everyone else lost someone in their battle." He looked at me, those deep eyes spearing mine, that scar peeking out from behind his heavy frames.

"Wow." I thought about how that would have felt. I couldn't imagine life without either Lance or Dante. Even considering it increased my heart rate and made it more difficult to breathe. Then something occurred to me. "What about Jimmy and Emma? They came here together too."

Lance nodded. "That's true. But they started their first challenge with two other friends. Remember the song they sang up at the cabin? It was about them."

"Oh, wow." I sighed. "Did Sabine . . . lose someone?"

"She didn't talk about it, but I can tell that she did."

Now I felt even worse for having been so petty. It was so

typically, disappointingly girlish for me to be the least bit upset that she was spending time with Lance.

"Anyway, she seems pretty cool."

"Good thing you saved her from a pack of hungry gators then." I smiled.

"You're the one who got her off the boat. It was a team effort."

I desperately wanted to stop talking about Sabine and yet I found myself asking, "Where is she now?"

"Watching some TV show." He shrugged, as if the topic bored him. "Oh, wait." He lit up. "I'm supposed to ask you a question. There's some concert coming up she wants us all to go to. Zydeco or something." He gave me a look that told me he *had* been paying attention to my trivia question the other night.

"Oh really?" I smiled back. "And what do you know about zydeco?"

"I know plenty: Creole origins, Clifton Chenier was the granddaddy of it." He turned over and crept toward me.

"I'm impressed. What else ya got?" I said, just coquettish enough.

"He designed that crazy washboard sorta thing we saw the other night—"

"Is that right?"

"I can keep going. But I'd really rather listen to some." He pulled out his phone and it was cued to a clip of a zydeco band playing "Happy Birthday," washboards and all. He had me from the first few notes. "Happy birthday, Haven"—he looked at the time—"in two minutes and twenty-five seconds. I have something for you." He lunged for me, giving me the kind of kiss—slow, sweet, nearly endless—that would have been enough. Then he pulled a small, red-ribboned box from the pocket of his hooded sweatshirt.

"Really?" I wasn't so accustomed to getting gifts from guys. I wanted to savor this.

"It's your birthday. What kind of boyfriend would I be to show up without a present?"

I slipped off the bow and lifted the lid to find a golden fleur-de-lis pendant nestled inside. "I love it, thank you." I beamed at him, petting it delicately.

Lance adjusted his glasses, shy for a moment. "I'm glad you like it."

"I mean, if it's good enough for French royalty—" I twinkled.

"Right. And Charlemagne and that crowd—" he finished my thought and helped me free the pendant from its box.

"Then it's definitely good enough for me." I smiled.

"Here." He gestured for me to turn around. I held my hair up above my neck as he unclasped my necklace, sliding the pendant on the chain and fastening it again. "I actually got it back home, which I think makes it even cooler, since these aren't as easy to find there, you know?"

It secretly thrilled me to think of Lance spending time looking for something for me. I pulled it in front of the angel wing charm and looked at the two together.

"It's so perfect."

"Like you," he said with a kiss.

When I had seen *Tour of Superdome* on the schedule for my birthday, I thought that sounded like a fine way to spend the day, even if I wasn't the biggest sports fan. Who wouldn't want to see that place? We would be hosting a huge group of area school kids to meet some of the Saints players and get a tour of the stadium, from locker rooms to skyboxes. I hadn't expected that our visit, at least for the dozen of us, would begin at four in the morning. A uniformed security guard, cap pulled over his dark hair, had let us in, making no eye contact. He hadn't said a word as he led us to the floor of the arena, depositing us there and giving Connor a nod.

And I certainly hadn't expected this view.

"Two hundred fifty-three feet," Lance informed me, grunting. His muscular arms were about to surrender at any moment.

"Well, at least we're not at the very top." I struggled to speak while still maintaining my slowly slipping grip. "We're probably, what, two-thirds of the way?"

Beside me, on this long metal track below the central scoreboard, the rest of the group dangled.

"What's two-thirds of 253?" Dante asked.

"That would be 168.67, rounded up," Lance answered, instantly.

Every tendon and bone in my hands gripped with a ferocity I didn't know they were capable of, but still I felt my sweaty palms sliding from the metal. I tried not to look down.

The official tour, the wrangling of children, the good times, all of that would come later this morning, Connor had informed us. First, we had some fears to conquer.

"C'mon! Y'all look so scared. The only way down is to jump," his voice boomed in the loudspeakers, his commands richocheting around the empty stadium. "So you might as well jump. That's the point of this, you know."

It was a hard thing to get used to, this idea that we really couldn't be hurt.

Brody went first, howling the whole way down. The *BOOM* of his body hitting the ground echoed in a way that wasn't particularly encouraging.

"I'm goin'. Who's with me? Birthday girl?" Dante asked in a cracking voice, his strength draining.

"Uh, strongly considering it," I offered, sweat dripping down my face.

"Me too," said Lance.

"I'm in," Max said.

Sabine yelled and let go, with no warning. I found it shocking that she could be so helpless on the swamp boat and yet so gutsy here. So, I went for it too, gasping as I fell. For a moment, I enjoyed the speed and the wind and the rush of it. The air whipped at me, my nerves and skin tingling.

I had planned to land on my feet, but I hit the ground so hard, the impact knocked me over with enough force to make me roll several feet. I finally turned onto my back, panting and proud. I ached, but I was alive when I otherwise shouldn't have been. A good lesson, to be sure.

13

I Couldn't Stay Away

Dante and I had spent much of the next day elbow-deep in soil at the community garden in the Mid-City neighborhood. It was a relief to have a less strenuous day for a change. Half the kids who came over from the nearby elementary school had seen their homes flooded by Hurricane Katrina, though we never would have guessed that from their smiles and the joy they brought to digging in the dirt. I couldn't help but think that if I had lived through that disaster, I would have had trouble pushing its memories out of my mind. I had experienced my share of trauma and I felt like I thought about it in some way every day. My horrors lurked at the back of my mind, hovering, always prepared to spring out. But they also, I supposed, pushed me forward.

With their small, curious hands, the kids built cylindrical tomato cages. We staked the structures into the soil, training the plants to grow up through the wires and out. On another strip of land, we planted basil, thyme, sage, rosemary, and a host of other herbs, and at the day's end, we sent the kids home with packets of seeds, all donated by the New Orleans Botanical Garden. When the last of the students had left and we had cleaned up after hours of digging and watering, soil matted under our fingernails, Dante pulled from his pocket a few star-shaped, quarter-size, deep red seeds, a handful of turquoise pinwheels, and a trio of violet reeds the size of cigarettes. He nestled them all in a section of the garden camouflaged by a protective wall of begonias.

"Are those from where I think they're from?" I asked.

He nodded, pushing each specimen into the soil and covering it up. "They're the last of their kind—or at least, I'm not planning to go harvesting in the underworld to try to get more."

"Will they grow here?"

"They'd better, because every *recipe,* every spell I know, requires some combination of these things."

"Well then, abracadabra." I waved my fingers over the soil. "Poof."

"Thanks, yeah, I'm sure that did the trick." He laughed.

Since Dante and I were on night watch later, we got to opt out of tutoring for the day. Connor picked us up and took us home. We showered and I walked Dante to Mariette's, where he had promised to put in an hour or two in the evening, and then wandered back to the house on my own. I had had so little time to myself since arriving here, I felt like I saw the city differently when it was just me walking through it and I could breathe.

As I passed the LaLaurie mansion, the muted glow in the front window ensnared me: that candle. If I hadn't been alone, would I even have seen it? Could I just ignore it? Would I dare try to go in? I stood out on the sidewalk staring at it for so long, I thought my gaze alone might extinguish it. But finally, since I knew I wouldn't be able to stop thinking about it, I made my way up to the door. I placed my fingers on the handle and with only the slightest push it creaked open. I took a deep breath and stepped slowly inside.

It was perfectly silent, nothing like it had been that other day with so many machines rattling and roaring. The foyer grew dimmer by the minute as the sun set. The flickering votive beckoned me. And once again, I spied a corner of alabaster paper poking out beneath the holder. I pulled it out, unfolding it. Inside it read, simply: *Hi, Haven.*

It was his handwriting again, I was sure of it. The blood rushed to my head and my heart.

I then felt the lightest tap at my back, like a leaf falling from a tree. Shivering, I touched my shoulder.

And found a hand there. Strong fingers perched gingerly.

I spun around and gasped.

Lucian.

He squeezed my shoulder. I could feel my eyes flashing supreme fear at him. Was it even him? Or was it the Prince? "Please don't scream, Haven. Please," he said with troubled eyes. But it didn't matter. I couldn't find my voice; the shock paralyzed everything. With one hand on my shoulder and the other on my arm he pushed me back, away from the window. Was I hallucinating? Dreaming? I had the feeling I had floated up and was watching myself but not actively participating in this scene. If I'd had full control, wouldn't I have run, or fought him, or even yelled? *Wake up, Haven.* I found enough strength to struggle against him, wiggling my arms, kicking my legs, as he backed me to the wall. "Please. I promise I won't hurt you." This wasn't the first time he had said this to me. He had to know I was terrified. He had to feel me shaking.

He was so close to me, whispering, but he looked nothing like he had the night I'd thought I'd seen him at that party, when it had really been the Prince. He didn't have that polish and sheen. Now he looked worn, weathered, beaten down. His dull gray eyes had lost that mysterious sparkle that used to be potent enough to be seen even in this kind of darkness. Those eyes that had always known how to lock on mine and reel me in now looked pained. He wore that same tuxedo he'd had on when I saw him last, on that dreaded night back in the spring when he had forced me to send him to the underworld, to push him through that door where he would face his penance for not having killed me. He had been too humane then to carry out his assignment and he had surely been suffering for it since then.

I couldn't control my breathing; it heaved and echoed in my head so that I could barely hear his soft whisper. "Please listen, Haven. Be careful. Be on guard. They have you in their sights. And beware who you tell about me." He looked away for a moment. I closed my eyes, trying to focus on my scars, which I had ignored that night in the garden. I didn't think I could feel them stinging. "I shouldn't be here now," he went on. "But it's the only place I can see you and I . . . I couldn't stay away. I'm going to help you, but I need your help too. Please. Soon." He let go of me and backed up, his footsteps making no sound, not even the slightest tap on the wood floor. He placed his finger to his lips, telling me to be quiet, then turned and stalked off. I watched, rooted in my spot. At one point he looked back over his shoulder toward me again and then I felt heat rise to my skin, like it used to back when I had just met him and knew nothing about who or what he was.

I heard a voice in the distance, in that murky way everything sounds from the bottom of a swimming pool. I forced myself back into the present.

"Hey there. Thought I heard someone. You're lucky—almost locked ya in." It was Lance's boss. "They're not here today, your friends. We should have 'em back next week. I was just closin' up."

I was almost too shaken to speak. "Oh, of course, I . . . I forgot. Thank you," I stammered, and slipped out the door as fast as I could.

Outside, it was all I could do to keep from running. When I reached the gates to our house, I let myself clumsily drop to the ground, no strength left to stand. I had broken out in a sweat. I slicked back my wet hair and put my hands around my head, closing my eyes for a moment to keep the world from spinning.

Eventually, I gathered the strength necessary to return inside on unsteady legs. Connor intercepted me as soon as I came in.

"Haven! Come take a look at this," he said spiritedly, gesturing for me to follow him down the hall. I hoped I didn't look as shaken as I felt. Part of me wondered if I should tell him what had just happened, if perhaps I was actually endangering the whole group by keeping quiet. But it was just too soon; I wasn't ready. I needed to hold it in, keep it close to me just a little longer until I could make sense of it. I wanted to believe that Lucian wasn't a danger and I didn't want anyone to convince me otherwise yet. *Lucian.* To see him again, the real him, confused my heart. It opened up that old wound, my old feelings for him stinging like salt.

" . . . don't you think it's a great idea?" Connor was saying. I hadn't been paying attention, so I simply nodded in agreement. He stopped before a room I had never been inside. "So I just finished and I think it'll be a great place to practice," he said, opening the door and flipping on the lights to a windowless room, every wall, floor to ceiling—floor *and* ceiling—padded in a layer of white cushion.

"Uhhh, how crazy do you think we are?" I asked, my fingers grazing the soft wall beside me. Opposite the door sat a basketball, dumbbell, boxing glove, and a couple books.

"Very funny." He rolled his eyes. "C'mon now, this took a while. What do you think? Y'all needed a place to practice your levitation."

"Ohhhh," I said. "It's . . . nice. But I don't get it. Why the padding?"

"Trust me, when you're learning, all sorts of crazy stuff can happen. I like to be prepared. Wanna test it out?"

"Well . . ." I scanned the few objects piled in the corner. No, I didn't really want to. I wasn't feeling particularly powerful at the moment.

Connor seemed to sense this from my slow response. "No sweat. Didn't mean to put ya on the spot," he said easily. "But it's here, so use this room anytime you like."

"Thanks," I said, following him out.

"And Haven . . ." He paused, as if debating whether to continue with his thought. "I hope you keep at it, okay? You'll get it." He smacked my shoulder in a brotherly way. "And when you do, they'd better watch out. Trust me."

"Oh, yeah, right, thanks." I tried to appear nonchalant. I knew Connor intended to sound comforting but for some reason I felt worse. I didn't like being the one who couldn't keep up with the group, someone in need of extra attention. I watched him wander the hall toward his room and, thinking for a moment, I turned back around, slipping into that odd padded room alone.

I hopped on the cushioned floor. It felt like jumping on a firm mattress. Then I stood in place, my stance strong, and I focused a laser-like gaze on the boxing glove, hopeful. It shook for a second or two as though it might launch, but then it stilled just as quickly. My heart fell. I tried a few more times with no luck, then returned to my room.

I must have watched that house next door for a good hour until Dante returned home, breaking only once to glance at that stash of printed photos (finding nothing new) and to discover a new text message on my phone:

> You no doubt have many questions in light of recent events. You have done well on many fronts, even if you don't feel it. Be patient with yourself and your progress while still pushing forward with all of your strength. You will see that, physically, the results will come fast. Throw yourself fearlessly into your training and you will reap swift rewards. The power you seek will manifest in no time, and when it does, it will be almost overwhelming.

I had to pause at that. Overwhelming? I couldn't quite imagine that. But there was more. I scrolled down.

> A note on the matter of trust. You are, no doubt, having difficulty knowing who is worthy of yours these days. You are right to wonder and to worry. As always you will need to find answers for yourself, but I will offer you this much to start, out of necessity: You can trust Connor, despite his methods. And Mariette. She is on your side. You may not like what she has to say, but she has your best interests at heart. Let her in.

That was all. I wanted more, though. Connor and Mariette weren't the ones I was most concerned about right now. Why couldn't I get answers on the one I really wanted to know about? But there was never any use in getting upset at these messages. It seemed they would always be riddles, prompting so many more questions for every answer they gave.

Before long, the group had returned. Lance gave me a kiss on the cheek and offered to take Dante's place on night watch, but Dante, perhaps sensing my need to talk, refused him. I considered for the briefest of moments whether to tell Lance about Lucian. Each minute that I didn't tell him felt more and more like this was a weighty, poisonous secret. The longer I waited, the harder it got to mention it. We reached his door and I decided I would let it be just mine for now. I wondered if he could tell how distracted I was as we said good night.

And so, with all that batting around in my mind, Dante and I had begun our rounds, walking the hallways together, upstairs, downstairs, and then ducking out onto the balcony to monitor the courtyard. Once or twice, to test ourselves, we steadied our jittery feet upon the wooden railing of the balcony and leapt down to the ground as Connor had instructed us to do as often as possible. Cool air whipped through my hair, giving me the illusion of flying, but I landed every time with an ungraceful, ankle-crunching thud, falling forward and scratching my palms. Dante had no better luck, but he didn't seem to mind—he was too engrossed in stories of Mariette.

"So she's starting me on the easiest ones: love spells," he said after we'd climbed the stairs back inside.

"Those are easy? Really?" I had to ask.

"I know. Who woulda guessed, right?"

"It could have drastically changed our entire high school experience."

"You're telling me," he said. "So I'm working on this one. It's basically a mixture of these wild ingredients—you saw that pantry! —to make another one of those little bags, you know, a gris-gris bag? And apparently I have the power to transform that stuff into something that can actually rock someone's world."

"Well, I mean, you do that anyway."

"What can I say." He laughed. He thought for a moment. "It's sort of like the flip side of what I was learning from, you know, Etan . . ." He said the name with a heaviness and was quiet for several long seconds, his eyes fixed somewhere far away. I could only imagine he was thinking about the devil at the Lexington who had wooed him, almost stolen his soul, and nearly killed him. In some ways, Dante had endured even more than Lance and me. We had had to survive a battle against them all, but Dante had really been submerged in their world, fighting it from the inside out.

He piped up, upbeat once more, "Anyway, all I have to do is stash this thing in the intended's room, hidden somewhere in his stuff, and it should do the trick."

I smirked. "I take it you have your target picked out."

"Well . . ." He hesitated. "I suppose . . . I was thinking maybe . . . Max," he said, like it was no big deal.

"Personally, I don't think you and Max need it. I think you guys look like you're on your way already."

"Really?!" He perked up at this, looking at me with wild eyes. "You're not just saying that?" I shook my head.

"Mariette said she sees good things for us, Max and me. She was saying . . ." He went on as we patrolled the property, but again my mind wandered.

" . . . and then she's working on this thing that'll basically let a person disappear and . . . *Hav!*" he shouted at me, so loud in the still hallway as we passed Connor's room that I worried he might wake up, thinking we were in some kind of trouble.

"What?!" I jumped. "What, Dan? Sorry." I shook my head. "You were saying?"

"Please, you haven't heard a thing I've been saying. What aren't you telling me?"

Dante always knew when I was holding back—that was the danger of being around a true best friend—and I felt him glaring at me for answers. I turned slowly to face him, staring into his eyes, and took a deep breath.

"I saw Lucian today," I said with the weight it deserved.

His jaw dropped.

By the time I finished telling him the story, we were outside again, on the balcony, leaning over the railing and surveying the grounds below.

"I don't like this at all, Hav," Dante said, shaking his head. "He wants your help? I just don't like it at all."

I breathed in the cool night air. I didn't know what to say. I felt like I needed to defend myself. Before I could, the murmur of other voices floated up from below, quieting us for a moment—it sounded like Tom and, could it be, River? They appeared to be curled up on the chaise below. It never ceased to amaze me how people paired off—there was just no guessing sometimes. I gazed up at that corner window of the house next door. Pitch-black right now.

My mind replayed each moment of my encounter with Lucian. It came in flashes accompanied by feelings, impulses, all spinning out of sequence: his whispered words in my ear; that parting glance as he walked away; the pain in his eyes; that firm hand gripping my shoulder; having him so close to me again. That feeling was what I most wanted to relive over and over again, and what I still had trouble believing. This figure that had been living only in my mind for months had now appeared before me again, in the flesh. Even in that poor lighting, I could sense a newly withered quality about his presence, a frayed spirit. I figured it was probably akin to what you might find in a soldier returning from a war zone. I couldn't begin to imagine what he had been enduring in his time below, and it killed me to know that he was there because of me; I had had to send him there to save myself. So now the light that had once radiated from his eyes —so powerful that it would just seize you and not let you go—had dimmed. I tried to search for it in his gaze in those fleeting minutes we were together, and thought I found it, or the memory of it—just enough for my pulse to race and my stomach to flutter once again.

But now I forced myself to cut through all of that and focus instead on what he had actually *said.* And when I dissected those few words, it seemed that he was on my side. Didn't it? Didn't it seem that, despite whatever he might have had to brave below, he hadn't entirely let himself be brought back into that fold? He had been trying to warn me about something. Why bother otherwise? If he had wanted to hurt or kill me tonight, he could have. His powers were so far beyond mine. But still, I had to watch myself. Much as I wanted to believe the best about him, I had to keep an arm's length away until I knew for sure, just to be safe.

A cackle below broke me out of my introspection. I leaned over, squinting, and caught sight of two figures emerging from the darkness of the carriageway into the twinkling courtyard, laughing and giggling so loudly that I probably would've heard them even if I'd been inside my room. Dante smacked my arm, gesturing toward the duo, home hours after curfew. They clung to each other, arms entwined, heads thrown back in hysterics, and they stumbled, their heels clicking against the cement patio. It was Sabine and Emma.

Dante and I continued our rounds until nearly five a.m., when Connor would be taking over, as he did each day. When we finally said good night, Dante had opened up the door to his room, ready to get a few hours' sleep before reporting for duty at the food bank, and there was Sabine. Sprawled on the floor, my roommate was fast asleep in their room, still wearing her dress from last evening. My heart blackened; I felt instantly ill. That Lance was tucked into bed, dozing peacefully, did little to settle me. A look of concern, frustration even, flashed in Dante's eyes when they caught mine.

"Hey, Sabine, you've got a great room down the hall. Let's go, lady," he said flatly, tapping his shoe against her bare foot. Her eyes fluttered open and set on me. She smiled as if there was nothing wrong.

"Hey, roomie." Woozy, she yawned, struggling to get up. She grabbed her heels off the floor and stumbled out the door, taking my hand in hers. "So sleepy," she said, her voice slurred.

"Night, Hav," Dante said, in a troubled tone I seldom heard, as I got pulled away. I could feel my mouth setting into a frown, my brow furrowing, and my patience dwindling, though Sabine didn't seem to notice.

"Fabulous night!" she said, bumbling toward our door. "How 'bout you?"

I didn't answer. My mind raced in too many directions. She simply continued talking as we stepped inside and I flipped off the light. "Omigod, so much to tell you! Jimmy is a total dog. But gotta sleep now." She pitched forward into her bed, still in her dress.

As I settled under the covers, I could feel my blood boiling. I wished to climb back down, creep into Lance's room, and curl up beside him, make him tell me that nothing had happened, that everything was fine. He was mine, wasn't he? And didn't that entitle me—us—to move at whatever pace we chose without the threat of some sort of outside force wedging itself between us? In my heart, though, I knew that something hadn't felt right since we arrived here. We were just a shade . . . *off*.

I thought of that text message on my phone again. Yes, it was true. My trust was in short supply.

I rolled over onto my side, trying to push these thoughts away, hoping they might be colored by fatigue and anxious to correct that. I let my eyelids shut. But as I drifted off, I felt a strobe effect coming from the distance, a few flashes registering even behind my closed eyes, reaching out for me. I knew it was that light across the way, and I knew who was behind it. And for the first time since it had begun signaling to me, I was grateful for it, comforted by it. That was the last thing I remembered before falling into a deep, dreamless sleep.

14

Her Name Is Clio

It probably wasn't the most mature thing, but I didn't really feel like looking at or talking to Sabine the next day. So I pulled myself out of bed much earlier than usual, dressed, and made my way to the levitation room. I would simply lose myself in activity. This brand of productive avoidance was how I operated, and it had always done the trick. The house slept as I let myself into that cold, wholly intimidating white room with the padded walls.

I stared down at the boxing gloves first, then the basketball, then, just to feel entirely hopeless, the dumbbells. I shook my head, jumped up and down, shimmying my limbs. Starting small, I tossed my keys on the floor and watched them, dreaming of them soaring through the air. They began to jangle, then stopped. I tried again, focusing with all the concentration I had. Again, they clinked but this time they floated up, slowly, slowly. I watched them, so steady and strong, until they reached a good foot above my head before dropping. A rush washed over me, followed by a wave of peace from the exhaustion. I allowed myself a minute's rest, then I tried again. I set my gaze and all my strength on those keys, once more tuning out all other thoughts until I heard the click of the door. Startled, I gasped. As I whipped my head around, the keys, gloves, ball, and dumbbell all went flying, knocking with force against the padded walls.

"Whoa!" Connor called out, arms shielding his face. "And that's why this room is padded." He shook his head, smiling.

I was still catching my breath, panting. "Sorry," I said, shy. "Or, I mean, did I do that?"

"You sure did, and apology accepted. Keep it up," he offered. "Your roommate and Lance were worried, didn't know where you were. I'll let 'em know we can call off the search."

"Thanks," I said, my voice drained of all life.

"Or, you know, I'll let 'em wonder a little longer," he said, and winked as he let himself out. I stayed there until it was time to leave for the food bank with Dante. On my way to his room, I ran into Sabine in her pink bathrobe, heading for the shower.

"Haven!" she called, sunny as can be, sashaying to catch up with me. She grabbed my sleeve and said, "I feel like you're mad at me." Her exaggerated pout made me feel bad.

"No, what do you mean?" I asked, barely believable, even to my ears.

"We need girl time. Can we go out tonight? Pretty please?"

I sighed internally. "I've got the hotline."

"Tomorrow then," she insisted. "It's a date, okay?"

"Sure," I said, not masking my lack of interest in the plans.

"Perfect. We'll have fun," she promised as she floated away back down the hall. I waited until she was tucked away in the bathroom before knocking to collect Dante.

"Ready to go?" Dante opened up. In the space behind him, Lance pulled on his favorite Cubs T-shirt, getting ready for another day of building homes.

"Morning!" he said, twisting the sleeves in place over his

biceps. He felt far away from me somehow. I just kept thinking of him there last night, Sabine on the floor. "You heading out already?"

I nodded, trying to smile like all was fine.

"I'll see you tonight for counseling though, right?" he asked. We would be manning the phone lines back at the library. Though I felt a bit like I was the one who needed counseling. I nodded again. His eyes darkened. Dante watched this exchange silently.

"Totally." I struggled to sound upbeat. "See you later."

"Well, those meals ain't gonna wheel themselves," Dante said, ushering us out and swinging the door shut. As soon as we had walked a few paces away, he turned to look at me. "I hate when Mom and Dad fight."

I just rolled my eyes. "I'm allowed to be, I don't know, confused, right?"

"You are, seriously. But I still think you have nothing to worry about," he said as he linked his arm in mine and led me out into the cool morning air.

I had been dreading our peer counseling session all day, which I knew wasn't a good sign. Lance breezed in just after five, kissing the top of my head as he took the seat beside me.

"We've built five houses in the past week. It's insane and amazing," he said, excited.

The phones were almost completely quiet, save for a nameless female caller in search of confirmation. "Is middle school supposed to be hell on earth?" she asked, just enough edge to her voice to not sound too desperate.

I sighed. "Yes, I'm afraid it is."

"So it's not just me?" She sounded comforted.

"Definitely not."

"Is high school better?"

"Um . . . it depends, but again, no one is alone in having lousy days. Take it from me."

Lance waited until Drew, who was stationed at the phone on the other side of me, excused herself on a vending machine raid downstairs, before giving me the look I'd been waiting for since the morning.

"What?" I asked.

He shook his head, looking like he wanted to say something. "Okay, are we . . . good?"

"Yeah, of course." I drummed my pen against my pad of paper, thinking, thinking, fighting it and then crumbling. I just didn't appreciate being put in a position like this—one in which I was possibly being made to look foolish so I had to ask these awful questions and look like some sort of jealous stereotype instead. "Well, I mean, it was just kind of, you know, *weird* to see Sabine in your room last night."

He slouched in his chair and looked at me. "That? I was asleep, I heard a knock—I thought it was you, if you really want to know."

"Oh."

"Yeah. 'Oh.' She passed out on the floor, end of story. I don't know why she came by." He paused a moment, as though deciding what path to continue down, but then Drew returned, snacks in hand, and we both seemed to resolve to forget it, at least for now.

We made no reference to it until we said good night at my door that evening. In the empty hallway, the two of us completely alone—a rarity these days, it seemed—Lance wrapped his arms around me, so tight, and spoke softly into my hair.

"I hope you're not *really* upset," he said. "You know me better than anyone and you know that you're what matters to me, don't you?"

"I'm just . . ." I started. Not sure how to go on, I decided to be honest: "I think being here, with everyone like us, all of this, it's making me, I don't know—"

"Crazy?"

"Thanks, you flatter me."

"No, because it's making *me* a little crazy," he clarified.

"Really?" I asked, feeling better. He nodded and I did too. "Well, then, let's get uncrazy," I said, like it was decided that this was all we had to do. "That's the new battle cry."

"Not the most rousing call to action." He smiled with the slightest laugh, pushing up his glasses. "But it'll do."

Sabine had proposed we meet after work the next day outside a tattoo parlor just off Bourbon Street. I hoped it was simply a landmark and not actually part of our evening plans. "Hey, roomie!" she greeted me as she descended the steps from the sliver of a shop with grimy, barred windows.

"Oh, Sabine, what did you do?" I asked, with a laugh.

"Have you met Kip?" She gestured to the top of the steps, where a stocky, bearded man with chin-length dark hair leaned against the doorframe. His fingers brushed at his scruffy chin. I waved. "He's a true artist. Anyway, he did this . . ." She tugged at the sleeve of her top to expose a tiny pair of wings, no larger than a paper clip, on her left shoulder.

"Omigod!" I leaned in to check out the darkly sketched symbol. "Joan would kill me. But I gotta admit, it *is* really cute."

"Kip, I think we've got a live one," she said, nudging me up the stairs.

"No, no, no, maybe another time," I said, playfully pushing her away.

"You got it." He smiled and waved goodbye to us and we set off down the street.

Sabine informed me that we would be doing some shopping, and I could tell from her strong, quick stride, set to the jazz soundtrack of the street musicians, that she was on a mission. She cut a sharp path through Bourbon Street, as we dodged crowds of more sedate daytime patrons. Soon the raucous nighttime groups would move in, taking their place on barstools and dance floors along this strip. "So where are we going?"

"You're so going to thank me—I heard about this amazing place from Clio."

"Clio?"

"That blonde! You know the one from that bar the other night? The one dancing? Her name is Clio. Here, this way." We turned down a quieter, narrower street.

My skin chilled, but the dusk air wasn't entirely to blame. "What do you mean? You *talked* to her?"

"I did!" She lit up, so proud. "She's amazing. So, anyway, she told me where she goes. It's right down here. It's supposedly kind of out of the way, like at the back of some courtyard. Never would've found it on my own. Wait, what are we on?" She looked around for a street sign.

"Dauphine?"

"Yeah, one more. I think it's right there." She pointed to the end of the block.

"So, where did you—"

"It's this place that's part vintage and thrifty and part new stuff, but, like, not new that's everywhere, new *unique*. You're gonna love it."

"No, that's great, but where did you meet her? Clio?" I didn't like that she had a name. It brought her too close to us. I didn't trust her.

"With Emma," Sabine said. "The other night. We went back to that place."

"How'd you get in?"

"Trust me, it's not that hard."

"Good to know. So you just started talking to her?"

"Yeah, I guess." She shrugged. "Omigod, this is it!" We stopped before the narrowest of alleyways between two brick buildings. Both sides of the passage were lined with souvenirs for sale, all manner of T-shirts and magnets and shot glasses and framed photos and fleur-de-lis everything.

"Here?"

"C'mon!" She grabbed my hand and led me back through the long corridor. There was barely enough room for us to pass other shoppers without seriously violating their personal space. But eventually that claustrophobic strip opened out into a courtyard that forked into two tucked-away boutiques. Pausing for only a split second, Sabine yanked me in the direction of the one on the left. Outside its open doorway was a headless mannequin wearing a hot pink 1960s shift dress. "Love!" Sabine said to it as she entered.

Inside, there were many more racks of clothing than I would have guessed could've fit in the small space. Sabine let go of me and walked the aisles holding her hands out on either side of her to sweep the clothes as she passed. I followed close behind, slowing down from time to time to admire the many flouncy tops and skirts and perfectly tailored designer jeans. She worked her way to the back of the store and then halted before a rack of strapless dresses in an array of colors and patterns.

"Yes," she said to them. She whipped through the frocks, flicking at the hangers and pulling a few out. She handed three to me.

"Okay, thanks. Cute."

She took an armful herself and pointed to the far wall. "And we need those." She drifted, as though being pulled by an unknown force, to the shoe section and planted herself before a display of cowboy boots. "Here." She handed me a pair of buttery beige ones, then grabbed a black pair for herself. All of this was accomplished with absolutely no eye contact. I had to admit I was impressed with her focus. If I could zero in like that more often, I could probably conquer just about anything.

We retreated into adjacent fitting rooms and only then did I get to inspect what Sabine had selected for me: three strapless dresses, all hitting at the thigh, with a sort of cinched-in bustier-corset effect. There was a black dress, a blue one patterned with those paisleys you usually find on bandanas, and a red gingham that made me want to go on a picnic. "I want to see those!" Sabine's voice ordered through our shared wall, followed by a knock, like some sort of secret code.

"We'll see," I said, not masking my uncertainty.

"Yes, we *will* see!" she called back.

I took a deep breath. Strapless was never my favorite; I had learned to accept that scar of three slashes above my heart—as well as all the rest of my scars—but I still didn't especially like to draw attention to them. But what did it matter? I wouldn't actually be buying anything, I was just along for the ride. I tried on the black dress first. Even though the material seemed to be cotton—no sequins, shine, or bells and whistles—it just didn't look right. I looked like I was trying to be someone else. I shimmied out of it. The red felt too girly and delicate for me, so, with low expectations, I went for the blue. A knock shook the door this time.

"Let's see it, c'mon!" Sabine beckoned. I could see her boots under the door.

I pulled the dress on fast and slipped on the beige boots. Then gave myself a quick glance in the mirror: not the worst outfit, though I couldn't imagine an occasion when I would actually wear it. I opened the door. Sabine had her back to me, sizing herself up in the three-way mirror, twisting and turning to look at herself from every direction. Her hair was swung over one shoulder, those scars on her back, like mine, peeking out above the top of the dress.

"You look amazing," I said. Sabine wore the black one I had so quickly and surely rejected. But she looked completely comfortable in it. It hugged her like it had been painted on.

"You think? I'm still not sure."

"I don't know how much better that thing is supposed to look. I mean, it's kind of perfect."

She turned around to face me. "You're, like, the best shopping partner," she said, with true appreciation.

"Thanks."

"And I'm sorry, excuse me, but I think this is screaming for you to buy it," she ordered, pointing at me in the blue dress. "Do you love it?"

"I guess it's all okay."

"Okay? You're getting it. And you're getting this one, too." She tugged at the dress she had on.

"Well—"

"But do you really think this looks good on me?" She cut me off.

"Yeah, it—"

"Because I have a confession," she said, her eyes dancing. She stepped closer to me as though about to let me in on something big. "I have a date. Tonight!"

I felt a smile break out, encompassing my whole face. "Wow! Details please!" My voice could not have sounded more genuinely excited. As long as this date wasn't with Lance, we were about to begin a lovely new chapter in our friendship.

"With Wylie!"

"Wylie?" She had to have seen my complete shock.

"You know, the hot guy from the other night? The hurricanes?"

"Right, of course, the hurricanes. Hurricane Wylie."

"Hurricane Wylie! Love that! That's what I'm going to call him."

I wrestled with whether to say something, defeating the impulse only to have it rise back up again. If she had set her sights away from Lance, I hated the idea of discouraging her, but I couldn't shake the feeling I had about this guy. "He seems, I don't know, like he runs with a . . . *fast* crowd maybe." It sounded like a word Joan would use, but what I really wanted to say, something along the lines of "potentially devilish," just seemed too absurd and unfounded even to my ears. "And isn't he kind of . . . *older,* and . . ."

If I was supposed to be dissuading Sabine, I was going about it the wrong way. She just nodded, confirming it all, and grinning so widely I could tell she was proud of reeling this one in. "Totally, totally my type," she gushed.

"Oh, yeah, of course." I would obviously need to try a different approach. "But, you know, he may be just too"—I racked my brain and came up short—"fun."

She laughed. " 'Too fun.' Listen to you! Haven, you're hilarious." I pretended that that had been my intention. "Lance must love that about you. Guys love a sense of humor. Or at least some guys, from what I hear." This wasn't really sounding like a compliment, so I just ignored it. "We're probably different that way, you and me."

"I'm sorry?"

"For instance, I like hurricanes. Like you said, Wylie is a hurricane—I'm totally, totally into him and, like, powerless against that force. But I would bet that you and Lance"—I found it noteworthy that she was acknowledging that there *was* a me and Lance—"you probably prefer more of a slow-and-steady, wait-and-let-things-develop kind of guy. I don't know what that would be called . . ." She fixed her eyes upward, as though the answer were there in the ceiling.

"So Lance is like, maybe, a tropical depression? I think that's what they call things that may turn into hurricanes, meteorologically speaking."

"Wow, okay, yeah. Lance is a tropical depression," she said. She studied me, head cocked to one side. "You're looking at me funny."

"Who, me? No. What?" It must have been an involuntary sign of relief that she saw creeping into my expression.

"You think I'm being mean or something."

"No way. C'mon, let's try on some more clothes. So tell me more about hurricanes."

"I'm just having some fun. I mean, we're seventeen. I think you need to have a little more fun, Haven."

"Maybe you're right."

"We've got enough to be serious about." It was the first time

Sabine had really alluded to our shared status since that weekend at the swamp. I wanted to pounce on it but here in the middle of this store didn't seem the right time. And in a flash I lost my chance, anyway. "It's decided then. Let's get these and get outta here," she said. "I have an idea."

Get Off My Back

*T*his is where we should be working," Sabine said, gazing into the window. Behind the glass, men in matching hats and T-shirts tossed dough into a deep fryer, where it sizzled, then drenched each crispy piece in mounds of powdered sugar.

"No, this would be much too dangerous," I countered, equally mesmerized. "This is too much of a good thing."

"Is there really such a thing as too much of a good thing, though?"

"I think, in some cases, yes. And in matters of beignets, I think, definitely yes."

"Well, I need some right now. That's all there is to it." Sabine marched over to the cashier to place her order, her giant shopping bag swishing against her thighs.

"You convinced me," I said, joining her, my own shopping bag dangling from my arm.

She had been similarly persuasive at the store, somehow managing to coax me into buying not only the blue dress but the black one that matched hers, and the cowboy boots, too. "Don't you see how the beige is exactly your skin tone? Your legs look like stilts in those. Or taffy! Long, tan strips of taffy! They're endless," she had cooed at me. A bit of hyperbole, but it had worked. Sabine bought the black boots and three dresses: in black, fire-engine red, and a sparkly halter-top. New outfits, boots, beignets—this was turning into an unusually indulgent day for me. I felt an uptick in my mood, some of Sabine's high-spiritedness rubbing off on me perhaps.

We grabbed our paper bags full of beignets in heaps of sugar and our matching iced cafés au lait, then found a path stretching out along the riverfront. The bright sky was just beginning to dim, the sun still glowing red in the distance. Sailboats coasted slowly in the water as a steamboat chugged in the background.

We walked quietly for several minutes, sipping our drinks, until Sabine led us to a bench looking out onto the water. Once we settled in, setting down our goods, she opened up one of the bags and held it out to me. I pulled out a still-warm beignet, a soft spray of sugar floating over me in the breeze and sticking to my skin. She grabbed one for herself and curled her legs up underneath her.

"These are kind of amazing," she said finally.

"I know, good call." I decided to give it another try. "So, Wylie. It's just you two tonight? What are you up to?"

"I don't know. He's planning it. But I think it'll be pretty fabulous," she said between bites.

"I'm sure. You'll have to tell me *everything*," I said in my gushiest voice.

"Of course! But don't wait up!" She smiled and laughed.

"Got it." I nodded knowingly. But an alarm sounded in my mind. I had to push. "So you're kind of, like, in with that group now?"

"I wouldn't say *in* in," she clarified. "But I'm working on it."

"What's the deal with Clio, anyway?"

"She's cool. We were in the same circle all night, but I really only had a short conversation with her. I know her name and I know where she shops and that's about it." She licked the sugar from her fingers and went on. "She was pretty busy being hit on every five seconds."

"Tough life, right?" I popped the last of the beignet in my mouth. Sabine was already peeking in the bag for her next victim. She grabbed one and shook the bag at me. I hesitated for a beat then plunged my hand in.

"Anyway, they're all really fun. Emma and I were totally surprised that they let us hang with them."

"So what was up with Emma?"

"Emma, omigod, and Jimmy, check this out." She shifted to face me now. "So they've been together a year or something crazy and apparently they got here a few days early, and had this, like, coupley time." She rolled her eyes. "But then he just told her out of the blue, this week, he totally fell for someone else and I guess he's been staying at this random girl's place."

"How does that even happen?"

Sabine shrugged. "I'll tell you when I find out," she said with a mischievous glint in her eye.

I thought of that first morning when Jimmy came back to the house so early, and we found that body discarded in front of our place. "She has no idea who it is or anything?"

"Nope. He just told her yesterday and then disappeared again. It's pretty crazy. So obviously, Emma needed a night out. But you have to hang out with us!"

"Thanks, I'd love to," I said. Much as I didn't like the idea, I knew I needed to get closer to Clio's group, to see what I could find out. A cool breeze blew, dusk setting in. We would need to head back soon. "So, what was it like in Boston?" I sipped my coffee then lowered my volume so there was no mistaking what I was getting at. "I mean, in terms of leading you here and all?"

She shifted, turning back to the waterfront, squinting into the distance as she took a long drink of coffee. Finally, in a rigid voice: "I don't really feel like talking about it."

"I understand. That's usually how I am. But it's just so amazing to suddenly find someone, a whole group, going through the same thing. The three of us thought we were the only ones."

Pausing for a moment, she sighed, softening the slightest bit. "I guess we did too," she offered with a glance out of the corner of her eye. The *we* wasn't lost on me.

I realized I was going to have to give a little something to get something in return. "We were living at that hotel and we were with these people who were really glamorous and promising us this certain kind of life, these dreams, thinking they would hook us." She looked at me, expressionless, but I could tell she was taking it in. "And you know, they had their ways of trying to control us, with the poisons and things, which it sounds like you had to deal with too." She nodded. After a few seconds of silence, I went on. "Luckily Lance and I caught on to that soon enough to work around it. But Dante was really in the thick of it, so it was tougher for him." I tried to be as vague as possible, still unsure whether I really wanted to share this all with her. But part of me felt that I needed to, for both of our sakes. "He had an incredibly close call."

"We had more than a close call," Sabine said finally.

I didn't say a word, leaving plenty of space for her to fill. She took her time and at last: "We started working on the docks—it was on one of these tourist cruises that would go back and forth to

Cape Cod. I grew up doing all sorts of sailing, boating, yachting with my family, so it was perfect. There were events on the boat sometimes. It made a few stops. There was food and entertainment. We mostly stayed on the boat, or sometimes on the Cape or in Provincetown or Newport."

"It must've been fun, at least in the beginning, before you realized—"

"Yeah, they were going after the souls of everyone who came onboard. They made them all sorts of promises. Us too. First they poisoned us all, hoping it would be enough for us to just agree to anything, but instead we got so sick. We thought we were going to die—and we probably should have, but, you know, we're not like other people . . ." She trailed off for a moment. "Then we slowly started getting better. And when we did, the one in charge told us each that our dreams would come true and we could be really powerful too, for just a small price."

"How did you find out what you were?"

"He said that's why they wanted us, more than any of the other people whose souls they were taking. He made us seem so important. We didn't believe him at first, but then there was some stuff that happened." She folded her arms across her chest, as though protecting herself from the memories she had unleashed.

"Like what?"

"There was this one girl who warned us. She told us why we all had these scars. She was one of them but had started to snap out of it. She told us to stay strong and resist them. The day after she warned us, she disappeared. Some of her things washed up on the shore but they never found her." Sabine spoke slowly, as if in a trance, staring out at the river. "They had given us these contracts to sign but we ripped them up and left them in our rooms and ran away one night. Just jumped off the boat and swam away. I've never been the best swimmer, but for some reason I swam for miles and miles in the dark and was okay. I was really proud of that. I felt kind of invincible, you know? But he didn't make it. I don't even know when or how they got him, just that at some point I stopped hearing his kicking in the water. He was gone."

Much as I wanted to slow her down, to ask about this *him,* I let her keep going.

"So I went home. I didn't know what I would say, but it turned out I didn't need to come up with a story. The next day, by the time I got back, news had broken of a ship sinking. It was them." Sabine shivered. I wondered what it must feel like for her to look out onto a nautical scene like this after enduring what she had. Now I understood what had happened on the swamp boat—why she had shut down like that.

"So that was it then?" I asked finally. "They were just gone?"

"That was it." She paused, then looked at me. "Mind if we head back now?" she asked with pleading eyes. The riverfront walkway had cleared out and the sky was a dark iridescent blue heading into night. "And maybe talk about something else? Just for a little while?"

"I'm worried about you tonight," I blurted out. "I'm worried about this guy, and I had something like this hap—"

She put up her hand. "Please," she barked, making me jump. Then, more controlled, but just as firm: "Later, okay?"

"Of course," I said quietly, respectfully. She had turned off. I'd have to try again.

We gathered our things and silently walked the path back to the comfortable familiarity of the busy streets.

We were halfway home before either of us said another word. But finally Sabine slowed her pace and then stopped walking altogether. I did too.

"Hav?" She glanced at me, then down at her fingers fidgeting with the handle of her shopping bag, like she was embarrassed.

"Yeah?"

"I'm sorry. I just get funny thinking about all that stuff, you know?"

"Sure, I mean, it's intense. I get it, trust me." I looked her right in the eye for a second, but she quickly looked away.

"I was just kind of messed up after all that."

"I was too; we were too. I still am. And I don't want to speak for the guys but . . . well, they still are too." She appeared comforted by this, her posture loosening just enough. "And if it's any consolation, you seem like you're just rolling with it so well."

"I'm not."

"Then you're faking it really well. I can't really fake it." It was true—swamp visit aside, she didn't appear nearly as tortured and edgy as I felt on a daily basis.

"No, I feel like you do. I think we're so alike. I mean, the real me." I didn't really know what that meant. I didn't know Sabine well enough yet to know exactly what side of her *was* the real her. But I didn't think we were all that alike so far. I wished we were. There were certain aspects of her personality I wished I could have seen reflected in myself. There was an ease about her that I longed to have. And certainly more confidence. I had come a long way, but that wasn't saying a whole lot. I had miles to go.

Her voice lightened. "But all that aside"—she took a deep breath—"we gotta perk it up around here. I've gotta get into date mode. So, on to happier subjects. Let's decide which dress

I should wear." And with that, the spring returned to her step, her whole being transformed into something airy, her aura and attitude matching those of the upbeat patrons now beginning to flood every bar and restaurant along our route. The cloud that had hovered over us for the past hour had fully and officially lifted.

Our room looked like it had been ransacked: two of the new dresses, a cardigan, and two wraps lay strewn across Sabine's bed; heels of all heights and colors were scattered on the floor, some apparently mateless; and a pair of lipsticks, a trio of eye shadows, and a buffet of brushes littered the desk. A curling iron, still plugged in, sat on the floor, emitting a burning smell. A rotation of pop and hip-hop, Sabine's "Going Out Mix" as she called it, thumped from her speakers.

"I'm not sure about this lipstick," she said to her reflection. "I think it's too red." She shook her head, blotting it away. Curled up on my bed, I pulled out a beignet—somehow it had already become stale, but I didn't mind. I took a bite and opened up the magazine I had hidden my photos in: camouflage. One by one, I studied every single face for any signs of change. As I paged through, they all appeared just the same as when I passed them in the hallways here. I came upon Dante's photo from outside that bar the other night and found the slightest glow around him, as well as the faintest halo above his head. I skipped ahead, flipping through to find Lance's—yes, it looked the same as Dante's—and then to Sabine's, which also had that similar light emanating, but no halo yet, as far as I could tell. I kept going through the remaining handful but didn't get very far before stopping again.

Jimmy. He had been smiling originally when I had blown this photo up and printed it. But now one side of his mouth drooped, like a comma. His eyes had dulled and the corners looked like they were being tugged downward. A small gray splotch had sprung up on his cheek. It froze my heart to look at his picture. Evil was already seeking us out, moving in on us.

And then I arrived at the photos of the Krewe. Last time I had looked, these had been normal. Now, I compared each one against Jimmy's, and Clio looked like she was part of the same grotesque family. Wylie and the others showed signs of disfiguration as well—a sagging bit of skin here, a lesion there; they would likely be in full bloom in another day.

"Haven!" Sabine called.

"I'm sorry?" I realized I had tuned her out.

"So what do you think? Okay?" She looked perfect in the black dress and boots and she had her hair expertly curled and fluffed, full of shampoo-commercial-worthy body. She spritzed perfume on her wrists and swiped at her neck.

"You look great," I said, my mind turning it all over. I bit my lip, gnawing on it to stop myself from saying anything to her but I couldn't help it.

"Thanks! You're sweet." She popped a mirror and lipstick into a black clutch the size of an envelope.

"But don't go tonight. You can't." It just flew out, making me sound crazy. I stumbled down the ladder with the pictures in hand.

"Ha!" She actually laughed. "You're hilarious. Gotta go. I'll tell ya all about it." She looked at me with those wild eyes again.

"Wait. Seriously, I know you don't want to hear this, especially now, but it's Wylie—all of them—they're as dangerous as the group you ran away from in Boston. They are the same. Or they may be worse. You have to listen to me," I insisted, grabbing her by the wrist. She furrowed her brow in disapproval. I just launched in, anyway. "I didn't tell you enough today. There was a guy in Chicago. He was . . . incredible, everything anyone would want. And I fell for him, but it turned out he was someone who was after people like us. He wanted our souls, he collected them. I fell for him and it almost cost me everything—"

"Haven—" She tried to interrupt me, but I just kept going.

"We didn't have it like you in Boston. We didn't get to run away. We had to fight them, so many of them, and it almost killed us. They were either going to convert us or kill us—there was no other option. We shouldn't have won. I shouldn't be here now. I don't know why I am." I searched for any understanding or compassion in her eyes, but found them rocky.

"You've gotta get off my back, Haven," she said icily.

"I just don't have a good feeling about—"

"Look, I get it. You were traumatized by all that. I understand, trust me. But I sort of feel like I can hold my own," she assured me. "And I'm not about to sit at home just because a gorgeous stranger asked me out and we're worried he's too gorgeous and too much of a stranger."

"I just don't think you realize what they're capable of. He's one of them, I know it." Her eyes told me I hadn't been the least bit persuasive. "Look at this picture. You have to see this." I held it up in front of her face and she swatted it away.

"Leave me *alone*," she said, perfectly controlled, and yet the word felt like it was studded with spikes. "I have to go. Good night."

She stalked off. I remained rooted in my spot, bracing myself for a slamming door. Instead I heard her say in her most sugary-sweet voice, "Hi, Lance! How *are* you?" It was punctuated by the wet smack of a kiss, on the cheek or the lips, I couldn't see from where I stood. "Saturday night concert . . . still on?" I couldn't make out his answer. I think it was a very weak "Mmm-hmm." I could picture him stunned by her forwardness, her clothes, her whole persona right now.

When he stepped into the room, his body was facing me, but his head was still in the direction of the doorway, as though fascinated enough to watch the air Sabine had just occupied. Finally he looked at me. "She's in a good mood."

I didn't like her much at that moment, but still, I couldn't just let this happen. I sighed. "We have to talk to Connor."

Tucked away in the privacy of his room, Connor had looked at the pictures, all of them, with hard eyes. I had intended to keep those photos, that ability of mine, a secret, even from this group, but I couldn't just sit on this. My mind had flashed to that text message: if Connor could really be trusted, then I would let him see. "You don't know where she was going?" he asked gravely.

I shook my head. "They're always at that bar, you know, the one on St. Peter?"

"I'll go there. I'll also see who else is home and tell them to go looking. You guys head out, but be careful."

I called Dante, who was at Mariette's shop, before we even walked out the door. "Purely hypothetical: Name five places you'd take Max on a date night."

"I love your hypotheticals, Hav! Easy: Arnaud's, Galatoire's, Brennan's . . ." I jotted down the names and promised to tell him everything later.

Lance and I leapt up onto the balcony railing and jumped to the ground. Ouch. I fell forward on weak ankles again. But it was getting easier. Then we shot out into the dark night, looking into every window and doorway, our eyes scanning every face we passed. I filled him in as we surveyed.

"And the Jimmy photo?" He shook his head. "That's a really bad sign. He seemed fine at work today, but now that I think about it, he hasn't been around the house in the evenings much."

We trekked quietly for a few blocks, taking in the music and good times on every sidewalk, all these people with no cares. We stopped at an intersection, waiting for the cars to go by, some honking their horns spiritedly. I glanced at the corner restaurant beside us. It was one Dante had mentioned. Inside, flower-dotted tables sparkled with crystal as well-dressed diners nibbled fancy versions of Cajun delicacies. Through the honey glow of the long windows, I could see a grand swath of the place. Some patrons leaned against the bar, waiting for their tables with drinks and smiles. I noticed one couple standing so close to each other, sharing a laugh about something, the woman with her hand on her date's arm. It was Sabine and Wylie. I grabbed Lance, pointing.

"Speak of the devil," he whispered. We crept to the side of the window, to watch from the shadows in the hopes of going undetected. Luckily, Sabine seemed too engrossed to notice. I knew that look: she was smitten. I had given that look to someone myself on several occasions.

We watched them silently their entire date. It could not have looked less suspicious: a beautiful couple sipping drinks, eating from each other's plates, gazing into each other's eyes. It occurred to me that Lance and I had never quite had this. Our union had been born of such life-altering events that we had fast-forwarded past this stage. For us, it seemed romance came from the adrenaline surge of defying death. I supposed that every relationship was different.

At last, they rose to leave and as he pulled out her chair, Wylie glanced in our direction for the briefest of seconds. My breath stilled. Lance and I lunged out of sight.

"Do you think . . ." Lance was about to ask.

"Hope not," I said as we crept away from the door and prepared to follow them to their next destination. We waited and waited, the combined force of our gaze enough to burn holes in the sidewalk. It felt like they were taking too long. We watched a few couples emerge from the restaurant into the energy of the street. The sidewalk outside the restaurant wasn't so crowded that we should have lost Sabine and Wiley. Could they have been swallowed up by that group of drunken college boys here, or that bachelorette party there? Could we have missed them amid the bustle of that trumpeter packing up after a day of playing for change? Or did the novelty of that grungy-looking artsy man walking arm in arm with a statuesque trophy of a woman distract us? Lance left me to stand watch as he took a lap inside the restaurant, but found nothing. They had vanished.

I couldn't bear the failure of going home so soon, so we wandered down every dark street, barely paying attention to where we were going, just searching madly. Before long we found our way to quiet Rampart Street. There were empty sidewalks and darkened storefronts for blocks and blocks. But then I heard in the distance a woman's laugh, high-pitched, birdlike, carefree. Then the hushed tone of a man whispering. And footsteps getting softer as they walked away from us. Lance looked at me, catching it too.

We tried to follow and the voices led us to the cemetery.

～ 16 ～

I've Seen That Guy

Lance flicked his head toward the gates. I had never seen the cemetery closed, its black metal bars theoretically keeping potential trespassers at bay. But he was right—it sounded like the voices were inside. We heard a thump that could have been someone finding his or her way over that wall. There was a rustling and then I heard the woman's giggling.

I thought of Sister Catherine's warning—not that I needed to be told that a cemetery at night probably wasn't the coziest hangout even under the best of circumstances—and then I nodded to Lance with a shrug and roll of the eyes that said, *Sure, let's break into the cemetery. That's a great idea.* He just smiled.

I grabbed two of the bars and tugged, careful not to rattle them. This gate was solid—it wouldn't be pried open. A few chips of paint peeled off beneath my fingers. On the other side of the barrier, security lights bathed the whole city of the dead in an eerie glow.

We looked up. The gate wasn't really all that high, maybe ten feet. We had done our share of climbing. I gripped two bars, planting my right foot flat against another bar, then pushed off, managing to swoop up, pulling with my arms and landing my left foot firmly on a horizontal bar situated across the gate halfway up. From there, I jumped, yanking myself up onto the top of the gate, another horizontal bar. I sat there for a moment, waiting as Lance followed. He was so tall, it seemed easy for him with those long, muscular limbs to swing up so gracefully.

On one side, the cemetery stretched out before us, all those rows of tombs. On the other glowed the lights of Bourbon Street a few blocks away. "Nice view," I mouthed. He smiled. I swung myself over the gate, shimmying down and landing hard on my feet, almost silently. I shook the life back into my legs as Lance leapt to join me. Perfectly still, we listened closely, locating the voices. I pointed toward the back of the cemetery.

I led the way, charting a course studded with large crypts perfect for hiding. The voices grew louder and at last we spotted a couple wandering clumsily through the grassy land near Latrobe's grave. We sought refuge behind a towering tomb, poking out our heads to watch. We could only make out their silhouettes.

"Why do you like to come here?" the man slurred.

"Are you kidding? It's soooo romantic," the girl gushed. "Don't you *love* it?" A smack echoed, a kiss somewhere in these dark corners, and then her birdlike laugh and the coltish clop of her trying not so hard to run away. She landed in a spot illuminated by moonlight. It was Clio. Her paramour reached out and grabbed her hand and she yelped playfully as he pulled her into another kiss.

"So you're gonna make me come back here?" he barely protested.

"It's my favorite place. There's a party coming up. You'll love it," she assured him, adding matter-of-factly, "You'll be here, all right."

"It sounds like I don't have much choice," he said. I didn't recognize him, but he had that generally familiar collegiate look, as if he could have been one of Connor's friends, a typical French Quarter reveler. The pair tumbled to the ground entwined. It took me only an instant to realize Lance and I weren't going to learn anything else here right now, and we were going to feel incredibly voyeuristic in another minute. A heat had risen to my skin and it was so distracting that I almost didn't realize my scars had flared up. I gestured in the direction of the exit, Lance nodded, and we slunk away as quietly, and quickly, as possible.

We vaulted back over the gate and walked home, giving up for the night. Few were out on Royal Street and it was quiet enough for me to notice as we passed the LaLaurie mansion that a window had been left open, wind whistling through. The candle was out, but my heart stopped as I caught the outline of a hand. It held up what looked to be a bottle, then pulled it away out of sight. I thought of Marie Laveau's grave, all those offerings, some bottles among them. Somehow I knew this was an offering for me. I wanted to run up to that window now. Beside me, Lance was lost in thought; his heavy eyes had fixed on something in the distance. He stopped walking and just stood there. I stopped too, waiting for him to say something, but he didn't.

"You okay?"

"I think I need to get some air," he said finally.

"Really? I mean, we've kind of been getting air all night," I said gently.

"Yeah. You go on ahead. I'll be back soon."

"I can stay out too—"

"No. I'm just going to walk around the block, clear my head," he said, backing up in the direction we had just come from. "See you later." And with that he turned around, hands in his pockets, and strode off into the night.

I didn't like it but I could tell he wanted to be alone, so I let up on him. "Well, don't stay out long, okay?"

Back at the house, I found my room dark and empty. Connor and the others hadn't had any luck looking through the bars and clubs. When I told him how we had found Sabine and then lost her, he said, "Get some rest," reading the defeat in my eyes. "You did everything you could."

I changed into my scrubs and pulled out my stack of photos. Jimmy's had deteriorated in those few hours since I'd last looked. Now his features melted down his face, lesions covering his skin. I shoved it back into the nightstand, slamming the drawer shut. I fished around in my backpack to locate both of my Swiss Army knives—I always liked to have a spare these days. I tucked the extra one into the drawer beside the pictures, a shiver overtaking my body. As I turned off the lights, I discovered a new message on my phone:

Your eyes didn't deceive you tonight. Go looking tomorrow. You'll find something.

I dozed off with thoughts of Lucian running through my mind, invading my dreams.

The rapping on the door wouldn't stop. I groaned. Why did Connor need to do this? Couldn't he train us at normal hours of the day? It was still completely dark outside. Since the pounding showed no sign of subsiding, I crawled down the ladder. More awake now, I noticed the knocks came at slower intervals, as though someone was hurling his body against the door repeatedly. I opened it up with a yawn.

Lance practically fell on me, stumbling over the threshold. "Whoa!" I exclaimed.

"I'm so sorry, just me," he slurred his words, whispering. It sounded like he'd been drinking. Or what I imagined he would sound like drunk. I'd never actually seen him show much interest in alcohol. He tripped, toppling over Sabine's night table and landing on the floor along with it. "Can I lie down here? Few minutes? D'you mind?"

"Are you okay? Where have you been? Did you find Sabine and Wylie?"

"I'm fiiiine, I think. I dunno," he said woozily. "Just need to sleep."

"Maybe you need some water or something? You look like you're gonna be sick." I stood over him, a pile of bones crumpled on the floor in the dark.

"No, just sleep, just need sleep," he said, not moving, eyes closed, moonlight bouncing off his glasses. I crouched down. He lay on his back, which seemed like a bad idea if he was going to get sick, so I rolled him over onto his side. Then I noticed it: his right bicep was slashed, right through his shirt and down to the flesh. A dark claret ribbon of hardened blood had dried there.

"What happened to you?" I said loudly, waking him.

"Huh?" he mumbled, going back to sleep.

I bolted to the closet, rummaging through my first-aid kit to find a bandage and some ointment. I yanked up his sleeve. It was certainly ugly: ragged and raw. As I smoothed the bandage over the top of the wound, the antiseptic bubbled, a popping sensation, beneath it. If the room hadn't been so silent I wouldn't have heard or believed it, but a hiss rose, sizzling like an egg on a hot frying pan. Still asleep, Lance shook his arm as though trying to flick a bug away. I grabbed his hand to settle him and eventually he stopped. I dragged the trash can over beside him and trekked out to the kitchen to get him a bottle of water.

Before heading back up to my own bed, I leaned into his chest listening to his breathing. It sounded okay, maybe a little jagged, but he was very much alive. It all worried me, though, in a way it wouldn't have concerned me to see pretty much anyone else in this house stumble back in this state. Lance just didn't do stuff like this. He liked to be in control; he prided himself on it. He made fun of the kids at school who got wasted on the weekends. I climbed back up to my bed and glanced at my clock. It would be time to get up soon.

I didn't hear Sabine come in, but when I woke in the morning, she was tucked neatly into her bed and Lance had left. I checked and found him in his room getting ready for work, seemingly back to normal. I didn't have time to ask him what had happened last night before we all had to rush out to our jobs. On the walk to our work sites, Sabine regaled Dante and me with tales of her date.

"And then after dinner, and the music and everything, he said he wanted to walk for a little while, so it could be just us. Isn't that amazing?"

"Yeah, amazing," I said sarcastically. "Sabine, what aren't you understanding?" Dante sighed, an angry sigh.

"We went to Jackson Square. It's *so* beautiful at night, and we just found a little secluded bench and . . ." She gave us both a mischievous look. I shook my head. "I don't know why I have to believe your photography project," she spat at me. She was getting frustrated with us now. "Anyone with Photoshop can do that. *I* can do that with Photoshop. Dante, back me up." I whipped my head toward him.

"Sorry, Sabine. I'm Team Haven on this one—"

Thank you, I mouthed to him.

"Even if I told you Max was *just* talking to me about you?" Sabine said, in her most persuasive tone.

Dante lit up. "Oh? And what did he say?" He did his best to play it cool, but I could tell he was jumping up and down on the inside.

"Just that you guys grabbed dinner since you were both working late," she said, very nonchalant. Dante hung on her words as though secretly dissecting them for subtext.

"True," he said, sounding a little disappointed.

"And . . ." She drew it out, as if about to bestow a great gift. "He didn't *say* this, but I totally know he's into you. Just in case you were curious."

"I suppose I might be," he said with a twinkle in his eye.

I tuned them out, my mind wandering. I couldn't stop thinking about looking for whatever Lucian might have left. But something in the distance intruded on my thoughts. At the end of the block, police tape boxed off the tattoo parlor. A few gawkers stood by, watching, as two cops, lights flashing on their parked police car, called for backup.

"Hey," I interrupted Sabine and Dante, who had been too locked in conversation to notice. "What's going on there?" I pointed, slowing my pace. Sabine crinkled her eyebrows and walked ahead of us to where Kip stood, his back to us. She tapped his shoulder and he put his hand on her back protectively, saying something. Standing on her tiptoes, she looked past the few people in front of her and then snapped her head away, covering her eyes.

As soon as we got closer, we understood why: a man lay on his back soaked in a pool of blood. He looked like he'd been torn open. I grabbed Dante's hand, on reflex, squeezing hard. Sirens shattered the still morning air and an emergency vehicle pulled up. Two uniformed men dashed out, throwing a sheet over the body. But I had already seen enough: it was the guy I'd spied in the cemetery last night with Clio.

"I've seen that guy—" I started to say to Dante, but Sabine was on her way back over to us, the shock clear on her face.

"What happened?" I asked.

"Kip said he just found him there when he got in." She shook her head. "No one knows who he is," she said to the ground, arms folded. "I'm gonna hang out here for a while and then go home. I can't handle work today." Her face had gone ashen, her spirit paralyzed, not unlike the day in the swamp.

"You sure?" I asked. She just nodded, turning to go back to Kip, but she quickly spun around again.

"What was he like? That guy? You know, in Chicago?" she asked me in a heavy tone.

I took a deep breath. "Perfect, in every way. And in an unreal way," I said finally. "And also completely, dangerously wrong. All at the same time." In my head I added: *And now he has resurfaced, in that way that boys seem to when you have moved on.*

I waited until Dante and I were alone and then it flew out of me. "I saw that guy at the cemetery last night," I blurted out. "He was with that Clio person. It's them; it's definitely them. Her group. The Krewe. I know it."

"Are you serious? What were they doing? Did she kill him?" he whispered.

I didn't know. I didn't even want to think about it. But I feared that I could guess the answer.

⤳ 17 ⤳

Meet Me at Midnight

D ante and I spent the first part of our workday in the kitchen
at the food bank, me as his sous-chef, chopping vegetables,
heating meals and packaging them for the drivers to take later that
day. River had beat us there, missing the crime scene, and demanded to hear all the gory details. When she was outside loading
up the van, Dante and I resumed the debate we'd begun on the
walk over: deciding whether to go to the police about Clio. Since
I didn't really want to have to tell them that Lance and I had been
trespassing in the cemetery, we thought it might be best for me
to call in an anonymous tip, even though I had so little information: I had a first name and I could tell them where she liked to
drink her hurricanes, and that was all I could really provide them
on the mysterious Clio. The cop, who called me "sweetie," took
down those few details and promised to look into it.

Since Dante wanted to update Mariette, I went ahead to catch
the streetcar to the library by myself, but first I had a bit of business to tend to. The afternoon sun did its best to clear my darkened mind, but certain sights I would never quite shake. I wound

my way back home, standing before the house next door long enough that passersby probably wondered about me.

Unable to wait any longer, I let myself in. The buzz of saws and whir of machines performing their various tasks, lifting and slicing and hammering, greeted me. The Habitat for Humanity home construction now complete, the guys had returned to their work here today, so I braced myself, hoping I could find whatever it was I was in search of before any of them—Lance especially—made an appearance.

Even in daylight, the foyer was dim, full of shadows, making my job more difficult. Last night the object had looked like a bottle from my vantage point: dark, with a long neck that he had grasped in those slim fingers. I looked all around the window where the candle had been. I sorted through piles of discarded, chopped wooden beams. I even pawed around a heap of full black garbage bags, and there I found it. I didn't recognize the label, but something caught my eye on the back: in the block of text listing the ingredients, five letters had been circled in the first line: *H, A, V, E,* and *N.* And in the second line, eight more letters, this time spelling: *PLEASE READ.*

No one was around, so I decided I would just go for it. I intended to pop the top with the bottle opener of my Swiss Army knife, but then I realized there wasn't a top. This bottle had been sealed shut as though someone had melted the nearly opaque glass to close it off. I shook it, trying to see what lay inside, and thought I could make out something attached to the bottom: a folded slip of paper. I had to get it. With the construction equipment roaring, I wound up my arm and thrust the bottle to the floor, shattering it. My scars tingled, perhaps at being so close to this vessel that had been brought from the underworld. I crouched to the ground, carefully picking through the shards to find that scrap of paper.

Then a voice calling out made me jump back to my feet. "Everythin' all right out here?" It was the supervisor, John. I heard footsteps coming out to greet me. I froze.

"Hi!" I waved, overly friendly. "Sorry, I'm clumsy. Just knocked something over. I'll clean it up, promise." With my shoes, I tried to direct some of the jagged pieces into a pile, to convince him it was under control and there was no need to come any closer.

"Don't worry about it. We'll get it later. Don't want ya hurtin' yourself there."

"Thanks." I simply smiled, hoping he would go away. But he went on.

"You here for Lance, too?"

"Um, yeah, thanks, if he has a minute."

"Sure is popular," he said, shaking his head.

"What do you mean?" I couldn't help calling after him.

He turned around. "That other one."

"Sorry?"

"Dark hair, sweet, but real upset about that scene over on Toulouse."

I opened my mouth to speak, but my thoughts were too unformed. Finally, when he was almost out of earshot, I managed: "Can I see him for a minute?"

"He's not here. He left with the other girl." He turned around to face me. "Don't shoot the messenger." He put his hands up, returning to the construction zone in back.

So Sabine had come by? I struggled to push that to the back of my mind. I knelt down, sifting carefully through the pile, but

I was so distracted, I nicked my index finger on a piece of glass. Blood trickled down, but I didn't have time to deal with it. I gingerly sorted until I found that folded piece of paper: thick, cotton soft, familiar. I opened it up fast, leaving the slightest streak of crimson on it. It read:

H-
    You're right about Clio. Sabine will be next.
Meet me at midnight. Please.
    L

I read it again, letting it all sink in. *Sabine will be next.* It haunted me, that line. I felt the blood drain from my face, as though it was all pouring out of that small, stinging slice in my finger. My hands burned like they were being brushed with hot coals. Without warning, my fingers tossed the note. The second it hit the floor, the paper burst into flames.

A crackling ball of fire the size of a grapefruit began to grow, dancing over the shards of glass and shooting out rays of light. I watched in sheer disbelief for a moment, then my foot, acting on its own, stomped on the flame. Three hearty stomps and it was out. Nothing left at all, not even charred bits of the paper. I took a deep breath, prepared to gather the broken glass and be done with this. But it was gone. All that remained of the dark glass shards were quarter-size puddles scattered at my feet. I studied them and they seemed to be evaporating. They shrank until there wasn't even the slightest trace of them. No sign that a bottle had shattered, or ever even existed.

On automatic pilot, the flash of that flame still burning in my eyes, I went next door in search of Lance. I knocked on his door, but no response. I let myself into my room, but found it empty as well. Where were they? Since I was home anyway, I decided to take another look at those pictures. I'd made it only a few steps up the ladder to my loft when a crash jangled my thoughts. My heart lurched. It had come from somewhere outside. I went to the window to peek out, but I got stopped in my tracks.

Something—no, some*one*—came flying through the glass. But he didn't even fall to the floor; he kept running, right into me, knocking me over. I felt myself scream but I couldn't hear myself. I just kept hearing the sound of that shattering glass over and over on a loop in my ears. The guy was too fast and furious for me to even get a good look at him. He was a long, lean flash of blond and tan.

He jumped off me literally, his sneaker pushing off my stomach, and launched himself at Sabine's bed. With one hand he lifted it and flipped it over, then ran up the wall and propelled himself to the other side, landing on our desk and breaking it in half, a pair of its legs snapping off in the process. He looked at me then, and his whole form compressed a few inches. The angles in his face changed, his hair went dark, even his clothing morphed—his T-shirt from black to white, his pants into jeans— but his mad rage remained: now it was Jimmy. But not the Jimmy I'd previously encountered. This Jimmy had wild, angry eyes, like a jungle cat midattack. His hair was mussed as though it hadn't been washed in days. His clothes were dirty, bloody, ripped. A gash on his upper arm had dried into a fat tar-colored wound, but there was no mistaking its shape: it was a scabbed-up, flaming fleur-de-lis.

He threw the desk chair at me and I retaliated with the alarm clock from Sabine's bedside table. It soared through the air and he punched it as it came his way, shattering it. I needed to get past him up to the loft so I could destroy the photos of him. I grabbed the floor lamp and swung it at his shins, managing to knock him off his feet. I took a few long strides to the ladder. He yanked my foot as I scurried up, and I tried to shake him off but he just gripped tighter. I pulled myself up one rung and then clocked him in the head with my other foot.

For another hiccup of a second he flickered back to being that blond man, and then back to Jimmy. My eyes couldn't make sense of it. I ripped open my night table drawer, the entire thing coming off its track in my hands. I grabbed the knife and stack of pictures as the rest of the drawer fell, everything spilling out. Jimmy's photo was still at the top. He seized both my legs, tugging them out from under me. I landed on my chin. He tried to pull me back down the ladder. I sprang open the blade, held his picture against the loft floor, and sliced. Slice, slice, stab.

But his grip didn't loosen at all. I looked at the picture again. It was grotesque and disfigured, evidence of his corrupted soul, but my violence against it wasn't having any effect. This had never happened before. He was laughing now as he pulled me down the ladder. I gripped the top rung with one arm and swung the knife at him with the other. I sliced him once but he didn't flinch, didn't even seem to feel it. Instead, he let out a howling, wild roar, mocking me. My legs scissored trying to buck him away. I scanned the room for anything that could help me. If he managed to get me down the ladder, then I could go for one of the desk legs that had been stripped off and try to fight him with that. I continued swinging and kicking and I kept that sharp, strong metal leg in my sights. The more I stared at it, the more attainable it seemed. And then, in a flash, it flew up at me. I whipped the knife away and caught the leg in my one free hand.

I beat Jimmy back, swinging the leg at him, striking him as

many times as I could, trying to tire him, though it seemed impossible. He landed on the floor but popped right back up. I hopped to the ground, wound up, and shot the leg at him like a spear. It landed in his chest and hurled him against the back wall with enough force to elicit a grunt. He slumped to the floor.

The door to my room burst open. Connor and Brody stormed in. Brody charged at Jimmy as Connor ran to my side. But Jimmy sprang to his feet again and took off, zipping past Brody, back through the window he had destroyed and out onto the balcony. We ran to look out and made it in time to see him leap straight down from the railing to the courtyard below, startling Emma, who had just walked in the front gate. By the time she saw who it was, he had grabbed her and then flung her away, so hard she landed on the ground by the fountain. Brody and Connor jumped over the railing to chase him. I followed a few steps and then felt the trauma of the past few long minutes catch up with me and my legs buckled. Jimmy tore off through the gate and out into the darkening evening streets. A little while later, Brody and Connor came back through the gate, panting and hanging their heads low at having lost him. He was gone.

18

I Should Have Been There

All of us assembled in the common room, in nearly the same places we had our first morning here. Except there was no Jimmy. And Sabine sat beside Lance. I hadn't gotten to talk to him yet. Connor had called over to the library to order everyone home immediately after the tutoring session. Lance, as it turned out, had texted me that he and Sabine were meeting me at the library after work, that she had been upset so he was keeping her company. But I didn't get that text, of course. I had been too busy sparring with Jimmy, or whoever this version of Jimmy had been who had crashed into my room and tried to kill me. Every muscle ached and every nerve throbbed now.

Brody and Emma, who were supposed to be on night watch tonight, had had the afternoon off and had witnessed bits of Jimmy's rampage. "I was watchin' SportsCenter and heard the crash," Brody explained to the group. "Jimmy was crazy, never seen anything like that. Out of his mind." He shook his head and ran his fingers through that blue streak in his hair, tense. Across the room, Emma sat on the sofa beside River, who had her arm around her protectively. Emma clutched a balled-up tissue in her hand; her freckled face had gone red and puffy from so many tears shed. Even now, her glassy eyes looked like they just might spill over again.

Connor stood at the front of the room, addressing us with a serious expression and tone. His T-shirt and jeans were rumpled and torn in a few places.

"I don't have any answers to all the questions I'm sure you have," he said, pacing. "What I can tell you is that Jimmy's soul has been captured." A soft collective gasp swept the room. He looked at Emma, who fixed her eyes on the ground.

"Does that mean he's not coming back?" Dante asked.

Connor breathed out a huge sigh, hands behind his head, perplexed. "There's no way to know yet if it's reversible. But if he returns to us and we can keep him here, then we can attempt to reclaim him." I scanned the room. Everyone seemed to be hanging on his words, as though he were pulling us through a storm, our only hope for survival. "This is what I've been warning you about. They will find you, and we need to keep close to one another, to know where everyone is all the time, in order to defeat them. You are all going to be sought out, that is a given. Do you hear me?" He looked at each of our faces to make his point clear. "This is part of your test: separating out the defeated part of your soul."

"How do we do that?" River barked at him, angry, still holding Emma.

"We lift it out, which is why I expect to see everyone practicing their levitation." He pointed down the hall in the direction of the padded room. There's one person in there every night, and she is the only one who will stand a chance, unless you all get your sorry asses in there and start getting strong." I felt myself blush. I had been quietly working levitation into my routine, a necessary daily task, like brushing your teeth. It had paid off today.

"Emma says Jimmy had been spending some time with someone new lately—" As Connor said that, I could feel how that line must have sliced through Emma. It was as if she lost him twice: first his body to this other person and now his soul. "Beware of everyone. Report anything suspicious to me. We'll pool our information. Catching your attacker quickly and having a will to fight back, these are the things that will protect you. There's a group we've learned of called the Krewe, and we now know they're who you need to watch out for. I've posted descriptions here." He smacked a few typed sheets of crisp paper taped to the wall behind him.

I had offered Connor my morphing photos, but he had ultimately decided he didn't want to share them with the group. "Can we keep this just between us, Haven?" he had asked me, making me feel, for the first time since I'd arrived here, that I did have something special. "These," he had said, tapping the stack of photos, "can help me keep tabs on all y'all." At his request, I printed a set of photos for him to keep under lock and key in his room.

"Be careful," he went on now at the meeting. "Travel in pairs, keep an eye on each other. If anyone asks, tell 'em Jimmy decided the program wasn't for him and took off. He's eighteen, so I wouldn't've been able to stop him, anyway. Discretion is the name of the game, okay?" With that he clapped his hands, a few quick rousing claps. "That's it for now." He dismissed us, adding with serious, scolding eyes, "Sabine, can I see you?" A look of worry clouded her face as she sashayed over to him.

Lance glanced in my direction, but too nervous, it seemed, to look me in the eye. When we all got up to leave, he grabbed my elbow as I tried to walk ahead of him.

"I should have been there," he said, the heavy tone in his voice evidence that he was censuring himself. "I should've known when you didn't text me back."

I shook my head. I hadn't needed saving; that wasn't the issue here. "I'm fine. I didn't need you. Don't worry about it," I said. I was bruised and scraped up—I had pulled a piece of glass the size of my index finger out of my upper arm, which I'd bandaged —and with my torn clothes I looked like something that had been dragged in off the street, but I hadn't actually gotten hurt. "I mean, it wasn't the way I'd prefer to spend an afternoon, but I'm still alive, so it's all good." But there was no masking the iciness lacing my words. We neared Lance's room and I made no motion to stop, so he walked on with me until we reached my door.

"I hope your arm is better," I said coldly.

"How did you know about that?" he whispered.

I glared at him. "Are you kidding? Who do you think cleaned you up last night?"

"What do you mean?"

"No, you're right. I guess you were drunk or whatever. What was that about?" I felt like he was a completely different person lately.

He thought for a moment, then whispered some more. "I don't really remember last night. At all. And I'm pretty embarrassed that I got this." He wore a T-shirt over a long-sleeved shirt, which he pushed up to expose that spot on his arm. He peeled back the bandage and the wound seemed to have taken on the shape of a fleur-de-lis, but it had scabbed up in such a way that you couldn't even see the actual ink, only this odd-shaped injury.

"It didn't look like that last night. It was just a gash." I leaned in, studying it. Just like Jimmy's. "You need to tell Connor about that. Like, right away."

"Maybe you're right," he said quietly, pulling his sleeve back down. He leaned against the doorframe, his face close to mine watching as I fumbled with my key. He looked like he wanted to say something. I felt it in the pit of my stomach even before he spoke, somehow knowing from his deep breaths and the way he pulled at the bottom hem of his worn T-shirt that I wasn't going to like whatever he planned to say. "Sabine just showed up next door, all upset, from everything this morning, you know? She didn't want to be alone. So we hung out until it was time to hit the library and then we went there. That's it."

"That's fine, Lance," I said, weary, unlocking the door at last and pushing it open.

"I just want to explain . . . everything, you know. Not that there's anything to explain, but . . ."

"You don't have to. It's fine." He followed me in, scanning all around at the disaster area of splintered, shredded furniture, tattered bedspreads, ripped clothing, and a mosaic of broken glass across the floor near a spiky hole where the window once was. "I'm not fighting with you. I didn't even say anything about . . . that . . . her." But even as I said it, part of me wanted to fight, because maybe in some strange way that would show Lance that he mattered to me, that I would fight for him. But why didn't he know that already? Was he forgetting all that we'd been through? Had his feelings for me changed? I didn't understand this unraveling that seemed to be happening. "I've just had a long day."

"I know. I'm sorry," he offered softly. "I can see that." He shook his head, as though trying to erase the mess around him. "You're obviously staying in my room."

"Thanks." I exhaled. He took a slow, studied tour of the surroundings, as though noting every single bit of destruction.

"How are you okay after this?" he asked, somber, as he knelt and cleared away larger pieces of glass.

"Yeah, it was kind of a wild afternoon," I said matter-of-factly, rummaging through my dresser to collect some clean clothes. I pulled out my favorite jeans, a tank top, and a blue cardigan and climbed up the beat-up ladder on sore legs. "First, I found out the hard way that it doesn't seem to work to just defeat them by destroying the pictures anymore." I tossed the clothes on the slashed comforter of my bed and dug around the scraps of paper on the floor until I found it: Jimmy's picture. I handed it down to Lance.

"What?" He looked up at me, studying the photo closely. His fingers brushed across the fringe left by my blade. "So, all of this" —Lance waved the tattered shot—"and nothing?"

"Not for lack of trying, right?" I sighed. "I just about wore out the knife on that thing." I piled up the rest of the photos scattered on the loft floor and handed those down too.

"You should shoot one of yourself again too, as a sort of baseline, you know? Just in case," he said. He had a point. I didn't have a photo of myself, now that I thought about it. Lance slowly shuffled through the group of pictures. He was engrossed enough that I managed to pull off my ripped T-shirt and jeans, changing into the new clothes without attracting notice, even though that wasn't the sort of thing he had witnessed all that often. "Are you losing your powers, Haven?" he said, glancing at the photos and pushing his glasses up.

For a moment I thought he had somehow read my thoughts—I had been wondering that myself lately—and that we were about to have a talk about us, as ill-timed as it was in the middle of the day's upheaval and the larger life-or-death issues at stake. But then I realized he was speaking exclusively about my effect on the photos, not on him. I didn't answer for a beat too long.

"Haven?" He looked up at me now, expecting a response, shaking me out of my inner monologue.

"My powers?" I shook my head to get the blood and thoughts flowing again. "No, I mean I don't think so, but I don't know. I think maybe these devils are just different or something."

He tilted his head, nodding like this was a distinct possibility.

"Because, I'll have you know, my powers are just fine," I said taking offense, a fire lighting in me. "And it turns out I'm a lot better at that levitation business than I thought."

Fully dressed, I swooped back down the ladder, purpose behind every step. Lance followed me out the door and back down the hall. We had nearly reached his room when he grabbed my bicep—the uninjured one—and stopped me. "Wait a second," he said quietly, his eyes searching mine for what lay beneath the surface. I did my best to project peace and neutrality in every feature and clear my face of any hint of the storm that I was really feeling. At that moment, I just wanted to be left alone. He felt far away even though he was touching me. "Where are you going?" he asked in a way that seemed to plead with me not to go anywhere.

"Levitation room. I want to practice before I lose whatever it was that was working this afternoon."

His grip loosened. "I'll see you later?"

I nodded and walked ahead. "Later. I don't know how long it's going to take."

I had nearly reached the levitation room when I saw Sabine shoot out of Connor's room. Her eyes were steely, her glare like a stake to the heart. Her voice came at me fierce and barbed, unlike any time I'd ever heard her: "Thanks a ton for ragging on me to Connor. About Wylie? You're a great friend."

"I . . . I didn't mean—"

"Save it," she spat the words, storming past me down the hall. "Is this about the kiss? What did Lance tell you? It was a peck, please. I was drunk. Give a girl a break. It was a couple nights ago. Let it go already."

My mouth opened but the words didn't materialize. Finally: "Good to know, thanks."

"Oh, he didn't tell you? Sorry," she said flatly, completely unapologetic as she stomped away.

When I recovered, many long seconds too late, it occurred to me what I should have said: I had told Connor because for some reason, I cared. I didn't intend to let Sabine, or anyone, slip away on my watch. But now I wasn't sure how I felt about her anymore. I only knew that the day had wounded me, in body and spirit.

I let myself into the practice room, anxious for a distraction. Once there, I couldn't quite replicate what had happened earlier. I got close: I could lift all the objects, but I just couldn't direct them to myself. Dante had poked his head in at one point, but I had sent him away with talk of needing to focus and a promise to see him later. My progress tonight didn't really matter, though. The exercise kept me busy and when my watch signaled five minutes to midnight, it was certainly easier to sneak out of there than it would have been to leave from my own room, since it was so close to the front door. Lights were still on in the rooms surrounding the courtyard, but no one was out to notice that I was leaving. I tiptoed down the stairs.

Even as I crept along the shadows of Royal Street to that imposing house next door, I knew this meeting wasn't necessarily the best idea. My judgment felt so clouded after my encounters with Jimmy and Sabine and that talk with Lance that left so much unsaid. Lucian had hinted that he was ready to take me up on that standing offer I had made so many months ago to help him escape the underworld. But if I was being honest with myself, I didn't quite feel prepared for that kind of challenge. Part of me wished I didn't have to deal with that so soon, or maybe even at all. I already felt I was being pulled in so many directions and pushed to my breaking point. I wasn't sure I could handle adding Lucian, and the weight of his curse, right now. And then there were those very legitimate concerns I couldn't entirely swat away: Could he be trapping me? Did he know Jimmy was going to come after me today? And, worse, had he sent him? I didn't know what it would take for me to truly be able to trust him.

I neared that doorway enshrouded in the black of night and stopped before it, resting my hand on the doorknob gingerly, as though it might bite, then taking a deep breath. Just as there was the part of me that didn't want to be thrust back into that world of his with its deep terrors, there was another part that had felt an uptick in my pulse, a quickened heartbeat, the minute I unfolded that first note from him. With Lucian there had always been that tug, that push and pull, that spark that made me want to see him, along with that voice of reason that knew the danger he always brought with him.

I cracked open the door, slithering in, engulfed by the smothering darkness of the haunted house. A mustiness mingled with the scents of charred wood and sawdust, making the air thick as it settled in my throat. The space looked and felt nothing like it had when I had been there earlier in the day. Now, I supposed, it was all filtered through such a different prism, a whole new variety of fear and also adrenaline. The silence fluttered my nerves.

Then I heard it, so soft, somewhere far above me: "Haven . . ."

Dense clouds shifted in the night sky, as moonlight streamed in the front windows, painting patches of the foyer's floor and walls a honey color. It set aglow the blond wood of a newly constructed grand staircase, at the top of which stood Lucian.

19

I've Been Waiting Months to Do That

He still wore that weathered tux, the tie hanging undone and loose around his neck and his top buttons unfastened. "Haven," he said softly, a layer of quiet relief in his tone. He took each step slowly, carefully, his eyes set on me, unwavering. I felt held in place by his gaze. He moved so smoothly and yet it felt like it took an eternity for him to reach me. "You came," he said, sounding surprised. The moonlight dimmed again. I had forgotten how tall he was. "Thank you," he said, sincerity knitting his brows. He stood so still and at a distance before me, perhaps to suggest we wouldn't have the struggle we did the last time we met here.

"Sure. I mean, I wouldn't stand you up." I tried to stifle the quiver in my voice and smiled a cautious smile, still on guard. I searched for that worn look in his eyes, anything to prove once more that it was really him.

"Well, welcome." He gestured to the construction site around us. "I guess you could call this my home away from home."

I looked around again, nodding. "They told us this place was haunted but I never thought it was you doing the haunting."

He laughed coolly. "It's not always me. That's just the past month or so, since you got here. It's sort of a halfway house for misdirected souls, like mine. I've tried the other portals but this is the only one open to me." I had so many questions, but I couldn't be sure my voice would remain steady, so I just let him talk. "I made the others leave, though. I've still got some seniority, you know, in that world." His voice got a degree heavier and I understood what world we were talking about. "For better or worse."

"I guess we've got a lot of catching up to do."

"Yeah." He smiled sadly and shook his head, looking away a moment. "I guess we do." He looked at me, into me, his eyes dancing like he wanted to tell me everything all at once and didn't know where to start. "Come here," he said, and waved for me to follow him to the stairs.

"How did you . . . with the lights?" I pointed up in the direction of that window.

"Oh, you know . . ." he said, sheepish. He held out his hand, watched it intently, and flames lit above his fingers as though they were candlewicks. Just as fast, he snuffed them out, closing his palm into a fist.

"Ohhh. Got it."

He walked halfway up the staircase and sat down, motioning for me to join him. A beam of light from outside fell across the step and made it one of the few spots where you could see at all. "This okay?" he asked. I nodded. "There's so much I have to tell you, Haven." He exhaled, as though the thought of it all overwhelmed him. He spoke into the space in front of us. "And I shouldn't be telling you any of it, which is why it's even more important for you to know."

My mind drifted through every memory I had of Lucian.

Yes, there was something muted about him, but if I had only ever known this version of him, I might have still thought he was plenty perfect. And then a new concern found its way into my heart: what did I look like to him? How did I compare to what he remembered about me? I felt like I had changed so much since last spring in Chicago. I was a different person. That night of the fire, the last night I had spent any real time with him, was the start of my becoming this new being.

He paused, his eyes locking on mine again, and then he said, in an easier tone, "It's good to see you."

"You too," I offered. But it didn't seem enough. I searched for something more, anything. "Though I feel sort of under-dressed. I didn't realize it was a black-tie affair."

"Oh, this." He looked down at his clothes and seemed embarrassed for a moment. "You get kind of frozen in time when you're sent back there . . ." I felt a pang that I had done that to him. "So I'm stuck in this tux until my penance is up." He slipped off his jacket and tossed it onto the railing.

"And when might that be?"

"That's what I need to talk to you about." He hung his head for a moment, the words trickling out slowly as though it might diminish their collective sting. "I don't know why it's got to be like this with us, Haven. For some reason our lives are intertwined." A mix of exhaustion and frustration darkened his face. "My life always comes with the threat of your death."

He must've seen my face go ashen.

"No! I don't mean now." He smiled widely, his hands up in surrender. I breathed a sigh of relief. "I'm not going to hurt you, I promise. And if it helps, I think you're the one who will ultimately be doing the hurting." He had lost me. But at least I felt like he hadn't brought me here to kill me, so that was something.

"Even so, your"—I searched for the right euphemism—"assignment . . . hasn't changed. You have to capture my soul or kill me whenever the powers that be see fit."

He closed his eyes for a moment, starting over. "Last time I hesitated, as you know, and I considered making the wrong choice. But I made the right one in the end," he said. He had helped me then. Rather than plot against me, he had sacrificed himself to let me win in my fight against his fellow demons. That's why he had paid so dearly. "And you remember . . ." I saw the pain in his eyes and thought of the promise I had made.

"I'll help you. Of course, I'll help you," I said, not making him ask.

His face softened in gratitude and surprise. "You'll fight them with me?"

"With you, for you, yes, I will," I said in the sure, clear voice of a business transaction. And for that moment, strengthened by the hope I saw reflected in his eyes, I felt capable of this. "I'll do all I can."

"To be honest, at the moment I don't even have a formal assignment. I suppose it's still true that if I were to . . . take your soul, your life," he whispered, disgust washing over him, "my power and authority, my status, would be reinstated." He paused. "But I'm not going to do that."

"Good. Thanks," I said, as lightly as I could muster.

"If they knew I was here, they would be subjecting me to even worse than . . ." He trailed off, shaking his head, not wanting to go down that path. "They wouldn't like it."

"So you're a double agent now."

"Yeah, I guess I am. I promise I'm on your side, Haven. Even if it's hard to believe, I'm going to tell you everything I know. The irony is that they don't fully trust me either, so there may be things going on that I'm not even aware of. They keep a lot from me now, about their intentions, the details of what's in the works. But together, I think we can figure it out."

"So, what now?" I wanted to believe everything he told me. I wanted him to break free from them. I had wanted him to do this before and he wasn't ready. Now that he was, I had to hope that I wouldn't let him down, that we wouldn't both be made to suffer if I failed.

"There's a transformation ritual. Friday night."

"What do you mean? Like the Outfit?" My mind flashed back to the formal ceremonies I had witnessed in Chicago.

"It's different. We weren't saints there, but here the Krewe, they're savages, the things they do. And they shape-shift—" The thought of that made me shudder, especially the concept of not knowing what I was fighting against. "I'm still trying to learn their other identities. And I—"

Something else occurred to me: "Wait, where do they do the rituals? Here in this house?"

"No, no, no, they don't come here. I would never let you come here if they did. They have their favorite spots. They do these rituals in the cemetery—"

"Saint Louis? I'm going," I said. There was too much to be learned. I had to.

"*No*," he said, his voice firm, scolding even. "Why would you want . . . *No*."

"If you want my help, then you have to let me do things my way," I countered, surprising even myself.

"I shouldn't have even told you where it was," he said almost to himself, angry.

"Friday night," I said matter-of-factly, as though entering it into my schedule. "I'll see you there."

"I don't want you going because I can't be there to keep an eye on you."

"What do you mean?"

"This . . . here . . . is the only place I can see you. Everywhere else I try to go or want to go, it's as if there are invisible shackles keeping me from getting very close. It's part of the punishment." He said the last part as though he were ashamed.

"Well, then I'll just have to go and report back to you."

He paused for a good long while, then finally: "I can't believe I'm dragging you into all of this." He sighed, quiet for a moment, looking up to the ceiling and then back at me. "I owe you, Haven. I owe you so much." I could hear in his voice just how much he was beating himself up.

"I don't know about that. We can call it even," I said with a soft smile.

"If it weren't for you, I wouldn't really have known that I should be breaking out of all this, I was so far gone."

"How are you surviving there? I mean, what is it like?"

"There's really no need to talk about it," he deflected my question. "It's what you would expect. The kinds of things you read about, the circles, the dazzling array of unpleasant ways to make the time pass." He tried to smile, but he must have seen the horror on my face. "But don't worry. I'm fine and I've found my ways to work the system."

He leaned into my line of vision, lifting my chin to look at him. I hoped I didn't have tears in my eyes, but I could feel the first seeds of them blooming.

"You didn't do anything wrong. You're the one getting me out of this. Don't say another word, okay? Okay?"

I nodded and looked away from those gray eyes I had missed more than I even realized.

"Honestly, you've got plenty to worry about already. Your plate is rather full," he said, trying to pull me out of my sadness. "Not sure if you've been paying attention, but it's about to get a lot worse around here." He tried to laugh. "Trust me, you'll be far too busy to even think of worrying about me."

I smiled.

"In fact," he continued, "if you're planning to worry about someone, start with Sabine. They're anxious for her to join and she's weakening. The Prince is hopeful. She's a powerful one. It would be a huge coup for them to get her."

"What am I supposed to do? How do I stop that?"

"Keep her on your radar as best you can. There's usually a little bit of time before they're officially taken, when you can still win them back, but it's a small window." He nodded with finality. "So that's all I've got right now. But it's a start." He grabbed my hand to look at my watch. "I should probably let you get back; it's late. I'm going to have to see you again soon, though, if that's okay. Yeah?" He stood up and walked a couple steps down. I followed.

"Yeah, sure."

"How about Saturday, same time and place?"

"It's a date," I said solemnly.

"It's a date," he repeated. "You know . . ." He shuffled down a couple more steps and stopped, the light filtering in from outside and framing him. "I'm glad you left your boyfriend at home," he said, just the right mix of flirtation and needling to keep me from getting too offended. "That guy is here all the time."

I matched his tone. "He works here. He's making it a pretty place for you to haunt." The mention of Lance brought back all the wrong memories of the evening. "And, anyway, things with us are . . . complicated." It was out of my mouth before I had time to stop it.

Lucian looked surprised and a little sorry to have taken this turn. "Well, then, it goes without saying, he must be insane," he said sincerely, as though apologizing to me on Lance's behalf. He took a step closer to me now. "It's the only possible explanation."

But I was lost in thought, running through all that had consumed me in the past couple of weeks: Was it me? What was wrong with me? Now I was feeling defensive. "Well, I mean, I . . . I don't know," I stammered, my fingers fidgeting. "I think it happens, right? And, you know, it's one of those—"

But I didn't get to finish. My words were snuffed out by Lucian's lips landing on mine. I stood one step above him, but he was still taller than me. He wound an arm around my waist and pulled me tightly to him, his other hand in my hair. It caught me so off-guard I felt my balance go. A head-in-the-clouds vertigo set in, butterflies and dizziness and a sense that I was floating. My feet didn't even feel rooted to the stairs anymore. My arms snaked around his neck to steady myself, every bit of me wanting to pull him closer. I backed up a step and ran into the wall but I didn't care. It all happened so fast that I couldn't catch my breath. I just let myself drown in him.

I had kissed him before, back at the Lexington, after that one date of ours, but it hadn't been like this. This was otherworldly, endless. All I knew for sure was that my body felt like it belonged here and had no desire to be anywhere else or doing anything else in the foreseeable future. Every time I feared he might be pulling away, his lips would simply land instead on my neck or at my collarbone, and then return to my mouth once more.

Finally, when it seemed like it had been hours but had probably just been many sweet, slow minutes, he did inch back. He was still so close, his arm looping around my waist. I loosened my grip on his neck, and then let my arms fall to a place behind me, against the wall. We had stumbled into a patch of total darkness between those slim ribbons of light.

"So what was I saying before?" I whispered.

He leaned into my ear. "I have no idea, but I'm sure it was very important."

"It'll come back to me," I said. And he gave me one more lingering kiss.

"I've been waiting months to do that," he said, his fingers still woven into my hair. It seemed unfathomable. I wanted to question his kiss—or, at the very least, make him repeat it—but I knew better. I tried to act like this wasn't as core-shaking as it was. I searched my mind for some sort of response, but came up short. I was too occupied trying to slow the runaway train that was my heart. Somewhere within, the silenced voice of reason broke through at last, telling me to go now, that the best time to leave had to be when you were feeling like this.

"So Saturday then?" I asked with a smile and then tried to move away. Still, it took a few seconds for him to disengage from me.

"Saturday," he repeated, punctuated with a kiss on my ear.

Slowly I slipped away, leaving him leaning against the banister. I had secretly hoped that he might watch me leave, a sign that he was still thinking of me even though our evening had come to an end. And as I pivoted to close the door behind me, I saw that he hadn't moved an inch.

I floated out into the street, but with each step closer to the house next door, I let go of what had just happened. I couldn't quite make sense of it. The courtyard was empty, thankfully. I felt rattled and turned my gaze up to the night sky, speckled with stars, in search of some calm. Peeking through the window near the entrance, I spied Emma and Brody inside, making their rounds, and decided it would be best to crawl back in what was left of my window. Before I did, I looked back up to the LaLaurie mansion, and it anticipated my thoughts: a light flared, stopping my heart. I contorted myself creeping through that glass jaw, managing to avoid the toothlike spikes still poking up at odd angles.

I had forgotten the state my room was in. The main level was strewn with broken bits of furniture, papers, clothes, and glass, but my loft was another story. My night table had been righted, my spilled belongings gathered up and returned to their drawers, my bed had been made . . . and Dante now lay tucked into it. His eyes opened immediately.

"I know you weren't in the levitation room all this time, so don't try to sell me that line," he said, not missing a beat. "You'd better tell me the truth." I could see from the way he looked at me he already knew.

There was no use lying. I flopped onto the bed, ashamed. "Lucian."

"Next door?"

I nodded.

"You can't do things like that, Hav!" He sat up, truly cross with me. "I'm not covering for you either. You're going to tell Connor and Lance. You can't trust that guy and you can't go running off into abandoned buildings looking for him."

"Not even if he told me some stuff that can help us all?"

"He probably endangers your life, like, ten times for every one good thing he does. What happened?" He studied me. I had to look away. "Ugh, I knew it. You kissed him, didn't you?"

"Well, I mean, he kissed me and I kissed him back. I think that's the order it happened in but I don't know." Now I was angry with myself. I felt unmoored. I didn't do things like this.

"I don't like this at all. Let the record show"—his tone was as firm as it had ever been with me—"that I'm trying to look out for you."

I hung my head. I knew he was right. I rubbed my hand over a slash mark on my comforter. "It was just, I don't know, a Pavlovian-dog response."

"What?" he spat.

"You know they ring the bell and the dog gets food and then after a while the dog feels hungry just hearing the bell because—"

"*Yes!*" he barked, annoyed. "I know what the Pavlovian-dog response is, but how could you have this with Lucian?"

"I don't know, I wasn't thinking. I saw him and we were talking and then it's like I just needed to be throwing myself at him or having him throw himself at me because that was, like, the state of mind I was used to being in around him." I sighed. "Look, it had been a pretty bad night." I thought for a moment. "Wait a second . . ."

"What?"

"Why did you come looking for me in the first place?"

Now Dante looked sorry. "To tell you Sabine's in our room. Again." He sighed. "I'm sorry, Hav. She came in earlier in the night and then she dozed off in there. That's it. She told Lance she feels safe there with him."

"That's a good one." I rolled my eyes. The pain from earlier was rearing up again.

"I know, total soap opera line, right? Playing the safe card. Please. He was asleep and she just sort of curled up on the edge of his bed, like a pet or something. He asked for you—"

"How thoughtful—"

"She told him you were in the levitation room. That's when I left, to find you. But he was telling her to go, so maybe she did." He looked at me. Neither of us considered that a possibility.

Dante told me to get some rest, that no good would come of fighting this out tonight, and, since he had a point, I told him he might as well stay. Needing little convincing, he curled up on Sabine's empty bed and drifted back to sleep. My eyelids, like my heart, felt leaden so I followed his advice. But first, I reached for that smartphone that had been returned to my bedside table. A new message flashed onto the screen:

As you can see from today's events, more of your powers are setting in. This will require you to graduate from some of the powers you enjoyed before, like the ability to destroy demons by attacking their photos, but only because you are gaining a much greater strength. Continue working and practicing these new abilities, and in time you will learn to control them. Until then, trust that they will rise to the surface when necessary. Grave challenges lie ahead. The days will only grow more difficult.

20

We Need to Focus

Lance and I both emerged from our rooms at precisely the same time the following morning, each of us wearing the same guilt-ridden expression of criminals.

He spoke first. "Hey, so, what happened to you last night? Practicing late?"

"Kind of." I hadn't fully committed to lying yet. But trying it out now, I didn't like the taste. "What about you? What did you end up doing?"

He danced around it. "Wait, did you get a message today?"

"Last night, but it wasn't all that groundbreaking."

"Because mine says that you and I have to go to the cemetery. Friday. Does that make any sense to you? Isn't that the night we overheard Clio telling that guy about a party?"

Caught. So fast. "Yeah, I do know what that's about actually." We started walking together. I focused my attention straight ahead. "It's the Krewe. They're doing some kind of ritual; we need to check it out," I explained.

"Wow, whoever's writing my messages is really slacking. I

didn't get any of that." He pulled out his phone, in case he had just missed something.

"No, I heard that somewhere else."

He held the front door for me as we stepped out onto the balcony.

"I heard from Lucian," I said, trying my best not to sound like I had done something wrong. He froze, though, staring at me, betrayed. I felt trapped. Brody ran out the door, right between us, munching on a Pop-Tart.

"See you over there, Lancealot!" He leapt over the balcony.

"What?" Lance's eyes were set on me, not even noticing Brody.

"He wants to help us against the Krewe. So he's going to tell us stuff—like about this ritual." It came out in jagged bits. "But in exchange, he wants help breaking free."

"And you're the person to do this?" Lance asked, appearing calm but there was an undercurrent of frustration running through his words.

"Yeah, I guess so," I said, steeling myself for the inevitable blowup.

He took a deep breath. "Haven." He said my name with such bite it sent a tremor through me. "We live in a house full of angels." His volume amped up, control slipping. "Are you telling me there is *no one* else who could take this on? We'll tell Connor."

"No. I can't outsource it," I said, angry now. "It has to be me. I'm the one who banished him, remember?"

"Whatever, Haven." He shook his head. "We'll talk later." He climbed onto the banister railing and stood above me.

"Good. Then I can ask you about your night with Sabine." I tried to steady my voice. Now he looked boxed in, as if the interrogation lamp hovering over me had swung to him.

"Great. Looking forward to it," he said, stone-faced as he leapt off.

"And I'll be looking forward to Friday," I said more to myself than him, since he had already stormed out of the gateway.

"What's Friday?" Connor ambled out the door, cereal bowl and spoon in his hand.

I told Connor what I had learned of the evening's plans and how I knew, but managed to omit the part about seeing Lucian in person. Still, he warned: "Be careful with this one. A source like that is useful but not if he gets us killed. Got it?" I would be spending the morning at the community garden again but he gave me the afternoon off from tutoring. "Case the cemetery today. Find the best hiding spots. You'll go in pairs Friday," he ordered.

I had a few minutes before meeting Dante, so I leapt down, landing on solid footing, and let myself out the gate to wait on the sidewalk. I couldn't resist roaming next door. Lance was in there now, brooding no doubt, but as I stood, staring down the place again, last night came flooding back. I felt a blush rise, coloring my cheeks. My eyes swept the porch, a last look before going, and noticed the window had been left open; beneath it, hiding under some scraps of wood, lay a bouquet.

Perfectly exotic and a variety I'd never seen, the luscious tropical blooms burst forth, each easily the size of my fist and boasting a shade of red so rich and bloodlike they appeared almost black. A delicate black ribbon had been tied in a bow around them and attached to it was a blinding white slip of paper burrowed in among the stems, marked *H*. With a quick look around to be sure no one noticed, I nestled the bouquet quickly into my backpack.

Showing tremendous self-restraint, I managed to wait until after our trip to the community garden to look at that note. When Dante and I parted—he set off to tutor—I made my way to the cemetery as Connor had instructed. There I pulled out all my painting supplies, for cover, and settled in, taking a seat behind one of the larger, more decrepit crypts far from the tourist attractions, before finally digging out the flowers. I unfolded the note, my pulse speeding up. In Lucian's precise hand, it read:

H—

A token of my gratitude. You are an angel. Truly.

Be careful this week. I regret that I can't be there with you Friday. I've learned it will begin at midnight. Arrive in advance, find a high, secluded perch in view of the back lawn, wait and watch. Until Saturday.

Yours,

L

I leaned against the tomb for support, my heartbeat pulsing in my chest as I read it through again. My scars tingled, and then my fingertips twitched where I held the note. I dropped it and backed up and sure enough, within seconds, the paper combusted. A flame crackled at my feet but before I could even decide whether to bravely stomp it out, it just flared up and turned to smoke, leaving no trace behind. Though I knew the flowers had probably been plucked straight from the underworld, I buried my face in their sweet fragrance and then set them back in my bag.

A second later, I heard a familiar voice from behind a nearby crypt, just down the alleyway.

"Why, hello, Haven." Sister Catherine appeared, hands folded before her and that delicate smile on her lips. "Just passing through. You're making lovely progress."

"Hi there. Thank you."

She didn't even stop; she just kept going.

I painted only until I could be sure she was gone, then I pulled out my camera and, because I couldn't resist preserving them, the flowers too. I found a waist-high tomb that seemed the perfect height. I positioned the flowers in front then I set the camera atop a crypt opposite it. Timer set, I hopped up on the tomb, posing with my legs dangling over the front of the stone. *Click.*

I checked my work—just fine—and under the guise of an amateur photographer with a camera in tow, I wandered, scoping out the likeliest hiding spots. My favorite: a mammoth circular crypt that rose to a point, as though wearing a hat. It seemed we could crouch behind that and probably get a fine view of the lawn.

I had already made it past the church and halfway across Rampart Street, the enflamed copper-hued winter sun dipping low into the horizon, when I realized I had left the flowers beside that grave. I turned around before my head had time to overrule my heart.

As I wound my way toward the front gate, I couldn't miss the scent of something burning. I ran, but I was too late: I found no more than a charred mass where the flowers had been, the last few embers flaming out. I watched what was left of those blackened blooms disintegrate until there was no trace left of them. I thought it might be intense disappointment that I felt burning my heart at that moment, even though it shouldn't have really made me all that upset.

Then it dawned on me: it was the burn of my scars that I felt. And they were so fiery that my legs took off into a jog through the empty cemetery to the exit. I turned the corner, my footsteps echoing in the quiet evening, and my heart stopped. The gate was now closed and locked. Scars stinging, I leapt up onto it to climb over.

But, just as quickly, I was swatted down.

Two hands ripped me off that gate with great force. A slender arm hooked around my neck, getting me in a chokehold as I kicked and squirmed, trying to breathe but unable to catch any air. My captor wasn't large; the person felt like my size in fact, but was unbelievably strong. My breathing was snuffed out so swiftly, my head felt like it might explode. I would have very little time before passing out. My eyes fixed on a small rock just ten feet away. I focused on it, and it lifted from the ground, smashing into whoever was holding me. The grip on me loosened just enough for me to get in a shallow breath and take two steps closer to the gate. I gasped and the arm tightened again but I summoned my last bit of energy. My legs took off, up the narrow bars, as though it were a wall, running straight up and then kicking off with enough quick, sharp power to break free from this chokehold. I would have flipped backwards, clear over my attacker, but when I launched myself back, suddenly there was no one there. I landed messily, nearly pitching myself onto my knees. But I was free and in one piece. I popped up in a fighting stance and spun around, checking in every direction. Nothing. And not a sound. No footsteps. My racing heart and aching neck were the only signs that I hadn't imagined the whole thing. My backpack had been thrown off in the struggle, so I grabbed it and tossed it over the gate.

Then I scurried up that metal barrier, throwing myself over

with such fierce strength I thought I might land clear in the street. Instead, I came down hard on the sidewalk pavement. I darted across the street without looking, dodging cars as I went.

It took me almost a block to realize ringing was coming from my backpack. I slowed my pace enough to pull my phone from the outside pocket. Dante.

"Dan, you won't believe—" I picked up, panting.

He just cut me off. "Did you get Lance's text?" he launched in, his voice chilling enough to literally stop me in my tracks.

"No, I . . . we—"

"They found a body outside the library," he said in a flat tone. "It was a student volunteer from one of the other houses."

I burst into my room. It had been put back together. We had a brand-new desk and a few new lamps. The window had been replaced. Everything felt in order again—except for me. I closed my eyes, trying to calm my rattled nerves. I dug my camera out of my bag, and grabbed the cord I needed. I retreated to the computer room and fired up my camera, loading the pictures taken in the cemetery and blowing each of them up to fill the monitor. I studied them, one by one, looking for any trace of someone lingering or loitering in the background today, waiting to attack me. But I found nothing, not even so much as a shadow.

Back in my room, I climbed up to my bed, texting Lance back— *I'm home. Come by when you're back*—and pulled out that stack of photos. Sabine's glow had definitely diminished. The others in our house all still seemed to be surrounded by a fairly strong light.

Within minutes, the door opened and Lance appeared, looking shell-shocked, like he'd just been through a war. He sat down at the desk, not a word. I crept down the ladder toward him.

"You okay?" I leaned against the ladder, hovering over him.

"Maybe you need some electrolytes?" I said to fill up the dead air. I climbed back up, shimmied under the bed, and pulled out a cherry Gatorade from my secret stash.

"It was in those bushes, the body, you know? Hidden back in there, sort of camouflaged. Some kid spotted the hand poking out," he said, looking through me instead of at me. "And he wasn't just dead, he was . . ." He shook his head, looking for the right words. "Mangled. Parts were missing. The guy had been filleted. I've never seen anything like this—and I've . . . we've seen a lot." It was true, we had. "That's three of them since we've been here, right?" I nodded, even though Lance wasn't looking at me anymore. "So there's no way these deaths are unrelated, right?" He leaned forward, elbows on his knees.

"Right, gotta be," I said, sighing. "I had kind of a crazy—" And was about to tell him about the afternoon I had had but he cut me off.

"Brody actually knew this guy," he launched in."His name was Jeff. We've seen him, those first couple nights?" He said it as a question, even though it wasn't one. I thought for a moment then climbed back up the ladder once more, grabbing the stack of photos and flipping through to some of the group shots. I pulled out the few taken from that bar on the same night I got shots of the Krewe. Lance took them from my hands and paged through until he found who he was looking for.

"This is him; this is Jeff."

I leaned in to a photo of Brody—glow surrounding him—talking with a group on the patio. I focused on the blurry Jeff in the background. He had dirty blond hair and a wrestler's build. He stood, hurricane in hand, laughing.

The door opened again: Sabine. She and I hadn't spoken since last night. She didn't even look at me.

"Lance, can I talk to you?" she said in a meek, helpless voice.

Lance glanced at me for the slightest second, then stood up. "Sure," he said, leaving my side without even a look back.

The next couple of days flew by, as they do when you're dreading the passage of time. Lance and I had barely spoken and so, not surprisingly, when Friday night arrived, our walk to the cemetery was marked by more painful silence. We had given ourselves ample time to get settled, leaving the house just before ten then breaking off from River and Tom, whom Connor had enlisted to keep watch with us. They would be positioned on the treetops overlooking the other side of that grassy expanse where Lucian had said the ceremony would take place.

I had finally managed to tell Lance about my run-in there earlier in the week and though concern had burned in his eyes, after he had asked if I had been hurt, he had quickly shifted to more incendiary conversation topics.

"So he's not going to be there tonight?" Lance asked as we reached Rampart Street, nearing the cemetery.

"Nope," I said, the frustration thick in my voice.

"Well, that's the best news I've heard all day."

I chewed on my lip and just let it go. I couldn't afford to expend energy fighting with him right now. I was already jumpy, too jittery at the idea of having to return to this place just days after someone or something attempted to make me a new resident of it.

A few cars whipped past us, speeding blurs of light, music pulsating. I could feel every nerve tensing as we got close. The shops near Mariette's had all closed up and switched off their lit signs; the church sat dark and empty, its spire now sinister-looking. The upshot of my few terse words with Lance had been that I now felt the anger coursing so strongly through me that I was almost looking forward to burning it off by scaling that giant tomb.

We made our way over the gate easily, familiar with it now.

"I didn't get to look around last time," he whispered, as if issuing a détente, as he ran his fingers along the chipped façade of one of the tombs. He stopped before a smooth, white pyramid-shaped crypt. "No two look alike here." He petted it like it was a large animal at rest. It had to be at least nine feet tall and seemed to shine, reflecting and amplifying what little light there was.

"Yeah, they're like snowflakes. That's a good one. I think there are only two people in that huge thing." He moved his hand away, as though he might be leaning on a body. "It's okay. We're not bothering them." I smiled, though I felt hollow and joyless.

"So these are all pretty shallow, none of that six-feet-under stuff? Too swampy, right?" He bent down to touch the gravelly ground and expected it to be wet.

"Yeah. I guess people get buried in here and after, like, a year they take 'em back out and burn what's left and then they shove their remains back in there."

"Nice use of space," he observed.

"Yeah, it's pretty economical. They can jam whole families into some of these." I trained my pocket-size flashlight on the darkened path ahead of us and led the way between a series of crypts about my height. Eventually the alley opened up and we came out at that circular marble monolith, at least sixteen feet tall, a sleeping giant in the darkness. A carved arch in the center housed a statue of a woman in draped dress who appeared to be keeping watch over the whole cemetery. Lance walked the perimeter, checking it out from every side.

A filing cabinet for dead people, it probably housed dozens and dozens of bodies. Around the entire circumference, neat rows and columns of rectangles had been precisely spaced out. Each appeared to be large enough for a casket to slide in and all were decorated with a door-knocker type of handle.

"I've got a good idea," Lance said, arms folded across his chest, sizing up this beast.

"Use the handles as footholds and climb and swing up on them?" I proposed.

He looked at me as though he'd just set up a joke and I gave the punch line. "Yeah, actually."

We scoped out our targets: we would ascend columns on either side of where the sculptured woman sat.

On my first try, I crashed, falling so fast and hitting the earth with enough force to kick up a cloud of dust. I landed on my side. Everything from my right shoulder to my right foot felt like it had been flattened.

But my muscles would have to ache later. We powered through, and by 11:45, we had both reached the top, dragging ourselves up at nearly the same moment. That was how Lance and I were: every time one of us figured out how to conquer something, the other one couldn't help but shift into overdrive to master it too. We were equally matched in skill and strength and ambition. I felt a pang of regret to think about that now, when we otherwise seemed to be so terribly out of sync. We lay on the lumpy stucco of the tomb's upper reaches, catching our breath. I stared into the opaque sky, no stars penetrating through tonight but just a sliver of the moon. We could see over the few nearby rows of graves, straight through to the lawn area blanketed by the soft glow of the security lights. Lance shook his wrist, straightening his watch for a good look. "Fifteen minutes to spare. Not bad."

We settled into place, crouching behind the small dome that the unknown saint was perched upon. This felt like us; we were in our element. I wasn't sure if it was the adrenaline or the time alone with Lance, listening to his breathing in the darkness, or if I was just feeling a little bit more myself again, but I wanted to set things right with him.

"Listen," I started. "About earlier this week and . . . everything." My voice, whispering, carried with it the white flag of disarmament. "I'm sorry. Things have been a little . . . out of control, right?"

"Yeah," came his soft voice, finally. "I know. It's been a lot. I think we need to focus for the next couple weeks or months, or whatever, while this is going on."

"Focus . . ." I repeated, gauging where this was headed.

"Right. On, you know, not getting killed?"

"Of course. Yeah."

"And maybe forget the extracurricular . . . stuff."

I sensed it, this turn, and the feeling settled in my stomach, making me ill. No. I wasn't going to let this happen to me. "The drama. Right."

"Right."

"So we should just kind of . . ." I was searching for the word; I didn't want to say it but I really didn't want it said to me. Those being my only two choices, I went ahead as though we were in some kind of awful agreement. "Pause?"

"Pause. Exactly," he said, sighing, as though he had put a bookmark in and closed up this chapter of us. "And then you know, figure stuff out afterward."

"After the whole survival thing is resolved?"

"Yeah. Okay?" He looked at me for the first time in this whole exchange and it was so quick, no more than a courtesy. But at least then he couldn't see the mist in my eyes. I was grateful for the darkness.

What choice did I have? I nodded, steadying my voice. "Sure, it's better than trying to multitask right now."

"Hey," he said now, even quieter. "Do you hear that?"

I hadn't. I had to struggle to turn up the volume on the rest of the world, on the things I needed to pay attention to in order to continue living and breathing. But right now I didn't feel like I was doing either of those.

I had been hurt that night I kissed Lucian. Part of it may have been a secret thrill, I suppose, but a larger part was surely retaliation. I didn't want *this* to happen. Lance felt so far away from me, like he wasn't mine. And now all the good flooded back. Escaping the flames of the Lexington together, that kiss in the alley after we survived. Or even here, before we became so engrossed in the madness of this place. I didn't understand when or how this slipping away had happened. I wish I had asked, but how do you ask something like that? And is it worth it when the answer won't change the outcome?

But this much was certain: I didn't want him if he didn't want me. I deserved to be wanted, didn't I? I wasn't going to convince someone to be in love with me. Much as it hurt, I had too much pride for that. And I couldn't afford to feel so weak in my relationship at a time when I needed to be so physically strong in order to live. To guard my soul, I had to first guard my heart and my mind.

And so right now, I would have to be strong. I would have to tuck Lance and all of this away somewhere deep inside. I needed to be fully awake and alive to absorb whatever it was that was about to unfold before us on this cruel night.

21

The First of Many Soul Captures

A t midnight on the dot, we heard the first sounds of stir-
ring below: footsteps, so faint, falling like a soft rain. We
had been leaning against that pedestal and now we sat straight
up, attuned to every noise and movement, even though so much
remained shrouded in darkness.

Within minutes, they started trickling in, coming from every
direction. Some dropped over the walls of the cemetery, alight-
ing to the ground gracefully. But many others crept out of the
crypts. I heard the slow scrape of rock against rock and felt the
slightest vibration from beneath where we sat. I looked to Lance,
who wore the same confused expression. A few seconds later, I
spotted one of them directly below us: he had emerged from this
very tomb. A shiver swept over me.

There were at least two dozen of them in all, floating over to
the lawn area silently, as though everyone knew his or her role
and performed it effortlessly, the cogs in a perfect machine. They
abandoned their shoes in neat rows, like parked cars. They peeled
off layers of street clothes so that the women were left in either
white dresses—from long flowy ones to short wispy ones—or tank

tops and camisoles with skirts. The men wore white T-shirts and white linen pants. Everyone's attire shared a looseness, beachlike and free. As a whole, the group had an incandescence, their clothes picking up what light there was and reflecting it at a higher wattage. Two men laid out a woven tapestry in a swirling array of colors that glittered even in the dim haze. It stretched nearly the entire length of the lawn, roughly the size of a tennis court. A pair of barefoot girls in billowing skirts and tank tops knotted up above their navels set candles out along all four sides, the dancing flames fencing it in.

From the darkness came a drumbeat, and then a long, low hum, so soft at first I thought I had imagined it, until it grew louder, stronger, more guttural as the beats echoed with greater force. Below, everyone stood perfectly still surrounding that tapestry, then slowly began swaying, raising their hands, as the hum evolved into a chant, though the words weren't in any language I had ever heard. Another drum sounded in the distance, playing a game of call and response. Slowly all the bodies turned to face the direction of this drum. Lance and I craned our necks trying to find the mysterious source of this sound.

The man with a drum stood beside a tall, boxy crypt at the far end of the cemetery, with a straight path to the gathering. It was one of the crypts that I had recently painted. Slowly the passageway in front slid open and a cloaked figure emerged. Only delicate ivory hands and feet were exposed beneath the gauzy black floor-length covering, sheer enough to reveal her knee-length black slipdress underneath. A hood concealed her head and face. She glided, accompanied by the drum, to that spot where they all stood waiting for her, chanting to welcome her. The closer she got, the faster the tempo of the chanting became. As she approached the group, those lined up closest to her split their chain in half and moved with such precise coordination it looked like two sides of a gate opening. All the while, they swayed and clapped and waved their hands in the air, keeping their music going.

With ethereal poise, she passed through them onto the candlelit tapestry. The human gate closed, reuniting the chain of revelers, as the hooded woman took her place at its dead center. As she settled into that space, the abstract patterns of the silky lawn covering glowed red and transformed into a mammoth pentagram around where she stood. It looked as though embers had risen up from the ground, singeing this symbol into the material.

Her drummer joined the chanting masses, and the woman slowly raised her arms up into the sky as though conducting all these unified voices. She stood frozen there for a few seconds, then, she spun around slowly, then fast, faster, spinning and spinning until she leapt out of her spin and launched into a dance. The layers of her draping cloak trailed behind her movements, like a shadow, as she pranced and whirled across the entire space, filling it up with her motions. Arms waving in grand and graceful sweeps, legs kicking and swooping into the air, she leaned and swayed, carried away by the music. I couldn't look away. I was aware of nothing but her until stinging waves washed over my scars. Every few moments they would dissipate only to flare again. I tapped at that spot above my heart and then felt for my charm necklace as though grasping those pieces of metal could soothe anything.

The chanting picked up into a frenzy of clapping and foot stomping. The hooded woman began spinning once more, this time ending as abruptly as the music did, back in the center of that tapestry. The silence came so suddenly, it made my heart lurch. I felt as if I had been the one dancing and needed to catch my own breath. I imagined this was how everyone on that lawn felt, as if she had tapped into each of them and was living this out on their behalf, taking them with her through her movements.

Through it all, somehow, her cloak had managed to stay put, that hood never exposing her face. But now she carefully unfastened the ties in front and held out her arms straight on either side of her. As she stood there, without a word, two women stepped forward out of the line. Flanking her, they delicately pulled down the hood and slid off the sheer drape, taking it away.

It was Clio, barefoot in her slim dress, gazing at her loyal subjects. The light shimmered off her skin. She said something I couldn't understand, arms outstretched toward those in front of her. I noticed now that the fleur-de-lis tattoo on her wrist burned bright, glowing to a crimson shade, as though it had been newly branded by a hot iron, matching the pentagram on the ground. The entire group answered her with another mysterious word. Then, as if that had been the cue, several of the onlookers stepped forward, placing ceramic bowls and urns of all shapes and sizes around her in a circle and then sitting at her feet. I didn't know where they had gotten these, but it must've happened while I had been transfixed by her dancing. It worried me that I had managed to get so swept up that I had stopped paying such close attention to the full picture. There was something hypnotic about these proceedings. I looked at Lance out of the corner of my eye and wondered if he was thinking the same thing.

At last, Clio spoke and in words we could understand.

"Welcome, *mes chéries*," she cooed, in a slow, sweet voice. "We have been harvesting for weeks, far and wide, around our fair city and its surroundings, as you know. We have been cultivating much-needed ingredients from the strongest of sources: the recently departed." That phrase gnawed at my mind—did that mean what it sounded like? But she went on and I had to listen. "It is from these glorious building blocks that we are synthesizing some particularly potent toxins, as we speak."

She held her arms out toward the urns at her feet and one by one, beginning with the woman seated directly in front of her, each pulled out whatever lay inside the vessels. First came a bone—it didn't look like one of Mariette's, but more substantial . . . human. Another produced scraps of clothing. A few had small jars of a dark liquid that I knew, even from where I sat, had to be blood. Some had jewelry—one bearing a ring that still had a finger attached, which was so gruesome I had to look away. Another had an ear. And the last held a blood-splattered baseball cap. At that, Lance averted his eyes and found mine. He leaned toward me. "Jeff. That was Jeff's," he whispered in a shaky voice. "It was in your photo." He shook his head. When all of these items had been presented and displayed, those manning the urns slipped back into their spots in line.

Clio went on: "We will be able to take many souls in the coming weeks, if we all do our part. We should have plenty to boast about when we make the pilgrimage to see our brothers and sisters of Père-Lachaise." Père-Lachaise. I turned it over in my mind. Yes, I knew it. From AP French. Paris. It was a cemetery there. Full of artists and writers and even a rock star or two, if I recalled. I tucked it away for now and kept listening. ". . . and so tonight we celebrate the first of what will be many soul captures." She dragged out the phrase, letting its importance linger in the air.

She then gestured to those along the tapestry edge to her right, holding out that elegant arm to summon with the slightest flick of the wrist. "Come, my lovely," she said. The line parted and a guy stepped forward, serene and dreamlike, floating toward her. He wasn't dressed in white garb, though. Instead he wore his street clothes. Which I recognized. Even from this distance I knew him: Jimmy. He looked just as he had when he had burst into my room. The wild hair, the torn shirt and worn jeans. He seemed completely entranced. His gaze never left Clio's face. He stopped beside her.

"Today we are privileged to be welcoming someone new to our fold. We expect great things," she said. Jimmy didn't quite look like anything was registering. A man came forward from the back row and on bended knee presented Clio with a black satin bag. It was Wylie. She took it from him with both hands, as though it was something sacred.

Beginning with the bone directly in front of her, she used nothing more than her index finger to slice off the slimmest sliver and place it in the bag. She made her way around, taking bits of each ingredient, pouring in a few trickles from the jars of blood, until she had each item represented in her bag. She gave it a shake, then put both hands around it until the bag glowed red. Reaching inside, she pulled out an incandescent scarlet orb the size of a baseball. The bag fell to the ground and she held one hand out, fingers fanned, focusing her eyes on part of the burning pentagram symbol closest to her. It grew brighter and brighter, then the flame kicked up, rising to meet her hand. She held the orb in both hands again and the blaze licked at her, turning her hands and the ball itself a fiery orange. Finally, she pulled away and held a handful of molten ash. With a master craftsman's careful fingers, she molded the fireball into a sharp point, like an ice pick.

She nodded to Jimmy and he obediently took off his shirt and turned around, his back to us now. Even from so far away, I saw those scars, stubbornly embedded, the ones all of us angels in training had across our shoulder blades. Those marred patches of flesh awaited something so lofty and divine and beautiful, if we could only get to that point in time: wings. Clio lifted the sharp stake into the air, its point twinkling like a diamond. Then her arm swooped down. In two sharp swipes, Clio slashed at each of those scars. *Whoosh. Whoosh.* It sounded like the feedback from a microphone. Jimmy's back arched at the pain, but you could see, even from here, the muscles tensing, trying to fight it off, and he quickly straightened out. Two slash marks, black and thick, oozed from his shoulder blades now. Beneath them, those scars bubbled and sizzled and then, in seconds, evaporated. It happened so fast I thought I had missed something. His back became an entirely smooth canvas, his rippled muscles the only texture. But when he turned around, he wasn't Jimmy anymore. He was that other figure, that blond man I had seen flashes of as I had fought him in my room. Lance leaned forward, crouching now, anything to get a better look. I touched his arm.

"You saw that too, then?" I whispered.

He nodded, his lips pursed.

Clio gave the slightest bow. I worried things were wrapping up before I'd had a chance to really mentally record it all. I scanned those figures surrounding her. Who were all these people? Where had they come from? As my eyes passed over them, I caught a few familiar faces clustered near Wylie, the handful of his Krewe cohorts I'd seen in my photos.

Clio kissed Jimmy on the forehead and handed him the weapon that had done her dirty work, transforming him. "Now we thank the great Prince for the powers he has bestowed upon us for our service." He held it up into the sky as she clapped her hands three times and the women who had presented the ingredients returned to retrieve them. The group stood in a circle surrounding Clio and Jimmy. Clio clapped twice more and now everyone flowed onto the tapestry with her. The drums sounded again, beating another spirited rhythm. The women with the urns held them above their heads, waving them in the air, moving to the beat as the whole group began dancing. They hopped and skipped and threw themselves around, so free. Some danced together, while others were in their own worlds. Some of the men pulled off their shirts, tossing them to the side. The women with the long dresses lifted them up to their knees and thighs as they moved. Clio remained at the center of the tapestry with her new recruit, dancing with him, the others leaving a ring of space around them, reverentially.

It should have looked like chaos, but there was something intoxicating about the freeness of it all. A primal, tribal wave swept that space and traveled as a current in the air. I felt my tensed muscles loosen, my posture ease, my mind let up from its racing and its fears as I watched. The dancers' skin glistened with sweat and their clothing clung to them now, but none of them seemed to mind. All that seemed to matter to them was this need to move to those resounding beats. I could feel them thumping in my heart. I looked at Lance leaning against the pedestal, watching intently.

It's hard to say how long it went on. The night felt endless, and yet, when the drummers drifted slowly off that mat and others began to follow, it seemed too soon. The drums played on as everyone collected any items they had left along the periphery. A handful of them helped fold up the tapestry, moving with such coordination the process almost looked like a choreographed dance itself.

Once that task had been completed, the drummers began

their recessional, leading the group through the cemetery. Along the way, several peeled off to slither inside a tomb, then seal it back up. The group snaked around near our perch and Lance and I crouched behind the pedestal, so still that neither of us was breathing. That man who had crept out from here earlier left the group and pried open one of the casket vaults to return. I didn't dare move or breathe until I heard the heavy marble slide back into place as the winding tail of the group traveled on farther. The members of that core group we knew as the Krewe's leaders hung back, Jimmy among them, with Clio at the very end of the line. They reached the part of the wall nearest to us and a few scaled it.

Wylie scooped up the woman beside him in one arm and scurried up the wall, clutching her tightly. When he reached the top, Clio stopped in her tracks, looking up.

"Wylie," she called, her voice so soothing. He paused and took a seat atop the wall with the girl on his lap, her long arms wound around his neck. She wore a slinky white dress and certainly hadn't been standing along the edge of that tapestry—I would have noticed. Maybe she had been in the shadows somewhere observing it all quietly. Even from here, I could tell from her lethargy and how she hung on him that she was in some kind of trance.

"Yes, love?" Wylie called down to Clio, flirtatiously.

"I believe there's someone who would love to meet her," Clio said purring.

"So soon?"

"Trust me."

"Lucky us," he said sincerely. He looked into the girl's eyes, brushing the long golden brown hair from her face. She barely moved; she just beamed at him dreamily. "We're taking a field trip, my sweet," he said, planting a kiss on her lips. She nodded and smiled, clinging even more tightly to him. He swooped back down the wall, landing lightly on his feet. He set her down, but kept one arm around her, pulling her close as they walked now. "Just so you know, we should probably make it quick," he said to Clio. "I think the toxins will soon be wearing off." The girl's head lolled forward, as if she were drunk.

"We'll be fast," Clio promised. "But it will absolutely make his night. And besides, you know you're going to love taking credit," she teased him, squeezing his arm. She flitted down into that crypt from which she had emerged earlier.

"You know just what to say, don't you?" he said, helping the girl inside, then climbing in himself. In seconds, the passage sealed up behind them all as though it had never been disturbed in the first place.

It gave me a chill. I knew where they were taking her.

Lance and I neither spoke nor moved for several minutes. It seemed like we both wanted to be sure they had all been sufficiently swallowed up into their respective portals to the underworld before we dared to do anything that would put us at risk for being detected. But when it finally felt safe to speak, I didn't know where to begin. There was so much to sift through, so much jumbled in my mind. So much I couldn't make sense of.

"I guess Wylie's got someone new. I wonder if Sabine knows," I said.

"Why would she care?" he snapped, his voice attacking me like a blunt object. "She's done with him. She knows what he is." It stung to see Lance so upset about her.

"I don't know. I told her to stay away from him. Connor told her too. She wasn't thrilled with us; that's all I'm saying." He wasn't looking at me. He sat with his elbows perched on his knees, playing with a leaf, peeling it into tiny pieces. I went on: "Do you really not remember how hard it is to get someone out from under the spell of these . . . these creatures?"

"Of course, I remember," he said bitterly, shooting daggers at me. "Tell me again about that note from Lucian."

I was seething now. It built up in me and I knew I had to try to stifle it or I would explode and make this so much worse. I was ready for this night to be over. "I was talking about Dante, but whatever."

By the time he finally spoke again he had cooled down just enough. "Well, we're going to have to do something. This is only gonna get worse. I don't know what they did to Jimmy, but it seems like they intend to do more of it."

We went straight to Connor's room when we got home and found River and Tom already inside debriefing him.

"That was some messed-up stuff," River said as we walked in.

We filled in what few blanks there were, earned a "Good job, team" from Connor, then all filed out. I was too worked up to go back to my room so I followed River and Tom out to the courtyard, where the three of us recounted the night's events, taking comfort in the shared horror of what we'd seen. Lance opted to stay inside. He and I didn't even say good night to each other.

When I finally went to bed, my room was dark, and Sabine was nestled in her bed, asleep.

I awoke the next morning from such a deep sleep that I wasn't sure where I was when my eyes opened. My dreams had been wild and freewheeling, populated by those characters I'd watched in the cemetery. But instead of Clio at the center of that tapestry dancing and leading her group, commanding all those eyes, it was me. What seemed the worst about this dream was that it wasn't a nightmare. It should have been. After what I'd witnessed last night, I had braced myself for waking up in a cold sweat, being scared to even let my eyes close. And instead, to have found my subconscious plucking out some part of that experience and twisting it into any sort of pleasant dream was terrifying.

I let my arm drop over the edge of the bed, like a dead tree branch, and fished around in my bag blindly until I found the cool, hard shell of my phone. I brought it to life and, as expected, found a new message waiting. The latest directive filled the screen:

Last night was no doubt eye-opening. You may have not even fully realized how much you learned. What may be most important is the feeling it evoked. That is the strength of this group—they can infatuate and entice like no other. This is how they operate—in a visceral, emotional way that can catch a person off-guard and then seize them before it has even occurred to them to fight back. This realm is less intellectual than what you encountered in Chicago and more physical. You may not be able to think and reason your way through —you will have to feel your way. It may very well be a more formidable fight than before. That's why this is the second of the tests. It gets more difficult.

I turned it over in my mind: I wasn't entirely sure what that meant right now, but I didn't like the notion that this thing was telling me flat out to expect a tougher battle. I had barely made it out alive the last time.

Part Three

≈ 22 ≈

We're All Winners

Dante and I spent much of Saturday strolling the city together, camping out in the courtyard of a coffeehouse.

"Dan, I'm so impressed you've got such a classic date night ahead of you," I said, picking a pecan from a praline the size of a hockey puck. Ever the thoughtful friend, he had shown tremendous restraint, barely mentioning it, since he knew my romantic status had deteriorated quite literally overnight.

"I know, right? Dinner and a movie. And you won't believe it, but I totally let Max make the reservations," he said, proud of himself.

"Wow! You must really like him to give up control of your dinner location."

"You know what?" He stirred his iced coffee and looked up, whispering, "I really do. Like, so much." He stopped for a minute, sighing. "And, as for him, I know it's probably just that gris-gris bag at work, but I'm having so much fun I almost don't care."

"Hey, now," I comforted him. "I actually don't think there's any extra magic going on. I think it's you."

He thought for a moment. "Thanks for that, Hav," he said, sincerely. Then, in his gentlest tone: "So, are you and Lance really . . ."

I exhaled. "I don't know what's going on. We're taking a 'pause.' "

"Are you going to Sabine's group thing tonight? That concert or show or whatever?" He rolled his eyes dismissing it, which I appreciated. She had organized some sort of outing—inviting me as though things were actually normal between us—that I had been pleasantly noncommittal about all week. Now I shook my head. I didn't want to tell Dante about Lucian. I knew what he would say; I knew that I probably shouldn't be seeing him at all, but I couldn't help it. Something just pulled me to him. Even though, deep in my heart, I still wasn't sure what to think of all this, or what had happened when I saw him. That kiss shouldn't have happened; it was just too sudden for me to properly process then. I couldn't help but wonder if that would happen again tonight. Or perhaps it had just been a case of him being so relieved to hear that I had agreed to help him, as I had pledged to do. I thought the latter, to be honest, which might be for the best.

I smiled at Dante. "Promise to give me a full report on your date, so I can live vicariously?"

"Of course!" He didn't say another word about Lance all day.

That evening I stayed tucked in my room alternating between reading my collection of Robert Louis Stevenson short stories and levitating it (it flew from the desk up to me on my bed, its covers like wings, and connected with my outstretched palm with such a hard slap, I had to shake out my hurt hand) as Sabine primped and filed out with her group. I thought of going, but I just couldn't bear to see her and Lance in such close proximity to each other now that he was no longer tethered to me. Instead, when I had had enough levitation for one day, I convinced Drew to help me pop copious amounts of popcorn and settle into the common room to cue up a mini-marathon of chick flicks. At one point Connor strolled by on his way to the kitchen and stopped, watching for a moment, then plopped down on the sofa between the two of us for the rest of the film, falling victim to the charms of an assuredly happy ending.

We were finished long before midnight, and at 11:57, I stood on the doorstep of the LaLaurie mansion, the streetlamps casting a dim glow on the porch. Hand perched on the doorknob, I took a deep breath, adjusted my sweater, and turned the handle to let myself in.

Locked.

I rattled it, shaking the door in its frame, but it didn't budge. Peeking through the windows, I saw nothing more than inky darkness and the reflection of the lamplight in the glass. I knocked. And knocked and knocked, but there was no response. Finally, I tried the windows and found one stuck but unlocked at least. With just a little struggling, I managed to push it up enough to slither through, getting dirty and dusty.

The darkness of the foyer engulfed me. I stepped forward into it, feeling my way. "Hello?" I called out, getting no response. With the help of the streetlight filtering in, my eyes adjusted, and I noticed the place was somehow nearly finished. Light fixtures dotted the walls—they were inoperable, with tangles of wires exposed. The second-floor landing was complete and it looked like there were actual rooms up there, as well as a staircase leading up to the top floor, it's freshly polished banister gleaming even in such low light.

I took the creaky stairs up to the second floor and rather than explore there, I continued on to the third floor. "Hello?" I tried a couple of times but got no answer. Moonlight poured in through the windows of the top floor, casting a glow but still leaving many corners dark. The space was just one big open room, a great place for entertaining, with its sparkling hardwood floors and high ceiling. I tried once more: "Are you here?"

"Are you looking for me?" I heard from the shadows. It wasn't Lucian's voice. I stepped back toward the darkness of the staircase as he stepped forward: Wylie. My blood turned cold in my veins. And then I ran down the staircase, stumbling in the dark and nearly tripping down the whole flight to the foyer. Behind me I could hear his footsteps. I fumbled with the lock at the front door finally opening it before he came into view, and I flew out into the street sprinting so fast my legs throbbed. I glanced back over my shoulder but no one was there. He hadn't followed me.

I didn't stop running until I was safely back in my room. But Sabine hadn't returned yet and being alone there hardly felt comforting.

On my way to the common room, intending to watch TV until my heart stopped racing, I knocked on Dante's door, just in case. It opened up; I had never been so happy to see him.

"Wow, you really do want the scoop. I just got home, like, two minutes ago!"

I invited myself in, curling up on Lance's bed, my nerves still jittery. "Tell me everything." He hopped up next to me, lying back to look at the ceiling.

"So, I won't leave you in suspense: we had that awkward end-of-date moment where someone has to make a move, you know? So no smooch. *But* the date was a-maz-ing," he said. "So, first on our way to dinner . . ." The sound of Dante's voice was so comforting and the subject matter such a pleasant departure from everything on my mind that I felt my nerves begin to settle at last and lost myself in the details of his night out.

We were awakened, unexpectedly, the following morning at three o'clock. I had finally fallen asleep despite the sound of Sabine's group talking spiritedly in the courtyard below. I had crept to the window only once and found Lance and Sabine seated on the chaise talking. It had been that simple, that innocent, but it had made me feel sick nonetheless.

Connor herded us up in the van and we nestled in for a long ride, expecting we might be making a return trip to the swamp. Instead, we pulled to a stop only minutes later at a dock along the Mississippi, not far from the Riverwalk where Sabine and I had sat and watched the ships pass. A steamboat reading NATCHEZ in giant letters along its side loomed there now in the darkness, its giant form in silhouette as it slept. The river looked like ink at this hour, lapping softly against that wheeled monster.

We stood at the dock in the cool morning air. A man walked past us, averting his eyes but giving Connor a nod as he boarded the boat and made his way to the captain's quarters. He looked familiar; I remembered him from the Superdome.

"Who is that guy?" I whispered to Dante.

"Facilitator," Connor, overhearing me, said in a clipped, all-business tone. "He handles logistics, so that I can handle you all. Like a getaway car driver. You never saw him." And we never mentioned him again. Connor paced before us now.

"The steamboat races are a big deal around here," he barked out. "So we're doing our own sort of race this morning. And there's a catch, folks. You're going to be turning the wheel to propel this boat."

Lance's hand shot up. "I thought that the mechanics of the steam engine would make it impossible to—"

"Lance, I love it. Whatever you're about to say, I know you're right. But the point of this exercise is to show you guys how strong you can be when you toss aside your fear. Could you theoretically get crushed by the wheel? Sure. But y'all aren't going to die, so you gotta get in there and figure out how to manipulate a situation where you have an incredible amount of force and discomfort coming at you and be able to fight against it. You're gonna be on two teams. Each team is gonna take the boat out to that bridge—the Crescent City Connection—and loop back. I'll start it moving at a low speed, so you can get a feel for what you'll need to do to keep it going, but then I'm cutting the power and it's all you working that wheel and keeping the momentum going. I'll give it another blast when we make the turn. The team with the fastest time gets bragging rights and my utmost respect."

I got put on a team with Dante, Brody, Drew, and River. Connor led us onboard, getting our opponents settled on one of the upper decks overlooking the paddle wheel, then taking us onto the lowest deck to a place I imagined passengers didn't usually get to explore. We followed him all the way to the stern, where the pathway split and narrowed, framing that imposing wheel, which must've reached up a dozen feet from the water's surface and a good twenty-five feet across.

Connor was explaining how the paddle worked to propel the boat and how we would need to accomplish this feat ourselves. As the wheel moved forward, its giant horizontal slats would cut through the water. The more I studied them, the more those paddles, equally spaced about four feet from each other across the wheel, began to take on the look of a motorized ladder.

"So if we position ourselves here sort of standing up on one rung and holding another above it"—I gestured to the side of the wheel nearest us—"and then we move like we're climbing up those slats with enough force, jumping off and pulling up, then theoretically we should be able to move?" I proposed to our group, working it out aloud. It was exactly the kind of conversation I would've loved to have had with Lance. I could imagine him upstairs already thinking about the physics behind this challenge.

"Totally, right?" Brody seconded, staring down that wheel. "We just need to throw our weight around, make the wheel spin. This is gonna rock." He shrugged, as if this simplistic strategy made perfect sense, and earned nods of agreement from our teammates.

Connor had hung back listening but not participating, when Sabine called his name. She had found her way down from the upper deck and pulled Connor aside, out of earshot. Even in the darkness, I could see how frantic she was, hopping from one foot to the other, hand on her forehead, her mouth set in a pained grimace. His arms folded, he looked away, seemingly unsympathetic. She tugged on his sleeve, pleading. I figured she would do just about anything to avoid getting in the water. After a moment, he sighed and then gave what looked like a reluctant nod. She jumped up and down in appreciation, following him as he walked back toward us. I could just make out what he said as he neared: "You can stay up top and watch but next time I'll expect you to get in there." She thanked him and turned around, prancing back upstairs.

"Okay, guys, we're gonna get started. Time to get on that wheel. Rolling out in five!" he called. Four of us traded looks. Brody was the first to climb onto the metal guardrail and reach out to those narrow beams along the side of the wheel. With cautious agility, we crept out, taking our places on the slats of the enormous wheel. We stood there, our backs to the boat, as we looked into the wheel's steel inner workings. My limbs trembled. Any moment this boat would begin to move and we would be forced to throw our bodies at this wheel to keep up with it. Success seemed unfathomable on such a slick, slippery mechanism. We would likely lose our footing as soon as the vessel pulled out and fall into the river to be batted around as the wheel rolled over the top of us. We probably wouldn't die, but we could surely come close.

The five of us stood gripping our arms around the oak plank above our heads, our toes curling to remain steady on the one below us. The whistle sounded, blowing a burst of steam into the sky. I could feel vibrations as I held on so tight I thought I might lose circulation in my arms. At once the boat set off with a lurch, the wheel jerking us down faster than I expected. My stomach fell. I heard a few screams, but was too shaken to tell whether my voice had been among them. The motion, slow as it was, submerged us knee-deep instantly. We scrambled up, water flying so we couldn't see where the surface of the river stopped and the air began.

I launched myself on the slippery planklike paddle, the tactic we had all discussed. My arms and legs burning, I shot up to the next paddle as fast as I could before being smacked back into the water, holding on to the support beams on either side of me. There was barely enough time to recover from one leap when I needed to do it again just to keep from being yanked underwater. Slowly I got ahead, making my way up that slick paddle wheel, back where we had begun, where it was easier to breathe. Brody was up there already, an animal, seemingly able to accomplish this effortlessly. I was glad to have worn my running leggings and not jeans. As I jumped, I glanced quickly to my side. Dante was still holding on but Drew had been bucked off and River, engaged in a wild dance of flailing arms and legs, was struggling.

We were strong, though, picking up speed now. The idea of what we were managing to accomplish made me want to push even harder. I felt my limbs figuring it out, getting into a rhythm. As the boat's power slowed, I had the sense of ours revving up: my muscles registered the satisfaction of forward motion, the results and slow burn of our pulling as we pounced from one rung and grabbed hold above, swinging our legs up for leverage. In no time, the boat began to veer, we were nearing the bridge, and I was at Brody's side keeping his pace, as though we were on neighboring stair climber machines at the gym. Yes, I wanted our team to win. I wanted to beat Lance and to be stronger, gutsier than Sabine. Was there anything wrong with that?

I breathed in the cool, wet air, feeding my adrenaline, channeling it into more power to help me climb and leap and pull myself up. Wind roaring through us, the port nearing, we pushed on as the whistle sounded. Only when we coasted to a stop did I realize how soaked we were and what a feat it had been just to have hung on the entire time. Poor Drew and River had slipped off and were still out there, two specks in the distance, swimming to shore. Connor politely waited for them before heading back out with the other team perched on the wheel.

Still buzzing with leftover adrenaline, we toweled off and made our way to the upper deck to watch them. We could just make out their silhouettes as the sun began to glimmer on the horizon. The boat set off, surging, Lance's team propelling us at a quick enough clip that I couldn't tell whether they just might best us. They lost Tom, but from where we sat, the other three looked astonishingly solid and sure-footed.

Before long, that whistle had sounded again and we pulled to a stop, all gathering on the lower deck awaiting Connor. "I know I encouraged bragging," he said, as he joined us to declare the victor. "But let's not have too much gloating because y'all did pretty good and the teams were separated by just seven seconds—"

"Yeah, yeah, we're all winners," Brody joked. "Give it to us, Mills."

Connor just smiled. "But the winner is . . . team two!" He pointed at Lance. We all congratulated them, offering slaps on the back and high-fives. They cheered mildly and respectfully. But much worse than losing the race had been the image of Sabine, perfectly dry and lovely, jumping up and wrapping herself around Lance in a celebratory hug. The final traces of adrenaline drained out of me. My only mild consolation came when Lance almost grimaced, that particularly overzealous public display making him just uncomfortable enough to give me a glimmer of hope.

23

You've Been Consorting with Them

It wasn't until the next day that I dared to look next door. I was alone when I walked by the mansion after a morning at the food bank and noticed that candle burning and the window open wide. A bottle had been left on the sill and I knew it was for me. It made me queasy to be so near to that house after being chased out of it. Each time I felt myself falling for Lucian, something happened, a hiccup in our plans to leave me questioning him all over again. I couldn't afford to be reckless, especially when it came to love. Had he set me up, stationing Wylie there to attack me? I wished that I could just walk on, leaving that bottle there and not giving another thought to what might be in it. But I just couldn't. I reached in the open window to retrieve it and stuffed it in my bag. I knew what would happen when I opened it and I had no intention of doing that yet. I was due back at the library, which had just reopened after the grisly discovery of last week, but I called Connor asking for a reprieve in order to help Mariette with a project. That excuse wasn't entirely true . . . yet. I headed off to Rampart Street.

I know you've been consorting with them," Mariette said gently, the way girlfriends confront each other when one is truly concerned, as soon as I stepped into her shop. Her eyes fixed on me with an intensity that made me feel she had instantly read my entire soul.

"Not them, so much as *him*," I clarified, guiltily.

Now, as she looked on, I shattered the glass bottle directly into a stone basin on the table of her altar room. She had covered it with a black velvet cloth that she said would help absorb some of his essence before the message and its vessel disintegrated. She read aloud from the note in my hands, as we sat opposite each other on a silk tapestry. It sounded even more mysterious in her hypnotic voice:

H-

FORGIVE ME FOR LAST NIGHT. I WAS DETAINED UNEXPECTEDLY. IF THERE HAD BEEN ANY WAY FOR ME TO GET BACK TO THE HOUSE, I PROMISE I WOULD HAVE BEEN THERE. I DON'T HAVE THE FREEDOM THAT I WOULD LIKE THESE DAYS. I HEARD THAT WYLIE WAS THERE, THOUGH, AND THAT HE ENCOUNTERED SOMEONE, BUT HE DIDN'T SEE WHO. I CAN ONLY IMAGINE IT WAS YOU THERE TO MEET ME, AND IT SICKENS ME TO THINK I PUT YOU IN DANGER.

I'M HOPING WE CAN TRY ONCE MORE. WE SHOULD WAIT A FEW DAYS. I WANT TO BE SURE WE WON'T HAVE ANY UNINVITED GUESTS AGAIN. WEDNESDAY, MIDNIGHT. I SHOULD BE ABLE TO SLIP AWAY THEN WITHOUT A PROBLEM. THE DOOR WILL BE UNLOCKED,

BUT, TO BE SAFE, DON'T COME UNTIL YOU'VE SEEN ME
SIGNAL YOU WITH THE LIGHT. I DON'T EVER WANT YOU
IN THAT HOUSE UNLESS I'M THERE.
    YOURS,
    L

I dropped the note as soon as it began to spark and Mariette quickly folded up the velvet, smothering the flame.

A dish of red dust sat between us on the tabletop. She dipped her long fingers into it, extracting just a pinch, and sprinkled it into the velvet, closing it up again, and onto her palm. She rubbed her hands together and held them out to me, wordlessly asking me to give her mine. I did and she closed her eyes. Holding my hands in hers, she sat perfectly still for a few long seconds, then opened those piercing eyes and speared me with that look once again.

"You think he can help you?" she asked, finally.

"My gut tells me he's trying to help me rather than hurt me, but I just don't know." As I said it, I hoped I didn't sound as naïve as I felt right now, with this wise woman staring me down. "I know that may not sound so convincing but—" She pulled her hands away for a moment, holding them up to stop me.

"Your markings . . . what do they tell you? Tell me honestly."

"My scars?" I thought about it now, taking stock of every interaction in the past several weeks. "I don't know, some mixed messages, I suppose. There was one time I was reading one of his notes at the cemetery and got a sharp twinge, but it's not always that way." Then I thought some more and it dawned on me: "But the one night I spent a lot of time with him, I felt nothing." I meant, of course, that I had felt nothing from the scars, but in my heart? In the pit of my stomach? In every nerve ending? There I had felt a lot, but it seemed best to keep that to myself.

"Then let that be your guide," Mariette said with a serene, assured air, surprising me.

"Really?" It seemed too easy.

"You know best your skin, your own radar. You are an illuminator, am I correct?"

"Yes." I was proud to be able to say that, even if I wasn't always so sure of my abilities.

"That is a strength to be reckoned with. Trust yourself. Your instincts are only growing sharper."

"Okay . . . thanks." Her words were reassuring.

She held up the black cloth now, the red powder gone. "This is clear for now. True evil would not have absorbed the dust. It would have shown its true colors, you see. But don't become complacent," she warned, her tone suddenly darkening. "It can change in the blink of an eye. We have to beware, and keep that at the back of our minds: they can win our trust and lose it again so quickly." She spoke as if she knew this from experience. "Have you had much more interaction with the others?" she asked. "The Krewe?"

"I'm worried that a friend of mine has already fallen in with them and another of our housemates has definitely become one of them." At this, she hung her head, as though grieving at the news. "I watched their gathering at the cemetery a few nights ago. It looked like some sort of voodoo ritual."

"I'm afraid I do know a bit about their rituals," she said with gravity. "But that isn't what voodoo is about. Voodoo can heal. My great-great-great-grandmother Marie Laveau was a nurse, you know. She saved so many who would have died of yellow fever.

And others who would have died a spiritual death. What those creatures practice is not our voodoo. That is the devil's work. You must be careful if you happen upon such an event again."

"So that was a regular sort of thing?"

"When they take a vaunted soul, for instance, one of yours, an angel's soul, they rejoice."

This landed like a lead weight in my heart. She continued. "But when you are immersed in extreme evil like this, you can fight this cancer from within."

"But . . . how?"

"With your will for good. With your essence. It's that simple. Each of you angels has the ability to fight off an attack from these creatures, but it requires a tremendous strength of the spirit. A commitment to the role that's been thrust upon you. It's not something that can necessarily be taught."

"So are you one of us then?"

"I'm not. I'm just a guide. Dante is my first charge. But if you and he survive, then he will be my greatest accomplishment. The two of you, your fates are linked. He's destined to be much more powerful than I could ever dream of being. It's an honor for me to teach him."

As if on cue, a knock came at the door.

"Come, Dante," she called. My eyes bulged. He wasn't supposed to be here today.

He entered holding a golden tray of three thimble-size vessels, each bearing a different powder, a tiny flask of azure liquid, a translucent pouch large enough to hold no more than a single marble, and a silver plate.

"Haven?"

"She came for guidance."

One by one, he set the items on the table and took a couple steps back, pausing for further instruction, as though he were a waiter. Mariette looked at these items and then over to Dante.

"Well, what are you waiting for?" she asked him with a bright smile.

"Who, me?" he blurted out, caught off-guard.

"Who else?" She moved aside to make room for him behind the table. He took her place, sitting on his knees and looking tentative, like he would rather be standing in the corner again.

"But this is a big one," he whispered, as though not wanting me to know this was important and he didn't want to be the one to foul it up. "Are you sure?"

"We have to begin testing you, Dante. Otherwise we'll never know if you're prepared for the challenges you and your friends are going to face." She nudged him. "So, go on now."

He looked at me quickly, almost apologetically, then flexed his fingers. Carefully, he tapped out a dash of each of the powders —white, yellow, brick red—into the silver dish and stirred them together with what looked like a chopstick. He whispered a few unintelligible words. Then, with a trembling hand, he let a single drop fall from the flask. The mixture flared, igniting the dish for a second. I jumped on reflex. But it burned out immediately, leaving the powder mixture just as it had looked before, not the least bit charred, nor with a hint of ash. He poured the mixture into the bag, tied it up with a piece of silky string, placed it on the table, and looked to Mariette.

"That was perfect," she praised him. "What should she do with it?"

Dante looked at me solemnly. "So this," he said, holding up the small bag, "is for you. Or, I guess, it's more for Sabine." I took it from him. It felt warm in my hands, perhaps from the fire. "Can you take an item of hers, like a T-shirt or something that we can keep and cut up?"

"Sure, no problem."

"Good," Mariette said. "Put it in a bag and pour this onto it and shake it around. Let it sit. Dante will bring it back tomorrow."

"What exactly will this do?"

"With any hope, it will break the hold they have on her. Disrupt the spell strongly enough to send her back into the light, away from them," said Mariette.

"There's a chance it won't work," Dante said, defeated.

She rested her hand on his arm to comfort him. "If that's the case, it's likely that they have her too tightly in their grip. It won't necessarily be a fault of your skills," she said to him. "Doubting yourself will do you no good." She turned back to me. "We'll look forward to receiving that article. We will root out this evil together."

Back at the house, I flipped through those photos again, finding everyone's glow still intact, with the exception of Jimmy —who was, of course, going to remain in a grotesque state now. And Sabine. Hers had begun to dull, her eyes deadening, lesions forming, her skin taking on a sallow, leathery quality.

I climbed down, studying the closet. It didn't even matter to me what garment I took. I just wanted this to work. I rummaged through her dresser, sorting through T-shirts and camisoles. But I stopped when I found something more interesting: a picture of her and what looked like her parents and a boy—she had never mentioned a brother, so I imagined this had been a boyfriend. The foursome were all dressed up and seated around a table at a restaurant. The guy looked as movie star perfect as I would expect and the more I stared at the picture, the more I realized he resembled a preppier, less dangerous version of Wylie. He could've been Wylie's little brother. Another picture had the same boy in formal attire with his arms around Sabine, who wore a satin evening gown. He planted an adoring kiss on her cheek. It had to have been prom or maybe homecoming; they both wore crowns. He looked so much like Wylie, no wonder she hadn't been able to stay away from him. I sorted through the drawer again, hoping for more photos, but found none. Instead, I grabbed a black tank top. I found a plastic convenience store bag under my bed, placed the shirt inside, and emptied Dante's mixture into it. After I tied it up, I shook it over and over again.

A knock came at the door. I felt like I'd been caught. I shoved the bag inside my backpack, hoping it would somehow work its mysterious magic, and opened up to find Emma in the hallway.

"Sabine isn't here, is she?" she asked. I shook my head no. "She texted me to meet her tonight," she said, fear shading her voice. "Corner of St. Peter, near that bar, where we first met all those guys in the Krewe. Ten o'clock."

"You can't go," I snapped.

"I know. I told Connor. Haven, what's going on with her? What is she doing?"

I didn't know, but I was determined to find out.

24

I've Been Flying

At ten o'clock, St. Peter Street was awash in excitement and drunken revelry. Midblock, a crowd swelled outside that bar, waiting to be granted access. Connor had drafted Lance to join me, not seeming to have noticed that things were a little rocky between us these days. We did a walk-by, slowly wandering past the bar as though we just happened to be out and deciding where to park ourselves for a carefree evening in the Quarter. Our eyes sized up the crowd in a flash. No. They weren't here yet.

Looping back around, we reached that street corner again. This was technically the meeting place, and we needed a spot to be able to watch for them. So we ducked into a restaurant—an expensive one by the looks of the opulent white tablecloth–covered tables, white-gloved waitstaff, and dressed-up diners—and milled around in the empty entranceway, pretending to read a menu on display nearest the window overlooking the corner.

"Can I help you?" the hostess asked us, with a smile that was kind enough while still telegraphing her doubt that Lance and I, in our beat-up jeans, really belonged here.

We looked at each other. "I'm suddenly not so hungry," Lance said, ushering us back out into the night. The sign for the antique jewelry shop across narrow St. Peter Street seemed to be out, but inside lights were still on, and the place had a ton of windows, giving us a perfect view of our target spot. We crossed and found the front door locked, but spotted a white-haired, mustachioed older man behind the counter, polishing a silver watch. I knocked and he unlocked the door.

"Is there any chance we could just take a quick look around?" I asked in my sweetest voice. He looked skeptical.

"I, uh, promised I'd get her something. It's our anniversary," Lance piped up. I shot him the quickest surprised glance, impressed with his cover.

The man sighed and then gave us a bright grin. "Well, who am I to stand in the way of young love." He opened the door wide.

Display cases and glass shelves bearing all manner of shiny gold and silver chains and trinkets and an array of colored gemstones and pearls lined the walls.

"Oh, these are pretty," I said glancing at some bracelets in the case that were made of turquoise stones. Really, though, I gazed out the window, my eyes set on that spot. Lance, on the other hand, had become fixated on a rack on top of the case. Hanging off its spokes were a tangle of thin leather strips bearing brushed nickel charms, all featuring either letters of the alphabet or astrological signs.

I kept my eyes focused out the window for several minutes, neither of us saying a word. And then, at last, I saw them. I grabbed Lance's forearm and he stopped looking through the rack. Wylie appeared across the street, hands in his pockets, smiling and laughing with one of his cohorts. A woman strolled up to them, the tall golden brunette from the night of the ritual. She wore tight denim wrapped around her mile-long legs, and had a wide smile. She threw her arms around Wylie's neck, kissing him. I hoped Sabine would appear, if for no other reason than to see this spectacle.

We stayed glued to that spot studying them, every once in a while saying something about the jewelry—"I like this one," "What about that one?"—just in case the shopkeeper was wondering about us.

The members of the group had slowly cooled to one another. They hadn't spoken for a while now. Wylie, arms folded in front of his chest, leaned against the façade of the restaurant, looking at his watch, for the tenth time, it seemed. I checked mine too. It was nearly 10:30. The girl touched his arm, as though to comfort him. She said something and looked like she was pleading with him, but his face was set firm. Then, from the direction of the bar, Clio, in another micro-short dress and a tight jean jacket, burst out, yanking the woman by the bicep to turn her around. Arms in the air, Clio shouted something so loud, we could just about make it out: "So where the hell is she? She should be here!"

The brunette hung her head, fingers fidgeting, mumbling something. Clio kicked her cowboy boots against the wall. Wylie simply took out a cigarette, gave a look around, and, seeing no one approaching, held an index finger to it and lit it. My blood chilled. From the corner of my eye, I saw Lance's head jerk back in shock. The cigarette end burned red and Wylie put it to his lips, blew a smoke ring, then pulled it out and placed it in Clio's mouth.

She took a puff then pointed at the brunette, barking something else. The brunette pulled a phone from her bag and began furiously keying in a text message. Clio looked at her watch, then stormed off in the direction she had come from. After a second or two, the trio followed slowly behind her. We watched them head toward the bar, focusing on them until they disappeared out of sight.

"Should we try to get into the bar? Maybe Sabine is already in there."

"I bet she's at the house. Let's get outta here," Lance whispered, more optimistic, heading out.

Peeking back over my shoulder, I noticed the shopkeeper watching us. I flipped through the rack in front of us ready to take the first thing I saw, but then something special shimmered at me. It was buried in the back and I had to unloop a slew of bracelets to liberate it, but finally I did: four leather strips were joined by a chunky silver clasp, the size of a small dog tag. It featured a raised fleur-de-lis. I had to buy it.

As I jogged to catch up with Lance, I tapped his arm with the bag.

"Here," I said flatly. "You should have this." He peeked inside the bag, pulling it out.

"Thanks," he said sincerely.

I awakened to a steady and rhythmic pulse I couldn't quite place, a beating against my window like fingertips knocking softly. I opened my eyes and found the glass streaked with rain. I had somehow managed to forget what rain sounded like. We had encountered mostly sunny skies since arriving in New Orleans and to see the gray overcast now didn't seem to fit. I also couldn't help noticing that Sabine's bed was still made. Perhaps she was in Lance's room again.

I hadn't worked at the cemetery since that dreaded evening of my attack and I wasn't especially looking forward to it today. I stopped by River's room to see if she wanted to walk over with me, and Tom opened the door, silent and still sleepy. Somewhere in the background, River called out, "This weather blows. Forget it, I'm skipping today." *Why does it never occur to me to skip anything?* I wondered to myself. Nevertheless, I headed out into the wet morning.

The downpour picked up as I crossed Rampart Street, pelting me in sheets, my umbrella mounting no real defense against the onslaught. I was soaked, head to toe. I was so busy fighting the elements, I didn't even bother to wonder until I reached the church office to procure that tucked-away key what I was supposed to do when it rained. I certainly couldn't paint in this weather.

"It is nasty out there, isn't it?" Susan greeted me from behind her desk. "I've got some indoor projects you can help me with. I would love for you to touch up some of the gold leaf in the sanctuary. If you want to go ahead and change into your painting clothes, I can toss these in the dryer for you."

"Yeah, that would be great, thanks." It meant a trip back outside, to the caretaker's cottage, but it was probably better than spending the day like this.

"Sorry to send you out there again." She smiled.

"No problem, but that reminds me—if they're going to close the cemetery gates early, I wish they would look and be sure no one's in there. I had left something the last time I was here and went back, and the gates were shut while I was still inside."

"That's very odd. I'll certainly mention that," she said, jotting it down.

Something else occurred to me. "Oh, well, maybe don't say anything to Sister Catherine, though. I know she mentioned not to be there late. I don't want her thinking I didn't listen."

Susan smiled gently, as though dealing with someone who was certifiably insane. "You're very sweet to ask for Sister Catherine. I'm afraid I haven't seen her in quite some time either. Hopefully at some point she'll come back for a visit. I know she would be so impressed with all that you've done here."

My mind had gotten stuck on jagged bits of what she said. I needed to smooth it all out again before going on. "Come back to visit?"

"I admit it's not the same here since she got the calling to the Ninth Ward." She looked concerned now. "Haven, dear, are you feeling all right?"

"Sure, yes, of course. Just remind me again, exactly when did she leave?"

Her eyes fixed on the ceiling as she thought about it. "Oh, let's see, her last day was your first, I believe."

"But she drops by the cemetery almost every day . . . to check on me . . ." Susan was looking at me now like I had a life-threatening head injury. "I meant, she's there . . . in spirit." She nodded at this—a big, overexaggerted nod—so it must have been the right thing to say. I said a hasty goodbye.

I shot my umbrella up into the gray sky again, sheets cascading down on me, and made my way behind the church and across empty Basin Street. All the while, I ran through that conversation in my head. I hadn't hallucinated this—I had seen Sister Catherine on a regular basis, almost every time I'd been here. But the Ninth Ward was nowhere near here. It didn't make sense that she would be dropping by that often if she was stationed there all this time. Lost in thought, I turned into the cemetery, digging the key out of my pocket as I stepped through the gateway. As soon as I reached the caretaker's cottage, all other thoughts drained from my mind.

Slumped in a heap on the doorstep lay a rain-soaked Sabine.

A scream rang out from my lungs, a reflex I couldn't stop. I dropped the umbrella and lunged for her, falling to the ground to be at her side. She wore that sequined dress she had bought on our shopping trip together. It was soaked through and muddied. Her hair hung in wet strips matted flat against her head. I grabbed her wrist to check her pulse and leaned down to try to hear her breathing. It was nearly impossible to make out any sound above the crackle of rain hitting against the cottage. But I caught her shallow breath and felt a steady pulse. She was alive.

I grabbed her arm, shaking her with one hand. Then I rummaged in my bag for my phone and dialed 9-1-1. "Sabine! Hey! Wake up! Please!" I shouted. I shook her and shook her and even slapped her face, which I felt bad about, but she wasn't waking up. Her slick limbs were lifeless and heavy, as if they were the stuffed beanbag arms of a doll. And then, just as the operator picked up, I noticed a marking. She had what looked like a fleur-de-lis made of flames on her shoulder, but it appeared to be a thick scab. I hung up and called Connor instead.

"Sit tight, I'll be right there," Connor told me. "And don't call anyone else." I didn't put up a fight. Maybe I would have if we had been back home and I knew that we would be able to go to Joan's hospital with doctors I'd worked with and trusted, but here I couldn't trust anything or anyone. I wanted to drag Sabine inside the cottage—who knew how long she had been out here—but I was still scared to jostle her just in case there was some deeper internal injury. Her skin, which I would have expected to be cold and clammy in the rain, felt surprisingly warm. I just wanted a sign, any sign, that she was really in there and making her way back to the surface of consciousness.

Suddenly, Sabine's eyes fluttered, her long and clumpy

mascaraed lashes like chubby insect legs dancing; they had left trails of black streaming down her cheeks. They opened, tiny slits letting slivers of the world in. She squinted, shielding them from the rain, and let out a mournful moan.

"Sabine! Are you okay? Tell me how to help you."

"I'm so hot." She groaned.

"Can you move at all?"

Eyes closed again, she nodded. "Yeah."

"If I help you, can you get up?"

"Where am I?" she asked woozily.

"You're at the cemetery."

"Really? How'd I get here?"

"I was hoping you could tell me."

"Huh."

"Do you want to try getting up?"

She nodded. I put her arm around my neck, held her by the waist, and slowly rose to my feet, taking her with me and hoping not to slip in the mushy, saturated ground. She felt like a lump, content to be dragged, unable to contribute much strength to our efforts. I dug in my pocket for the key and after unlocking the door, I kicked it open and we stumbled in. I set Sabine down in the desk chair. She slumped there, looking like she might slide right off onto the floor.

"I don't know what happened or how I got here, but all I know is . . . it was amazing, whatever it was." She sounded dreamy for a moment.

"Amazing?"

"Yeah." She fixed her eyes far away and shifted in her seat, settling in again. "I feel like I've been flying. I can almost still taste it, but . . . something about it has worn off, you know? And I just want to get it back."

"I guess," I said. "So . . . you're really feeling okay? Because it looks like you might've been outside for a while." I didn't know whether to say anything about the tattoo just yet.

"Oh yeah." She flitted her hand. "I'm actually feeling better than—" She stopped short of finishing her thought and her face fell, a seriousness taking over her features. She slowly raised an arm to point. "What's that?" she asked, skittish. She focused on the space at my feet. I looked to the ground and saw nothing more than my beat-up sneakers and two sets of wet footprints. "That. There! What is that?!" She said it more frantically this time.

"What is it, Sabine?" I asked, looking all around me but unable, for the life of me, to figure out what had her upset.

She let out an ear-piercing scream that startled me so much I jumped. "Get him away!" she shouted. She turned her head, looking back over her shoulder, then squeezing her eyes shut. "Him! Get him out of here!"

"Who? Sabine, who?" I felt powerless.

She opened her eyes again, focusing on the ground to her right. Her lips looked like they were struggling to form the words. Finally: "What . . . what's going on here?" she stammered, looking at me like I had betrayed her in some way.

"What do you mean?" I stepped toward her. She lifted her legs up on the chair, hugging her knees. "What happened to her? What have you done to them? Who are they?" She shook her head, closed her eyes, and screamed once more. I ran to her and embraced her, trying to calm her down. I didn't know what to do. I wished I had called an ambulance after all.

"Shhh-shhhh." I tried to soothe her. "It's gonna be okay. Can you tell me what you're seeing?"

She cried softly into my wet hair, sniffling. At last, gathering herself and finding her voice: "Bodies. How did they get here? Who are they? What happened to them?"

"Bodies?" I looked around the room: as empty and boring as it had always been. Nothing at all resembling dead bodies to be found. I didn't know what else to say, so I just let her cry.

Connor arrived several minutes later, though it felt like much longer. He was soaked, with no umbrella, and there was tension in his expression. Sabine sat curled up in the desk chair, still hugging her knees, cradling her head in her arms.

He put his hand to her back.

"I can't go near the bodies. I don't want to see them."

He looped her arms around his neck and leaned in, scooping her up. She perked her head up, tensing her body and clinging so tightly to him I wondered if he could breathe.

"You have to go fast!" she ordered him, squirming in his arms and tugging him closer to her, as though he were a tree she was trying to climb. "Step over them! Fast! Don't step on them!"

"It's okay," he said. "It'll be okay. We'll get you home."

I was just locking up the cottage, rattling the door to be sure it was secure, when I felt my scars fire up into a fierce burn.

A hot claw clamped down on my shoulder. I snapped my head around and jumped back, so shocked to see her there.

Sister Catherine. Standing right before me.

"I'm sorry. Did I startle you, my child?" she asked peacefully but, if I wasn't mistaken, wearing the slightest smirk. She stood close to me, too close. I backed up a few steps. She must have noticed this, along with the look of sheer terror on my face.

"Ah, yes, so you heard about my 'calling.'" She made air quotes around the word, in a way that didn't seem to fit her, and then began cackling. Slowly her laugh changed in tone. Gone was the crinkly, weathered voice of a sweet old woman and in its place, something harsher, more taunting . . . younger. I thought I might be hearing things. She stopped abruptly, watching me with hard eyes. "You know my real calling, Haven?" she asked cagily. She leaned in, that hot hand burning my forearm. "Serving the Prince," came the sugary southern drawl of a beauty queen from her old body. I had heard it very few times but recognized it from the start. It sent chills through me and yet my feet remained rooted, not aware they should be running. "You'll soon serve him too, if you know what's good for you."

Before my eyes, she transformed within that habit: taller, slimmer, blond hair peeking out. It was Clio standing in front of me. I stopped breathing, wondering if I was hallucinating the way Sabine had. But I knew deep down that this was terrifyingly real. I set off running just as she whipped around, disappearing into a burst of fire. The flame slithered to the nearest tomb, oozing into the cracks of the sealed doorway, and she was gone.

I excused myself from work and called Lance on the way home. "Hey, I can't talk now," came his clipped voice. I was still fragile from the episode I'd just run from, and I couldn't help that it showed.

"Well, just thought you might like to know that I found Sabine."

"What?" Now he seemed to be listening.

"Passed out in the cemetery. Connor came to take her back to the house."

"Why didn't you call me?"

"I am calling you. Right. Now." He was frustrating me. I had called hoping for comfort. I didn't need this.

"Right. Sorry. I'm just . . . I've been worried." He sighed.

And after a pause, as though not sure he wanted to share it: "Did you hear about the bodies?"

I stopped in my tracks, wind swirling around me. "What?"

"Yeah. I heard there were a couple more around the city. Some of the guys here said they heard they were found in alleyways, courtyards, dumpsters . . ." He sounded distracted, his voice petering out. "So, I just couldn't help thinking maybe she was one of . . . Anyway, just be careful, okay?"

25

I Can't Handle This

Here's how this is gonna work, guys." Connor addressed us in his most serious, take-no-prisoners tone. He had ordered us all home, and we gathered in the levitation room. Sabine, still weak from all she had endured, barely conscious, and glistening from battling the rain and inner demons, lay in the center of the floor. "This is why I started you learning levitation from the very start. We didn't have enough warning when this happened to Jimmy. There's still time for Sabine. What you see here is a soul divided: there's the real Sabine, and then there's now another part, a vicious aspect, that was set loose by the Krewe. That part is threatening to take hold of her. She needs to fight it from the inside, or this'll never work. But I need you all to perform an extraction from the outside, to help her along."

He had us sit in a circle, evenly spaced around her. We all watched Connor hovering over her, each face around the circle wearing variations of the same terrified, confused expression. Slowly he moved toward the door. "You're all going to focus your energies on her, as though you're trying to raise her, like any of the objects you've been practicing on."

"How do we know if we're succeeding?" came Lance's concerned voice. He sat opposite me and I felt that sting looking at him. It was as though I no longer existed to him and he had transferred all of that care to this other person, who quite literally now lay between us.

"I'll be watching. If she lifts for any period of time, it's that diseased soul being pulled out. We go until we run outta steam," he said, like a coach. "This is grueling stuff, guys. But Sabine needs you, and one day each of you may need the same treatment."

With that, he turned off the lights, so we sat in suffocating darkness. Finally, he signaled, with that same foreboding tone of someone proctoring a standardized exam: "Good luck. You may begin."

Almost immediately, a flash flared and something hard and heavy smacked against the padded wall across from me, where Brody had been sitting. Footsteps rushed over and then Connor whispered, "You okay, man? . . . Okay, that's why you gotta learn to control this. You're done today. Hang back and rest." Gazing around the circle now, I saw soft hazy light, beginning to connect from each person to Sabine, like spokes of a wheel.

I closed my eyes. The petty side of me thought of holding back. Would Sabine have given herself so fully to me if the situation were reversed? But I had no choice. It would forever haunt me if I didn't try my hardest. And I channeled all my strength as I had so many times before in this room. I felt a pressure collect in my head behind my eyes. And then I felt a breeze behind me, blowing my hair around in my face. I let my eyes open a sliver: I was moving. A soft glow illuminated the space in front of me, where Sabine's reclining form now hovered a foot above the ground. That light seemed to be pushing me, back, back,

back until I reached the padded wall with a firm shove, but nothing like what had happened to Brody. Eyes closed again, I kept up until, without warning, I felt all my strength drain, the well dry. I toppled over, lying on the floor, as I heard Sabine hit the ground. I opened my eyes to a pitch-black room.

The lights went on—so bright, as if they were screaming at my eyes. I squinted and found everyone lying on the ground, spent.

"Good work," Connor said. He helped Sabine onto her feet. She seemed so much steadier than I would have imagined. Maybe just because I felt so entirely depleted, I couldn't fathom anyone having any energy at all.

"Where am I?" she asked as he walked her out. We all stayed in there until one by one, we regained enough strength to lift ourselves up and go back to our rooms. For me, it felt like hours. I was the last to go.

I heard the voices before I even opened the door to my room.
"But you told me to meet you. How can you not remember that?" Emma prodded gently.

"I told you, I can't remember a damn thing," Sabine responded, hostile and biting. "Why won't you back off? I should be mad at *you* for not showing up. If I told you to meet me somewhere and you didn't come, then maybe this is *your* fault." I lingered in the hallway, wanting to hear more.

"I can't believe you would say something like that." Emma sounded hurt now. "Like I would want you to go through something like this? Like it's not enough that I've already had this happen with Jimmy?"

"Whatever. Let's just forget about it."

I couldn't wait any longer. I wandered in, pretending, of course, that I'd heard nothing. "Hi." I addressed Sabine tentatively, as though approaching a tiger in her cage. Her weekender bag lay open, disgorging clothes and personal items, waiting to be stuffed shut. She and Emma stared at me blankly. "So . . . how are you feeling?" I tried.

"I'm fine," she shot at me. She was dressed in jeans and a T-shirt and appeared freshly scrubbed since I'd last seen her.

"Good, that's great," I said. Emma gave me a wary look as Sabine knelt to zip her bag. I could tell she was going to make me ask. "Um, so are you going somewhere?"

"I need a break." Sabine sighed.

"Me too," Emma shot back at Sabine. She hopped off Sabine's bed and let herself out, slamming the door.

I took her vacated seat on the bed. "So where are you going?"

"Look, Haven." She softened, but only the slightest bit. "I need a couple days away from here, okay? I'm just not cut out for whatever's going on. I don't know what this morning was about. I don't know what's happening and I'm sick of feeling this way. I don't want to be here."

"That's fine," I said easily. "But I was under the impression we didn't get to decide that, you know what I mean?"

"I'm sick of these rules. This is some club I'm trapped in that I don't even want to be part of."

"I know, I get it," I said, though, honestly, I tried not to think that way. It seemed a waste of time to be frustrated. I always tried to channel those feelings into something that would do me good. "I kind of thought either we accept these rules or we're drafted by the other side."

"Whatever. I need to run away right now, and so I am going."

"When are you coming back?"

"In a couple days," she said, exhaling. She closed her eyes, about to level with me. "Look, I didn't ask to be in this freak show. To fight anyone or earn any wings. My life was just fine without this." She continued jamming things into her bag.

"My life was fine too." I shrugged, a little on the defensive.

"I mean *really* fine. I had everything I wanted. I had friends and a boyfriend and much better things to do than go looking for ways to save other people's souls and lives and things. I know that sounds terrible—" She stopped zipping for a moment and looked at me sincerely.

"No, it doesn't," I said, meaning it. "It sounds understandable and normal."

"So I'm taking a couple days to go home and live my old life. I just need a break from this. From this version of me. I'm not like you . . ." She let it hang there and I didn't know quite what she meant. And finally: "I can't handle this."

I nodded. But I couldn't quiet that nagging feeling in my gut. "Watch yourself up there." She slung her bag over her shoulder. The wide neck of her sweater fell low enough to see a hint of that fleur-de-lis peeking out as she turned to go without another word.

Knowing I now had the room to myself had the opposite effect than I would have expected. It suddenly felt claustrophobic. The emptiness closed in on me. I pushed open the window and heard muffled voices from outside. I climbed out onto the balcony into the cool evening air, breathing it in to clear my head as I leaned over the railing and gazed into the darkening sky. But something below caught my eye instead.

There they were: Lance and Sabine, standing in the court-yard, facing each other. He held her bag, and she had her hand on his wrist, shaking his arm, telling him something I couldn't quite make out. He nodded and looked away, placing the week-ender on her shoulder. Then he leaned in and kissed her, one arm around her waist. I stayed only long enough to see that the kiss was returned, enthusiastically. My stomach dropped, nausea setting in and filling the emptiness inside: I felt like I had lost something dear to me. I didn't want to see any more. Even after these grave matters of life and death that had filled the day, I couldn't help that this still stung me.

The next morning, Drew and I had just changed into our painting clothes at the cemetery when Lance pulled up outside the gates in a beat-up once-white pickup truck, its bed overflowing with tools, huge shovels, waste bins, tarps, and slabs of marble. Drew went along to start painting, giving me a look that said she knew the potential for awkwardness would be running high.

"So does this mean we're gonna be coworkers again?" I asked, by way of greeting, as I neared him. We hadn't spoken since that scene in the courtyard and my voice couldn't quite decide on the proper tone to address him.

"I finished over at the LaLaurie mansion, so I'm building a crypt here." He pulled a few rolled sheets of paper from his back pocket, smoothing them out on the hood of the truck. "It's going to be one of the raised boxy ones, nothing too crazy, nothing like the scale of that one from the night of the ritual or anything." He said the last few words quietly, as if sorry to have alluded to that night, as he gestured to the blueprints. "It'll be more like maybe seven, eight feet?" He pointed out the dimensions on the grid, amid a sea of measurements and impossibly perfect handwriting. And then as if reading my mind: "Shouldn't take long."

I helped him unload his supplies and then left him to get to work. I tucked myself behind one of the nearby crypts for just a moment to watch him dig out his space. He had gotten immensely strong. He then carried a slab of marble nearly his height under one arm, as though it were a gigantic skateboard. He set it between two sawhorses, wound up and smashed the side of his hand into it, chopping it somehow into two with a perfectly clean, sharp break. Then he carted over another slab and did the same thing. He did it all with such ease, as though it were made of flimsy Styrofoam, giving no indication that it might have hurt in the least. Of course, he should have broken his hand.

Watching Lance so easily and openly using these newfound powers incited my competitive side. I looked around, finding no one, and I went for it. I stood beside the tomb, focusing all I had on one of the paintbrushes. My stare was firm, unwavering. Within seconds, the brush flew into my hand, its wooden handle hot to the touch. Thrilled with my success, I got another idea. Setting my eyes on the trees drooping over the top of the cemetery wall in the distance, I left my work behind for a moment, turning that brush over in my hands. One tree in particular was just the right height, with plenty of its trunk visible amid its leafy branches. I chose a spot about twenty feet away and settled into position, staring down this target. Then, as though throwing a pitch, I wound up, lunged, and flung the paintbrush. It cut through the air and landed with a sharp *CRACK* against a part of the tree trunk exposed above the cemetery wall. The pointy handle wedged itself right in and appeared to be embedded nearly up to the head of the brush. Unless I wanted to climb up the tree, I'd be using another brush to edge the corners of the Degas family crypt I was working on today. I couldn't help but be secretly pleased: my levitation power gave me hope. And though I hated to admit it, having Lance working nearby, being able to hear the dull crash of him fitting those pieces together and see him when I found a reason to walk past that spot, gave me a sense of comfort, even after all that had happened between us.

The evening could not have passed in a more mundane fashion: tutoring followed by the hotline, then returning to the house to look through those pictures (no new casualties, but Sabine's image had failed to improve) and do laundry. But it all served to distract me from what was to come. Even after what I had encountered on my last trip next door, I still couldn't quite manage to share my plans with Dante, or anyone for that matter. I knew I should—intellectually I knew that it was dangerous not to tell. Reckless, even. But I didn't want to be talked out of going, it was that simple. And I also didn't want to be saddled with chaperones. No one wanted to trust Lucian, and I could accept that, but I didn't have to agree.

Standing on the porch, hand poised over the doorknob, I braced myself and gave it a jiggle. Unlocked this time. Slowly I turned it, pushing it open as it creaked back at me. I stepped inside, closing the door behind me as quietly as possible but steadying myself should I find the need to strike.

"Hey," I heard from the space behind me.

Gasping, I whipped around, not expecting him to be so close by. He sat on the staircase, illuminated by the soft rays of light filtering in from the streetlamps outside.

"Sorry," he said. "I promise, it's just me tonight."

"Good." I exhaled but my pulse failed to slow.

"I'm impressed you found your way in the other night, even though I wish you hadn't. Are you okay?"

"Yeah, I was just . . . caught off-guard. I mean, I didn't realize this place had become a hangout. I thought you said the others didn't come here. Should we be expecting company now?" I didn't want to sound afraid, but I also didn't care for surprises like that.

"I'm sorry." Lucian shook his head, regretfully. "I don't know what he was doing here. They usually prefer being out where the action is. We'll keep our meetings short. And watch out for that guy, okay? He's a problem." I wondered what constituted a "problem" when you were already a native of the underworld, but I only nodded. "So, come 'ere." He gestured for me to join him on the stairs. I took a seat beside him, his gray eyes glowing in the near darkness, his familiar cedar scent making me a little woozy. "I don't have much time," he said, looking apologetic. "There's a meeting tonight. They're starting to assemble for Metamorfosi Day, the day of metamorphosis." He waited before going on, bestowing an extra importance to it.

"That sounds like a pretty big deal."

"It is. They're going to designate when it will be and then that'll be the time when you will all sort out and battle to determine who, of those of you in training, become angels and who become devils. This is also the one day when those of us who are consigned to our fates"—he put his hand to his chest, including himself in this group—"can sort of change our stripes, so to speak." He said it shyly, as if he were embarrassed.

I let this sink in and then offered gently, "Oh. So this is your chance then? To break away?"

"It is. So that's when I'll be needing some help, if you'll be kind enough . . ."

"Of course," I said firmly.

"Thank you," he said looking at me for only a moment and

then focusing in the distance, breathing a sigh. "Thank you. You have no idea . . ." He didn't finish, but he didn't have to.

"You'll just tell me what I can do and I'll do it."

"I'll know a little more after tonight, but the first thing will be to ensure you make it through your own battle. After that we'll worry about me."

"So I'll have to go against Clio and the Krewe," I guessed.

"No, actually." He must've read the surprise as it swept my face. "I know," he said. "You'll be battling someone who is your equal and has fallen to my side. A devil in training. The Krewe, Clio, that whole set, their work is being done now, trying to make the final conversions, grabbing whoever they can. They'll be helping whoever your nemesis will be, but they'll mostly be kind of sitting back and watching the mayhem play out."

"Okay, so then who am I up against?"

"We don't know yet. We won't know until everyone has been tagged and has sorted out into sides. I'm assuming that I'll find out and be able to tip you off. But they're still wary of me, and there's a lot that goes on that I'm just not included in." He shook his head. "I'm sorry. It's been hard to walk this line, trying to learn as much as I can without anyone knowing that I've found this way to see you."

"I know what you mean." I felt bonded to Lucian by this secrecy, both of us protecting each other by keeping quiet.

He looked like he was thinking and then, in a heavier tone: "I hope you don't think that . . . I mean, with Wylie. I hope you don't think I meant for that to happen, for him to find you, for him to be here instead of me. I promise it was just terrible timing and I should've found a way to warn you. It never would have occurred to me that you would have gotten in even with the door locked."

"Yeah, I guess I should learn to take a hint. It was a little pushy of me."

"I don't mind pushy." He smiled. "I just regret that that happened. Truly. I'm not stupid. I know you're looking for reasons to not trust me and I can't say I blame you, but I promise I didn't know he was going to be here," he said, the pleading clear in his voice. "And I hope you believe me."

"I do," I said simply and it was true. Right now, it was true.

"But what I really wanted to tell you is just keep strong, Haven. They will attack you with greater force than any of the others— don't let them wear you down. Know that you can fight them. You can." A deep gong sounded at the top of the stairs from a grandfather clock that had been added since I had last been here. We both looked up toward it. He sighed.

"I have to go." He shook his head, angry, then almost to himself he said, "If they notice I'm gone . . ." Instead of finishing his thought, he lunged, his lips landing on mine. I had wondered if this would happen again, or if it had been a fluke the last time, just an inevitability when you put two people with a history in a dark, empty room after midnight. "I have to go," he whispered again, still so close to me that I could feel his lips move when he spoke. "I don't want to, but I have to."

I nodded, making no other motion beyond that for a few seconds. And then, not wanting to overstay my welcome either, I got up to go. He grabbed my hand just before it was out of reach.

"I'll see you soon. I promise," he whispered. "Depending on the preparations that start tonight, I may be away a little while. I'll keep leaving you notes, okay?"

With that I drifted back outside, the chilly air slapping at my face, waking me up as I walked home.

I peeked in the front door, no sign of anyone to catch me, and I let myself in as quietly as possible, hustling to my room. I found him standing there, pounding on my door.

"Hey, what's up?" I said trying not to sound as guilty as I felt.

Lance turned around. He was sweating, with skittish, squirrelly eyes. "I was there," he started. I unlocked the door and he followed me in.

"What? Where?"

He paced, holding his head in his hands. "I was there for the partying, for the excitement and the fun and then the rest of it. I don't know if I did it . . . oh god, oh god, oh god . . . Tell me I didn't, but I was there. I saw those bodies. I saw those people killed. I saw them take what they wanted from them. I was there, and then I ran away with them. I was there that whole night. I saw it all. And I felt *good* afterward. How did I feel good after that? What's wrong with me? What kind of monster must I be?"

I just watched him, searching for a clue into what he was talking about. It made no sense. He was panting now. "How did this even happen? Why me? What did I *do?*" He ran both hands through his hair then squeezed his head as though trying to stifle all these cascading, mad thoughts. He stopped pacing, dropped his hands at his sides, and looked at me, expecting me to have answers. But I had nothing. I took both of his arms and gently walked him backwards to Sabine's bed, sitting him down and taking a seat beside him.

"What are you talking about, Lance?"

He took a deep breath now, closing his eyes, then looked at me squarely. "That night I showed up in here? With that thing on my arm? Seeming drunk and out of it? I had been with them. I was with the Krewe."

I shook my head. "But how do you know that? You couldn't remember anything. How can you be so sure?"

"I don't know, I just am. I can't explain it but I fell asleep reading just now and I had these dreams that weren't dreams. And I felt the same way I had that night—that rush and that excitement, except this time, that feeling came with all these other images. Remember the bodies that turned up the next day?" I nodded. "I could picture all of it like I was there when it happened. And I know that I was. I also know that there was other stuff, too. I thought Sabine was there too, but it's weird. The image started as Sabine and then I saw this sort of hazy silhouette that I can't describe. It's like a blank spot even in this dream, except I know it was her." He grabbed my arm now, squeezing so tight. "Tell me I didn't do this stuff, that I'm wrong. What happened to me? Why did I think, at the time, that this felt like the most exciting night of my life? Because it did. And that terrifies me."

I let his words and descriptions tally up in my mind and then the connections started to make sense, linking it all to the kinds of things I'd already heard. "What happened to me?" he asked again.

"You got tagged," I said simply, studying his eyes. Confusion swept his face and he looked away, as though trying to understand. "They're trying to draft us, to steal our souls by getting us, I don't know, infatuated with this feeling of what life is like as one of them. That's the rush you felt. But if we fight it off then we've won and we get to continue on . . . as us, as angels. You made it through, Lance. You fought it and you're fine."

"But I can't stop seeing these images. I can't make them stop. And I can't live with myself if I did some of this stuff. Did I?"

"I don't know. I don't really know how it works." I felt like a fraud trying to talk him through it all when I hadn't been tagged myself yet.

I grabbed his hand and pushed his sleeve all the way up to his shoulder in one quick movement. "But do you see? That marking is gone. And if you looked at my pictures right now, you would look perfect."

"Well, it's little consolation unless I can find out what really happened." I could understand that. He trudged back to his room, slamming his door shut.

~ 26 ~

You Only Live Once

Lance had been especially aloof since the night he had those dreams. Connor had instructed us to levitate him, just to be safe and thorough. And then the others, too: River, Tom, Drew. They had all gotten tagged and we tended to them. Each incident was unique; one might barely be affected and find that marking disappearing quickly, while another would have been lost if not for the group performing its soul extraction. And then, regrettably, there was Brody, who simply failed to come home from the hotline one night and was never seen again. Gone. He and Drew had both gotten tagged that evening, but she had turned up in the courtyard and we got to her fast. That made all the difference.

Physically, Lance appeared fine now, but that was only half of the story. Despite spending more time together working, we were talking less than ever. It was frustrating. He had cut himself off and it hurt. My reflex, for better or worse, had been to fixate on Lucian as an escape. I found myself replaying our most recent encounter over and over like it was a song I couldn't get enough of. Even so, I kept trying with Lance and managed to convince him to come along for Max's birthday celebration—the whole house was going. Max happened to be universally adored and, besides, we all needed to rally around something *normal* amid the madness for a few short hours.

We crowded around weathered wooden tables and benches at a down-home Cajun hot spot Dante had suggested. Tulane pennants hung on the wall, a brass band played at the back, and the tables were littered with vats of barbecued foods, sinful side dishes, and plenty of fried fare served family style. The hurricanes—virgin, for us—arrived by the pitcherful. And best of all: the restaurant wasn't anywhere we had ever spotted the Krewe.

When we had finished feasting and settled the bill, a cake was brought out—a surprise orchestrated by Dante, which made Max blush—and the group sang "Happy Birthday," as a few of our neighboring tables looked on smiling and clapping.

We had just dug into our cake when the music stopped.

"Is there a Dante here?" a rich bass voice boomed into the microphone. "A Dante Dennis, by chance?" Dante's eyes bugged as Max stood up, pointing at Dante beside him.

"What? It's not *my* birthday!" Dante laughed, smacking him on the arm. He was so used to being the party planner that to see him on the receiving end of such celebration made me smile.

"No, but it's mine and you're my favorite birthday present." Max said it matter-of-factly, not saccharine at all, as if this were an everyday occurrence and people always professed their love with a brass band. I looked at Lance from the corner of my eye and couldn't help but feel a pang of longing. He smiled as we all cheered and whooped for Dante and Max, but I could tell his mind was far away. "By the way," Max went on, "this is for you." He handed over a simple blue gift bag. Dante looked confused but took it and peeked inside.

"You're kidding me," he said, without even pulling anything out.

"What is it?" I had to ask, leaning to peer into the bag.

Dante reached in and pulled out the gris-gris bag he had made and stashed among Max's possessions, which Max had apparently discovered, and a voodoo doll made to look like Dante. "Dude, you did a good job on this!" He held the doll, which was the size of his hand, up beside his face.

"It's cute, Dan!" I smiled.

The trombone player quickly drowned me out, launching the band into the first few notes of "Happy Birthday," then instantly morphed into a spirited "When the Saints Go Marching In." And march they did, right over to our table. One of the restaurant hosts placed plastic crowns on Dante's and Max's heads and made them stand up; our waiter stepped out waving two green parasols in the air and handed them to the guys. The whole place clapped along, and suddenly everyone at our table was on their feet.

"C'mon!" Connor gestured with a huge wave. "It's a second line!"

"What?" I asked, over the music.

"That's what they call it. Ya gotta follow! C'mon!"

Lance looked like he had no intention of going anywhere, but I waved him along. "Gotta follow!" I repeated, tugging on his arm. Led by the band, we all filed out of the restaurant, along with many of the other patrons, and right into the street. As the music blared, everyone in our general vicinity paused to take note of our celebration and several joined in.

"I can't believe you did all this!" I shouted my praise to Max.

"You only live once!" Max called back with a smile. Dante grabbed his hand, waving it in the air. In their other hands, they bobbed the parasols up and down to the rhythm. We danced along the streets, trailing the brass quintet and picking up more and more revelers as we went. Somehow, as the crowd surged forward, I ended up toward the back of the pack. The group grew so large, with so much jostling and elbowing, that Dante, Lance, and I got separated, like three pieces of driftwood carried off by a river's current. There was something energizing about being caught in the upheaval and good times. I decided to just soak it all in, the joyfulness, the thrill of this impromptu street party. I couldn't help but smile.

But then I felt the sting.

I couldn't place it at first, couldn't imagine what I must have bumped into. It wasn't that familiar sensation of my scars flaring up—I had had only a second of that feeling and then it was something much more intense. It felt as if a spot on my back had been sliced through, like a patch of skin had been sharply unzipped and now it was open and crying out to be soothed. I had to stop in my tracks as the crowd flowed around me and moved ahead. I put my hand to my back, feeling blindly for it, and found the wound—blood, sticky and thick, saturating my thin sweater. I felt the scene melting: the muffled music, the falling voices. I drifted, consciousness slipping, slipping, slipping, until darkness descended. But I was still moving, or something, someone, was moving me, pulling me along with it. Everything went dark and numb.

I was out.

A group of faces flashed above me, each more beautiful and terrifying than the one before it. They huddled together, closing in on me. They ranged from the perilously familiar heavies—Wylie and the formidable Clio—to ones more recently indoctrinated but equally feared: that tall brunette Lance and

I had watched from the jewelry shop, the blond creature that Jimmy had morphed into. And on the outskirts I made out a pair of leggy blond girls, a couple of buff, brutish athletic guys, and perhaps a dozen of the perfectly symmetrical faces, with their chiseled cheekbones and enviable physiques, I had seen at that bar and, more notably, during the ritual in the cemetery.

I was numb, lying with my cheek to the ground in an alleyway, my body against a brick building. All around me I could still hear the sound of revelry, of that party in the streets. I wanted to scream but I couldn't even summon the strength to open my mouth or gather enough air in my lungs. Even more horrifically, it dawned on me that because of those blaring horns and that pulsing drumbeat filling every inch of the air, and the roar of the crowd, no one would be able to hear me. The only sensation that registered at all came from my three sets of scars. Especially my right shoulder—that throbbed and raged as though something were trying to rip through my skin and escape.

The faces above me smiled.

"Hiiiii, Haven, we're so glad to have you joining us tonight. You've no idea how we've been waiting for this," Wylie said to me in an eerily sugary voice. "In fact, some of us have been so impatient that we almost took you too soon." He looked at Clio. She just shrugged, a wild grin taking over her face.

"Can't blame a girl for tryin'. I just knew we'd have so much fun." She kneeled down, cooing at me, her cowboy boots in direct line with my eyes.

"I'm sure you remember our dear Clio from your encounters in the cemetery."

That had been her, locking me in that one evening, trying to pry me off the gate, attacking me from out of nowhere.

"Ahhh, don't worry. You're gonna feel so good soon, honey,"

Clio said in a soothing voice. "We all have quite a night ahead."
The entire group traded looks with the same hungry eyes.

"Welcome to the Krewe," Jimmy piped up now, with a smile,
reaching out to stroke my hair.

My mind, my vision, my everything went black.

We were racing through the streets now, this pack. Lucian
was there too. He reached out and clasped my hand, running
with me. The wind whipped my hair and my dress. I felt like
I was flying, and had to look down to confirm that my feet were
still on the ground. What was I wearing? I hadn't put on a dress
for dinner, but now I wore an outfit resembling Clio's: short,
tight, with a flared miniskirt, and patterned with bursts of color.
And stiletto ankle boots—the kind I wouldn't have thought I could
walk, much less run, in. It was perfect for this warm night—it felt
so much hotter now than it had been when I set out earlier, or
was it just my body temperature that had spiked?—and perfect
in general if I were a different kind of girl, the kind who knew
how to have a good time, who always appeared at ease with herself. Who was afraid of nothing, able to seize anything and anyone
she wanted, the girl I sometimes wished I could be. Tonight, for
once, I felt comfortable inhabiting this persona. I didn't quite
know how that had happened or why, but it felt good and freeing.

On we ran through the lamplit streets of the French Quarter
together, Lucian pulling me off into dark corners to kiss me. He
whispered in my ear that he wanted us to be away from the others,
on our own, that we could be together. That a world awaited where
we had to answer to no one, a world devoid of these divisions or
these rules and levels to attain as angels or devils, where we could
exist. We could just *be*. That was all he wanted and dreamed of,

and all I had to do was follow him into that realm and we could have that.

I couldn't get my bearings, though. It looked like we had reached that leafy park, Congo Square, where Dante and I sometimes ate lunch. But then, next thing I knew, we were along the waterfront. Lucian let go of my hand and kept running, disappearing into the distance. Before I could make sense of it, in a blink, I was on one of the steamboats as it cruised the river. Music played as the passengers danced and sipped drinks. My mind felt too slow to process everything bombarding it—the sights and sounds and the wild, thrilling adrenaline that accompanied it. And yet, despite the confusion, it felt as though something had been unlocked, allowed to lift and lighten and let this new brand of freedom in. My soul rose up from somewhere deep within to meet the world, to run wild.

Lucian had yet to return, but this, like everything else right now, didn't bother me. Clio and Jimmy were sequestered on a bench overlooking the water but paying no mind to the view. She broke away, sidling up beside me as I gazed into the dark harbor with dreamy eyes. I was content to watch it all pass by, living in the moment of it, my mind slowed down to match the easy pace of our boat journey, but my heart and every nerve ending revved up to take it all in—from the sweet, sticky scent of the river air to the wind sweeping through me and the hypnotic ripple of the water below us. My senses and soul worked in overdrive, extracting each ounce of feeling from every second of every minute.

"You know he loves you, don't you? You've got to know," Clio said wooing me.

"He does?" I didn't know why we were talking to each other like we were friends. Why wasn't I afraid of her? But just as quickly

I whisked those thoughts away from this landscape, like a bird might swoop down to snap a fish from the water's surface and fly away all in one smooth movement.

The brunette appeared. "He's so beautiful and he loves you. Why aren't you with him?"

"It's complicated," I heard myself say.

"Why?" asked the brunette. "You're seventeen. What needs to be complicated? Because you're an angel?" The word, spoken by this relative stranger, should have registered as a shock in my heart, but instead it felt no more different than a conversation about the weather or what happened on a favorite TV show. "You're not really, though. Not yet, anyway. Not completely."

"You have a long way to go," Clio offered. "And you probably won't get there. They don't tell you how hard that path is. They act like it's easy, that it's destiny, meant to be. It's brutal and the journey there is littered with those who failed." She paused, smiling in that way that she had to know was a great weapon. "It would be so easy to just go with him. To be in his world instead. Wouldn't you love that? Wouldn't that be so much easier than what your life is like now?"

"Do you actually like your life right now?" the brunette asked.

"Now that you've already seen some of what it takes to become an angel?" Clio finished the thought. They were on either side of me, each filling my ears with these ideas that sounded so true, as though they had tapped into some very hidden part of my subconscious that never wanted to voice any of these concerns for fear that acknowledging them would ruin what drove me and kept me alive.

"Have you noticed how you have it harder than everyone else? How much more is expected of you? Why is it that way? It seems pretty unfair."

"When do you get to live? When is it your turn to enjoy the things that others get to do every day instead of being mired in constant worry and dread?"

"Don't you wish those scars would stop stinging?"

"Things don't have to be this way. There's an easier way. A better way."

"We're just so excited to have you as part of us. Aren't you having fun? This is what every night feels like here."

"I suppose I could get used to this," I heard myself say and just as instantly I felt betrayed by my own words. I felt a division within myself, a line being drawn, splitting my soul into halves, but I felt powerless to stop it. These words were coming out of my mouth; there was no filter. I was at war within and I couldn't find the sane me; it was being buried. But it was being buried by bits of truth. I *had* grown weary of the pressure on me, of following such a difficult path. What I said wasn't a lie. These were things I felt, even if I tried so hard not to.

Right now was certainly something far better than I'd felt for as long as I could remember. It was invigorating. I felt like my eyes had opened: I hadn't realized the extent to which this fate of mine, this role forced upon me, weighed on me. I didn't realize how it infected every cell and muscle and bone and thought and every scrap of my existence. I didn't grasp the full capacity of that pressure and how frustrated and fearful I had been until the veil was lifted. Yes, I could get used to this. I could even get addicted to this.

I barely had time to put these thoughts together, though, and I was swept up in another mad rush. This night was a near constant whirling, the kind that enlivens every ounce of your being and you don't want it to end—even if, for some reason, I wasn't completely aware of what was going on the whole time. It was as if someone had hit shuffle on the night's events—nothing seemed to unfold in any linear way and huge chunks seemed to go unaccounted for. I had no idea how I got from point A to point B or what other points I might have hit along the way.

I vaguely recalled, for instance, that Lucian and I had been in that haunted house with everyone, and that he and I had made some sort of pact that bonded us together and left me feeling like he did care about me and he did want me and was as drawn to me as I was to him. It had been a revelation. But I just didn't know any of the details; none of them could quite push to the forefront of my mind, except for the residual joy. The pervading sense of invincibility, power, strength, peace, coursing through me at once, couldn't have been more all-encompassing or intoxicating. There was a freewheeling, freefalling, otherworldly charge to it all. It took over, wooing the nervous, wary parts of my consciousness that originally set out questioning everything then ended up surrendering. What had I been so afraid of?

The last thing I remember was catching sight of my reflection in a store window as we passed in the wee hours. I brushed the hair out of my face, just as the reflection did. But the reflection wasn't me. The reflection was of someone else, some sort of ideal: flowing flaxen hair, willowy limbs taking graceful strides as though on a runway, and commanding, sultry eyes. Who was this? Where was I?

27

This Isn't Even You

I heard the bells first. They were so loud and booming they shook my entire body, echoing in my head like they were pealing from somewhere within me. Then came something at a different pitch—sirens? But I paid that no mind. I felt too at peace for that. It all faded blissfully into the background.

My eyes opened to the smallest slivers, letting in the pale light of the sun just beginning its ascent. The chilly morning air encased me. I didn't know where I was or how I'd gotten here, but it didn't matter right now. I wasn't ready to open my eyes any further, anyway. Why bother? What was the rush? I couldn't quite move, couldn't really feel much of anything, except for the sense of pure calm running through me as if I was floating through time and space. All seemed right with the world, like I was experiencing a sweet serenity that had eluded me my whole life so far. And I thought of Lucian. I wished he was here right now. Why did we have to follow any of these rules that kept us from each other? It felt so absurd. It seemed so clear that we should be together. Where was he? Where was I? I had no idea where I had been, who I'd been with, what I'd been doing. I was only aware of this sort of nirvana. I wanted more of it. I drifted, letting my eyes fully close again.

The bells. Those bells again. *Make them stop,* I thought. What were they? Why were they so loud? They made my body tremble and my eardrums feel as though they might burst. Finally, I pried my lids open against the burning sun. It blinded me, so that I couldn't see anything at first but a white flash. Then objects began to take shape: someone on a horse, frozen in time, somewhere below me; leafy trees rustling in the chilly breeze; and straight ahead, sky, clear out to the river. I sat up, jittery, unsteady. My head throbbed, my muscles ached, and my bones felt like they'd been mangled in a grinder. But my legs felt free, loose. I looked out again. I was on the level with the clouds. I looked down and then my breath stopped. I knew that man on the horse—that was Andrew Jackson. Below me was Jackson Square. *Below me.*

My heart lurched. I sat on a ledge, my legs dangling in the air, nothing fencing me in. I could easily just keel right over onto the pavement below. Had I slept here? I could have killed myself simply by rolling over. I gripped the edge with my sweaty hands. The bells stopped. I tried to take a deep breath but it came jaggedly, making me cough. I had to get off this ledge, but how? I felt paralyzed, scared to move, and yet my heart jumped out of my chest, pulsing so hard and fast I thought that alone could propel me from this spot. I was sweating, shaking, hot and cold. I couldn't look down again. So instead, I looked up. Just above me, stretching into the stratosphere was the central steeple of St. Louis Cathedral. But . . . how?

I couldn't begin to make sense of it. I just had to get down. Now. The numbers ran through my head, every single fact I'd ever read about this landmark: dedicated to King Louis IX of France. Destroyed in a fire in the late 1700s and rebuilt; Latrobe worked on it. But the one statistic I kept coming back to was that it was 130 feet high. So I had to be about 80 feet up right now. I clutched the edge again. But then I recalled another interesting fact: I could not be killed by a fall from here. I didn't know how I had gotten up here, but I wouldn't die getting down. I looked down once more, slowly, so slowly, so I wouldn't overwhelm myself and fall over. About 20 feet below me was a wider landing and a pair of windows. I needed to be there.

I steadied myself but then, without any setup or strategizing, I just pushed myself right off the ledge. I hit the landing with a thud that seemed far louder than I expected for my weight and it felt as if I might go right through and end up inside the church. I stumbled forward onto my hands and knees, scraping them. My feet and ankles throbbed as though something may have snapped inside, and everything felt banged up but I was too relieved to be too bothered. And I felt manic. I needed to keep going, get inside, get somewhere safe. The narrow sills of the mammoth windows jutted out about three feet up from where I stood. I climbed the big step and stood there, framed by this glass structure and gazing into the mezzanine of the cathedral. No one was there. These windows were for show and not meant to be opened, so there was no easy way in. Too bad. I would simply have to create my own entryway.

I angled my sweater-covered elbow, and, using my other hand to push my arm like a battering ram, plowed it into the glass. Once, twice, three times. *Crack.* The glass buckled, and there were several fault lines etched into it. One more hit and it shattered, raining chunks and shards inside. I fell through onto the pews with a crash. Organ music filled the air, followed by a crush of dissonant, wrong notes and everything went silent, except for a few gasps. I righted myself, scrambling to my feet, and caught sight of the main floor of the church: the pews were nearly full. So many curious, horrified faces looking up at me in the mezzanine. I froze.

And then I ran. Straight down the staircase in the corner, blowing past the ushers and right out the front doors into the pedestrian plaza before Jackson Square, where artists were already setting up their booths and horse-drawn carriages awaited the day's first passengers. I kept going, so fast that pieces of glass flew off me and I felt the breeze rushing through my clothes. Only then did I realize I was bleeding and my sweater was ripped along the arm and across the back. But I kept on. It was early enough that the streets had yet to awaken, with shopkeepers just beginning to open up and few tourists out and about. But on every block, I encountered the same thing: an area cordoned off with police cars and yellow crime scene tape. I didn't want to look any closer as I passed, but there was no ignoring the body-bag-shrouded lumps on the ground at each of these locations. It only made me run faster, panting.

Finally I made it to the house, climbing in through the window. My room felt too cozy, like it couldn't contain me. And my body couldn't contain this mania; it overwhelmed my system. I hit the floor, and everything went black again.

The voice was familiar. "Haven! Haven!" It got closer, and then it was right over me. "It's Dante! How long have you been here?" Something tugged on my arm, patted my forehead. Everything sounded like it was happening in another room to someone else. "Wait. Thirty seconds. Okay? *Connor!*" I tuned it out. Outside the window, it was dark now; the day had apparently come and gone. My nerves, my pores, every inch of skin buzzed. A fury rose swirling within me, lifting me up to my feet. It started on my shoulder, where I could feel something foreign sizzling, and it spun out from there, permeating every cell in my body, a wild anger setting my blood aflame, demanding action and movement, like a question in search of an answer. My entire body wrapped itself around this violence to embrace it, and, ultimately, become it.

I flung open the closet door so hard the mirror inside came unstuck on one side, hanging now at an angle. I ripped off my sweater and pulled at the strap of my tank top, looking over my shoulder. I stood so close to the glass of the mirror that its coolness threatened to quell that burning scar. But now as I watched, the intense sharp blade of that pain transformed into a comforting warmth. A fiery fleur-de-lis glowed on my shoulder.

It was beautiful. It belonged there, begging to be admired. I marveled at it, and at the girl in the mirror with the fire in her eyes and that piercing gaze. Look. At. Me. A calm washed over me, mingling with madness; a confluence of adrenaline and peace.

Something else caught my eye in the mirror. Outside in the black of night came that flash, the reflection of the window across the way. That light. It called to me.

I searched through the items hanging in the closet and found it, tugging at it so sharply I broke the hanger in the process. I ripped off my tank top and jeans, pulled off my shoes, and poured myself into the long-neglected dress—the black one I had gotten with Sabine—zipping it up, feeling it cling to my body. I clomped down into the boots I had purchased that same day. I felt ten feet tall.

With a crash, I threw open the door to my room, smashing

it into the wall. I felt superhuman. I heard another voice, but I didn't bother to listen. I kept walking.

" . . . you're back. You're . . . where are you going? . . . Are you . . ." The tall guy followed me, talking to me still. The look of him made me furious. Eyes set straight ahead, my body shot down the hall on automatic pilot, determined to get next door as soon as possible and sweeping aside anything that impeded that progress. He kept talking and trailing me. He seized my arm to stop me. I just swung it up, bucking him off like he was no more than an insect and sending him flying back a few feet. I kept going.

As I turned the corner, more obstacles came at me. I smiled for a moment, then let their faces fall away. I looked through them. All that registered on my radar were stony eyes that seemed intent on stopping me and outstretched arms ready for attack. Only bits of their worthless words reached me, mostly coming at me like static.

" . . . not what she was wearing a second ago . . ."

" . . . look like you want to kill someone . . ."

" . . . Watch out! . . ."

" . . . need to get her into the room . . ."

They blocked my path but as I neared them, I raised my hands, pushing through them as though they were saloon doors. One fell over. The tall one lunged at me.

" . . . *not safe to go* . . . want to help . . ." His arms grabbed me from behind. The scream tore out of me, mad and manic. I thought I could rip his flesh off of him with my teeth to get him to let go. I kicked my legs in the air, scissoring wildly, and knocked him off balance. He dropped to his knees, letting go while I whipped around and rammed my fist into his jaw. It was made of stone, but the crunch was so pleasing to my ears, the impact so satisfying against my hand, my lips curled in a smile. That etching on my shoulder rewarded me for my efforts, and I felt my veins being pumped full of euphoria.

My legs took off, carrying me lightning fast to the LaLaurie mansion. I was there before I heard any footsteps, no time for anyone to even see what direction I had headed. I rattled the doorknob with enough force to shake the door right off the frame if I wanted to. It annoyed me, this locked door. This house deserved greater destruction for trying to keep me out. My hands smacked the door, as though I were pushing away some brute. The window. Yes. I wound up my leg, kicking it hard and fast. My chunky heel spiked the glass, shattering it all around me. It was beautiful, all those pieces twinkling to the ground, like a music box. I knocked in a few jagged shards and stepped right inside.

The darkness and the silence surrounded me. Safe. Where I belonged. And then that voice, the one I wanted to hear, filled my head, touched my heart. As the volume turned back up, my entire being registered the shift now to something dreamlike.

"Haven?" Lucian said gently, in disbelief. Then louder. "Haven. What . . . ?" He didn't finish his thought. He materialized at the top of the staircase, stopping in his tracks.

Again, I launched my body up those stairs, gliding to him, pulled as though by an ocean current on a stormy day. The burn of my shoulder lit a fire, propelling me. He had time only to take one step in my direction before I reached him.

"What are you doing here?" he whispered, smiling. But I leaned into him, pulling him by the collar into a kiss. I wrapped my arms around his neck and we floated, it seemed, up those last few stairs, feverish, collapsing onto a cushy bench near the railing overlooking the foyer.

He pulled away for a moment to say, "I've been so worried about you I don't even know where to start." Soft beams of milky moonlight filtered in, setting him aglow in the enveloping dimness. "Have you gotten my messages?" He ran his fingers through my hair.

"No, I—" I had trouble assembling my thoughts into sentences.

"I found out you got tagged. I was the last to know. They're still keeping me in the dark about so much." He shook his head, regretful. "Are you okay?" The electric currents of blue in his gray eyes lit up, radiating waves of calm that had a hypnotic effect on me.

"I'm fine," I whispered, pulling him in to kiss him again. "Stop talking."

"That doesn't sound like you," he said softly, sharing the slightest laugh. "Not that I'm necessarily complaining. But . . . what's all this?" He looked me up and down. "What's going on with you?" He rested his fingers on my chin for a moment, staring into my eyes, tunneling in for clues. I felt a mischievous smile blossoming. I pulled off that unloosened tie around his neck, held it over the railing, and let go, watching it flutter to the ground. "We don't have much time. We have to talk about Metamorfosi Day at some point," he said with a sigh.

"No!" I didn't want to hear about logistics or planning or what fate had in store for either of us. I was sick of all that. Lucian was talking now, but I wasn't listening. I lay my head on his shoulder. His voice lapped at me but none of the words stuck. He tucked my hair behind my ear and swept my long locks over one shoulder. Then his hand froze. He jerked away, startling me, and twisted me with force, turning my back toward him.

"What's this?" he barked, his chilly tone snapping me out of my trance. I sat straight up, shaken by this sudden shift. I could feel his breath on my back as he leaned closer, examining it as if it was alive. I looked over my shoulder and found that marked spot glowing a burnt-orange hue in the darkness. I tried to swivel it away from him.

"You know what it is," I snapped back. "It'll go away. Relax."

"Not if you don't try to fight it off." He spat his words. "Didn't I warn you, you can't let it take over or it will destroy you?"

"No." I leaned back against the railing now rolling my eyes, already bored with this talk. I let my head rest against the banister and stared straight up into more darkness. My lids closed, my mind lost in a haze for a moment. Scenes flashed back to me at once, waves of memories I didn't know I had until right now. Lucian and me, here, talking, just like this, except it had gone so much differently. We had come to some sort of decision that I remember finding comforting. I racked my brain for what it was but hit a wall. "Didn't we have this talk before?" I asked.

That feeling I remembered so vividly was the same sensation that had enveloped me just a few minutes ago, right until he discovered my marking. It was an ease; I was so infatuated with that feeling, I wanted more. Now. Forever.

"What are you talking about? When would we have discussed this? I haven't seen you in days."

"I was here last night. With you."

"You were not here last night with me." He made no attempt to mask the anger in his voice.

I was losing patience, that madness rising up again. "No, we *did* talk about this," I snapped in his direction. The scene played in my mind now, like a movie. "You said I could just stay with you, in your world, find a way to be there that suited us both."

"Why would I say that?" He sounded offended now. "And why would you ever agree to something like that?"

I leaned back again, a dreaminess setting in, swirling outward from that spot on my shoulder. "It would be so easy." The words flowed out of me peacefully, like I was channeling someone else. "That's what you said. 'Don't you want something to be easy when everything is always such a fight for you? Aren't you tired of struggling?'" I quoted him from this memory of mine, my eyes locked somewhere back in this dark abyss as I thought of how he'd looked at me when he had said it. "Yes. I am tired," I responded to his question and closed my eyes again. "Yes. I want something to be simple, finally." I felt myself drifting, slipping from the here and now.

"Don't you get it? This is what they do!" he said. "They prey on every insecurity and desire. That's how they get you. This"—he touched that marking and it stung, sending a sharp shiver through me—"creates a fantasy for you to hang on to. You weren't here last night. We didn't talk. If you fight it, like I told you to, then you'll learn the truth about your time with the Krewe. I guarantee that whatever really happened with them, it wasn't anything pleasant. Trust me on that."

"Trust you. You. Sure," I sniped.

"Look, we should cool off for a minute."

"Cool off? I'm still waiting for us to heat up!" I shot back.

He backed away from me on the bench, scowling at me, horrified. "This isn't even you right now," he said. "It's this . . . this corrupted, manipulated version of you. I don't know who I'm talking to." He sounded more than just disgusted: he sounded let down. It should have woken me up, but my anger only ignited more.

"Really? Because who you're talking to is someone who's pretty sick of being told what ridiculous feats are expected of her. So maybe joining you doesn't sound as bad as it used to, how about that? When the other option is that I could lose you entirely?

And lose you because I have failed you, because I can't save you? How do I live with that?"

"I thought you could handle this, but maybe I should just forget it," he said, bitingly. He tugged me by one arm, yanking me off the couch.

"You're gonna throw me out? You can't. You need me."

"Not like this," he barked, making me shiver. "I can't talk to you like this, and I won't talk to you at all until you fight this thing." He flattened his palm against the fleur-de-lis marking and I felt it sizzle up to meet him, singeing me in the process. He took his hand away again, looking shocked that it had done that. His voice softened: "I'll send word or a light in a few days, and we'll try all this again."

All that tranquility erased. "Don't bother," I snapped, the rage burning me from the inside once more. I had to get away. Far away. I pushed him aside, sprinting down the stairs. Midway down, I jumped onto the railing and threw myself over. I landed on the floor just as the door below opened, revealing Dante, Lance, and Connor. I wanted to run through them out into the night. I took off, but made it just a few steps.

The side of my face smacked against the ground.

28

Good to Have You Back

I could feel the struggle within me—something trying to suffocate my soul: sealing its mouth with tape, throwing plastic over its head, binding its hands, tying weights to its feet, submerging it, leaving it to drown. And doing it all so joyfully as my soul kicked and screamed within my body, begging to be heard and brought back to the surface, to gulp giant breaths of sweet air again, to open its eyes, to live. It fought and fought, working and wishing to expel this foreign force, this attacker that had taken up residence.

You need to destroy this, Haven. Extinguish this before it kills you and everything you are from the inside out. Before you lose everything. You don't want this.

And then, just as the struggle became too much and I could picture myself lost at the bottom of that lake, I was floating. I was quite sure of it. I didn't know where I was, only that it was dark and I was weightless, suspended. My eyes struggled to focus, but there was nothing to see except for a golden glow surrounding me. One by one the lights burned out and I landed—the wind knocked out of me, gasping for air—on a padded floor. A silence was trapped in the room, penetrated only by faint breathing.

Someone scooped me up and my body crumpled in his arms: Lance, I could tell from the scent of his skin, like freshly laundered cotton.

"I'm fine. Let me walk," I whispered.

He ignored me.

W e just turned around and you were gone," Lance said. I had opened my eyes and found myself tucked into my bed, Dante and Lance by my side and the sun setting outside my window. I had apparently slept the day away. They had just finished filling me in on my rampage. It's a strange feeling to know you've been doing and saying things of which you have absolutely no recollection. It's as though someone else has taken over your body, like stealing a car, and then they park it back in your garage with dents and dings and mysterious extra miles racked up. And these were just the things the people at our house had witnessed. Who knew what else had happened.

My memories were incredibly sparse: really, all I remembered was waking up above Jackson Square. It was a detail that Dante had found astounding ("But how did you get there?") and Lance had found inspiring ("Do you think you actually climbed up there?"). Apparently after raging through the house, I had passed out on the threshold of the LaLaurie mansion just as the two of them and Connor had come searching for me. They had seen Lucian, who had simply said, "She's been tagged, and she needs you. I'm shackled here or I would bring her over myself." And they had taken me back, gathering the group in the levitation room.

"There were so many people all of a sudden joining in the second line, you know? It was out of control," Dante explained, pulling something from his pocket, a green sprig that almost looked like mint. He handed it to me with a bottle of water.

"Here. Mariette says this will help you get your strength back. It's just an herb." I took it, crunching on the leaves, which were more brittle than I expected and tasted of vanilla.

"Not bad, thanks." I smiled and searched for the words. "You guys, I'm so sorry for . . . everything. I don't even know what to say."

"We're fine." Lance brushed it off. "It's just, you know, good to have you back." His tone was heavy, with the slightest crack in his voice. He pushed his glasses up. "But forget about us. It's Connor you really ought to apologize to."

I put my hand over my mouth, stifling a misplaced laugh. But what they had told me just seemed so unfathomable. "I really punched him?" I whispered.

"Dude, you've got a killer right hook." Dante laughed.

"Yeah, don't get me angry, right?" I shook my head.

Dante's eyes darkened. "Hav," he started, his fingers fidgeting and a pained expression sweeping across his face. "I feel so guilty. I got so caught up in Max's birthday, I should've been paying better attention. I shouldn't have lost you."

"That's crazy, D." I bumped my shoulder into his. "This was going to happen no matter what. I mean, it's happening to all of us like some kind of hazing ritual, right?"

Lance nodded. "Well, a little more serious than, like, some kind of fraternity hazing, but yeah. Everyone."

Dante raised his hand, looking sheepish. "Except . . ."

"You don't count," Lance said. "That's why you feel guilty."

I turned to him. "Why don't you count?"

"The night you went missing, we were talking to Connor, and he knows some stuff. Like he said, from what he's been told, I'm kind of exempt from some of what you guys are being put through right now. It turns out I'm in, like, advanced-placement angel training."

"You've gotta be kidding." I laughed. Dante always was an overachiever.

"Yeah, so I guess I had this happen in Chicago, with Etan, you know?" He still sounded wistful when he said the name. Etan really had been his first love, even if he was trying to steal his soul. "So I'm kind of a level ahead. Max is too, actually. We're supposed to aid the rest of you now."

"Wow. Lucky."

"Yeah. Lucky. I almost had my soul taken back then, as you may recall. But lucky," he said.

"Anyway," Lance jumped in, "so Connor seems to know about our pasts and everything. He said Dante is a 'born angel' rather than a 'made angel,' and that's why he's a step ahead of us."

"What does that mean?" It had never occurred to me to ask Connor about our pasts—I'd always been too concerned with trying to learn about our future and survive our present.

"Something about our souls finding our bodies and Dante's soul being born in his body."

"Huh?"

"I think my dad was an angel!" Dante glowed, proud.

"You never knew your dad."

"I know. I think that may be why."

"Anyway, he said not to bother getting hung up on it, because we'll be finding out more if we make it past this phase." Lance caught himself. "*When*. When we make it past this phase."

"Ohhhkay." I shook my head. "So did I miss anything else around here?"

"Oh, yeah!" Dante said. "Totally insane killing spree. Like seven, eight murders in one night."

The sound of it made me shiver. "That's awful."

Lance just adjusted his glasses with a serious expression and changed the subject. "And besides that, we're doing a Mardi Gras float," he said.

"The whole volunteer program gets to do its own float and march in the parade," Dante added. "We just started working on it today."

"So I think you're all up to speed," Lance said, standing. "Now as soon as you can tell us what you were doing that we missed, then we'll have all the blanks filled in."

"Right," I said with the proper sarcasm.

"Oh, wait, I have one more question," Dante piped up. "Who or what or where is Savannah?"

Now I was really confused. "Uhhh, in Georgia?" I offered.

"Yeah, but, I mean, what's its significance?" Dante probed.

"How should I know?" I shrugged.

"That was apparently the last thing you said before you passed out," Lance explained.

"Oh."

"Let us know if anything comes back, okay? Because it will. Like it did for me." Lance shook his head now as he recalled the horrors that had flashed back. "Maybe we can learn something." I just nodded. They got up to leave.

"No more gallivanting, Haven the Terra-ble," Dante said, pointing at me in warning.

"Oh, and call Joan," Lance ordered.

"Ugh." I groaned. Joan, of course, her radar must be up. I wondered if there would come a day when I would need to tell her about all of this. It had begun gnawing at me lately: it was getting harder and harder to keep this secret from her. I didn't have a lot of practice lying. My life hadn't really been exciting—or rather, dangerous—enough to warrant lying about anything until this past year.

"She called a bunch of times and we told her you had a bad cold and lost your voice," Dante said proudly.

"She bought that?"

"Enough to not get on a plane and come down here." Lance laughed.

I would call, but first I had one more thing I had to do.

Connor opened the door. I saw the army-green bruise tinting his left cheek.

"I come bearing gifts," I said in my sweetest voice. In one hand I held out a bag filled with ice, in the other, a tin of caramel popcorn.

"As long as you're not planning to throw any of that at me, c'mon in." He laughed and swung the door wide.

"About that—"

"I'm past the icing stage. It's healing fast. But this I'll take." He grabbed the tin, tearing off the lid and peering inside. "Hey, this is half-empty—"

"I like to call it half-full. Best I could do on short notice."

"Half-eaten stale popcorn?" He pulled out a handful, hopping up to sit on his desk. "Not bad."

"I'm really sorry, I didn't mean—"

"Don't worry about it." He swatted my apology away. "Like I told the others, you got hit harder than anyone else here. It's what happens when you're the strongest. With power comes a certain burden, right?"

"I'm the—?"

"And you were probably depleted to begin with because don't think I don't know that you've been carrying the team on the levitation and soul extraction."

"I have?"

"I know I've been tough on all you guys, but I believe in everyone. And in you, especially, Haven. I'm pretty invested in your success. If—" He shook his head, starting over. "No, when—when you make it through to the completion, you're pretty much going to end up being my boss."

"What?" I actually let out a laugh, it sounded so ridiculous. "That's funny."

"No, seriously." He didn't look like he was kidding.

"That's kind of awesome." I meant to only think it, but it came out of my mouth.

"But one day at a time, okay?" Connor said. "You know at some point soon, you'll have to do battle against *them*." I nodded. "We've got to learn as much as we can about how it's all gonna go down. We're all up to speed on the guy next door now."

Lucian. "Yeah," I said, guiltily, for so many reasons.

He put up his hands. "Hey, you were protecting your sources, fine, but now we're on the same page, okay? We can keep you safe better that way. Got it?"

I nodded. "Got it."

"That marking gone?" he asked, pointing to my shoulder. I hadn't even looked. I tugged at my T-shirt and tried to look over my shoulder. He leaned toward me, spun me around. "Yep, just a little red. You're good."

"Thanks." I couldn't hide my relief.

"Now watch it, okay?" I nodded again. "You're certainly full of surprises."

"Yeah. I kind of wish I could go back to being boring," I said as I opened the door.

He smiled again. "Somehow I don't think it's possible."

When I felt I could fake sounding back to normal enough to pass Joan's finely tuned ear for detecting trouble, I finally called her. She answered on the first ring, as though she were waiting by the phone.

"How's your cold, honey? I can't believe you survive these Chicago winters and we ship you somewhere warm and then you get sick. What did I tell you about keeping up with your vitamin C, Haven? Are you eating, I mean, anything good for you? I need to send you more care packages. I was thinking of enrolling you in the fruit of the month club even though you're not going to be away all that long but still—" She veered off on one of her tangents.

"No, I'm fine, really," I lied.

"I'm sure you're working yourself too hard," she scolded lovingly.

"Yeah, something like that."

"You treat everything like it's life or death. Go easy on yourself."

"Thanks," I said, my eyes rolling. "I will, promise. How's everything at home?"

"Fine, fine. The girls at the hospital say hi. Everyone still keeps asking if you've heard from colleges yet but I just tell them—"

"No," I said, bristling a bit. "When there's news you'll all be the first to know." It still felt odd, this college charade, going through these motions of applying and waiting and wondering. It was impossible to imagine that I would be permitted to go to school, to go through that rite of passage that I had been so excited about for so long. But recent events had reminded me in no uncertain terms that there were aspects of my future that I had far less control over than college admissions.

"I know, I know, it's too soon, but we just all know you're going to get in everywhere and they're all pulling for you to not go far away. You know how it is, they miss you so. And I do too."

"I know you do," I said softly.

"I was thinking, what if I came in for Mardi Gras?" Her voice kicked up an octave and a decibel.

"Oh, Joan, that's sweet, but it'll probably be super expensive and it'll be crazy here. Maybe another time would be better."

"Oh, but I found some incredible fares, some kind of special promotion. And I've always wanted to go." There was a pause, as though she was waiting for me to speak, then she just went on. "I know, I know, you're worried it'll be hectic with your work, but I promise to stay in a hotel and not get in the way . . ." When she got this way it could be difficult to dissuade her. But I vowed that she wasn't coming to visit, even if it meant having to get her name placed on the No-Fly List to keep her away.

She was still making her case when I heard my door open. I looked over but my eyes couldn't make sense of what they saw: Dante stood there but he wasn't all there; he was a translucent hologram of himself. He materialized fully and then flickered again.

"Uhhh, can we talk about it in another couple days? Dante just came in and . . . he . . . doesn't look so good."

"Oh no, honey, is he getting what you had?"

"Who knows what this is."

"Give him my love. Take care of yourselves. I love you, sweetie."

"Love you. Bye." I hung up the phone.

Dante stood there, hands on his waist. "You can see me?" he asked in disbelief.

"What's going on with you?"

He held an eyedropper and squeezed a bit of liquid into his

hands, coating them and shaking out his arms and legs. "Can you see me now?"

"Yes."

He squeezed more liquid, this time rubbing his hands all over his body, as though trying to shake off a swarm of bees. "What about now?" He wasn't even a hologram anymore; he was his usual self.

"Dan, yes. Stop that. Please."

He muttered a series of expletives, clenching his fists.

"I can hear you too." I laughed.

"Gimme your charm, from Lance." He wiggled his fingers at me, insistent.

"Are you serious?" I took off my necklace and handed it over. "Are you going to use this power to rob people? Don't make me your accomplice."

"Too late." He coated the fleur-de-lis charm with an eye-dropperful of the liquid. A thin trail of smoke sizzled from it. He handed it back to me. "Hold on to that charm and picture yourself invisible." I closed my eyes, focusing, imagining my form and figure being erased by the air. It was the same power of thought I used to levitate things, but it was now focused through a different lens.

"Whoa, Hav. You're really good at this."

"Whaddya mean?"

"Look in the mirror." As he gestured toward it, I turned around and in place of my reflection, I saw only a dark, hazy smudge. A silhouette, a stain. It set my mind racing.

"Wow, I've never looked so good," I joked.

"It's funny," Dante said. "I can cook this stuff up but it never works on me like it does on you. You've got skills, Hav."

"You're not so bad yourself."

"Try to change back," he said with the glee of a child watching a magician.

"If I'm stuck this way, you're in major trouble." I laughed as I felt for that pendant and focused once more.

"See, that's what I'm talking about," he said, gesturing to the mirror. I looked, and there I was. "Skills. It's a good thing we didn't lose you to them, to the other side." He sighed. "I forgot, with all of this going on, that I'm really mad at you."

"You are?" I couldn't tell if he was serious or if he was simply about to say something funny.

"Yeah. I am." That came out like a bullet, stopping me. I sat down.

"When we went over there and found you on the doorstep and him there . . . Haven, I wanted to kill him.

"But he didn't do anything. At all. If anything he really is try-ing to tell us whatever he can find out to help—"

"I know, I know." He raised his voice, cutting me off. I had to look away. "I *know*. But the point is, I didn't know that *then*. And I could have killed him; we all could have killed him. *Lance* could have killed him."

Dante gave me a few long seconds to let that sink in fully.

"He wanted to kill him, Hav." He said the words very slowly. "When he thought Lucian had hurt you. Just think about that." He let himself out.

29

You're Kind of a Troublemaker

Images flew at me as I descended into this hell: flashes of blood-splattered bodies in dark alleyways. A series of faces of guys and girls beaten, attacked, knifed. It was a show I wanted to turn off, a movie I wished I could walk out of. But I couldn't make it stop. Even as these fluttered through my subconscious and I told myself, *Wake up, Haven, you can just wake up,* the terror took over. I wished I could claw it out of my head, scratch it from my eyes.

My lids opened, but my breath and my heart kept racing, and my skin was slicked with sweat, matting my hair to the side of my head. There was no relief here in the familiarity of this darkened room or the comfort of this house shared with others like me —the visions were still there, playing on a loop. And somehow I knew that these weren't nightmares but rather memories. These were scenes I had viewed, not fears concocted by an overactive imagination and rattled nerves. Besides the victims, everything else appeared in a complete haze; just this pack of vulture-like figures descending on bodies and pulling from them belongings or locks of hair or, worse, digits and eyes yanked from sockets, gruesome bits and pieces. It all assaulted me just as the thrilling memories had earlier.

I squeezed my eyes shut, trying to fill my head with anything else to root out this evil, but instead my mind fixed on another scene: a snapshot of the cemetery, a long line of shadowy figures queued up before someone whose face I couldn't quite make out. They bowed before him, presenting him with these artifacts and scraps of people who had been left for dead. He stood in front of Lance's newly constructed crypt, collecting them all in a black velvet pouch the size of a potato sack. By the end it bulged with so many trophies from these terrors.

Pounding rattled the door. Only then did I realize I had been screaming. Lance burst in, arms poised for battle, in search of an assailant and easing up only when he realized I was alone. He ran up the ladder to where I lay, paralyzed, the screams ripping from my chest, and he grabbed my hand. Finally I felt the shrieking stop. I had run out of breath, but my eyes still couldn't settle. My gaze bounced manically around the room, and I felt my eyes bug out as I looked at Lance, who squeezed my hand in his.

"I know," is all he said.

"That crime spree, those murders—"

"I know."

"I was there. I saw it all happen. I didn't do anything to stop it."

"I know," he said again, each time his voice growing heavier and yet more comforting.

"But up until now I only remembered a weird excitement about that night."

He nodded wisely. "You've come out the other side," he said

softly. "But the visions will still haunt you, I'm sorry to say. They still haunt me."

"But did I actually . . . ?" There was no disguising the pure panic in my eyes, the tremor in my voice.

"No," he said with conviction, reading my mind. "No. We didn't. We couldn't have." He sounded less certain now, adding with regret, "But I don't know. And this has been worthless on this matter for me." He pulled my phone from my bedside table and scanned the screen. "I haven't gotten a single message with useful information about the night I was tagged. Maybe it'll be different for you." He held it out and I let him read it along with me:

By now you probably have discovered the true nature of your time spent with the Krewe.

So it confirmed one thing: this feeling like we had been on a thrill ride with the Krewe when actually we had viewed this night of terror from the center of the murderous storm. But then it changed course.

If you can bear the horror of being with them again, the plan you are considering is worth enacting.

It was true. I had already been thinking it over. Now I felt I couldn't *not* go.

"This plan," Lance said, tapping the screen, "can I get in on it?" His piercing gaze told me that he didn't intend to take no for an answer.

"I wouldn't have it any other way," I said.

Lance stayed in my room the rest of the night, curled up beside me until the morning sun streamed in the window. My eyes opened bright and strong to greet it. My body felt awake, finally awake, fully myself again. The dull ache of my shoulder was at last subsiding, but the horror of my dreams remained fresh.

Still in my scrubs, I sat down at the desk, pen in hand, and transcribed the words I'd been going over again and again in my mind.

L-

Please forgive me for the other night. Can we start over? I do want to help you. But first, I need your help: Can you find out where the Krewe will be taking their next victims?

And also, I just need to know, for me: What happened on the nights when Lance and I were both tagged? Did we hurt anyone? I need to know whether we actually took part in the Krewe's activities.

With affection, H

I dressed and wandered over next door long before anyone else in the house was ready to start the day. The window hadn't been repaired yet so a clear plastic tarp had been secured over the outside of it. I could see the candle inside, along with another one of those bottles. The door was locked and now that the project inside had been completed, who knew when it might be unlocked. The few passersby seemed to pay me no mind, so I quietly dug the Swiss Army knife out of my bag and sliced open a small flap. I reached my hand in, pulling out the bottle, and in exchange, I wedged my note beneath the candle. Hopefully he would find it.

I waited until I was safely ensconced in the comforts of our courtyard before shattering the bottle. Inside, I found two crisply folded sheets of parchment.

The first was dated the day of Max's birthday:

H–

> SINCEREST APOLOGIES FOR BEING AWAY, BUT I HAVE MUCH TO TELL YOU NOW. METAMORFOSI DAY IS IN THE OFFING. IT HAS BEEN SET FOR THE DAY OF MARDI GRAS. LET THE PLANNING BEGIN. I REMAIN FOREVER INDEBTED TO YOU FOR YOUR HELP. I WILL UNDERSTAND IF, AT ANY POINT, YOU DECIDE IT ISN'T WORTH IT TO YOU TO DO THIS FOR ME. YOU'VE ALREADY GIVEN ME MORE THAN I DESERVE: HOPE. MEET TONIGHT? I'LL SIGNAL.
>   YOURS,
>   L

I read it through twice before the inevitable happened and it began to warm my fingers. Then I held it a few seconds longer and, when I couldn't take it anymore, let it fall to the ground, where it caught fire and crackled before quickly turning to ash and disintegrating entirely. Then I unfolded the next note, dated just a day later:

H–

> I'VE HEARD FROM THE DENIZENS OF THIS

CONDEMNED WORLD OF MINE THAT YOU HAVE BEEN
TAGGED AND I'M RACKED WITH WORRY AND GUILT.
PLEASE LET ME KNOW THAT YOU'RE OKAY. YOUR SAFETY
IS ALL THAT MATTERS TO ME RIGHT NOW. I WILL NOT
REST UNTIL I KNOW YOU'RE WELL.
  LOVE,
  L

I studied it, committing it all to memory. So this is what it had taken to get a valediction like that: extreme danger and an imminent threat to the health and stability of my body and soul. At least the trauma of the past several days had earned me some sort of perquisite. I would take it. In a flash, that note, too, became ash.

L ance found me waiting for him in the courtyard. "You did it?" he asked as we set off along Royal Street.

"Yep."

He sighed with relief. "Okay. So now . . . ?"

"Now we just wait for him to answer my note. And we'll need to talk to Dante because if you can't shadow—"

He held up his hand to stop me. "Not a problem. Just tested it."

"Really?" I stopped walking for a moment to register my surprise, which wasn't lost on him.

"See, you're not the only one who can pull off these tricks." He smiled.

"I'm glad, trust me. I certainly don't need this thing with the Krewe to be a solo act."

"Yeah, I don't think you can be trusted to be left alone for a little while," he said. The quick glance he gave me from the corner of his eye showed me he was kidding, mostly. "It turns out you're kind of a troublemaker." He smirked.

"I get that all the time." I smiled back.

Lance looked different to me now after the horrors of last night's dreams and the madness of the tagging. I felt the shift; I felt close to him, as though we had been in quicksand, pulled away from each other, and now we were on solid footing again. I thought of what he had said last night and wondered, was it possible that *he and I* had come out on the other side of what threatened us, too? Could it be that we had made our way through that turbulence? I hoped so, because I didn't like the way my world looked without him. I hoped he had discovered the same about me. I wanted to know for sure, but it didn't feel right to ask. For now I would just revel in this hope that a piece of me had returned.

We made our way through the French Quarter to the dividing line at Canal Street—near Dante's favorite shopping spot—and on toward the Warehouse District. The crowds soon diminished but the area, happily, didn't live up to the image conjured by its name. I had pictured deserted structures in disrepair and street corners populated by unsavory loiterers. Instead, it seemed most of the storefronts housed charming art galleries and up-and-coming restaurants. As Lance and I moved along, so did our conversation to lighter, less loaded topics.

"The idea is to illustrate a bunch of the places where we're all working and make the joke that we're working so hard we're always on the graveyard shift. Then tie in the cemeteries since they're such a focal point of the city," Lance explained of the float designs the group had begun work on while I had regained my strength.

"So, judging by your speed at this sort of thing, it should take another ten minutes to finish, right?" I joked. He had apparently managed to wrap up work on the crypt yesterday morning. "We can totally catch a movie or something before tutoring."

He rolled his eyes. "Sorry to disappoint you, but we're working with the whole city-wide volunteer program, not just us—"

"Ohhh, so you have to dumb down your skills a little. No hammering nails with your bare hands."

"Yeah, and you may want to cool it with the flying objects," he swiped at me sweetly.

"Duly noted."

It wasn't until we reached the area's outskirts that we happened upon a real warehouse worthy of the district's name, a huge hangar-like monolith with sides that opened like garage doors. We slipped around back as Lance led the way in through a loading dock. The sound of drills, hammers, saws, and all manner of mechanized tools greeted us. Inside, the place teemed with our fellow interns—as Lance promised, not just from our house, but the entire group, all bustling with purpose, swarming around four multiwheeled platforms to be pulled by trucks on the big day. So far these four floats were all black. But surrounding them, our peers toiled on miniature versions of the city's landmarks— from Jackson Square to the Superdome to the Lake Pontchartrain Causeway. A banner unfurled on the floor read NOLA NATIONAL HIGH SCHOOL VOLUNTEER NETWORK stenciled in giant letters. Meanwhile, our fellow angels had annexed a corner of the space to work on scaled-down replicas of some of the more famous crypts in Saint Louis Number One.

Lance had begun building the trees for the cemetery portion of the float and drafted me to help him. "Try not to saw off an arm, okay?" he said as he planted me in front of a table saw.

"You've got to be kidding me," I said. He thought about it for a moment.

"Yeah, never mind." He shook his head. "Just look busy and when it's time to nail these together and paint then we'll put you to work." That sounded a little more doable.

Someone tugged on my sleeve and I turned around: Emma stood beside me, a clipboard and pen in her hands. "Okay, you two. Costume committee," she said. "I'm taking a poll. Should we be skeletons or some sort of zombie-like creatures or lost souls or . . . ?" We both stared at her blankly. "What do you want to be? On the float?"

I was on the way to the community garden with Dante the following morning when I found another bottle waiting for me next door. The message inside:

H-

WHATEVER YOU'RE THINKING, I DON'T APPROVE, BUT I PROMISED TO HELP YOU. THEY ALWAYS BEGIN THEIR SPREES AT CONGO SQUARE, MIDNIGHT. I SUSPECT THEY'LL BE GOING TONIGHT. PLEASE PROMISE ME YOU WILL BE CAREFUL. IT KILLS ME THAT I CAN'T BE THERE TO GUIDE YOU. LEAVE WORD HERE TOMORROW SO I KNOW YOU'RE ALL RIGHT.

AS FOR THE OTHER MATTER: I'VE BEEN ASKING AROUND AND I HAVE IT ON GOOD AUTHORITY FROM THOSE WHO WERE THERE THAT NEITHER YOU NOR

Lance committed any of those heinous acts. You were spectators but not participants. For the most part, those in your group have been exceptionally strong and haven't been active players in the crimes during their tagging episodes.

Yours,

L

30

Don't Say Another Word

Dante fortified Lance's fleur-de-lis charm and reinforced mine. "You'll be fine all night, but at sunup, or in any direct light, you're obviously in trouble," he warned, as Max looked on, his expression grave.

Connor had come by before we transformed to wish us luck. "Just be smart, guys, okay? If you're in danger of being detected, bail out," he ordered. A crease had begun to form between his eyes in the past few weeks, a sign that the weight of this war was taking its toll on him.

"One last thing," Max piped up. "This is something we've been working on. It's not there yet but if you scatter this at their targets right before they're attacked, it may protect them. That's our hope, at least. Test it out for us, okay?" He handed each of us a red-powder-filled bag.

As there were no other directions to be given, Lance and I looked at each other. "Ready?" I asked. He nodded. He put one hand on the leather bracelet at his wrist and bowed his head. I held my pendant and focused as I felt my form slip away into that haze.

W^e made our way to Congo Square, stealthily creeping along the more deserted streets, blending into the night so that we could barely even see each other; Lance and I were just dark smudges. If we stayed away from lamplight, we really were invisible. Our greatest challenge would be to not lose each other throughout the course of the night.

As we neared the meeting place, we heard the murmur of voices. Ahead of us, a few figures made their way over the top of the gates. But just because we were camouflaged didn't mean we could go slipping between the bars of the park's fence. As Dante had explained it, "It's like a paper bag has been thrown over you— you're still there, but you just don't look like you."

So, as we had so many times at the cemetery, we scaled the entryway. We ran up to the gate and grasped at the metal bars, trying our best not to rattle them. I heard Lance's soft footsteps land on the pavement on the other side. Mine followed a second or two after. The light of the archway caught his shadow for a moment and the sight comforted me. We ventured farther into the leafy park until we happened upon them at last. There were at least two dozen people huddled together, talking, chanting, swaying as though to the same silent beat. Spirits bright, they had the buzzing pulse of a crowd waiting to be revved up and set loose.

Stragglers joined the Krewe: an older man walked up from the direction we had come and with each step closer his form metamorphosed from gray-haired and hunched over to vibrant, young, and strong. He greeted them with handshakes. Others leapt catlike into the trees, then dropped down onto nearby benches, only to spring up again onto other branches. Many shape-shifted before our eyes, assuming entirely new physiques. A familiar man, blond and slim, wandered in on the arm of a tiny figure shrouded in black; as they neared the light, we could clearly see Sister Catherine transforming into Clio, assuming the young demon's enviable statuesque form, even borrowing her usual costume of minidress with cowboy boots. Her escort was our own fallen compatriot, Jimmy. I reached for Lance to point this out, but it took several tries until my hand grazed what I thought to be his shoulder. I felt him squeeze my arm in understanding as Jimmy took his place beside a guy with a familiar blue streak in his hair: Brody. Jimmy smacked him on the back as they spoke, like he was giving him encouragement. Ever so slowly, Brody morphed from the long-limbed, laid-back skater we knew into a musclebound all-American quarterback with a square jaw and short-cropped red hair.

Without warning, Clio sprang up into the air, landing atop a bronze sculpture, which was the bust of a jazz musician. She perched on his head like a bird, her legs crossed, gazing down at her followers, that manic smile playing at her full lips. Lance tugged me to the base of the nearest tree. We stood invisible beneath its full canopy, free to watch.

"*Bienvenue!*" she greeted them, and they called back the same welcome. "I see some have begun celebrating before the work has been done." She pointed in our direction. Dangerously close to us, beneath another nearby tree, an embracing couple locked in a kiss appeared disengaged from the gathering. "Wylie, you should know better," Clio said playfully. He stood now, bowing his head at her respectfully. "Save that for later. It'll be even sweeter after the thrills that lie ahead." Barely breathing, I drifted nearer to the couple. It was that woman, the tall one with the cascading brunette mane.

"You all know about the quota, right? While we always need new members, we need supplies as well. Choose wisely, *mes chéries.*

Save the best, use the rest," Clio trilled as though it were their own personal advertising slogan. "New recruits, don't be shy. Enjoy, and I'll see y'all back home with your trophies," she said in the sweetest drawl—if you didn't know better you'd think she was the perfect southern belle hosting a garden party. She clapped twice, which seemed to be the signal they had all been waiting for. They let out a communal roar, and then scattered into the night like a pack of wild dogs, everyone racing to throw themselves over the gate.

It took Lance and me a moment to move, overwhelmed by the sudden mass exodus into the Quarter. Together we darted out from our spot, trailing Clio. She pushed to the front of the group until they reached Bourbon Street. Then her masses fanned out, like planets orbiting the sun. She circled a trio of men clutching beers as they walked down the middle of the street and made eye contact with one, then skipped ahead of him and glanced over her shoulder, lassoing him with a look that begged him to follow. And he did. The closer he got, the faster she walked, backwards, smiling, weaving through crowds, leading him along as she darted down street after street. Within just a few blocks, she had maneuvered him into an alleyway between a pair of storefronts. Alone. We hung back and I flattened myself against a brick wall and felt for that bag of powder, getting ready to throw it.

"You caught me," she said to him.

"I guess I did. Hi. What are you doing out all by yourself in a place like this?" he slurred.

"You from around here?" she asked, running her fingers along the wall, as she walked slowly toward him. She glided, trancelike, until a quick loss of footing made her trip—but she caught herself with a smile. Her quarry was so transfixed he probably didn't notice. But my stomach dropped as it occurred to me that she must have stumbled over a shadowy Lance.

"You're a cute one, aren't you?" she purred at the man. He was barely her height and his body was soft, without being plump, rather just encased in a layer of insulation where muscle tone may once have been—someone perhaps who had replaced playing sports with watching them. She wound her arms around his neck as though about to kiss him, but something shiny glinted in her hand.

It happened too fast, all at once. I reached into my pocket, gathering a handful of the powder to throw as the masses descended. One of her female followers knocked right into me. I dropped the powder just as Clio plunged a knifelike spike into her victim's neck. I tried to stifle my gasp, stumbling away from the pack. Vultures, they swooped in, picking him apart. Then just as fast, they dispersed, some transforming into various alter egos.

But a few hung back. "Clio, I almost thought you were going to keep him around." It was the girl who had bumped into me. Her long hair hung in a wispy braid swept to one side.

"I know." Clio sighed, lighting a cigarette with her index finger. "I thought about it. He seemed kinda sweet. But I prefer to start the night with a body, not a soul. Just sets the right mood, y'know? Plenty of captures out there to be had. They need to be really somethin' special to be one of us." They seemed to float back out into the night. The man lay on the ground in a pool of blood, his chest split open. I wished I hadn't looked.

"I was too slow," I heard from the shadows across the alley from me. A regretful Lance.

"Me too," I said, the words sickening me.

"Next time," he whispered, his footsteps nearing. "C'mon,

before we lose them." We began running until we landed back on Bourbon Street. Clio had reconnected with Wylie and his paramour, and this time we stuck close to him. He clutched the girl to his side, his arm holding her against his hip, shielding her as they wandered through the crowd, scanning faces. Bourbon Street was so bright, we had to be careful, keeping our distance from the neon bar signs. We found it was safest amid the crush of people walking in the street, near enough to Wylie to catch bits of his conversation.

"You choose, my pet," he said into her hair. She pointed, smiling broadly, as though selecting a new puppy. And then their pace picked up. They floated toward a twentysomething woman modestly dressed in jeans, a tank top, and fitted blazer, walking with a handful of friends. She seemed the type that had been dragged along on a girls' night out, succumbing to the pressures of the wilder ringleader of the group: a disheveled reveler, who pranced down the street singing along to one of the songs drifting out of the loudest bar on the block. I couldn't imagine how this seemingly sensible sober young woman would be captured.

But Wylie and his partner walked past this target and quickly exchanged glances and that's when I saw it. They pinpointed every Krewe member within a twenty-foot radius and all those eyes transfixed their prey in her place, rooting and trapping her there. She appeared at ease as her friends wandered off a few steps ahead, and then Wylie and his partner looped back around, coming up behind the young woman, and took their places on either side of her. He threw his arm around the target's shoulder and I lunged, pushing past the bodies in front of me, to toss a handful of the dust, just as Wylie sunk something into her bicep. It looked like a long black spike, laced with poison, I could only imagine. He stabbed sharp and quick then yanked it out, tucking the evidence back into his pocket. For the briefest moment she lost her footing, like any other tipsy bar-hopper might have. But the two of them anchored her, leading her away.

I had failed again, and the night had only begun. I stopped moving for a moment, jostled on all sides by people out to have a good time amid others out to destroy them. How could we keep going on like this? I felt Lance at my side, pulling me. It was so loud everywhere, the music and the people and so many conversations happening at the same time when he spoke. "Brody looks hungry," he said. I scanned all around and found him, this new version of him, stepping out of a bar. He stood tall, inhabiting his new physique like a coat of arms. I was certain he could outrace anyone. The transformed Jimmy was at his side.

They didn't say a word; they just began following a petite blonde, who looked about my age. She waved goodbye as she stepped out of a restaurant, wearing what appeared to be a work uniform of a white shirt and black pants, her hair in a ponytail. It wasn't Bourbon Street, but it was still plenty crowded—enough that she wouldn't have noticed the pace of footsteps picking up behind her, or the two members of the Krewe among the others lazily gazing in darkened store windows as they wandered along the opposite side of the street. She pulled out a cell phone, launching into an easy, spirited chat. I took off, running ahead, not caring if my footsteps or panting were heard. I wouldn't miss my shot this time. She passed under a streetlamp as I neared her, and I darted out, as fast as I could, throwing a handful of dust at her side just as Jimmy and Brody tripped over me and lunged at her.

The girl spun around, a beast unleashed, as she looked right at the two of them, running backwards now. *"Stay away from me!"* The words tore out of her in the most terrifying, bone-chilling scream. "Stay away!" She sped off, her feet hitting the pavement so hard her steps sounded like gunshots. Someone across the street could be heard speaking to a 9-1-1 operator: "I'm not sure, but it sounded like an attack or something . . ."

"It's okay. You're a first-timer. Next time, next time," came Jimmy's voice as he and Brody scrambled to their feet. I followed them a few blocks but by the time the sirens pierced the air, they had transformed back to their other selves and disappeared into the night. The police would never find them now.

Somehow Lance had managed to remain close. "That was all you, wasn't it?" he whispered.

"Do you think?"

"Well, I didn't get there in time, and I don't think she would have noticed them on her own," he reasoned. "I also don't think she would have been that fast." It was true: the girl had gotten away with such speed and force, she could have been one of them. I made a mental note for Dante and Max that their red dust seemed to work.

As the night wore on, the Krewe split into groups, making it impossible to follow everyone, or to thwart all the attacks. They were never that far away from one another, and they all seemed so telepathically attuned. We would manage to disrupt one near kill, only to find those same Krewe members joining up with another band in the process of pillaging another victim a few blocks down. With each kill and soul capture, the members of the Krewe grew more euphoric, as though these acts fueled them, making them stronger and wildly joyous. Even Lance and I could feel their collective frenzy, the freeness of it. The feeling emanated from each of them, traces of it getting under your skin, even if you fought it off as actively as we did. They had physical advantages too, these creatures: They were impossibly fast and agile. At the first sound of sirens they would scatter, scaling buildings like bugs, slithering into dark spaces. The most skilled ones could transform in less than the blink of an eye. You might see someone walking toward you, and never take your eyes off them, then suddenly lose them so instantaneously you could only assume you had looked away or that someone else had stepped in front of them, obscuring your view.

Most chilling was all they could accomplish without saying a word. They could be yards away from one another and one would choose a target and the others would sense it and focus their gaze on that person too, and then it was as though the victim was caught in their web. It felt like invisible laser tag—the combined effort of that focus could root a person in place or send him veering off in a direction he might never have gone on his own. I remembered that feeling of being separated from the group on Max's birthday and not seeming to mind, and I understood it now.

The bodies. There had been a level of gore I had never wished to see. And there were so many. The few souls I'd seen taken inspired a different brand of fear. Those people were now drafted into this army. I shivered at the notion that I would encounter them again and they would be out for my blood. By the end of the night, Lance and I had racked up a mental flipbook of the double identities of many Krewe members, useful knowledge to be sure, but we had also accumulated so many new, horrific images. They were burned into our brains and I knew there could be no cure for the lifetime of nightmares they would provide. The guilt, too, was inescapable. I had not saved them all. There were people who wouldn't go home tonight, who would be assumed missing because I had neglected to save them; others would turn up tomorrow and need to be identified by family members. These thoughts made my heart ache. All I could hope was that having seen this evil up close, and learned how they operated, might help us know how to fight them next time.

But I knew our time was expiring, too. The streets had begun to clear, the predawn hours setting in. Lance found my arm, guiding me toward the house. We were now just a block from the alley where we had witnessed the night's first tragedy. And then I heard it, the scrape and scratch and slice of another body being picked apart. There was no mistaking it. I set off.

"No," Lance whispered.

"Yes," I hissed back.

Together we followed it, until we reached the gated courtyard of a restaurant that had been closed for several hours. Four of them were there, two guys, two girls, all familiar to us now, taking their hideous trophies to be used in the next ritual no doubt. They all stepped back at once, blood on their hands and clothes. Then they transformed. They were suddenly clean again in these new forms but still clutching their dark souvenirs. They tucked them in purses and backpacks—scraps of clothes, a watch, a digit here, an ear there, a small vial of blood. Then, with smiles on their lips, they leapt over the gate and walked on so easily, leaving the ravaged body amid the flowers.

I couldn't take this anymore, this killing spree that I hadn't stopped. The rage boiled inside me, insulating me from my fear. I followed them. I needed to know where they went. What happened after this rampage? I could feel Lance burning about this choice, even as his shadow walked silently beside mine. But I also knew he wouldn't let me go on my own. And so we trailed behind the group of them as they wound their way back toward the park where the evening had begun.

But they peeled off before reaching Congo Square. Instead,

they scaled another set of gates we knew well: those guarding Saint Louis Number One. Back, back, back they ran, weaving through the alleyways, leapfrogging over the low-lying tombs, and hopping atop the higher ones until they reached their destination: Lance's crypt. The pristine white tomb glowed, a beacon. They pushed in the marble slab and disappeared inside a two-foot-tall doorway. We managed to slink in behind them, so close that I bumped into one of the girls. "Hands to yourself, Marcus. There'll be time for that soon enough," she cooed to him.

"Whatever you say." The one with the crooked smile grunted in pleasant confusion.

Inside, the space was tight—about seven feet high and nine feet long, the walls and floor all smooth marble and oven warm.

"Do we just leave this all here? I want credit. I got some good stuff," the other girl said, her tone spacy, clueless, as she emptied a tote bag with all manner of human parts. The other man's backpack landed on my right foot. I felt the warm weight of its soft, freshly harvested contents and wished I could move my foot but I feared any motion would reveal us. My skin crawled; my mind struggled to focus on anything else.

"Yeah, leave it in your bag for now. He'll get it all. He's good," Marcus explained. "He used to be a big deal but he had a falling-out with the Prince or something."

"*Don't* let that happen," the other man snapped, his voice gruff, cold.

"Now what?" asked the girl.

"We celebrate, of course," said Marcus. He set off running into the darkness at the back of the crypt. I had assumed that there was a wall there, but he kept going, his footsteps growing more faint. The other three whooped and cheered as they rushed to join him. Part of me wanted to let them get far enough away to be free to talk to Lance—he had built this place. Had he known what lurked here? Where did this lead?

I heard his footsteps now. "Should we?" he asked, tension pinching his words.

"Yes," I answered, without thinking.

That corridor of suffocating darkness sloped down so steeply I thought we very well might slide to the bottom. I held my hands against the damp, bumpy stones of the wall. The path forked and the direction we took quickly spilled out into a landing lit with a red hue from below. The stone beneath our feet had been replaced with a long strip of glass, a window onto a scene somewhere far below us. It looked idyllic at first glance: a tree-studded lake, its banks lined with lounging figures. But the color settings needed adjustment: the trees were all black and gray, the grass dead and decaying. The lake itself was red. I looked at Lance, as though for confirmation, but my thoughts were interrupted by something worse. I gasped and he looked up from the sight below. He saw our bodies reflected in the window, and then he understood: we were no longer shadows here; we could be seen.

We ran on the glass, deeper into this tunnel until the windows below were again replaced with a stone walkway. The path ahead forked again to another corridor with cutouts on the wall, bathed in a crimson glow. These, too, were windows, and in one we saw another view of that lake. Now the four Krewe members we had followed here appeared, stripping off their clothes as they ran to the lake and leapt in, splashing. Someone emerged from it, red-tinged and resplendent: Clio.

"Let's get outta here," Lance said. I didn't need convincing. I only now realized I had barely been breathing for the past several minutes.

"This is a stupid question—" I started as we jogged back the way we had come.

"No, none of this was here. I built a very boring crypt of four walls, no basement, no windows into the underworld," he whispered back, a tremor in his voice.

"Just checking."

We turned a corner. I could have sworn it was the direction we had come from, but we found ourselves instead in another loop, reaching another fork. A new window appeared. In this one, two men submerged another in the same viscous red liquid to the point of drowning. He flailed his arms and legs and was pulled up just in time, only to be sunk down again. Over and over. In the distance, bleachers were full of a cheering crowd. The air had grown so hot now, the sweat trickled down my back. Panic set in.

"This was not the way we came," I whispered.

"It was the only way, though," Lance answered.

And then we froze: footsteps approached. We slunk back away from the window.

"Don't say another word," the voice ordered us, sharp, not to be contested. I knew it well. Lucian stepped into the light. He carried an empty black sack. "It's not you. It *is* a maze here full of optical tricks to trap trespassers. Come," he signaled. His eyes were dead, two dull stones. Fear lined his voice. He didn't have to say it—if we were found, none of us would ever leave. We jogged after him, past more windows onto horrific acts and others that were meant to contain joyful, hedonistic times but looked equally heart-stopping, as that frolic in the bloody lake had been.

He led us, darting down dark pathways we never would have found on our own, and finally we reached that steep ramp. We had begun running up toward the entrance to the crypt when a woman's voice rang out, stopping us in our tracks.

"Luuuuucian!" she called. "What's taking so long? We're waiting to award the night's winner!" I felt Lance's strong hand at the small of my back, protective. I could sense him wanting to pounce.

Pain flashed in Lucian's eyes. "Coming, Clio. Forgive me, your grace. I was just about to collect the offerings." It hurt me to see him answer to this creature. He grabbed my arm and pulled me, Lance following.

He whispered urgently, "Run as far as you can down here, turn right, and look for a cutout in the wall, showing a staircase. Climb through. Go."

I opened my mouth to thank him and he put his finger up to his lips, signaling me not to. He ran, disappearing up the ramp, that black sack in hand to collect what had been deposited at the mouth of the crypt.

Lance and I took off, speeding down that endless track, following his directions until we found it: a dim, hazy cutout we could've just as easily missed, looking out onto a familiar staircase. It wasn't enough that we would try to escape ourselves. I wished we could take Lucian with us. He did not belong here among these killers. But we climbed through, falling, falling so much farther than we expected. Finally, we landed with a thud and twisted, entwined limbs on the second floor of the LaLaurie mansion.

~ 31 ~

She Really Wasn't Trying

It wasn't easy reporting back to Connor. Lance and I raced out of the mansion just as the early-morning sun was beginning its ascent. We only stopped running when we reached the confines of our courtyard and then we collapsed on the cold ground before the fountain, unable to even make it to the chaise. Lance stretched out his arms, and I nestled my head in against his chest, closing my eyes for a moment and trying to push the night away.

We found everyone together in the common room, all still in their clothes from the day before, waiting for us. When we caught our breath enough to speak, we didn't quite have the words. Slowly, Connor drew it out of us in bits and pieces as the others leaned in listening close.

"The cops came right away, but it was still too late, always too late."

"They shape-shift so fast, even when you're watching them, you still can miss it."

"The sirens were constant. I think they had the whole police force out."

We recounted everything at our speed, numbed by the trauma as we were. When we were finally through, Connor dismissed the group, ordering us to get a few hours' sleep, but stopped Lance and me before we made it too far.

"Have either of you heard from Sabine? I would've thought she oughtta be back by now."

I looked at Lance, bracing for his answer. He glanced in my direction and spoke quietly to his feet. "I left a message or two right when she left." Then a shade louder, as though defending himself: "But that was it and I never got her."

"I texted her," I said, with a shrug.

"You did?" Lance asked.

I nodded. "She just said everything was fine." The truth of the matter was, it would have been impossible for me to get a solid reading on Sabine even under the best of circumstances. I was too skeptical of her every move to begin with, and I stopped fully trusting her after her first date with Wylie. "Have you tried calling her?" I asked Connor.

"Thanks, Haven, revolutionary idea," he said flatly. "Yes, and I got her and she told me exactly what I wanted to hear, which is why I don't believe a word. I don't want to sound the alarm yet, so I thought it would make the most sense for you to call her parents, Haven."

"And say what?" I scowled.

"Whatever. Just find out where the hell she is," he barked. He jotted something down on a slip of paper and handed it to me. "Here's their number."

Dude, I'm gonna need a full report on what worked later, okay?" Dante said when Lance and I got to their room.

"Max is even more of a perfectionist than I am and I promised him I'd call Mariette's today to fill him in."

"Some definite successes." I nodded, waving goodbye. "I'll be by in a few." I didn't care to be alone right now, after the night we had had, but I was anxious to change my clothes.

As soon as I let myself into my room, I heard the beeping. Who knew how long it had been going on. I climbed up to my bed, grabbing my phone, which had never buzzed at me before, from the night table. When I clicked the bottom button, the noise stopped and a message overtook the screen.

Dearest winged one, You may be weary, but this is important.

As Metamorfosi Day nears and you begin your final preparations, don't lose sight of the scope of the challenges that lie ahead. You may be more interested than ever in repaying Lucian for his favor of last night, which is admirable. But he has warned you that success in this mission will be difficult. As you strategize, look at that night from every angle. Leave no question unasked. Remember that with victory of any kind comes sacrifice.

You will be fighting for your survival and his, too. Don't lose sight of your own progress. Keep close watch over your soul's health or you will be no good to anyone. So much is at stake, but it's within your power to rise above all that threatens you.

My eyes set on a few curious bits: asking the right questions, making sacrifices. I turned that over in my mind. *Sacrifice.* I didn't like that word. Its weight settled firmly onto my shoulders, pushing down on me, the way my heavy backpack, filled with so many textbooks, used to. I wished to go back to a time when all that—

finals and papers and college applications — represented the most harrowing of obstacles. But it didn't matter really, did it? Even if I had never been forced down the path to angelhood, I still wouldn't have ever felt content or in full control of my life. I still would have worked myself to the bone to reach my goal, whether that goal was earning a good grade, a college acceptance, or the chance to live another day with my soul preserved. That was just how I operated.

After pulling myself together, I finally punched in the number Connor had given me. It rang and rang until a man's voice answered. It had to be her father.

"Hi, is Sabine there, please?"

"I'm afraid she isn't. Can I take a message?"

"Oh, hi sir, this is her friend Haven. Could you ask her to call me?"

"Haven, New Orleans Haven?" His gruff voice suddenly took on a friendly, familiar twang.

I was touched at the recognition. "Um, yes, that's right."

"I thought you were the roommate, but I must be thinking of someone else," he said, almost to himself, then continued before I could correct him. "Go ahead and give her a ring there. She got back to New Orleans a couple days ago. She couldn't wait to get down there again."

My gut received this news with a certain grade of panic I worked to control. We said goodbye and I let the phone drop as I rummaged through my night table in search of those photos. I gathered the few shots I had of Sabine. Whatever minor improvement they may have shown after her levitation had been undone. Her photos had grown grotesque all over again. Her skin dripped from her hollowed face as though it were melting. Sores festered over every inch, bleeding and peeling. Her eyes were jaundiced and misshapen. Her picture somehow now looked even worse than Jimmy's, much worse than any of the ones that had morphed into horrific alter egos. I flew down the ladder, ran down the hall, and pounded on Lance's door. He opened up looking like he'd just gotten out of bed, cleaning the lenses of his glasses on the bottom of his Cubs T-shirt.

"Her dad thinks she's here."

B y the time we walked the hall to Connor's room, we knew the truth. But we let him say it out loud.

"She's got to be one of them," he said.

"But we did the extraction," I argued. "And Dante performed a spell too. I don't understand."

"This hits everyone differently." Connor shook his head. "There's Brody, who got hit and never returned at all, just got sucked into their sick world — as we know now." His voice dropped in defeat before recovering. "And then look at Lance and you and the others who have made it through. But Sabine must have turned even before we knew she'd been targeted."

"But it shouldn't matter when you go to the lengths we did to protect her, should it?" Lance asked. "Didn't we do everything we could?"

Something occurred to me. "She was totally fine right after the extraction," I said. "I don't know about you, but I was wiped-out for a while after mine. And you" — I gestured at Connor, who folded his arms, listening closely — "you said that it was supposed to be real work on the part of the person who's undergoing the soul division."

"That's right," he confirmed.

"So it's possible that she really wasn't trying," Lance proposed.

Connor paused a long moment, hanging his head, and with a new tenderness said, "It sure is."

On our way to the Warehouse District, we passed by Kip's shop, and I felt a pang. Not in the emotional sense but a sharp physical jolt in my chest that stopped me for a moment.

"You okay?" Lance asked.

"Yeah, I just—" But I had lost my train of thought. I peeked in the window and saw a woman walking to a backroom, the soft waves of her long mane bouncing. Lance followed my line of vision.

"Hey, did you see that?" he asked. "Isn't she the one who's always with Wylie?"

I nodded. I thought of Sabine and how she hung out at the tattoo shop the day the body was found there. A horrible thought occurred to me, but I pushed it aside and walked on.

We reached the warehouse and found the usual flutter of activity, hammering and sawing and idle chatter filling the air. We wound our way back toward the area where our tiny group of Royal Street angels worked on constructing foliage for the cemetery float. Along the way I couldn't help observing our peers from the rest of the program. They seemed so at ease, talking and laughing as they worked. A few had even begun playfully flinging paint at one another, the kind of thing that always happens in movies but had never happened to me despite all the painting I'd done at my various jobs the past year. As I watched, I felt a longing for the normalcy of their lives. And then it intensified, transforming into that sharp, stabbing pain I'd just fought off at Kip's shop.

I thought at first it might be a run-of-the-mill panic attack, which would certainly be warranted the way everything felt like it was closing in on me, but this was something more. It started in the scar on my chest but it seeped from there and infected my entire body, lodging itself in my heart and slowing its beats; wedging into my lungs to constrict my breathing; impaling itself in my brain until my head felt like it had been severed into two throbbing hemispheres. My pace slowed and I fell a few steps behind Lance until finally I had to stop. I rooted myself beside a boy cutting planks of wood with a circular saw. Its hungry buzz echoed in my ears as it chewed through, each piece spitting a spray of dust that settled on my sweaty skin. I closed my eyes and held my head in my hands. Then I forced my eyes open to find the boy looking at me, puzzled, from behind his plastic goggles.

"You okay?" he asked over the roar of construction equipment.

I just nodded, wiping the sweat from my brow. Still struggling, I took a few tentative steps away as he returned to his work. What was wrong with me? Now was not the time for me to be feeling weak.

The same stinging feeling overtook me again just a few yards away. I came up to the costume department, a section cordoned off with a few clothing racks and a table with a pair of sewing machines humming. A trio of girls flipped through Polaroid pictures. "I think we need more color. Everywhere," one of them told the others, rolling her eyes. "Seriously, they just want red and black on that last float? The cemetery one? It's gonna be such a snooze." I had to stop in my tracks once more and focus on breathing. They halted their conversation to stare at me. As I looked at each of them, a shooting pain flared in my chest for an instant. But, with a heavy gait, I forced myself to continue on, finally catching up with Lance.

"Where'd you disappear to?" he asked as he pounded a board into place, almost finished with his replica of that enormous circular crypt where we had decided to take a "pause" a while back. I hated that thing. Before I could answer, he studied me and said, "Hey, no offense, but you don't look so good."

I leaned against the structure and it slid away from my weight. I stumbled but recovered.

"This isn't made out of marble and cement like the real one. What's up?"

I took a few deep breaths and tried to stand up straight. "You're probably still a little drained, that's all," he said, concern lacing his words.

"I hope you're right."

A voice interrupted us. "I'm taking a poll: How do we feel about sequins on the costumes?" It was Emma. "For them or against them?" We just stared at her blankly.

"Are you serious?" Lance asked.

"Emphatically against," I answered.

"But you don't even know how they would be used."

"Emphatically against," I repeated.

"We'll see." She marked something on her clipboard and continued on to her next victims.

I had one other near-fainting episode before our time at the warehouse was through. Lance ordered me to rest when we got back to the house. "It's been a wild few days, and we can't have you pulling this swooning act at Mardi Gras," he said, true worry behind the joking. So I tucked myself into bed early and decided to calm myself to sleep by practicing my levitation skills. I focused my gaze on one of my sneakers on the floor below, watching,

watching. In seconds it flew at me. I reached one hand out from under the covers and grabbed it. Not bad. I was getting faster. My eyelids closed and I began to drift off, but just as fast, that pinging sounded. I thought of letting it continue, but it seemed to get louder the longer I waited. I reached over and found a new message on the screen. Girding myself, I started to read, but the very first line filled me with relief instead of fear.

You will be pleased to know what you felt earlier today wasn't any kind of illness: it was a warning. You're accustomed to feeling the presence of danger through your scars. Now you are beginning to develop an even greater ability to forecast trouble. Pay attention to this feeling. Today, without the need for photographs, you succeeded in locating souls that are flirting with the dark side. Consider this a new radar for you: From this point forward, when you come in contact with anyone whose soul is at risk or in the process of being stolen, you will know. You will feel it. And while it may have overwhelmed your entire being today, in time your body will learn not to be overloaded by this kind of pull.

I replayed those episodes. Where, exactly, had I been when I'd felt those sharp jabs? Who had I been near? Who did I need to look out for? How could I protect these people I didn't even know? But I read on:

You're becoming more powerful, Haven. Today should give you confidence.

I tried, for a moment, to stop and savor that.

But despite this, your path is growing thornier. Now your sense of responsibility will only grow heavier. You'll want to save these people and others. You'll feel their fate is in your hands, but you won't always win. Still, this knowledge will afford you the opportunity to possibly change their course. These are the Krewe's next targets. A rampage is afoot with bloodshed the goal. The scale will be greater than even what you witnessed during your tagging. But now you will have the power to intervene.

My frustration bubbled up. I read faster, more urgently.

More than ever, you, the illuminator, will need the architect and the alchemist. Though you hold the greatest power, without their aid you are virtually powerless. The three of you are a unit; you function best together. Let nothing stand in the way of your bond. Your survival depends upon it. The day of reckoning is fast approaching, winged one.

Let nothing stand in the way of your bond. That line resonated. It was the only time a message had told me something I was positive I had already discovered on my own. I needed to be sure that one of them knew, without a doubt, what he meant to me.

~ 32 ~

What Happened with Us?

When we returned home from tutoring the next day, there was no denying it: Mardi Gras had nearly arrived. Sequined and feathered masks bearing those signature shades—green, purple, and yellow—had been left outside each of our rooms with flyers reading:

⚜

You're cordially invited

to the NOLA Student Volunteer Network

Mardi Gras Masquerade Party!

Celebrate in style

with a classic New Orleans fête and feast!

The LaLaurie Mansion

⚜

I was reading it when Dante burst in my room, no greeting, just talking. "I'm having a voodoo emergency!" He had that crazed skittishness of someone who's been cramming for finals in classes he'd zoned out in all semester.

"So this party is mandatory, I guess, right? Even if you're supposed to be saving lives that day?" I dropped the invitation on my desk. He ignored me.

"I need some last-minute ingredients. I just got these ideas." He was pacing, not looking at me. "Things I want to add. Even though they're not usually in voodoo spells. But these are *my* spells. And Mariette says I need to follow my heart and my impulses and experiment. And I need more than sage and jalap root and dragon's blood resin already, you know? I need to branch out. I need something more exotic to complement the herbs from the underworld."

I shrugged. "Well, that certainly makes sense."

"Can you get them for me?" Now he stopped moving and looked at me with his wild eyes.

"What?"

"Max is busy tearing up all my stuff at the community garden," he said, fluttering his hands. "And I don't know who else to trust. I just need this as strong as can be, with flowers potent enough to go with the underworld blooms."

"Don't send me back down there!" I blurted out. I couldn't go back to that crypt right now. I couldn't risk it so close to Metamorfosi Day.

"No, aren't you listening? I've got those covered; the flowers are *here*." He rifled through the books on my desk, tearing a sheet of paper from my notebook and scribbling a list.

"Oh, okay. I'll go to the florist over by the French Market."

"*No.* I need you to go to the botanical garden. Like, tonight. And take some clippings."

"Isn't that kind of, I don't know, theft?"

"All's fair in love and war—this is war."

I couldn't disagree with that.

"You're better at breaking and entering than I am, Haven. This'll be a snap for you. And with all I've got going on at Mariette's, I need every minute I can get. You'll see. Take Lance. And this." He held the list out to me with nearly a dozen flower names and descriptions.

By twilight, Lance and I were standing outside the gates of the botanical garden, the leafy expanse stretching out endlessly inside and just a ten-foot wall of metal bars keeping us out. No problem. With minimal rattling, we were up and over it, not even breaking a sweat.

"Not to celebrate too soon, but we're getting really good at that," I joked.

"I was thinking the same thing." Lance smiled. He pulled the map Dante had given us from his back pocket and studied it as we wandered back along the paved path, past proud towering oaks, blossoming rosebushes, an array of palm trees whose thick, broad leaves whispered as they brushed against one another in the cool evening breeze. In the distance, the glass dome of the conservatory sparkled, reflecting the lights from the security lamps. Even in the dim glow, the sprawling grounds, with their leafy wonders and bursting blooms, made such a peaceful oasis I almost forgot there was business to tend to. I dug Dante's notes out of my bag. He had ordered his shopping list from most vital ingredients to least.

"I vote we hit the tropical section first." I leaned over Lance's map. He had flipped on a tiny flashlight and shone it on our target.

I read the list out loud to myself as Lance navigated, our

footsteps and the chirping cicadas providing the only soundtrack. We spoke in hushed voices, as though in a church. "There's this starred one, 'Voodoo Lily, smells like rotting corpse.' That'll be a fun one. We've got a couple orchids. Yarrow, it says here, for healing—"

"So Dante thinks this stuff is somehow gonna be even more potent than what we used on the Krewe the other night?" he interrupted. He adjusted his glasses in that nervous way of his, then pointed at the path around a reflecting pool.

"Here's hoping, right?" I continued reading: "Hyssop to ward off evil spirits. Thorns from a few unusual hybrid roses. Love-lies-bleeding—" I stopped. "Whoa, that sounds ominous."

"Wonder what that would look like."

"It says here, 'small red blooms, weeping, looks like a broken heart.'" My mind wandered, the name of the flower sticking in my thoughts, held there by the thorns of the past couple months. I realized neither of us had spoken for a while. Lance watched his feet as he walked. I felt the weight of silence, nerves setting in as the minutes stretched. I wondered if he was thinking what I was. I stared off into the distance, tropical plants fanning and waving several yards away.

Somehow we both decided to speak at precisely the same time.

Lance started, "So, I—" just as I began, "What do you—"

We laughed in a painful, nervous way. I nodded for him to go ahead. "I was going to say, with these battles ahead and all, that we're sort of a team, so we've got to start acting like it . . . again. Or else we'll never get through this stuff."

I smiled softly, appreciatively. It occurred to me, I might as well go for it. "I'm going to ask a question I never thought I would have the guts to ask," I said. "But, you know, we always get bold when our lives are on the line, don't we?"

"I suppose we do," he answered.

"What happened . . . with . . . us?" All the blood rushed to my head as soon as I said it, but, still, I was proud of myself for trying.

"Us?" he asked, like he didn't know what "us" I was referring to. I worried this was going to go even worse than I had imagined. But sometimes you just need answers, even if they won't change anything that happened and won't necessarily change anything going forward. My life was populated with so many things that were out of my control, I couldn't help wanting to try to understand this.

Finally Lance sighed and mussed his hair, exhaling. "I don't know."

It was strangely reassuring somehow. I felt emboldened enough to press for more, my gaze firmly focused on my fidgeting fingers.

"I mean . . ." I braced myself and bravely soldiered on like someone who might perish in a battle against devils in mere days, nothing at all to lose. "Did you . . . do you . . . did you"—I couldn't get it out—"love Sabine?"

"Do you?" He parried with me. "Love him?"

"So unfair, I asked first," I said with a fake pout, watching him from the corner of my eye. The air had grown chillier since we'd arrived, even as the heat rose in my skin. But I thought of that message last night, and about this, I wouldn't joke. "Love Lucian? No. Not really. I care about him. I know that he doesn't deserve what's happening to him now. But I don't know. I think there's probably a difference between sort of friend-like-love and not-wanting-to-condemn-someone-to-hell-love and . . ." I searched for the right way to say it, but I had never had a conversation like this and came up short. ". . . and *love*-love. I mean, I'm just guessing." I shrugged. "You know, from an objective stand-point."

"You're probably right," he said, eyes fixed straight ahead. I could feel him wanting to say something more, so I fought the urge to fill the painful silence. "So then," he started finally. "For instance, you might categorize your time with him as . . . what?"

"Well, aside from the official business of making good on a promise to try to break him free?"

"Aside from that."

I smiled to myself. "Then other than that, I think I just wanted to get your attention."

Now he smiled too, and looked at me. "Well, mission accom-plished."

"Thanks," I said, just a hint of pride. "Is it me, or have things been kinda weird since we've gotten here? I mean, with us, not just, you know, demons trying to kill us weird, but *us* weird?"

"Yeah." He sighed.

"I just laid my heart out. You gotta give me more," I said lightly enough to hide how serious I was.

"Sabine?" he said tentatively, like he was testing out a micro-phone. Then, matter-of-factly: "Sabine was a momentary lapse in judgment."

"I'm intrigued, go on." We reached the tropical plants, their fragrance wafting out, giant leaves creating a canopy and nearly assaulting us. Orchids, in purples and yellows and reds so vibrant we could see them even in near darkness, studded the lush green landscape like jewels embedded in velvet.

"She was like an escape." He kicked at the dirt along our path. "Maybe it's just that she seemed kind of . . . fragile? Like she sort of needed me . . . more, maybe?" He said it in an apolo-getic tone, his eyes fluttering to mine occasionally like someone pleading guilty to a crime. If I tried really hard, this could almost sound like a compliment.

"Oh." I hadn't seen that coming. I wasn't prepared to mount a defense.

"I was confused, you know? Everything that happened at the Lex, that messed me up." I could see him running through the memories in his head.

"Of course. I was too."

"No, you're not getting—" He looked frustrated and tried another tack. "It's pretty uncool to admit this. But in a weird way I feel like everything we went through made me weaker. When we went back to normal life, the roller coaster was too much. And I felt like I needed you to keep me stable, but I needed you too much. It's not a normal thing for me to feel that, like, ever. It was too much . . . you were too much. And then we came here and—"

"I was too much?" I didn't understand.

"You seemed to assimilate into this new existence easier, this angel status, like it was something you had to do, so you did. I didn't get it. Once I finally felt good enough to get outta bed, after everything that had happened, the fire, that whole battle, I felt like it was someone else, not me, who had done all that and lived through it. I couldn't imagine having to do anything like that again."

"Join the club. I mean, are you kidding? It's kind of not the easiest thing to adjust to. I'm messed up too. Why didn't you ever say anything?"

"Not the most impressive thing to tell your girlfriend." He rolled his eyes behind those frames.

"Well, you would have discovered that I felt—and still feel—completely out of control. If it's any consolation." It felt good to say that and to have it be okay that I felt this way.

"Yeah, I guess." He smiled. "So all I'm saying is, hanging out with Sabine seemed like an escape. But there is no escape. I know that now. And when you got tagged—" He paused a moment. "I realized . . . a lot."

I soaked it all in for a moment, not wanting to speak too soon, letting the heft of his words have space to breathe. We had stopped walking. Who knew how long we had been standing here amid these orchids, lost in thought. Lance turned to face me, smiling shyly now.

"So, I laid my heart out there. You gotta give me something." He nearly repeated my line, with finality. I just grabbed his shirt and pulled him to me, my lips finding his, his arms closing in around my waist, holding me tightly.

When we got back to the house, I tracked down Dante in Max's room. I unpacked my many Ziploc bags, handing over so many clippings of all shapes and sizes, dictating each as I went along. When I got to love-lies-bleeding, he smiled, giving me a mischievous look I knew too well.

"Oh, it turns out I don't need that one after all," he said with a smirk.

33

All Hail, Queen Haven

After our escape from the crypt, I had left Lucian a note thanking him and asking what I needed to do on Metamorfosi Day. I checked day after day for his reply, but each time I was greeted by a dark window. I couldn't shake the feeling that he had been caught helping us and because of it, he was now gone forever. At last, that Sunday, on the way to the warehouse to put the finishing touches on our float, I found the candle burning and this note snuggled into one of those familiar bottles:

H-

I'm just glad I was there to help you both. Thank you again for what you're about to do for me. I can't begin to tell you what it means to me. I'll meet you at our usual place in the morning on the day of metamorphosis. Until then, I know that you should follow Clio that evening. She will lead you to your nemesis. Lance should do the same with Wylie. I wish I had more for you right now, but it has grown

INCREASINGLY DIFFICULT TO LEARN ANYTHING NEW.
THEY ARE TOO WARY OF ME. I WILL TRY WITH ALL MY
HEART TO COLLECT MORE BY THE TIME I SEE YOU.
        YOURS,
        L

The next couple of days were a blur. I could feel a shell hardening around my body and soul, protecting and strengthening me. Nothing, it seemed, could surprise me anymore. Case in point: We had called in another anonymous tip to the police to search the crypt Lance had built, and sure enough, they had dug it all up only to find absolutely nothing. If I hadn't explored those corridors with Lance, I might've been convinced I had dreamed the whole thing. While we were at it, we called the authorities again and again—River, Drew, and Tom all doing the honors this time—warning of threats on Mardi Gras. At least the police would be out in full force, even if they hadn't been able in the past to fight the demons.

But it was another call that had been far more nerve-racking: the one I owed Joan. I had managed to avoid her long enough, plying her with short, harried e-mails and texts, letting her calls go to voice mail, and blatantly and boldly ignoring every mention of her potential travel plans. But, curled up on my bed now, two days until what could be my last on earth, I couldn't wait any longer. She answered immediately.

"Why, hello! You're a tough lady to get a hold of!" she greeted me.

"I know, I know, sorry. Things have been . . . crazy."

"Yes, crazy, crazy, aren't things just always crazy for you. Too crazy to call home," she said, upbeat enough that I knew she wasn't really angry. Yet.

"I'm sorry, I—"

"Never mind, sweetie. It's fine, I know you're busy." She paused for a moment, as though searching for an adequate segue, which made me nervous.

"Is everything okay?"

"Yes, but, well, now, don't be mad . . . but I have a surprise," she eased in.

"Ohhhkay." I braced myself.

"I booked a trip to come see you. It's more than I should spend, but I couldn't resist—I want to see you in the parade!"

An alarm went off in my mind: she was coming here. At the worst possible time, the most dangerous time. "Joan, you can't!" I blurted out, before thinking. It came out far harsher than I intended.

"What?" She sounded shocked, all of her sweet excitement suddenly snuffed out.

I backpedaled. "No, I'm sorry, I just mean—I'd love to see you but I can't . . . you can't. I just . . . I can't have you here, not then, not now." It broke my heart to say this and to do it so forcefully but I needed her to listen. I needed her to be safe and that meant staying as far away from here as possible. I was met with such pure silence on the other end that I thought the call might have been dropped. "Are you there?" I had to ask, softening my voice this time.

When she finally spoke, I could hear the tears being stifled. "I don't know why you're so upset with me, Haven. I just want to see you. Is that such a bad thing? I know you're busy, but . . . I didn't expect you would tell me not to come. I thought it would be something fun to share together. Soon you'll be off at college, and I know that's a wonderful, exciting thing, but I'm going to miss you. I miss you already." I had clearly hit a nerve.

I felt awful. The only thing that kept me going was the idea that keeping her away would ensure that she would be okay, that she wouldn't get caught up in whatever battle would be raging here. For the briefest moment, my mind wandered into territory I had been trying so hard to push away. What if I didn't make it? I had had to consider this once before, but then I had been fine. My first challenge had seemed almost easy in retrospect.

It hit me: what if I told her? What if I just spilled it all? Spelled it all out and told Joan the truth about me and Dante and Lance and what we really were, as difficult as it may be for her to comprehend? It would sound so outlandish I think she would worry I was delusional.

"I'm sorry, Joan, I didn't mean to be . . . Look, there's just . . . some weird stuff going on here," I started, testing the waters. I was so sick of having to weave these elaborate webs. I wished she knew the truth for the selfish reason that she would somehow have the words to make everything seem better and less scary than it was. I needed that now. Sometimes I was tired of having to be strong.

"Well, Haven, now I'm concerned, quite frankly. What's going on there? What are you talking about?" She sounded stern.

"No, I'm just being dramatic." I chickened out. "It's fine. I'm just stressed. I'm looking forward to being done and getting home, that's all."

"I don't like when you get like this. It can't be all that bad. You always put such pressure on yourself to do everything perfectly. You need to ease up. It's not good for you to carry on this way."

"I know. You're right."

"Maybe you'll let me come another time before your trip is through. Or at least promise me you'll rest when you get home in June? I'll take a few vacation days and we can goof off together."

I was silent, trying to fight back the tears. Would I be there? How much longer would I have to make these kinds of calls, worrying that they would be my last? I hadn't spoken for several long seconds. "We'll have fun," she said, trying to sound light.

I wiped my eyes with the back of my hand and hardened my voice. "Of course, of course. It's a date, I promise."

"That's more like it." She paused again. "You sure you're okay? Should I be worried? Because I feel like I should, so you're going to have to convince me otherwise."

I wanted to say, Yes, be terrified, just like I am. But instead I said, "Of course not, I'm fine. I'm really good."

"I don't think I believe you, but I have a feeling you're not going to tell me what's really going on until you're good and ready. So, for now, all I'll say is, take pictures at least, okay? I want pictures of you in that parade, that's an order. And I want you to have fun, got it?"

"Got it." I nodded to myself, smiling through the tears.

Maybe someday I really would find a way to tell her, but, no, I couldn't right now. There was just no easy way. All I could hope was that my will to survive, to see Joan again, would get me through and give me extra strength when the time came.

Dante and Max summoned Lance and me to Mariette's on Monday afternoon. "She wants to wish you good luck," Dante had said. We needed all the luck we could get, so we weren't about to say no. The guys were waiting for us, seated on the front counter when we arrived.

"So, how's your pitching arm these days?" Dante asked as he greeted me, eyes dancing.

"I'm sorry?"

He opened up his backpack and inside I found so many

sharp-tipped triangles and stars, all made of a delicate sort of tree bark and each featuring pointed edges dipped in a multitude of colors. They were wrapped up and protected in tiny individual Ziploc bags. "Each of these delivers a debilitating punch," he said, closing his bag back up. "I'll show you what they all do and then it'll be up to you to throw 'em at the right people at the right times."

"You make it sound so easy."

"It's going to be," Max said in encouragement, which I appreciated.

"That's the idea at least," Dante said.

"What about me?" Lance asked.

"Don't worry, we'll give you a crash course in all this back at the house," Dante assured us. "You've got a night to figure it out. No sweat, right?" We laughed nervously.

At that moment, Mariettte floated out from her backroom, as serene as ever. "Thank you so much for stopping by." She looked intently at both of us. "I wanted you to know my spirit will be with you tomorrow. And I know you are capable of defeating the evil ones."

We both mumbled reverential thank-yous and she turned to me. "Haven, could I have just a moment of your time?"

"Of course," I said, stepping forward. I felt the others slink back as I followed her into the pantry. There she took my hands and looked into my eyes, studying me. "Dante may have told you that we have prepared some very special things for you."

"Oh, thank you. He showed me some things already—"

"I would be remiss if I didn't ask one final time: did you want something specific against the one whose letter you gave me?"

I shook my head. "No, thank you. I won't be needing that."

"I suspected as much, but I wanted to know for sure. Dante has trained well. He is doing everything in his power to help protect you. But even so, we can't be sure these mixtures will work on these beasts. You have my apologies if anything fails you."

"I know you've done so much. Thank you. If I fail it'll have nothing to do with you."

"I have full confidence in you." She nodded, then she hung her head, almost bowing to me, let go of my hands, and turned to go into the backroom. But I thought of something and I couldn't resist.

"Mariette," I called, and she turned back around. "Is there anything else I need to know heading into this? Anything at all?"

She looked deep into my eyes again, stepping toward me once more. "I don't know whether you will survive or not. I can't see that far ahead for any of you, much as I have tried time and again." She shook her head. "I can't tell if the one behind the letter will survive either. But I know what you're trying to do for him and you are very brave to try. And while this may not be knowledge that can save your life, I can tell you this: they both love you. Truly. And in my experience, sometimes knowing something like that can make a difference. It can certainly make a person fight harder." With a smile and another nod, she disappeared into the backroom, turning off the light. I stood there a few extra seconds in the dark, alone, and I tucked away what she had said and held it tight in my heart.

By the time Connor gathered us in the living room after dinner, we all had begun getting punchy, jittery with that dreaded day approaching. He took his usual position at the front of the room and scanned our exhausted faces. Our house had grown silent; each of us, it seemed, had retreated into our own thoughts as we mentally prepared.

"I know that things are gonna get rough soon," he started. "But I want you all to know that you can fight this. You know what you have to do. Each of you will be targeted by one freshly transformed devil whose mission is to steal your soul and destroy your body, making you their personal recruit for an eternity in the underworld. And some of you will find yourselves up against members of the old guard of devils as well, looking to weaken you as you do battle. As angels, you're the ultimate prize to them. You won't know where or when they'll strike, only that it has to happen before midnight on this day of metamorphosis, so you've gotta be on guard. The three of you"—he addressed Emma, Tom, and River—"need to focus on subduing your attackers and slapping one of these on them before they manage to hit you with anything." He held up one of the triangular shapes I'd seen in Dante's bag. "These, as provided by Dante and Max, will weaken them and enable you to destroy them. You'll know you've won when they change forms and begin to take on the look of their decaying souls. Then just keep at it until they smoke and turn to ash. If you want to know what this all looks like, talk to Haven, Lance, or Dante. They've all been there."

I was surprised to be called out; it gave me a jolt of confidence, a feeling that I was an expert here, like I knew what I was doing. "The only catch," Connor went on, "is that you have to hit their targets: those markings on their bodies."

"Those tattoos, you mean?" Emma asked. She had a pad of paper out and diligently scribbled down notes as he spoke. "What if they're covered up or something?"

"You'll be able to find them. On Metamorfosi Day those

markings will glow—there will be no missing them. And they'll emit heat. Trust me."

She nodded solemnly along with the other two, all wearing serious expressions.

"For you two"—he pivoted to face me and Lance, both of us seated on the lounge chairs in the corner—"it's gonna be a little harder: you'll likely be paired with stronger adversaries. So you've got stronger weapons." He held up one of the star shapes. "These would burn straight through the skin of a mortal or a lesser angel. But you guys can take it. Dante and Max, when Metamorfosi Day begins, your job will largely be done. You just have to hope that your tools will have given everyone the fighting chance they need. And I know you're already on this, but you're laying the foundation to ensure the devils are in fact sealed away after midnight?"

"On it," Dante answered. "We've scattered gris-gris bags around the cemetery, focusing on the crypts most closely associated with the Krewe." I raised an eyebrow, impressed. He caught my look. "Told you I've been busy," he whispered.

Connor was still talking. "Just remember, guys, you can do this. Think about it, think about your time here: you've already held your own against heartless beasts, battled the elements, and learned how to take a fall. You've got all the tools to fight and you've got the fearlessness you need to win." I hoped he was right. "So, last thing. Wherever the night takes you, when—yes, when—you've passed your test, meet back here as soon as possible for a check-in with one another. You'll be running on adrenaline. You'll be in the middle of Mardi Gras. There'll be that party going next door. But do me a favor and, you know, let one another know you're okay before wandering out into the excitement. Midnight is when the devils bring their new recruits back to the underworld. If they stay any longer on Metamorfosi Day then they risk losing their powers entirely." Lucian's image filled my head now. I wished I could just skip ahead to 12:01 and know that everyone was safe, have this all behind us. "So expect to see one another here soon after midnight."

Something about the last thing he said sounded odd to me. But I was momentarily distracted by the glazed confection with purple, green, and yellow sprinkles being shoved in my face by Max. He and Dante each had their hands full with plates bearing slices of these sweets.

"Now, in the spirit of this week's more enjoyable festivities, Dante and Max whipped up a king cake for us. So, dig in, guys."

"And whoever gets the baby gets to be king or queen of the float!" Dante called out.

Everyone began nibbling and talking quietly as Connor slipped away to his room. Lance was talking to me, but I got up, without a word, and chased after Connor.

"Hey, wait!" I called after him, jogging to meet him down the hall. "You said we need to look out for one another and meet back here and all, but aren't you going to be here too?" I said when I reached him.

His face fell for a moment, telling me everything I needed to know. He shook his head. "I've done everything I can right now. Don't worry. Focus on you and what you need to do in the next twenty-four hours."

"But . . . wait. I'm having major abandonment issues here. I don't understand." I tried to laugh it off but I couldn't help but feel the start of a dull ache in my heart. "How can you leave? Don't you want to be here to see what happens? Don't you care about us?"

"Haven, of course I do. It's not up to me. This is how it is—I keep an eye on y'all and then I have to go. I'm not allowed to be here when y'all battle. I'd be champing at the bit to fight, and it's not my place to do that, so I have to go away on Metamorfosi Day, for a little while. Look, I have a feeling I'm going to see you again, okay? Just—"

"But how does that even work?" I cut him off. "How can you leave school and everything?" Desperate, I searched my mind for anything that could keep him here.

"Haven." He put his arms up to settle me down. "This doesn't matter. You want to talk logistics? I'll be gone on a 'family emergency' and then at some point I will show up again. Someone else —not one of us, a nonangel—takes over for a little while. My real job is done. But what matters is that you keep your head in the game and survive this test, okay?" He said this sternly, looking at me with hard eyes before they started to soften. "I'm telling ya, just get through this and you could be leading the guardians one day."

"The guardians?"

He just smiled. And with that, he grabbed the fork on my plate, speared a hunk of cake, took a bite, and then nabbed something from what was left on my plate.

"Congratulations. All hail, Queen Haven," he said, grabbing the tiny plastic figure from my plate and holding it up. I took it in my hands as he smiled warmly, reassuringly, and wandered back to his room.

After all the time I had spent in that empty, eerie LaLaurie mansion during its renovation, it felt strange to see the place dressed up for a party on the morning of Mardi Gras. It was as if it had taken on an entirely different persona, evolved. I felt like I had grown up in these few months too, like I'd faced down immense evil, and though it had been the struggle of my life, I was now prepared to spit in its face. I had proved I had the emotional strength to fight off this horror. Now I just hoped I had the physical strength.

"I don't like this idea," Lance had told me when I shared my plan to meet Lucian. "But I get it." Lance waited for me on the porch while I went inside. We were due to board the float soon so I didn't have much time.

The crystal votive in the foyer had been replaced with a candelabra, but there was no mistaking the figure standing before it, gazing outside onto the world he would hopefully be joining in a few hours' time.

Before I reached him, he turned around. He wore a mask, already prepared for the party that would begin later. Even with his face obscured I could tell from his eyes that it was him, not the Prince, but to be extra sure, before I said a word, I ordered myself: *Listen to your scars, your radar.* I closed my eyes and did a quick internal check: nothing. No flare-ups, no warning signals. This was Lucian, I was certain.

I was already in costume for the parade, dressed—in an outfit not of my own choosing—as what was intended to be a sexy devil. A table just inside the front door had been decorated with scores of Mardi Gras–colored masks. I picked one up and held it in front of my face, mirroring him. "That had better be Haven under there," he said sweetly. "Otherwise I'm going to have to ask you to leave, whoever you are, because I've officially got this window reserved." His gray eyes twinkled.

I smiled shyly. "Just me."

"Hello, just you." He lifted his mask.

"Do they know you're here now?"

"No," he said. "But I don't think the recruitment will begin in earnest until the parade starts. I'll be fast and then I'll come back later, as midnight nears. By then you'll have completed your battle." He spoke in the clipped cadence of someone trying to silence his nerves.

"And I'll have time on my hands," I said lightly. He smiled, appreciative.

"Exactly. As long as I can go AWOL and avoid either being captured and taken back down against my will or . . ." His voice softened, slowing down. "Well, I think you know the other possibility . . ." I did. I nodded, trying not to let the fear show in my eyes. "Then my soul is free."

"Then you're free, got it."

"No." His eyes connected with mine for just a moment.

"What?"

"My *soul* is free."

"Isn't that what I said?"

"Not exactly."

"I don't understand."

"Don't worry about it now. We just have to keep me alive and away from the rest of the Krewe until midnight and then I'll be mortal, at least. But my powers will slowly fade as it gets closer to midnight, and when they see I'm not at the crypt collecting their trophies, they'll come looking for me. I'll need you. I'll need all the help I can get."

"You'll just need some backup, no problem."

"I'll meet you back here after your battle." He hung his head for a moment, looking at me with heavy eyes. "I'm afraid I still don't know who you're fighting, only that Clio will try to wear you out beforehand, so conserve your strength if you can."

"Got it," I said firmly. I needed Lucian to believe that I wasn't worried. I didn't know much, but I was aware that if he let even a tiny part of himself give up, this was never going to work.

Suddenly, a vacuum cleaner started up a few rooms over and voices and footsteps grew nearer. The party planners were still there, preparing. Lucian flicked his head toward the staircase. I followed him up to the second-floor landing. He seemed to be in search of somewhere private, quiet. Somewhere for the kind of heavy goodbyes you feel the need to give when you know the stakes are this high. A gold-threaded tapestry of a fleur-de-lis hung against one wall. He stopped before it.

"How am I supposed to thank you for risking your life for me? I don't want to point this out, but you do know that they won't hesitate to kill you if they find out you're aiding me like this?"

"You can thank me just by, you know, living," I said.

"Deal." He smiled. The melancholy grandfather clock began its dirge. Just outside of the window downstairs, I could see Lance peeking in, keeping an eye on me. Lucian glanced down for a moment too. His hand on my arm, he spoke into my ear. "I understand how things are, of course. But if it's all right I may still have to love you forever. Okay?"

I didn't answer; I had no answer.

He pulled aside the tapestry and slipped behind it, disappearing instantly.

~ 34 ~

Prepare to Chase and Be Chased

By the time we boarded the float in costume, waiting in line to travel down Bourbon Street, where the crowds were swarming—mostly drunk, and, it seemed, happy to do just about anything for the chance to earn some sparkly beads from us—I had put on my game face and was ready. As ready as I'd ever be. Between the roar of the raucous paradegoers and the shrieking horns and thump of the zydeco music, I couldn't hear myself think. I let it all wash over me, only too willing to let the thinking part of myself be overruled by the feeling part. If I had learned anything, it was that today would be a time for instincts and gut checks to prevail.

Clouds had rolled in, and with them the damp, thick air of an approaching storm. Thunder crackled in the distance. "They don't know what they're talking about. Hurricane season is way over," I heard one of the girls on the costume committee declare as we all assembled, taking our places on our quartet of floats. She was right, but I had checked the weather reports while catching up on some e-mail that morning—since, of course, I had woken up long before the sun rose and had barely slept at all—and a storm was expected to hit sometime today.

A different kind of storm had been brewing in my inbox: I heard from three of my prospective colleges, Northwestern, U. Chicago, and Princeton, and I was in, in, and in. I couldn't believe it, but most shocking of all was that it felt nothing like I had expected. I had dreamed of news like this my whole life, and now I wished I could be more excited. I just wished I knew for sure whether I'd be lucky enough to even live to choose one, let alone to enroll. Making it all the more bittersweet, when I went to Connor's room to tell him, but mostly to say goodbye, I found the door unlocked and his things gone. He had left a note on his desk:

Good luck to you all. It's truly been an honor to train you. I know you'll all succeed and that I'll see you again soon, so I'm not about to get sentimental here. Give 'em hell! Later, Connor.

I took it and posted it on the front door so it might be the last thing we saw when we left. Then I called Joan but got her voice mail. I remembered she had a long shift today and I was almost relieved. I e-mailed her instead of leaving a message and, because it made me feel better, I tacked this promise onto the end: *If I don't catch you before the parade, I just want you to know I'm sorry about our talk the other day. I have so much to tell you and I want to tell you all of it. You may not believe it all, but I would love to share it with you. Thank you for always wanting to listen. I love you, Joan. Love, Haven.*

If I made it through today, I would allow myself to let her in, tell her everything. Keeping it inside was killing me. This was the deal I made with myself.

H ello, handsome devils," I said to my three fellow demons, Lance, Dante, and Max. We had staked out a spot behind a few tombstones toward the back of the float. The guys were in black pants and black T-shirts with swatches of red leather—or, rather, pleather—sewn in at the pockets and cuffs, and the girls were in black T-shirts, fringed to look like they were in tatters, and skirts with red pleather sewn into the pleats. "I want us all to look like we're clawing our way out of hell," Emma had instructed. It could not have been more appropriate. She had done our makeup, too, which, for the guys consisted mostly of black lipstick and for the girls involved an elaborate sort of sparkly red eye shadow and false eyelashes. These seemed especially unnecessary and were a tremendous pain to apply, but I resisted only to the point where she had finally snapped, "I may die today, and goddammit, I want to die with long, pretty eyelashes."

Emma also wanted to die in knee-high stiletto boots, which was where I had to respectfully draw the line. We needed something we could run in, so she had acquiesced and allowed us to wear more utilitarian combat boots. She also dictated that we carry red pitchforks and sequined horns—for both male and female devils—but I planned to ditch these accoutrements as soon as possible. I held, tucked into my chest, the only part of the ensemble not mandated by Emma: a folded-up photo of Lance and one of me. This way, if the two of us got separated, I could still check on the health of his soul, or, if I got taken, I could monitor how quickly I was deteriorating. Small comforts, but comforts nonetheless.

The float rolled on, rattling from side to side, shaking us along the parade route, brass band music filling the air, and I felt the adrenaline trickle through my system, like the slow and steady drip from an IV. Lance grabbed my hand and tugged me behind that mockup he had constructed of the circular tomb I detested.

"Before it gets too wild today, I just wanted to say we got this," he said, nodding.

I offered a new mantra. "Us against the underworld?"

"Us against the underworld."

With the music blaring, the rickety float shimmying, crowds roaring all around us, I pulled him into a kiss, as we leaned against that mock crypt. We let the world fall away for a moment, losing ourselves.

"Sorry to interrupt, lovelies," Dante said. "But the time to glitter-bomb is upon us."

"Suit up, let's go," River, stepping past us with her pitch-fork aloft, barked at Tom. Dante, Max, and Lance had rigged up the devilish accessories inside the architecture of a water Uzi. With the press of a button, they would spray the crowd with what looked like confetti but was actually one of Dante's glitter-cam-ouflaged mixtures for warding off devils. Dante handed out the pitchforks as Max held open a bag full of beads fortified with the same properties. We fanned out across the float and set to work, but I couldn't help getting caught up in the night's spirit.

All those people were yelling desperately for beads, shout-ing at us, cheering for us. We each had already loaded up our own necks with the sparkly plastic necklaces of purple, green, and gold, and now I reached into the sack to pull out snakes of them, tossing them out into the crowds below and up into the balconies of buildings we passed. We faced a sea of hands and arms and various other body parts flashing and shimmying. As we cruised through the Quarter, amid raging music and deafening screams, we had to laugh at all the wild madness, the nudity, the delicious unruliness of it all.

"I've seen more naked bodies in the past three blocks than I have in the past, like, ten years at the hospital!" I shouted to my companions, trying to be heard over the collective roar.

"I could get used to this," Lance called back, his eyes wide under those glasses.

"Me too!" Max agreed as we passed a whole pack of shirtless men, chests painted in Mardi Gras colors.

"Hey, now!" Dante chastised him, jokingly.

I scanned the crowd and was instantly pulled back to harsh reality. Clio, glowing in pristine white, was perched atop the roof of one of the buildings, watching the parade unfold. I broke out into a cold sweat. Lance saw her too. "So Wylie can't be far away," I said, studying the scene some more. But we found no trace of him.

"Wait a second," Lance said. His eyes were glued to something on the opposite side of the street. I followed his gaze up to another rooftop and found . . . Kip.

Yes. Of course. I received the revelation like a lightning bolt, jolting me.

"You think?" he asked.

"Absolutely," I said without a doubt. It made so much sense now. A chill overtook me as I thought of that first introduction to Kip. We had never seen Kip and Wylie at the same time and place. That was Wylie's cover. We were set now. My heart froze, the terror setting in, but I warned myself: *This is what you've trained for. You are prepared. You can do this.* I reached past Dante and Max and tugged on Lance's arm, yanking him to me.

He looked up and nodded. "Okay then, so it's time," he said, perfectly calm. I admired his control. Personally, I felt like I was about to jump out of my skin. Dante and Max had stopped throwing beads and were watching us now.

"You've got the stuff, right?" Dante asked.

We nodded. A gust of wind blew through, so loud I could barely hear him, swirling all around us, fanning my hair. The sky had taken on an unnatural candy-orange tinge, somehow sinister.

"It should be all you need to hinder their recruitment powers for the day. It should render them powerless to convert or kill nonangels, you know, civilians." Dante handed me one of the special silver spray-painted pitchforks he had coated in a freshly concocted mixture to temporarily impair their abilities. "Do it," he said. I wound up and launched the pitchfork through the air, watching it land on Kip's roof, knocking him down. For a moment his entire being flickered and flashed as he became Wylie, before shifting back to Kip.

"Bingo," Lance said. That was all it took. Lance could finish the job now and use Wylie to lead him to his real target.

"Be careful," I warned him. I felt a cool, wet drop on my cheek. Thunder crashed in the distance.

"Go!" Dante barked.

"Go," Max echoed.

"Later," Lance said. He and I nodded at each other, trading looks that offered luck and the promise that we would live to see each other again. I watched him take off, jumping down from the float and shooting through the crowd to an alleyway that led back to a courtyard, allowing him to clamber up to the roof. That wasn't what I had in mind, though. I needed to get up. Fast. Dante handed me another pitchfork and I ran toward the very back of the float, to its tallest point—the tree that Lance had constructed. I pulled my arm back again and launched the pitchfork at Clio. It arced up into the dark cloud cover and onto the roof. And it missed.

"Don't worry about it!" Dante called to me. I shook my head; no time to lament my poor aim. Instead, I grabbed onto part of the tree's plywood trunk and pulled myself up. As I balanced on the sturdiest of its lifelike wooden branches, I took a couple steps out, holding on to another branch above and somehow managing not to fall. Then I pushed off, jumping with so much force I snapped the branch right off, but not before using it to propel me off the float. For those few seconds, I soared, the air cool as I cut through it. Everything seemed to move in slow motion.

And then the skies opened up. Sheets of rain poured down, soaking the entire scene so suddenly that it didn't even seem to occur to anyone to take cover. In fact, it only made the throngs of people more excited. They whooped and hollered even more loudly, shaking the water off like dogs after a bath. I reached out to grab the railing of a third-story balcony. The fingertips of my right hand slid off the slick wrought iron, but my left hand caught it. Cheers rang out from the revelers lining the space, who gasped and squealed for me. It seemed they thought this was all part of the act, a show choreographed to add something new to the festivities, which meant none of them helped me up, but just made room for me and applauded. I swung my legs up onto the railing and leapt toward the overhang of the roof above their heads, grasping it and tugging myself up as the animated, frenzied crowd watched.

On top of the roof now, I spotted Clio three buildings down. She didn't seem to know I was up here yet. She continued gazing with wild eyes and a mad grin at the scene below. I took off running through the rain, swatting my saturated hair out of my face. To get to her, I'd have to jump across an alleyway between buildings. I sprinted, picking up speed, then slammed my feet onto the brick ledge of the first building, catapulting myself over the gap, which felt endless. I pumped my legs to drive myself farther, faster, doing all I could to be sure I could bridge the distance. With a thud that sent a shock through my legs, I hit the next rooftop, where a few people had gathered to look down onto the parade. They froze, watching silently as I ran across. One more alleyway to go, and I flung myself over the gap again and landed nearly on my knees this time, but it didn't matter. I'd made it. Clio stood up straight and tall, strutting over toward me.

"Wow, I'm so impressed you made it up here," she said sarcastically. The wet wind whooshed past, so strong I thought it might knock us right off. The storm blared as if it were a train speeding through. "Too bad you won't live to make it back down." She raised both arms and as they came down, she shot two cracking fire bolts in my direction. They swirled as they neared me, and I dove to avoid them. Even the torrential downpour did nothing to extinguish them. As I ducked, I reached inside my boot for one of the stars from Dante, then lunged forward and beamed it at her, shooting for that tattoo. I just missed, and it landed in the distance with a puff of smoke.

Clio threw her head back, cackling. "This is going to be even easier than I thought. You'll be installed as our new pet in no time," she gushed, spinning in the rain, childlike. "The Prince will be thrilled! You'll be so good for my reputation." She shot another bolt at me, and another, and they swooped behind me, glowing and elongating, fencing me in so I couldn't run away.

"The beauty of this," Clio said through the swirling wind and rain that, somehow, only made the fire grow stronger and angrier, "is that you're going to run toward your demise. Prepare to chase and be chased!" She seemed to have a fiery orange hue around her entire body, and her smile made my blood run cold. "Ready, set, go," she said, purring with an eerie calm.

I felt the heat at my back as the flames moved closer and she took off, pivoting to run across the rooftops along Ursulines toward Royal Street, skipping easily over the alleyways, like she was dancing. As I ran and leapt, I felt myself being carried by the wind, which howled with such ferocity I could hear various pops as it blew out windows and shattered glass. The flames grew closer and I sped up, stumbling over my feet and almost hitting the ground. I righted myself and managed to reach down and tug at my boot for another star. No matter that she was more than half a block ahead of me, I flung the star at her, lightning fast, and in seconds saw her body jolt in pain as she grabbed her injured wrist. She fell down in a heap, pools of rainwater splashing around her. Even from this distance I knew the star had connected with that fleur-de-lis marking. The fiery curtain at my back dulled, in the process of flaming out. I picked up my pace, and as I neared her, she rose up to her feet, turning to face me. Now she was really angry. But at least she wouldn't be stealing any souls tonight.

"You're gonna be sorry you did that," she yelled at me, shooting larger bolts at my legs. One burned up at my thigh. I stumbled but willed myself to keep going, painful as it was. I secretly cursed Emma for making us wear such short skirts. As we reached Royal Street, Clio pelted me with a few more blazing bolts before jumping off and gliding straight over to the opposite side of the street in one long, smooth motion, as though she were rigged up to wires that let her cut through the rain and the air, set to a soundtrack of roiling thunder.

My legs pounded the rooftop, my mind suspended all thoughts and naysaying, and I pushed off the ledge. Partway across, above the cars and the street, I felt myself dropping, gravity regaining its hold over me. I spotted a lamppost and zeroed in on it, landing on it only briefly, then launching again and flying toward yet another lamppost. I finally landed right in front of our home and then leapt up to the rain-slicked balcony of the LaLaurie mansion next door, where sounds of good times wafted out from the party already under way, and onward to Clio's destination: the rooftop.

As soon as I reached the roof, Clio greeted me. She was seated on the ledge, legs delicately crossed. "Believe me, if I could kill you now, I would," she said, studying her manicured nails, not bothered by the heavy rain soaking us to the point where our clothes looked like they were made of adhesive. "But it wouldn't be fair. She's all yours, Savannah," she shouted at a figure wrapped in a cloud of smoke in the distance, then took a swan dive off the ledge, disappearing into a fiery haze long before hitting the ground.

I neared the smoky silhouette as she walked toward me, and at last she came into full view. It was Wylie's girl. She stood there so tall and proud and looking unconcerned, confident that she would be the victor here. I felt wiped-out already: scraped and scratched, rattled and roughed up. I summoned all my strength, shifting from leg to leg like I was waiting for a tennis opponent to take her serve. But, really, I was sick of waiting, wasn't I? I could see a fiery glow emanating from a spot at her shoulder, an ominous crimson halo. I reached into my boot and grabbed another star, quickly whipping it at her. She lunged and it flew directly over her shoulder. She just shook her head pityingly.

She held her palms up and produced two burning orbs of fire then smashed them together as though packing a firm snowball. It glowed, floating there in the space before her, then she shoved it toward the ground, where it shattered into tiny shards of flame. These many drops of fire rose back up, creating a sizzling swarm that rushed through the rain to surround me, spitting at and singeing me. It felt like being attacked by so many fiery needles. I pulled myself into a ball, no idea how to fight this off. The best I could do was to try to roll myself away. She just stood there firing these tiny bolts with her hands from afar, and she smiled, looking pleased with herself. I contorted myself as they engulfed me, nipping at me, leaving bloody streaks on my skin. They homed in on my three sets of scars and I realized there was more than just fire at work here. I swatted madly, but felt these toxic flames burrowing into my scars and infecting me with whatever poison they might be laced with. But I felt different than I had when I'd been tagged the night of Max's birthday. This time, I could feel everything within me rise up and fight it, try to suffocate this pollutant. I collapsed onto the rain-soaked rooftop, but I wasn't finished. I dug into my boot and pulled out another star, this one with black tips, the most fearsome I had among my arsenal. I caught a glimpse of the glow from my attacker's marking and then I took my shot.

"Why don't you let me see who I'm really fighting?" I called out, flinging the weapon at her and striking her shoulder dead-on. She flickered for a moment and I almost couldn't believe my eyes. Deep in my heart I had known, but seeing it happen still stunned me: she shape-shifted for a split second, morphing into Sabine.

"And you thought you'd seen the last of me." She flashed a manic, mad smile before falling to her knees and then crumpling into a heap on top of the glass panes of the skylight.

The shock of seeing her paralyzed me for a moment and she used that to her advantage, reaching over to pelt me with another poison-laced bolt. It sizzled my scars and sent my body slumping, limp against the roof all over again. My eyes closed and I focused on the steady pulse of the heavy rain beating against my aching burned skin. *Get up. You have to keep going,* I told myself. *For Lucian.*

Across the rooftop, Sabine, as Savannah, was beginning to rouse, carefully lifting herself onto her sharp heels again. She pulled her head up and shot me a look that could fillet a person. I scanned for anything that could help give me an edge and caught sight of some loosened bricks against the far ledge of the roof, likely left over from the restoration efforts. I focused all I had on them. A mass of them, the size of a trunk, fluttered then lifted up in the air behind her. I channeled my strength so fully, I felt the sweat bead up on my forehead. The bricks rose higher in the air, steady, and then, as I concentrated, guiding them, they came crashing down on the glass, shattering the entire skylight and taking Savannah down with it. She landed with a crunch. I jumped to my feet, energy suddenly flowing back, and lunged at the gaping hole. She lay sprawled on her back, her long limbs extended, on the dance floor of the mansion's third-floor ballroom. A circle of stunned partygoers surrounded her, gawking, while others fled down the stairs, their screams loud enough to be heard even from all the way up here. Rain poured in, drenching them.

Savannah's eyes met mine and they burned now. That had done it. She sprang to her feet as though nothing were wrong and sent up a sharp, dagger-like bolt at me, knocking me off my feet, down to her level. It felt like falling through a wind tunnel. I got sucked down fast, meeting the floor with a hard, wet slap. Glass chips were wedged into my skin, and everything throbbed. I heard the rush of so many feet running away, the herd clomping back down the stairs away from us. But I saw one pair of shoes, hers, coming toward me. I couldn't move. My scars burned and I felt the toxins taking greater hold, wearing me down. I rolled onto my stomach, hoping to pull myself up, and spotted two long slivers of glass. I concentrated on them and they rose up swooping toward her. They pierced her on either side of her flowy top and launched her straight back to the wall, pinning her there like an insect. I had bought myself time. I stood up on trembling legs, just as she pulled her hanging body free, and she fell to the ground but landed on her feet.

Then she charged at me, throwing blazing torches as I dove out of the way. I threw one more glowing star at her. It glommed on to that marking and in a flash she became that grotesque figure from my photo, and then turned back into Sabine again, the real one. I kneeled over her still body, my heart suddenly breaking. I felt the tears well up. I had had to do this, hadn't I? She would have killed me, and I had had to defend myself. But now, looking at her, I could only see my friend, the girl who had once walked along the riverfront with me and shared beignets and talked about boys. How had this happened? I hadn't realized I had let my mind drift, let my guard down, until I felt Sabine's hand, warm and brittle. She looked in my eyes, hers so heavy. Then she crumbled right before me, turning to ash. I couldn't hold the tears back any longer. I felt them streak my face, mixing with the rain, as I sat there beneath the hole in the roof.

Slowly, though, I realized where I was, what I still had to accomplish tonight. I had no time to mourn. I gathered and steadied myself, and set my thoughts on the final obstacle ahead.

35

Is This Your Way of Making Me Feel Needed?

I ran down the stairs to the second floor, surprised to find the party hadn't shut down. It had simply relocated to the first two levels of the house—a testament either to the magic of Mardi Gras or some devil's trick, I didn't know. The place was still bustling, music still thumping. Partygoers in their gowns and suits, and all hiding behind feathered, glittery masks, still danced. As I made my way down, trying to ignore how worn out I felt, I pulled out my photos. I worried the toxins had already done too much damage to me. I could tell my body was weakened, but my photo told a different story. Not only was it perfect, but now I had a full halo and two sprawling and glorious white wings attached to my back. I had to blink a few times to be sure I wasn't seeing things. Did this mean I was safe? I glanced at Lance's photo and found him sporting a similar halo and wings. I could only imagine this meant he was alive.

Then it hit me: what time was it, anyway? I glanced over the railing for Lucian—was he here? I spotted Dante instead. He lifted his mask and with a look and a flick of the head he directed my attention to the window. A masked Max stood there now, tense, fading into a group nibbling on hors d'oeuvres. His laser-like focus was trained on the front door . . . where Kip stood. The demon gazed quickly above the heads of those surrounding him, as though he had already been searching for a while, and then let himself out. Max peeked out the window, keeping an eye on him, then nodded once at Dante: a signal. I hoped Kip would not be coming back. We just had to run out the clock until he would need to return below or risk losing his powers and his entrée back to the underworld. A glance at the grandfather clock informed me that it was nearly midnight already, only ten minutes to go.

A tall, masked man slithered through the crowd from the direction of the back wing of the house, joining Dante's side. Lucian. They whispered to each other, then Dante pointed at me and Lucian set off toward the staircase, which was full of people chatting, sitting, enjoying themselves, and generally blocking the way. No time to wade through the crowd, I climbed onto the railing and ran down along the slick, polished banister of the staircase until I reached the point just above Lucian, about halfway down.

"Hey!" I yelled, not wanting to shout his name lest there might be other devils in our midst. I crouched down, giving a wave as he looked up from behind his mask, his eyes lighting up.

"I was starting to wonder about you," he called. There was a skittishness about him. He motioned me down.

"Watch out," I said. He stepped aside to make room for me and I jumped down, landing squarely in the space beside him. He grabbed my waist, as though I might need steadying, but I was on firm footing. I had gotten good at this. "Sorry I'm late."

"You have no idea how good it is to see you," he said, looking relieved.

"Why? What happened?"

"Nothing. That's the problem. Nothing at all. It's been too quiet."

"We just have a few more minutes and you're in the clear," I said. But he didn't look convinced, and before I could even attempt to calm him, a soaking-wet Max was pushing through the partygoers toward us.

"It's a mess outside, so hard to see," he launched right in as he reached us, shouting to be heard over the festive roar. "But I swear I saw Kip coming back this way. Dante and I went outside to have a look and we thought we saw him a block or so down. Dante's on the roof, trying to get a better look."

Lucian shook his head. "I knew it."

"Stay here," I said to Lucian and I bolted to the front of the house, elbowing past the revelers until I made it out into the storm. Wind and rain raging against me, I ran out into the street. A tempest now roared: water coursing, soaking those parade-goers who were fleeing from Bourbon Street. The crash of metal against pavement — *bang, bang, bang* — echoed behind me as a burst of color tumbled along Governor Nicholls Street. One of the floats had careened away. Another one blew past on Ursulines. Confetti, streamers, beads all fluttered in the wet, windy air. Before I could fully process the chaos spinning all around, something dropped into the space before me. My heart stopped and I heard myself gasp. There was Kip, walking toward me, toward the house, from twenty feet away. Something else occurred to me now: where was Lance? If Kip was here and Lance wasn't . . . No. It was impossible. I wouldn't even think it.

"Hey, Lucian, what're you doin' here?" Kip shouted in my direction. "You know we're supposed to be getting back to the cemetery now." He stood there, arms folded across his chest, staring at me.

I didn't understand, until the voice came from a few yards behind me. "Yeah, you go on ahead and I'll be right there," Lucian called out. I whipped around. He stood in the open doorway, just inside the threshold, wind gusting. I was the only obstacle standing between him and Kip. To any of the faces bothering to look in our direction, the exchange registered as nothing more serious than the prelude to a bar brawl.

Kip laughed. "You've gotta be kidding. You think I don't know what's going on?" My eyes set on Kip, I backed up slowly.

Lucian was silent a moment and then said, "So what's it matter? What do you care if I'm with you or not? Get outta here."

"Really, man? You know as well as I do, there's a price on your head, and I'd like to claim it if you don't mind."

"You're sick of being the weakest one of the group? I thought you didn't mind being the Prince's whipping boy."

"You really want to do it this way?" Kip unfolded his arms now, looking like he was about to pounce.

Lucian laughed. "You've gotta be kidding if you think I'm afraid of you, of all people."

"Oh, sure. Well." He looked at his watch. "It's a minute to midnight and I'm not the one who's going AWOL."

"No, you're just on a suicide mission, aren't you?" Lucian said coolly. But I tensed up when he said that.

"You're making this too easy," Kip said calmly and in a flash he whipped something shiny in our direction. I couldn't tell what it was exactly, all I knew was that my reflexes kicked in. Somewhere in the distance, church bells tolled: midnight.

It all happened at once, too fast to process. I lunged back, knocking Lucian out of the way. He plowed through a group of guests and landed hard against a wall inside the foyer. I leapt up, pulled out my last star, tucked beside that picture at my chest, and flung it at Kip. I could tell my aim was off. But it didn't matter: Lance whipped around the street corner. Running at Kip and pummeling him, he shoved him directly into my weapon's line of fire. Kip yelled in agony.

Suddenly, something sliced into me, digging in and wedging itself so firmly in my skin it took my breath away. I felt myself falling, but my body refused to stop fighting. *You can't drop here. You can't let Kip come back in this house. You have to keep him away.* My legs stumbled, and I took a few long strides back out onto the sidewalk before they gave out. I landed on the wet pavement, rain pelting me. My head lolled to one side and then I saw Kip, or a heap that had once been him. He decayed first into a festering form, a monster, and then changed back to his Wylie façade, and then finally to a pile of smoldering ash.

But something got in the way of my line of vision. Lance. He hovered above me and suddenly I tuned out everything else: the madness of the crowds, the storm, the flooding street, the pavement against my face, everything. He was saying something to me, his lips so close to mine.

"Why did you do that?" he asked over and over again. His voice quivered, an edge to it. I realized it might be because I hadn't answered him. He kneeled over me, easing my head up from the ground, cradling me. And then, as if sensing I was coming back, "Is this your way of making me feel needed?"

Slowly, I was starting to think clearly again. "That depends. Did it work?" I asked, struggling to speak.

"Maybe." He smiled.

"Oh, good." My shoulder ached on the spot where I had once been tagged. I reached my hand over to the bare patch beneath my torn T-shirt sleeve and pulled something out: a black spike the length of my index finger and likely poison-laden. We had seen Wylie use it the night we shadowed the Krewe, and I must have been stabbed by it the night I had been tagged. But it seemed that it didn't work on angels who had passed their second test. "And, besides, I knew it wouldn't hurt me. I mean, in the long-term sense. In the short term: Ow."

Lance smiled and leaned down, running his hand through my wet hair and planting a soft kiss on my shoulder and then surprising me, his full lips finding mine. I felt the life force returning to me, pouring back into my veins, filling my lungs, pumping my heart. I reached up, gripping his damp hair in my hand to pull him closer to me. I breathed him in and could feel his heart beating against mine. My head spun, intoxicated by him, by this day, by all that had happened. As beat-up as I had been by this night, it had been worth it to get here. Time stopped; I felt I could have stayed there forever in that sliver of Royal Street, pelted by the rain, windblown, amid the fleeing masses.

"What happened? How did you get here?"

"Sorry I was late. I got a little slowed down by Jimmy and Brody," he said as he helped me up. "But I took care of them and then I was on my way here when Lucian found me and said you were in trouble. I came as fast as I . . ."

"How would he have—" My heart stopped. "Lucian?" My head nodded toward the mansion. He lay there, just inside the open doorway, slowly beginning to rouse. No. *No.* But I couldn't blame Lance; the timing had been so close. And he wouldn't have been able to tell the difference in those gray eyes—he wouldn't have known that the real ones were so pained by all they had been through. "No, Lance. No. Where?" In a flash, terror clouded his eyes and he understood.

"Here," the calm voice called to us through the storm. Lucian's voice in Lucian's body, coming toward us from the opposite side of the street. Thunder crackled and the figure changed instantly to the Prince, striding proudly. He kicked at what had become of Kip.

"If you want something done right . . ." he bellowed, anger shaking his voice. He bolted toward us. Before we could move, act, or fight, he whipped his arm around Lance's neck, pinning his arms back too. I lunged at him and a circle of fire lit around both of them, flaming up over their heads. I jumped back to avoid being singed.

It died down for a moment, so I could see their faces again. Lance struggled in the Prince's grip, only to have the fire flare up once more and extinguish, taking them with it.

I called Lance's name, my voice ragged, and dropped to my knees at that smoldering circle.

Lucian came up behind me, free from the shackles of that prison. "What have I done?" he whispered, tortured. "What have I done? I'll make this right."

I couldn't speak. I couldn't think. I replayed those few seconds, wondering how I could have kept this from happening.

The others started to arrive. They looked as tattered and soaked as we were, but they were alive. Emma, River, Drew, and Tom each marched toward us from different directions, converging on this spot in front of our house. Dante and Max ran out from the haunted mansion like nervous parents relieved to finally have their children come home. Until they saw that one was missing. Dante put his hand on my shoulder. "I know what we can do," he said. "I got a message today. It didn't make sense until right now." He looked at Lucian. "You're helping us."

"Of course," he said, his voice choked up with guilt.

I stood up now, still staring at that circle as though it were a well I was trying to see to the bottom of. Dante grabbed both my arms. "This is all just part of the next test," he said in a comforting tone.

"The illuminator, the architect, and the alchemist must stay together," I heard myself say, as though in a trance. I shook my head and rattled my bones, summoning my strength. Then I looked at them all and said, "We need to get Lance. *Now.*"

I wouldn't lose him, not without a fight.

Acknowledgments

J ust as Haven relies on her team of angels to help her out, so do I. Here are just a few of mine. Thank you, thank you:

To Stéphanie Abou, quite simply the most wonderful agent — and friend — a girl could ask for. And to the fabulous Rachel Hecht and my friends at Foundry Literary + Media.

To Julie Tibbott, the most fantastic editor a girl could ask for. I've learned so much from working with you and I'm so grateful for your brilliant guidance (and patience)! And to the lovely Rachel Wasdyke and the whole Houghton Mifflin Harcourt team for the love you've shown to Haven Terra.

To Stephen Moore, for helping Haven expand her reach.

To Richard Ford, for your endless encouragement.

To my biggest cheerleaders: my amazing parents, Bill and Risa; my awesome sis, Karen (who read all those early drafts!); and my super-supportive in-laws, Steve, Ilene, Lauren, Dave, Jill, and Josh.

To all my Louisiana pals: you guys taught me everything I know! And to all the friends and family who've been so incredible reading and listening, with an extra thanks to Jami Bjellos,

Sasha Issenberg, Jenny Laws, Ryan Lynch, Jessica and Andres Lucas, Poornima Ravishankar, Cara Lynn Shultz, Anna Siri, Kate Stroup, Jennie Teitelbaum, Kate Zeller; and Eric Andersson, Albert Lee, Kevin O'Leary, Jennifer O'Neill, and all my pals at *Us Weekly*.

To Brian and Sawyer, for all of your love and for making real life as fun as anything in fiction.

And, of course, to you, the reader: thank you so much for taking the time to watch Haven grow and for joining her on these latest adventures. I so hope you've been enjoying where her journey has been taking her!